D0189575

FAITHLESS

"Smart . . . [a] muscular thriller." —*Entertainment Weekly*

"[Slaughter's] best yet . . . Her novels smolder with reality. . . . She writes with confidence and precision as well as passion. . . . She's one of the best crime novelists in America." —*Washington Post*

"The people in *Faithless* are so real and so well-developed that the reader can't help but feel empathy for them, and thus we are drawn even deeper into the ingenious plot."
—*Chicago Sun-Times*

"A tasty mix of melodrama and mayhem . . . The book's climactic scene . . . is without question one of the sharpest and most tautly written set pieces to come along in a while. It's a payoff that will keep fans of the series awaiting more, especially with the cliff-hanger ending."
—*San Francisco Chronicle*

"A compulsively readable narrative." —*Booklist*

"Slaughter turns a compassionate eye on a brace of female victims and still manages to come across as the toughest cookie in Georgia." —*Kirkus Reviews*

"Gripping . . . A literate, readable story where the characters are multilayered and flawed."
—*Atlanta Journal-Constitution*

INDELIBLE

A FAINT COLD FEAR

"[One of the] best mysteries of 2003 . . . a tension-laden, often grisly tale about the vagaries of family, the psychology of abuse and the treatment of victims."
—*Fort Lauderdale Sun-Sentinel*

"This is one of those rare books that keep delivering surprises right up to the very last page. Slaughter doesn't coast, even if she makes it all look deceivingly easy."
—*San Francisco Chronicle*

"Brilliantly chilling." —*Heat*

"Readers who can stomach gruesome details and like fitting together multiple stories of physical and psychological abuse will savor the way Slaughter can evoke sympathy for perverse, even criminal, behavior by tracing its origins, and those who make it through . . . will be rewarded with a satisfyingly chilling ending."
—*Publishers Weekly*

"Slaughter returns with the third riveting entry in her Grant County series. . . . [She] knows how to ratchet up the psychological tension in a compelling plot with an unexpected twist. . . . Chilling and addictive reading."
—*Booklist*

ALSO BY KARIN SLAUGHTER

Blindsighted

Kisscut

A Faint Cold Fear

Indelible

Like a Charm
(EDITOR)

Faithless

AND NOW AVAILABLE IN

HARDCOVER FROM DELACORTE PRESS

Beyond Reach

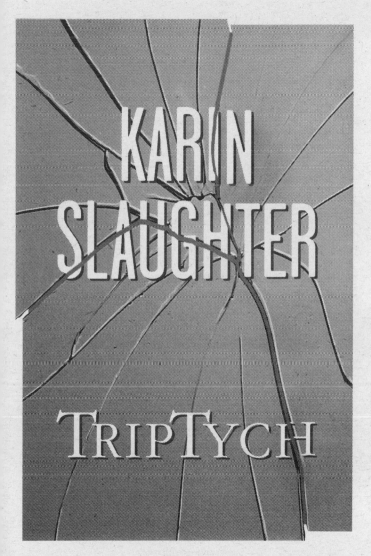

KARIN SLAUGHTER

TripTych

A DELL BOOK

TRIPTYCH
A Dell Book

PUBLISHING HISTORY
Delacorte Press hardcover edition published August 2006
Dell mass market domestic edition / August 2007

Published by
Bantam Dell
A Division of Random House, Inc.
New York, New York

This is a work of fiction. Names, characters, places, and incidents either are the product of the author's imagination or are used fictitiously. Any resemblance to actual persons, living or dead, events, or locales is entirely coincidental.

Library of Congress Catalog Card Number: 2006044475

ISBN 978-0-440-24292-5

Printed in the United States of America
Published simultaneously in Canada

www.bantamdell.com

OPM 10 9 8 7 6 5 4 3 2 1

For Kate and Kate

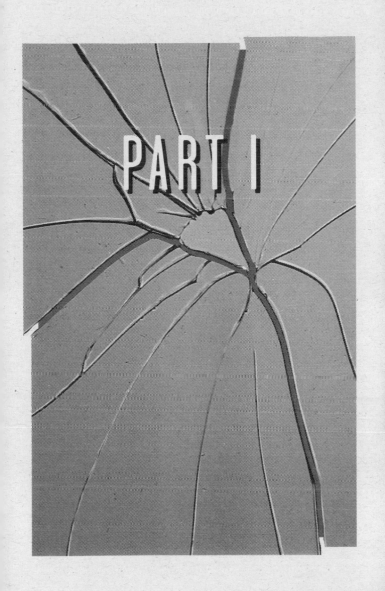
PART I

dicate
you...d be read

DECATUR TEEN MURDERED

Parents found fifteen-year-old Mary Alice Finney dead in their Adams Street home yesterday morning. Police have not released any details of the crime other than to say that they are treating this as a homicide and that those who were last seen with Finney are being questioned. Paul Finney, the girl's father and an assistant district attorney for DeKalb County, said in a statement released last night that he has every confidence that the police will bring his daughter's killer to justice. An honor student at Decatur High School, Mary Alice was active in the cheerleading squad and was recently elected sophomore class president. Sources close to the investigation have confirmed that the girl's body was mutilated.

CHAPTER ONE

FEBRUARY 5, 2006

Detective Michael Ormewood listened to the football game on the radio as he drove down DeKalb Avenue toward Grady Homes. The closer he got to the projects, the more tension he felt, his body almost vibrating from the strain by the time he took a right into what most cops considered a war zone. As the Atlanta Housing Authority slowly devoured itself, subsidized communities like Grady were becoming a thing of the past. The in-town real estate was too valuable, the potential for kickback too high. Right up the road was the city of Decatur, with its trendy restaurants and million dollar houses. Less than a mile in the other direction was Georgia's gold-encrusted capitol dome. Grady was like a worse-case scenario sitting between them, a living reminder that the city too busy to hate was also too busy to take care of its own.

With the game on, the streets were fairly empty. The drug dealers and pimps were taking the night off to watch that rarest of miracles occur: the Atlanta Falcons playing in the Super Bowl. This being a Sunday night, the prostitutes were still out making a living, trying to give the churchgoers something to confess next week. Some of the girls waved at Michael as he drove past, and he returned the greeting, wondering how many unmarked cars stopped here during the middle of the night, cops telling Dispatch they were taking a ten-minute break, then motioning over one of the girls to help blow off some steam.

Building nine was in the back of the development, the crumbling red brick edifice tagged by the Ratz, one of the new gangs that had moved into the Homes. Four cruisers and another unmarked car were in front of the building, lights rolling, radios squawking. Parked in the residents' spaces were a black BMW and a pimped-out Lincoln Navigator, its ten-thousand-dollar razor rims glittering gold in the streetlights. Michael fought the urge to jerk the steering wheel, take some paint off the seventy-thousand-dollar SUV. It pissed him off to see the expensive cars the bangers drove. In the last month, Michael's kid had shot up about four inches, outgrowing all his jeans, but new clothes would have to wait for Michael's next paycheck. Tim looked like he was waiting for a high tide while Daddy's tax dollars went to help these thugs pay their rent.

Instead of getting out of his car, Michael waited, listening to another few seconds of the game, enjoying a moment's peace before his world turned upside down. He had been on the force for almost fifteen years now, going straight from the army to the police, realizing too late that other than the haircut, there wasn't that much difference between the two. He knew that as soon as he got out of his car it would all start up like a clock that was wound too tight. The sleepless nights, the endless leads that never panned out, the bosses breathing down his neck. The press would probably catch on to it, too. Then he'd have cameras stuck in his face every time he left the squad, people asking him why the case wasn't solved, his son seeing it on the news and asking Daddy why people were so mad at him.

Collier, a young beat cop with biceps so thick with muscle he couldn't put his arms down flat against his sides, tapped on the glass, gesturing for Michael to roll down his window. Collier had made a circling motion with his meaty hand, even though the kid had probably never been in a car with crank windows.

Michael pressed the button on the console, saying, "Yeah?" as the glass slid down.

"Who's winning?"

"Not Atlanta," Michael told him, and Collier nodded as if he had expected the news. Atlanta's previous trip to the Super Bowl was several years back. Denver had thumped them 34–19.

Collier asked, "How's Ken?"

"He's Ken," Michael answered, not offering an elaboration on his partner's health.

"Could use him on this." The patrolman jerked his head toward the building. "It's pretty nasty."

Michael kept his own counsel. The kid was in his early twenties, probably living in his mother's basement, thinking he was a man because he strapped on a gun every day. Michael had met several Colliers in the Iraqi desert when the first Bush had decided to go in. They were all eager pups with that glint in their eye that told you they had joined up for more than three squares and a free education. They were obsessed with duty and honor, all that shit they'd seen on TV and been fed by the recruiters who plucked them out of high school like ripe cherries. They had been promised technical training and home-side base assignments, anything that would get them to sign on the dotted line. Most of them ended up being shipped off on the first transport plane to the desert, where they got shot before they could put their helmets on.

Ted Greer came out of the building, tugging at his tie like he needed air. The lieutenant was pasty for a black man, spending most of his time behind his desk basking in the fluorescent lights as he waited for his retirement to kick in.

He saw Michael still sitting in the car and scowled. "You working tonight or just out for a drive?"

Michael took his time getting out, sliding the key out of the ignition just as the halftime commentary started on the radio. The evening was warm for February, and the air-conditioning units people had stuck in their windows buzzed like bees around a hive.

Greer barked at Collier, "You got something to do?"

Collier had the sense to leave, tucking his chin to his chest like he'd been popped on the nose.

"Fucking mess," Greer told Michael. He took out his handkerchief and wiped the sweat off his forehead. "Some kind of sick perv got ahold of her."

Michael had heard as much when he'd gotten the call that pulled him off his living-room couch. "Where is she?"

"Six flights up." Greer folded the handkerchief into a neat square and tucked it into his pocket. "We traced the nine-one-one call to that phone." He pointed across the street.

Michael stared at the phone booth, a relic of the past. Everybody had cell phones now, especially dealers and bangers.

"Woman's voice," Greer told him. "We'll have the tape sometime tomorrow."

"How long did it take to get somebody out here?"

"Thirty-two minutes," Greer told him, and Michael's only surprise was that it hadn't taken longer. According to a local news team investigation, response times to emergency calls from Grady averaged around forty-five minutes. An ambulance took even longer.

Greer turned back to the building as if it could absolve him. "We're gonna have to call in some help on this one."

Michael bristled at the suggestion. Statistically, Atlanta was one of the most violent cities in America. A dead hooker was hardly an earth-shattering development, especially considering where she was found.

He told Greer, "That's all I need is more assholes telling me how to do my job."

"This asshole thinks it's exactly what you need," the lieutenant countered. Michael knew better than to argue—not because Greer wouldn't tolerate insubordination, but because he'd agree with Michael just to shut him up, then turn around and do whatever the hell he wanted to anyway.

Greer added, "This one's bad."

"They're all bad," Michael reminded him, opening the back door to his car and taking out his suit jacket.

"Girl didn't have a chance," Greer continued. "Beat, cut, fucked six ways to Sunday. We got a real sick fuck on our hands."

Michael put on his jacket, thinking Greer sounded like he was auditioning for HBO. "Ken's out of the hospital. Said come by and see him anytime."

Greer made some noises about being real busy lately before trotting off toward his car, looking back over his shoulder as if he was afraid Michael would follow. Michael waited until his boss was in his car and pulling out of the lot before he headed toward the building.

Collier stood at the doorway, hand resting on the butt of his gun. He probably thought he was keeping watch, but Michael knew that the person who had committed this crime wasn't going to come back for more. He was finished with the woman. There was nothing else he wanted to do.

Collier said, "The boss left fast."

"Thanks for the news flash."

Michael braced himself as he opened the door, letting the damp, dark building slowly draw him in. Whoever had designed the Homes hadn't been thinking about happy kids coming home from school to warm cookies and milk. They had focused on security, keeping open spaces to a minimum and covering all the light fixtures in steel mesh to protect the bulbs. The walls were exposed concrete with narrow windows tucked into tight little corners, the safety wire embedded in the glass looking like uniform cobwebs. Spray paint covered surfaces that had been painted white once upon a time. Gang tags, warnings and various pieces of information covered them now. To the right of the front door, someone had scrawled, *Kim is a ho! Kim is a ho! Kim is a ho!*

Michael was looking up the winding staircase, counting the six flights, when a door creaked open. He turned to find an ancient black woman staring at him, her coal dark eyes peering out around the edge of the steel door.

"Police," he said, holding up his badge. "Don't be afraid."

The door opened wider. She was wearing a floral apron over a stained white T-shirt and jeans. "I ain't afraid'a you, bitch."

Clustered behind her were four old women, all but one of them African-American. Michael knew they weren't here to help. Grady, like any small community, thrived on gossip and these were the mouths that fed the supply line.

Still, he had to ask, "Any of y'all see anything?"

They shook their heads in unison, bobbleheads on the Grady dashboard.

"That's great," Michael said, tucking his badge back into his pocket as he headed toward the stairs. "Thanks for helping keep your community safe."

She snapped, "That's your job, cocksucker."

He stopped, his foot still on the bottom stair as he turned back toward her, looking her straight in the eye. She returned the glare, rheumy eyes shifting back and forth like she was reading the book of his life. The woman was younger than the others, probably in her early seventies, but somehow grayer and smaller than her companions. Spidery lines crinkled the skin around her lips, wrinkles etched from years of sucking on cigarettes. A shock of gray streaked through the hair on the top of her head as well as the ones corkscrewing out of her chin like dreadlocks. She wore the most startling shade of orange lipstick he had ever seen on a woman.

He asked, "What's your name?"

Her chin tilted up in defiance, but she told him, "Nora."

"Somebody made a nine-one-one call from that phone booth outside."

"I hope they wash they hands after."

Michael allowed a smile. "Did you know her?"

"We all knowed her." Her tone indicated there was a lot more to be told but she wasn't the one who was going to tell it to some dumb-ass white cop. Obviously, Nora didn't exactly have a college degree under her belt, but Michael had never set much store by that kind of thing. He could tell from her eyes that the woman was sharp. She had street smarts. You didn't live to be that old in a place like Grady by being stupid.

Michael took his foot off the step, walking back toward the cluster of women. "She working?"

Nora kept her eye on him, still wary. "Most nights."

The white woman behind her provided, "She an honest girl."

Nora tsked her tongue. "Such a young little thing." There was a hint of challenge in her voice when she said, "No kind of life for her, but what else could she do?"

Michael nodded like he understood. "Did she have any regulars?"

They all shook their heads again, and Nora provided, "She never brought her work home with her."

Michael waited, wondering if they would add anything else. He counted the seconds off in his head, thinking he'd let it go to twenty. A helicopter flew over the building and car wheels squealed against asphalt a couple of streets over, but no one paid attention. This was the sort of neighborhood where people got nervous if they didn't hear gunshots at least a couple of times a week. There was a natural order to their lives, and violence—or the threat of it—was as much a part of it as fast food and cheap liquor.

"All right," Michael said, having counted the seconds to twenty-five. He took out one of his business cards, handing it to Nora as he told her, "Something to wipe your ass on."

She grunted in disgust, holding the card between her thumb and forefinger. "My ass is bigger than that."

He gave her a suggestive wink, made his voice a growl. "Don't think I hadn't noticed, darlin'."

She barked a laugh as she slammed the door in his face. She had kept the card, though. He had to take that as a positive sign.

Michael walked back to the stairs, taking the first flight two at a time. All of the buildings at Grady had elevators, but even the ones that worked were dangerous. As a first-year patrolman, Michael had been called out to the Homes on a domestic disturbance and gotten caught in one of the creaky contraptions with a busted radio. He had spent about two hours trying not to add to the overwhelming smell of piss and vomit before his sergeant realized he hadn't reported in and sent somebody to look for him. The old-timers had laughed at his stupidity for another half hour before helping get him out.

Welcome to the brotherhood.

As Michael started on the second flight of stairs, he felt a change in the air. The smell hit him first: the usual odor of fried foods mingled with beer and sweat, cut by the sudden but unmistakable stench of violent death.

The building had responded to the fatality in the usual way. Instead of the constant thump of rap beating from multiple speakers, Michael heard only the murmur of voices from behind closed doors. Televisions were turned down low, the halftime show serving as background noise while people talked about the girl on the sixth floor and thanked the Lord it was her this time and not their children, their daughters, themselves.

In this relative quiet, sounds started to echo down the stairwell: the familiar rhythms of a crime scene as evidence was gathered, photos taken. Michael stopped at the bottom of the fourth-floor landing to catch his breath. He had given up smoking two months ago but his lungs hadn't really believed him. He felt like an asthmatic as he made his way up the next flight of stairs. Above him, someone laughed, and he could hear the other cops join in, participating in the usual bullshit bravado that made it possible for them to do the job.

Downstairs, a door slammed open, and Michael leaned over the railing, watching two women wrangle a gurney inside the foyer. They were wearing dark blue rain jackets, bright yellow letters announcing "MORGUE" on their backs.

Michael called, "Up here."

"How far up?" one of them asked.

"Sixth floor."

"Mother *fuck*," she cursed.

Michael grabbed the handrail and pulled himself up the next few stairs, hearing the two women offer up more expletives as they started the climb, the gurney banging against the metal railings like a broken bell. He was one flight away from the top when he felt the hairs on the back of his neck stand up. Sweat had glued his shirt to his back, but some sort of sixth sense sent a chill through him.

A flash popped and a camera whirred. Michael stepped carefully around a red stiletto shoe that was flat on the stair, looking as if someone had sat down and slipped it off. The next step up had the perfect outline of a bloody hand gripping the tread. The next stair had another handprint, then another, as someone had crawled up the stairs.

Standing on the landing at the top of the fifth flight was Bill Burgess, a seasoned beat cop who had seen just about every kind of crime Atlanta had to offer. Beside him was a dark pool of coagulating blood, the edges spreading in rivulets that dropped from one step to the next like falling dominoes. Michael read the scene. Someone had stumbled here, struggled to get up, smearing blood as she tried to escape.

Bill was looking down the stairs, away from the blood. His skin was blanched, his lips a thin slash of pink. Michael stopped short, thinking he'd never seen Bill flustered before. This was the man who'd gone out for chicken wings an hour after finding six severed fingers in the Dumpster behind a Chinese restaurant.

The two men did not speak as Michael carefully stepped over the puddle of blood. He kept his hand on the rail, making the turn to the next flight of stairs, thankful for something to hold on to when he saw the scene in front of him.

The woman was partially clothed, her tight red dress cut open like a robe, showing dark cocoa skin and a wisp of black pubic hair that had been shaved into a thin line leading down to her cleft. Her breasts were unnaturally high on her chest, implants holding them up in perfection. One arm was out to her side, the other rested above her head, fingers reaching toward the handrail as if her last thoughts had been to pull herself up. Her right leg was bent at the knee, splayed open, the left jutting at an angle so that he could see straight up her slit.

Michael took another step, blocking out the activity around him, trying to see the woman as her killer would have seen her. Makeup smeared her face, heavy lipstick and rouge applied in dark lines to bring out her features. Her curly black hair was streaked with orange, teased out in all directions. Her body was nice, or nicer than you'd expect from what the needle marks on her arms indicated she was: a woman with a habit she fed between her legs. The bruises on her thighs could have come from her killer or a john who liked it rough. If it was the latter, then she had probably willingly endured it, knowing she'd be able to get more money for the pain, knowing more money meant more pleasure later on when the needle plunged in and that warm feeling spread through her veins.

Her eyes were wide open, staring blankly at the wall. One of her fake eyelashes had come loose, making a third lash under her left eye. Her nose was broken, her cheek shifted off center where the bones beneath the eye had been shattered. Light reflected against something in her open mouth, and Michael took another step closer, seeing that it was filled to the top with liquid and that the liquid was blood. The light overhead glinted off the red pool like a harvest moon.

Pete Hanson, the medical examiner on call, stood at the top of the stairs talking to Leo Donnelly. Leo was an asshole, always playing the tough cop, joking about everything, laughing too loud and long, but Michael had seen him at the bar one too many times, his hand a constant blur as he slammed back one scotch after another, trying to get the taste of death out of his mouth.

Leo spotted Michael and cracked a smile, like they were old pals getting together for a good time. He was holding a sealed plastic evidence bag in his hand and he kept tossing it a couple of inches in the air and catching it like he was getting ready to play ball.

Leo said, "Hell of a night to be on call."

Michael didn't voice his agreement. "What happened?"

Leo kept tossing the bag, weighing it in his hand. "Doc says she bled to death."

"Maybe," Pete corrected. Michael knew the doctor liked Leo about as much as everyone else on the force, which was to say he couldn't stand the bastard. "I'll know more when I get her on the table."

"Catch," Leo said, tossing the evidence bag down to Michael.

Michael saw it in slow motion, the bag sailing through the air end over end like a lopsided football. He caught it before it hit the ground, his fingers wrapping around something thick and obviously wet.

Leo said, "Something for your cat."

"What the—" Michael stopped. He knew what it was.

"Lookit his face!" Leo's shotgun laugh echoed off the walls.

Michael could only stare at the bag. He felt blood at the back of his throat, tasted that metallic sting of unexpected fear. The voice that came out of his mouth did not sound like his own—it was more like he was under water, maybe drowning. "What happened?"

Leo was still laughing, so Pete answered, "He bit off her tongue."

CHAPTER TWO

When he had returned from the Gulf War, Michael had been haunted by his dreams. As soon as he closed his eyes, he saw the bullets coming at him, the bombs blowing off arms and legs, children running down the road, screaming for their mamas. Michael knew where their mothers were. He had stood by helplessly as the women banged the closed windows of the schoolhouse, trying to break their way out as fire from an exploded grenade burned them alive.

Aleesha Monroe was haunting him now. The tongueless woman in the stairway had followed him home, worked some kind of magic in his dreams so that it was Michael chasing her up the stairs, Michael forcing her back onto the landing and splitting her in two. He could feel her long red nails sinking into his skin as she tried to fight him off, choking him. He couldn't breathe. He started clawing at his neck, her hands, trying to get her to stop. He woke up screaming so loud that Gina sat up in bed beside him, clutching the sheet to her chest like she expected to see a maniac in their bedroom.

"Jesus, Michael," she hissed, hand over her heart. "You scared the shit out of me."

He reached for the glass of water by the bed, sloshing

some on his chest as he took large gulps to quench the fire in his throat.

"Babe," Gina said, touching the tips of her fingers to his neck. "What happened?"

Michael felt a sting on his neck and put his fingers where hers had been. There was a rent in the skin, and when he got up to look in the mirror over the dresser, he saw a thin trickle of blood dripping from the fresh cut.

She stood beside him. "Did you scratch yourself in your sleep?"

"I don't know." He knew, though. He still hadn't caught his breath from the dream.

Gina wrinkled her nose as she pulled his hand to her mouth. For a second, he thought she was going to kiss it, but she asked instead, "Why do you smell like bleach?"

He'd had to scrub it off him—that smell, that stickiness, that came from being around the dead. Michael didn't tell her this, didn't want to open up that conversation, so instead he squinted at the clock, asking, "What time is it?"

"Shit," she groaned, dropping his hand. "Might as well get dressed. My shift starts in two hours."

Michael picked up the clock to see for himself. Six-thirty. After processing the crime scene, tossing the woman's apartment and going through the paperwork, he had gotten maybe four hours of sleep.

The shower came on, pipes rumbling in the wall as the hot water heater kicked in. Michael went into the bathroom, watching Gina slip off the shirt she'd slept in.

"Tim's already up," she said, taking off her panties. "You need to make sure he's not getting into anything."

Michael leaned against the wall, admiring her flat stomach, the way the muscles in her arms stretched as she took the band out of her hair. "He's fine."

Gina gave him a look, noticing him noticing her. "Check on him."

Michael felt a smile on his lips. Her breasts had kept their fullness after Tim, and his mouth was almost watering at the sight of them. "Call in sick," he told her.

"Right."

"We'll watch a movie, make out on the couch." He paused, then tried, "Remember how we used to just kiss for hours?" Christ, he hadn't had more than a peck on the cheek in months. "Let's kiss like that, Gina. Nothing else. Just kissing."

"Michael," Gina said, leaning in to check the water temperature. She stepped into the shower. "Stop leering at me like I'm a hooker and go check on your son."

She closed the shower door, and he waited a full minute before leaving, watching her silhouette behind the glass, wondering when things had started to go wrong between them.

He had met Gina before his unit left for the Gulf. No one was expecting to get hurt over there, but Michael and his fellow grunts had played it up, getting all the action they could before being dropped in the desert. Ellen McCallum was a petite, bottle blonde, not too bright—just the kind of girl you wanted to remember when you were stuck in some filthy, sand-encrusted tent a million miles from home, telling the guys about the girl back home who could suck the leather off a couch.

Michael had spent the better part of a week trying to get into Ellen's pants when up walked Gina, her cousin. She'd pretty much ripped Michael a new one for messing around with her favorite baby cousin, but when he'd shipped out a couple of days later, it was Gina he was thinking about. Her curly brown hair, her delicate features, the smooth curve of her ass. He started writing to her, and to his surprise, she wrote back—real mean at first, but then she calmed down a little, almost got sweet on him. He was in Kuwait, supposedly keeping the peace, when some dumb-ass teenager fooling around with a handgun accidentally shot him in the leg. The kid was a lousy shot, but the wound wouldn't heal. When Michael was sent to the base in Germany for surgery, it was Gina he called first.

They got married a week after he was discharged and two weeks later he signed up with the Atlanta Police Department. Gina graduated from nursing school at Georgia Baptist and got a good job at Crawford Long Hospital. Two years later, she went over to Piedmont where they paid her more. Michael got his gold shield and was moved from his patrol beat at Grady to Vice, with a pay bump to match. Soon, their life was rolling along better than Michael had ever expected. They bought a house just north of Atlanta, started putting money away for a rainy day, thinking about having a kid or two and making it a real family. Then Tim came along.

He was a quiet baby, but Michael saw a sparkle in his big blue eyes. The first time he held Tim was like holding his own heart in his hands. It was Barbara, Gina's mom, who saw the problems first. He never cries. He doesn't engage. He stares at the wall for hours. Michael fought it tooth and nail, but the doctor confirmed Barbara's suspicions. Tim had been deprived of oxygen at some point during Gina's pregnancy. His brain would never develop past the level of a six-year-old. They didn't know how or why, but that was just the way it was.

Michael had never liked Barbara, but Tim's diagnosis made him hate her. It was a cliché to despise your mother-in-law, but she had always thought her daughter traded down and now she saw Tim's problem as Michael's failure. She was also some kind of religious nut, quick to find fault in others, not so quick to see it in herself. She wasn't just the glass-is-half-empty type; she thought the glass was half empty and they were all going to hell for it.

"Tim?" Michael called, putting on a T-shirt as he walked through the house. "Where are you, buddy?"

He heard giggling behind the couch, but kept walking toward the kitchen.

"Where'd Tim go?" he asked, noting his son had scattered a full box of Cheerios all over the kitchen table. Tim's blue bowl was filled to the rim with milk, and for just a second Michael could see Aleesha Monroe's red, red mouth, the way it had been filled with her own blood.

"Boo!" Tim screamed, grabbing Michael around the waist.

Michael startled, even though Tim did this practically every morning. His heart was thumping in his chest as he lifted his son up into his arms. The kid was eight now, much too big to be held, but Michael couldn't help himself. He stroked back the cowlick on the top of Tim's head. "You sleep okay, kiddo?"

Tim nodded, pulling away from Michael's hand, pushing at his shoulder so he could get down.

"Let's clean up this mess before Ba-Ba gets here," he suggested, scooping some of the cereal into his hand and tossing it into the box. Barbara came during the week to watch Tim. She took him to school, picked him up, made sure he had his snack and did his homework. Most days, she spent more time with him than either Michael or Gina, but it wasn't like either of them had a choice.

"Ba-Ba won't like this mess," Michael said.

"Nope," Tim agreed. He was sitting at the table, legs pulled up underneath him. The fly to his Spider-Man pajamas sagged open.

"Tuck in your equipment, buddy," Michael admonished,

trying to fight the wave of sadness that came over him as Tim fumbled with the buttons.

Michael had been an only child, probably a little more than spoiled. When Tim came along, he didn't know anything about caring for a baby. Changing Tim's diaper had been embarrassing, something to get over with as quickly as possible and with minimal contact. Now, all Michael could think about was the fact that Tim would hit puberty in a few years. His body would start growing, changing him into a man, but his mind would never catch up. He would never know what it was like to make love to a woman, to use what God gave him to bring pleasure to another human being. He would never have children of his own. Tim would never know the joy and heartache of being a father.

"Who made this mess?" Gina asked. She was wrapped in the blue silk robe Michael had given her for Christmas a couple of years ago, her hair swirled up in a towel. "Did you make this mess?" she teased Tim, cupping his chin in her hand as she kissed his lips. "Ba-Ba won't like this," she said. Michael got a secret kick that the kid hadn't been able to call Barbara grandma like she wanted.

Tim started to help clean up, making more of a mess in the process. "Uh-oh," he said, dropping to his knees, picking up one Cheerio at a time, counting them out loud as he handed them to his mother.

Gina asked Michael, "You getting home at a decent hour tonight?"

"I told you I had a case."

"In a bar?" she said, and he turned his back to her, taking a couple of mugs down from the cabinet. He'd been too wound up last night to come straight home. Leo had suggested they get a drink, talk about the case, and Michael had taken him up on the offer, using the excuse to toss back a couple of bourbons and take the edge off what he'd seen.

"Eleven . . ." Tim counted. "Twelve . . ."

Gina said, "You smell like an ashtray."

"I didn't smoke."

"I didn't say you did." She dropped a handful of Cheerios into the box and held out her hand for more.

"Fourteen," Tim continued.

"I just needed some time." Michael poured coffee into the mugs. "Leo wanted to talk about the case."

"Leo wanted an excuse to get shitfaced."

"Uh-oh," Tim sang.

"Sorry, baby," Gina apologized to their son. She softened her tone. "You skipped a number. What happened to thirteen?"

Tim shrugged. For the moment, he could only count to twenty-eight, but Gina made sure he hit every number along the way.

Gina told Tim, "Go get dressed for Ba-Ba. She'll be here soon."

Tim stood and bounced out of the room, skipping from one foot to the other.

Gina dropped the Cheerios into the box and sat down with a groan. She had pulled a double shift this weekend to pick up some extra money. The day hadn't even started and already she looked exhausted.

"Busy night?" he asked.

She took a sip of coffee, looking at him over the steam rising from the mug. "I need money for the new therapist."

Michael sighed, leaning against the counter. Tim's old speech therapist had taken him as far as she could. The kid needed a specialist, and the good specialists weren't on the state health insurance plan.

"Five hundred dollars," Gina said. "That'll get him through the end of the month."

"Christ." Michael rubbed his fingers into his eyes,

feeling a headache coming on. He thought about the BMW and the Lincoln he'd seen at Grady Homes last night. Tim could see fifty specialists for that kind of money.

"Take it out of savings," he said.

She snorted a laugh. "What savings?"

Christmas. They had raided their savings for Christmas.

"I'm gonna ask for another shift at the hospital." She held up her hand to stop his protest. "He's got to have the best."

"He's got to have his mother."

"How about your mother?" she shot back.

Michael's jaw set. "I'm not going to ask her for another dime."

She put down the mug on the table with a thump that spilled coffee onto the back of her hand. There was no way to win this argument—Michael should know, they'd had it practically every week over the last five years. He was already working overtime, trying to bring in extra cash so Tim could have the things he needed. Gina took weekend shifts twice a month, but Michael drew the line at her working holidays. He barely saw her as it was. Sometimes, he thought she planned it that way. They weren't a married couple anymore; they were a partnership, a nonprofit corporation working for the betterment of Tim. Michael couldn't even remember the last time they'd had sex.

"Cynthia called last night," Gina told him. Their spoiled next-door neighbor. "She's got a loose board or something."

"Loose board?" he repeated. "Where's Phil?"

She pressed her palms to the table and stood. "Botswana. Hell, I don't know, Michael. She just asked if you could fix it and I said yes."

"Did you want to consult with me about that first?"

"Do it or don't," she snapped, tossing the rest of her coffee into the sink. "I need to get dressed for work."

He watched her back as she made her way down the hall. Every morning was like this: Tim making a mess, them cleaning it up, then some argument about something stupid breaking out. To top things off, Barbara would be here soon, and Michael was sure his mother-in-law would find something to complain about, whether it was her aching back, her paltry social security check, or the fact that he'd given her a retarded grandson. Lately, she had taken to leaving articles on Gulf War Syndrome taped to the refrigerator, the obvious inference being that Michael had done something horrible over in Iraq that had brought this scourge on her family.

Michael went into the bedroom and dressed quickly, skipping his shower so he wouldn't have to go into the bathroom and deal with Gina again. He saw Barbara's Toyota pulling into the driveway and grabbed his hammer out of his toolbox, sneaking out the back door as she came in the front.

Part of the chain-link fence around the backyard had been taken out by a tree during the last ice storm and there hadn't been any money to fix it. He hopped over the broken section, careful not to catch the cuff of his pants on the twisted metal and fall flat on his face. Again.

He knocked at the back door, glancing through the window as he waited for Cynthia to come. She took her sweet time, padding up the hall in a short, babydoll robe that was opened to reveal the camisole and thong she wore underneath. Everything was white, practically see-through. Michael wondered where Phil was. If Gina ever answered the door for Phil dressed this way, Michael would have fucking killed her.

Cynthia slowly worked the locks, bending at the waist,

flashing some breast. Her long blonde hair covered her face. The camisole was so low he could see the tips of her pink nipples.

Michael hefted the hammer in his hand, feeling an electric buzz in his head. He should just turn around right now and let her fix her own board. Shit, Phil had to come home sometime; let him do it.

Cynthia flashed him a smile as she opened the door. "Howdy, neighbor."

"Where's Phil?"

"Indianapolis," she said, cupping her hands around her mouth to hide a yawn. "Selling support hose to the masses so he can keep me in the style to which I've become accustomed."

"Right." He glanced over her shoulder. The kitchen was a pigsty. Crusty plates were stacked in the sink, take-out pizza boxes everywhere, cigarettes flowing out of ashtrays. He saw mold growing on a glass of what looked like orange juice.

He said, "Gina told me you have a loose board."

She smiled like a cat. "It needs tightening."

Michael put down the hammer. "Why did you call her?"

"Neighbors help neighbors," she said, like it was simple. "You told Phil you'd look after me when he was away."

Phil hadn't meant like this.

She pulled him inside the house by his shirt collar. "You look so tense."

"I can't keep doing this."

"What are you doing?" she asked, pulling him closer.

He thought of Gina, the way she never looked at him anymore, how it felt when she pushed him away. "I just can't."

Her hand pressed hard against the front of his pants. "Feels like you can."

Michael held his breath, his eyes following the slope of her small breasts to her firm nipples. He felt his tongue slip out between his lips, could almost feel what it would be like to put his mouth on her.

She unzipped his pants and reached in. "You like this?" she asked, moving her thumb in a circular motion.

"Jesus," he hissed between his teeth. "Yes."

DECATUR CITY OBSERVER
JUNE 19, 1985

dicate
jo... ...d be read

WITNESSES
SOUGHT IN
FINNEY MURDER

Police are asking witnesses to come forward in the Mary Alice Finney case. The girl was found slain in her Decatur home last Sunday. Police Chief Harold Waller revealed in a news conference that Mary Alice went with friends to Lenox Square Mall earlier that evening, then attended a neighborhood party in Decatur. The fifteen-year-old was last seen leaving the party with a stranger. Anyone who either saw the girl or has information about the stranger is encouraged to call the DeKalb County Police Department. The family has refused all interviews, but in a formal statement, Paul Finney, assistant district attorney for DeKalb County and father of the slain girl, has asked for privacy. Sources close to the investigation say that Sally Finney, the girl's mother, found her daughter when she went to wake her for church.

CHAPTER THREE

Michael felt like shit. Hell, he *was* shit.

The first time with Cynthia had been an accident. Michael knew that was a lame excuse, it wasn't like you could just trip and the next thing you know, you're in somebody's vagina, but he really did think of it along those lines. Phil had called long-distance from California one night, frantic with worry because he couldn't reach Cynthia. The man traveled all the time, selling women's hosiery to the big department stores and probably wetting his whistle along the way. Michael didn't have proof, but he had worked Vice for three years and he knew the type of businessman who availed himself of the local talent whenever he was on the road. The constant phone calls checking on Cynthia were more like guilt calls, Phil's way of keeping tabs on her when he couldn't keep tabs on himself.

Gina had been working nights then, already pulling away from Michael when he reached out to her. Tim's challenges were becoming more evident and her response had been to throw herself into work, doing double shifts because she couldn't stand the thought of coming home and dealing with her damaged son. Michael was sick with grief, exhausted from crying himself to sleep at night and just plain damn lonely.

Cynthia was available, more than willing to take his

mind off things. After the first time, he had told himself it wouldn't happen again, and it hadn't, not for a year at least. Michael had work and Tim, and that was all he thought about until one day last spring when Cynthia had mentioned to Gina that her sink was leaking.

"Go fix it for her," Gina had told Michael. "Phil's gone all the time. The poor thing doesn't have anybody to look out for her."

He wasn't in love with Cynthia and Michael wasn't stupid enough to think she had those kinds of feelings for him. At the ripe old age of forty, he had learned that a woman who was eager to go down on you every time she saw you wasn't in love—she was looking for something. Maybe Cynthia liked the thrill of banging Michael in Phil's bed. Maybe she liked the idea of seeing Gina out the kitchen window and knowing she was taking something that belonged to another woman. Michael couldn't let himself consider her motivations. He knew his own well enough. For those fifteen or twenty minutes he spent next door, his mind went blank and he wasn't thinking about paying the specialists or making the mortgage or the phone call from the credit card company asking when they could expect some money. Michael was just thinking about Cynthia's perfect little mouth and his own pleasure.

She would want something someday, though. He wasn't so stupid that he didn't at least know that.

"Yo, Mike," Leo called, rapping his knuckles on Michael's desk. "Get your head out of your ass."

"What's going on?" Michael asked, sitting back in his chair. The station was empty but for the two of them, Greer locked behind his office door with the shades drawn.

Michael indicated the closed door. "He jerking off in there again?"

"Got some Lurch-looking freak from the GBI with him."

"Why?" Michael asked, but he knew why. Last night, Greer had said he was going to call in help on this one, and the next step up the ladder was the Georgia Bureau of Investigation.

"He don't consult with me," Leo said, sitting on the edge of Michael's desk, scattering papers in the process. He did this all the time, no matter how many warnings Michael gave him.

Leo asked, "You get in trouble with the wife last night?"

"No," Michael lied, letting his eyes travel around the squad room. The place was depressing and dark, the wall of windows looking out at the Home Depot across the street thick with grime that blocked out the morning sun. City Hall East was a twelve-story building, a onetime Sears department store, that sat at the base of a curve in Ponce de Leon Road and took up a whole city block. A railroad track separated the structure from an old Ford factory that had been turned into pricey lofts. The state had bought the abandoned Sears building years ago, turning it into various government offices. There were at least thirty different departments and over five hundred city employees. Michael had worked here for ten years but other than the overcrowded parking garage, he had only seen the three floors the Atlanta Police Department used and the morgue.

"Yo," Leo repeated, banging the desk again.

Michael pushed his chair from the desk and away from Leo. Between the chain-smoking and constant nips Leo took from the bottle he kept in his locker, the guy had breath like a dog's fart.

"You daydreaming about some pussy?"

"Shut up," Michael snapped, thinking he'd hit too close

to home. Leo always did—not because he was a good detective, but because he couldn't keep his mouth shut.

"I was thinking about going to see Ken later on." Leo took a tangerine out of his suit pocket and started peeling it. "How's he doing?"

"Okay," Michael told him, though the truth was he hadn't talked to Ken in a week. They had been partners for a while, close as brothers, until Ken had clutched his arm one day and dropped to the ground. He had been talking to Michael about a gorgeous woman he'd met the night before, and for a split second, Michael thought the fall was some kind of joke. Then Ken had started to twitch. His mouth sagged open and he pissed himself right there on the squad room floor. Fifty-three years old and he'd stroked out like an old man. The whole right side of his body was gone now, his arm and leg useless as a wet newspaper. His mouth was permanently twisted so that dribble poured down his chin like he was a baby.

No one from the squad wanted to see him, to hear him try to talk. Ken was a reminder of what was just around the corner for most of them. Too much smoking, too much drinking, two or three failed marriages, all ending with your lonely last days spent catatonic in front of the tube, stuck at some crappy, state-run nursing home.

Greer's door opened, and a lanky man in a three-piece suit came out. He was toting a leather briefcase that looked like a postage stamp in his large hand. Michael could see why Leo had called the guy Lurch. He was tall, maybe six-four or -five, and whippet thin. His dirty blond hair was cut tight to his head, parted on the side. His upper lip looked funny, too, like someone had cut it in half and put it back together crooked. As usual, Leo had gotten the show wrong. Put some knobs on either side of his neck and the guy could be on *The Munsters*.

"Ormewood," Greer said, motioning him over. "This is Special Agent Will Trent from CAT."

Leo showed his usual grace. "What the fuck is CAT?"

"Special Criminal Apprehension Team," Greer clarified.

Michael could almost feel Leo straining not to point out that this actually spelled SCAT. Not much shut up his fellow detective, but Trent was standing close to Leo, looming over him by almost a foot. The state guy's hands were huge, probably big enough to wrap around Leo's head and crush his skull like a coconut.

Leo was an idiot, but he wasn't stupid.

Trent said, "I'm part of a special division of the Georgia Bureau of Investigation set up to aid local law enforcement around the state in apprehending violent criminals. My role here is purely advisory."

He spoke like he was reading from a textbook, carefully enunciating every word. Between that and the three-piece suit, the guy could be a college professor.

"Michael Ormewood." Michael relented, holding out his hand. Trent took it, not too firm but not limp like he was holding a fish. "This is Leo Donnelly," Michael introduced, since Leo was occupied with sticking half the tangerine in his mouth, the juice dripping down the back of his hand.

"Detective." Trent gave Leo a dismissive nod. He glanced at his watch, telling Michael, "The autopsy results won't be ready for another hour. I'd like to compare notes if you have a minute."

Michael looked at Greer, wondering exactly what had shifted on the food chain in the last two minutes. He was getting the feeling he had been relegated to the bottom and he didn't like it.

Greer turned his back to them, waddling toward his

office. He tossed over his shoulder, "Keep me in the loop," as he closed his door.

Michael stared at Trent for a beat. The state guy didn't look like a cop. Despite his height, he didn't fill the room. He stood with a hand in his pocket, his left knee bent, almost casual. His shoulders would be pretty broad if he stood up straight, but he didn't seem inclined to take advantage of his size. He lacked the presence of somebody who was on the job, the "fuck you" attitude that came from arresting every type of scum the earth had to offer.

Michael stared at the man, wondering what would happen if he just told the asshole to fuck off. Between the fight with Gina this morning and his run-in with Cynthia, Michael figured he should give somebody a break today. He waved his hand toward the door. "Conference room's this way."

Trent headed up the hall. Michael followed, staring at the man's shoulders, wondering how he had ended up in the GBI. Usually, the state guys were adrenaline junkies, their bodies so pumped with testosterone that there was the constant sheen of sweat on their foreheads.

Michael asked, "How long you been on the job?"

"Twelve years."

Michael figured Trent was at least ten years younger than him, but that didn't tell him what he wanted to know. "Ex-military?" he asked.

"No," Trent answered, opening the conference room door. The windows were actually clean in this room, and in the sunlight Michael could see a second scar running along the side of Trent's face. The pink lightened to an almost white as it jagged from his ear down his neck, following his jugular and disappearing into his shirt collar.

Somebody had cut him pretty deep.

"Gulf War," Michael said, putting his hand to his chest,

thinking that might draw the man out. "You sure you weren't enlisted?"

"Positive," Trent replied, sitting down at the table. He opened his briefcase and pulled out a stack of brightly colored file folders. In profile, Michael could see his nose had been busted at least a couple of times and wondered if the man was a boxer. He was too thin, though, his body lean, his face angular. No matter what his past, there was something about the guy that set Michael on edge.

Trent was paging through the files, putting the folders into some kind of order, when he noticed Michael was still standing. He said, "Detective Ormewood, I'm on your team."

"Is that so?"

"I don't want any glory," Trent said, though in Michael's experience, that was what the "G" in "GBI" stood for. The state boys had a reputation for coming in, doing half the work and taking all of the credit.

Trent continued, "I don't want to steal the spotlight or be on the news when we catch the bad guy. I just want to assist you in your job and then move on."

"What makes you think I need assistance?"

Trent looked up from the files, studying Michael for a few seconds. He opened a fluorescent pink folder flat on the table and slid it toward Michael. "Julie Cooper of Tucker," he said, naming a town about twenty miles outside Atlanta. "Fifteen years old. She was raped and beaten—almost to death—four months ago."

Michael nodded, flipping through the file, not bothering to read the details. He got to the victim's photograph and stopped. Long blonde hair, heavy eyeliner, too much lipstick for a girl that age.

Trent opened another folder, this one neon green. "Anna Linder, fourteen, of Snellville."

Just north of Tucker.

"December third of last year, Linder was abducted while walking to her aunt's house down the street from her home." Trent passed the folder to Michael. "Raped, beaten. Same M.O."

Michael flipped through the file, looking for the photo. Linder's hair was dark, the bruises around her eyes even darker. He picked up the girl's picture, studying it closer. Her mouth had been beaten pretty bad, the lip cut, blood dripping down her chin. She had some kind of glitter on her face that picked up the flash from the camera.

"She was found hiding in a ditch in Stone Mountain Park the next day."

"Okay," Michael said, waiting for the connection.

"Both girls report being attacked by a man wearing a black ski mask." Trent laid out an orange folder, a photograph paper-clipped to the top sheet. "Dawn Simmons of Buford."

Michael did a double take, thinking this girl couldn't be more than ten. "She's younger than the others," he said, disgusted by the thought of some sick fuck touching the child. She wasn't much older than Tim.

"She was assaulted six months ago," Trent told him. "She reports that her attacker wore a black ski mask."

Michael shook his head. Buford was an hour away and the girl was too young. "Coincidence."

"I think so, too," Trent agreed. "Guys like this don't hunt outside their comfort area."

Without realizing it, Michael had taken a seat at the table. He put down the photo of the ten-year-old and slid it back toward Trent, thinking he'd be sick if he looked at it one more minute. Jesus, her poor parents. How the hell did people live through this sort of thing?

Michael asked, "What's that mean? Comfort area?"

Trent went back to his professor voice. "Child sexual predators have a specific age group they go after. A man who's sexually attracted to ten-year-olds might think fifteen, sixteen, is too old. The same goes for a man who's interested in teenagers. He'd probably be just as disgusted as you are by the thought of molesting a girl that young."

Michael felt his stomach clench. Trent was so matter-of-fact about it, as if he was discussing the weather. He had to ask, "You got kids?"

"No," Trent admitted, not returning the question. Maybe he already knew the answer, probably from Greer. Michael wondered what the bastard had said about Tim.

Trent continued, "I've put in a call to the parents in each case to see if we can talk to the girls, perhaps get some new information now that some time has passed since the attacks. From what I've seen, victims of these sorts of crimes remember more as they get some distance from the event." He added, "It might be a waste of time, but then we might hear something that they couldn't recall during the initial interviews."

"Right," Michael agreed, trying not to sound annoyed. He had worked plenty of rapes on his own and didn't need a lesson.

"I think the perpetrator is probably a well-educated man," Trent said. "Probably in his mid- to late-thirties. Unhappy with his job, unhappy with his home situation."

Michael held his tongue. In his opinion, profiling was a load of shit. Except for the well-educated part, Trent could be talking about most of the men in the squad. Throw in banging his next-door neighbor and he'd be describing Michael.

"The files show a clear pattern of escalation," Trent continued. "Cooper, the first girl, was attacked outside a movie theater; quick, efficient. The whole thing took maybe ten minutes and all of it was out of range of the theater's closed-circuit cameras. The second, Anna Linder, was abducted right off the street. He took her somewhere—she's not sure where—in a car. He left her right outside the gates of Stone Mountain Park. Park police found her the next morning."

"Any tire tracks?"

"About twelve hundred," Trent answered. "The park had just started its annual Christmas lights show."

Michael had taken Gina and Tim to see the lights. They went every year.

"DNA?" Michael asked.

"He wore a condom."

"Okay," Michael said. So he wasn't a moron. "What does this have to do with my girl last night?"

Trent narrowed his eyes, like he wondered if Michael had heard a word he said. "Their tongues, Detective." He slid the reports back over. "They all had their tongues bitten off."

CHAPTER FOUR

The tongue is basically like a piece of tough steak," Pete Hanson said, slipping on his latex gloves. He stopped, looking at Trent. "I take you for a runner, sir. Is that correct?"

Trent didn't seem surprised by the question. Being on the job for twelve years, Michael figured the man had been around his share of eccentric coroners.

He answered, "Yes, sir."

"Long distance?"

"Yes."

"Marathons?"

"Yes."

"Thought so." Pete nodded to himself, like he had scored a point, though Michael had noticed that Will Trent hadn't volunteered any information about himself.

Pete went back to the corpse lying on the table in the center of the room. Aleesha Monroe's body was draped in a white sheet, her head exposed. The third eyelash was gone, the makeup removed. Thick sutures lined her forehead where her scalp and face had been peeled back to examine her skull and remove her brain.

"You ever bitten your tongue?" Pete asked.

Trent didn't answer, so Michael said, "Sure."

"Heals pretty quickly. The tongue is an amazing

organ—unless it's severed, that is. At any rate," he continued, "biting through the tongue is not a difficult endeavor." He rolled back the sheet, showing the top of the Y-incision but stopping just shy of baring Monroe's breasts.

"Here," Pete said. Michael could see deep black bruises over the woman's left shoulder. "The distribution of the livor mortis tells us she died where you found her. On her back, on the stairs. My guess," Pete said, "is that she was beaten, then raped, and in the course of the rape he bit off her tongue."

Michael thought about that, pictured her on the stairs, her body lax at first as she endured the rape, then tensing, convulsing in fear as she realized what was going to happen.

Trent finally spoke. "Can you get DNA off the tongue?"

"I imagine I'll get a significant amount of DNA off her tongue, given her profession." Pete shrugged his shoulders. "And I'm sure the swabs from her vagina will reveal a cornucopia of suspects for you, but my guess would be that your perpetrator used a condom."

"Why is that?" Michael asked.

"Powder," Pete answered. "There was a trace of cornstarch on her right thigh."

Michael knew that rubbers were often packed in powder to make them easier to use. All the condom makers used the same ingredients, so there was no way of tracing it back to a single manufacturer. Not that knowing whether he used a Trojan or a Ramses would narrow the search.

"I'm guessing it was lubricated," Pete added. "There were also traces of a compound not inconsistent with nonoxynol-9."

Trent seemed to find this interesting. "Were there any traces of this on the stairs?"

"Not that I found."

Trent surmised, "So, he must have had sex with her somewhere else, probably inside the apartment, before the struggle in the stairway."

Michael tuned them out. A whore like Monroe wasn't going to waste her hard-earned money on extravagances like lube and spermicide. Better to just grit her teeth and save the cash. Deal with the consequences later.

Michael said, "The condom must have belonged to the doer."

Trent looked surprised, as if he'd just remembered Michael was in the room. "That's possible."

Michael spelled it out for him. "The doer didn't mean to kill her. Why bother with an expensive condom, right?"

Trent nodded, but didn't say anything else.

"Well." Pete broke the silence. "As I was saying..." He went back to his lecture, opening the woman's mouth, showing the stub where her tongue used to be attached. "There aren't any major arteries in the tongue, barring the lingual artery, which spreads out like the roots of a tree, tapering at the ends. You would have to go into the mouth a few inches to get to it, in which case you couldn't use your teeth." He frowned, thinking for a moment. "Picture a dachshund trying to fit his snout into a badger hole."

Michael didn't want to, but he found the image playing in his mind, the yippy bark echoing in his ears.

"In this case," Pete continued, "the incision separated the frenulum linguae from the organ, bisecting the submandibular duct." He opened his own mouth and lifted up his tongue, pointing to the thin stretch of skin underneath. "The removal of the tongue in and of itself is not a life-threatening injury. The problem is, she fell onto her back. Perhaps the shock of the event or the various chemical substances in her body affected her. Subsequently, she passed out. Over the course of a few minutes, the blood from the severed tongue engorged her throat. My official cause of death will be asphyxiation due to the blockage of the trachea by blood, causing respiratory arrest, secondary to exsanguination from the traumatic amputation of the tongue."

"But," Michael said, "he didn't mean for her to die."

"It's not in my purview to imagine what goes through a man's mind when he is biting off a woman's tongue, but if I were a gambling man, and my ex-wives will tell you I am, then yes. I would guess that the attacker did not intend for her to die."

Trent said, "Just like the others."

"There are more?" Pete asked, perking up. "I've not heard of any cases similar to this."

Trent told him, "There are two girls that we know of. The first had her tongue bitten, but not completely severed. It was sewn back on and she was fine—relatively speaking. The second lost her tongue. Too much time had passed to safely reattach it."

Pete shook his head. "Poor thing. Was this recent? I haven't read anything about it."

"The first attack happened on state land, so we were able to keep it quiet. The second girl's parents shut out the press and the local cops held back the details. There's no story if nobody's willing to talk."

"What about the third one?" Michael had to ask. "The little girl?"

Trent filled Pete in on the case. "My opinion is she bit it herself," he concluded. "She's young, ten years old. She must have been terrified. The local PD is good, but they don't have a lot of experience with this sort of violent crime. I think it was probably very hard for them to elicit a statement from her."

"No doubt," Pete agreed, but Michael wondered why

Trent hadn't said any of this earlier. Maybe he had been feeling out Michael, seeing if he could pass the test.

Shit, Michael thought. He was tired of jumping through hoops. He asked the doctor, "How old do you think this one is?" He nodded to Aleesha Monroe.

"It's hard to say." Pete studied the woman's face. "Her teeth are a mess because of the drug. Given the hard nature of her life and her prolonged drug dependency, I'd put her in the late thirties; possibly older, possibly younger."

Michael looked at Trent. "But not a teenage girl."

"Definitely not," Pete agreed.

"So, we've got two teenagers thirty miles away and an old junkie in Atlanta and the only thing linking them is this tongue shit." He tried to stare his meaning into Trent. "Right?"

Trent's cell phone rang. He glanced at the screen, then excused himself with an apology as he left the room.

Pete gave a heavy sigh, covering up the body, tugging the sheet tight over her head. "Messy situation."

"Yeah," Michael agreed. He was watching Trent through the glass doors, wondering what the fuck was up with the guy.

"He seems on the ball," Pete said, meaning Trent. "I have to say, it's a nice change of pace seeing one of your compatriots dressed so smartly."

"What?" Michael asked. He'd been watching Trent, trying to hear the call.

"The suit," Pete clarified. "It makes an impression."

"Like a fucking undertaker," Michael answered, thinking Pete wasn't exactly ready to step into a *GQ* spread. His white lab coats were always starched and clean, but that was because the state took care of the laundry bill. Underneath, Pete generally wore jeans and a wrinkled button-down shirt, his collar wide open, revealing a patch of gray chest hair and a gold medallion that any of the Bee Gees would have been ashamed to wear.

"It is a tenuous connection," Pete said. "The three cases."

"You're telling me."

"But it does give one pause that the tongues were all bitten off. That's not a common twist." He picked up the evidence bag with the tongue and held it up as if Michael hadn't seen it plenty last night. "I'd have to say in all my years doing this job, I've never run across anything similar. Bite marks, yes. I always say if you want scientific proof that we have evolved from animals, you need only look at the average rape victim." Pete placed the tongue beside Monroe's arm. "Bite marks were all over her breasts and shoulders. I counted at least twenty-two. It's a base instinct, I suppose, to bite during a vicious attack. You see dogs and big cats do it in the wild." He chuckled. "I cannot tell you how many nipples I've seen bitten off. Five or six instances of the clitoris being severed. One finger..." He smiled at Michael. "If only these monsters had horns. It would be so much easier finding them."

Michael did not like the way the doctor was looking at him, and he sure as hell didn't want to hear his opinions on sexual predators. He said, "Tell Trent I'm downstairs when he's finished yapping on the phone."

He left through the emergency exit, taking the steps at a full trot. His instinct was to get into his car and leave Trent with his thumb up his ass, but he wasn't about to fuck around with the guy. Even if Greer didn't call him on it, Michael knew better than to make an enemy of the well-dressed asshole from the GBI.

"Where's the fire?" Leo asked. He was standing at the bottom of the stairs smoking a cigarette.

"Give me one," Michael said.

"Thought you quit."

"You my mother?" Michael reached into Leo's shirt pocket and took the pack.

Leo clicked the lighter and Michael took a deep drag. They were on the garage level of the building. The odor of car exhaust and rubber was overwhelming, but the cigarette smoke burning through Michael's nostrils cut the smell.

"So," Leo began. "Where's fucknuts?"

Michael let out a stream of smoke, feeling the nicotine calm him. "Upstairs with Pete."

Leo scowled. Pete had banned him from the morgue after a predictably ill-timed joke. "I went down to Records."

Michael squinted past the smoke. "Yeah?"

"Will Trent's file is sealed."

"Sealed?"

Leo nodded.

"How do you get your file sealed?"

"Got me."

They both smoked for a minute, silent in their thoughts. Michael looked down at the floor, which was covered with cigarette butts. The building was strictly nonsmoking, but telling a bunch of cops they couldn't do something was like telling a monkey not to throw its shit.

Michael asked, "Why'd Greer call him in? Him specifically, I mean. This SCAT team, whatever the fuck it is."

"Greer didn't call him." Leo raised his eyebrows like he was enjoying the mystery. "Trent was sitting in his office when Greer got to work."

Michael felt his heart start beating double time in his chest. The nicotine was getting to him, making him light-headed. "That's not how it works. The state boys can't just come in and take over a case. They have to be asked in."

"Sounded to me last night like Greer was gonna ask him anyway. What's the big deal how it came down?"

"Never mind." Despite Leo's disgusting people skills, the man knew a lot of people on the force. He had made an art out of developing contacts and could usually get the dirt on anybody.

Michael asked, "You able to find out anything about him?"

Leo shrugged, winking his eye against the smoke from his cigarette. "Sharon down in Dispatch knows a guy who dated a girl he worked with."

"Christ," Michael hissed. "Next you're gonna tell me you gotta friend who knows somebody who's gotta friend who—"

"You wanna hear or not?"

Michael bit back what he really wanted to say. "Go."

Leo took his time, rubbing his cigarette between his thumb and forefinger, taking a drag, then letting it out slow. Michael was two seconds from throttling him when Leo finally provided, "The news is that he's a good cop. Doesn't make a lot of friends—"

"No shit."

"Yeah." Leo chuckled, then coughed, then smacked his lips like he was swallowing it back down.

Michael looked at the cigarette in his hand, his stomach turning.

Leo paused, made sure he had Michael's attention. "He's got an eighty-nine percent clearance rate."

Michael felt sick, but not because of the smoke. In its infinite wisdom, the Federal government had called for measuring the clearance rate—the number of solved cases—in each police agency so that some pencil pusher in Washington could track the progress on his little charts. They called it accountability, but to most cops it was just a shitload more paperwork. Any idiot could have predicted that this would cause a massive pissing contest among the detectives, and Greer fed into it by posting their numbers each month.

Trent had them all beat by about twenty points.

"Well," Michael said, forcing himself to laugh. "It's easy to solve a case when you take it over from some cop who's already done all the work."

"This SKIT thing is new to him."

"SCAT," Michael corrected, knowing Leo was trying to bait him but unable to stop playing.

"Whatever," Leo mumbled. "What I'm saying is, Trent was working major crime before he was tapped."

"Good for him."

"He had a huge case a few years back with some gal over in kiddie crimes."

"Gal got a name?"

Leo shrugged again. "Couple of guys were snatching kids down in Florida, swapping them back and forth with their buddies in Montana. It was all going out of Hartsfield; they were moving them through there like cattle. Your buddy's team cracked it open in a month. Gal gets a big promotion, Trent stays where he is."

"He was head of the team?"

"Yep."

"Why didn't he get promoted?"

"Have to ask him that."

"If I could ask him, I wouldn't be here talking to you."

Leo's eyes flashed, like his feelings had been hurt. "That's all I got, man. Trent's a straight arrow, knows his job. You want more, you need to call somebody downtown and find out yourself."

Michael stared at his cigarette, watching it burn. Gina would kill him if she saw him smoking. She'd smell it on his hands as soon as he got home.

He dropped the butt onto the ground, grinding it in with his heel. "Is Angie still working Vice?"

"Polaski?" Leo asked, like he didn't quite believe his ears. "You don't wanna go fucking with that pollack."

"Answer the fucking question."

Leo took out another cigarette and lit it from the first. "Yeah. Last I heard."

"If Trent comes looking for me, tell him I'll meet him back down here in a few minutes."

Michael didn't give Leo time to answer. He ran back up the steps to the third floor, his lungs rattling in his chest by the time he opened the door. Vice was a mostly nighttime endeavor, so half the squad was in the room filling out paperwork from last night's sweep. Angie had obviously worked catch. She was wearing a halter-top that stopped three inches above her belly button and a blonde wig was splayed on her desk like a dead Pomeranian.

He waited for her to look up, and when she did, she wasn't exactly happy to see him. As Michael walked over, she leaned back in her chair, crossing her legs under a skirt so short he looked away out of decency.

"What are you doing here?" she demanded. "Jesus, you look like hell."

Michael ran his fingers through his hair. He was sweating from the sprint up the stairs. The smoke was still in his lungs and he coughed something that sounded like a death rattle. Christ, he'd be joining Ken in a wheelchair if he kept this up.

He said, "I need to talk to you a minute."

She looked wary. "About what?"

Michael leaned over her desk, trying to keep the conversation between them.

"Uh-uh," she said, pushing him back as she stood up. "Let's go out into the hall."

He followed her, aware that the rest of the squad was watching. The truth was that Michael had liked working Vice. You watched the girls, you picked up the johns, you seldom got shot at or had to tell a parent that their son or daughter had been found floating in the Chattahoochee. He hadn't left because he wanted to. Angie had been a problem for him. They hadn't exactly gotten along, and the fact that she was agreeing to talk to him now was up there with the world's biggest surprises.

She tugged at her skirt as she stepped into a nook across from the elevators. Beside her, an ancient vending machine hummed, the lights flickering. She asked, "You here to talk about Aleesha Monroe?"

"The pross?" He hadn't even thought to pull her record.

"You don't remember her?" Angie asked. "We banged her up a couple of times until she hooked up with Baby G."

Michael answered "Yeah," though Angie shouldn't really expect him to remember one hooker out of the thousands they had arrested on the weekend sweeps. Some Saturday nights, they called out a wagon just to transport all the girls to the station. Cabs lined up outside the precinct to take them right back out onto the street a couple of hours later.

Michael began, "I just—"

The elevator door dinged behind him. Michael looked over his shoulder and saw Will Trent.

"Shit," Michael muttered.

"Kit Kat," Trent said, and Michael's brain took its sweet time figuring out what the fuck the guy was talking about. Trent stood in front of the vending machine, digging in his pocket for change.

Michael decided to make nice. "This is Angie Polaski," he said. Then, as if it wasn't obvious from the way she was dressed, he added, "Vice."

Trent was sticking coins into the machine. He gave her a nod, but his eyes didn't quite meet hers. "Good morning, Detective Polaski."

"Trent's with the GBI," Michael said. "Greer called him in to give us a hand with the Monroe case."

Michael was watching Trent, waiting for the guy to point out that Greer hadn't actually called him, that he'd shown up at the lieutenant's doorstep on his own. Trent, for his part, was tracing his finger along the glass front of the machine, trying to read the code under the Kit Kat bars so he could press it into the control panel. He was squinting; Michael figured the guy needed glasses.

"Oh, fer fucksakes," Angie muttered. "It's E-six." She punched the code in herself, her garishly long fake finger-nails clicking on the plastic keys. She told Michael, "I'll get the file on Monroe."

She was walking back toward her squad before Michael could think to say anything else. He saw Trent watching her walk, the way her ass moved in the high heels.

"I worked with her a while back," Michael told him. "She's all right."

Trent peeled back the wrapper on the candy bar and took a bite.

Michael felt the need to explain. "She's kind of got an attitude."

"If I had to dress that way for work every day, I don't imagine I'd be very cheerful."

Michael watched Trent's jaw work as he chewed. The scar on his cheek seemed more pronounced. "How'd you get the scar?"

Trent looked at his hand. "Nail gun," he said, and Michael could see a pink scar cutting through the skin on the webbing between the man's thumb and index finger.

That hadn't been the scar Michael had meant, but he played along. "You into home repair or something?"

"Habitat for Humanity." Trent shoved the last of the Kit Kat into his mouth and tossed the wrapper into the trashcan. "One of my fellow volunteers shot me with a galvanized nail."

Michael felt another piece of the puzzle slide into place. Habitat for Humanity was a volunteer group that built homes for low-income families. Most cops eventually ended up volunteering for something. Working the streets, you tended to forget that there were actually good people out there. You tried to salve this wound in your psyche by helping people who actually wanted your help. Michael had worked at a children's shelter before Tim had been born. Even Leo Donnelly had volunteered with the local Little League team until they'd told him he couldn't smoke on the field.

Trent said, "I'd like to see the crime scene."

"We tossed her place last night," Michael told him. "You think we missed something?"

"Not at all," Trent countered. Michael tried to find any guile in his tone but came up empty. "I'd just like to get a feel for the place."

"You do this with the other cases?"

"Yes," Trent said, "I did."

Angie was back, her high heels click-clacking on the tile floor. She held out a yellow file folder. "This is what I've got on Monroe."

Trent didn't reach for the file, so Michael took it. He flipped open the cover, seeing Aleesha Monroe's mug shot. She was attractive for what she was. The hardness in her eyes was a challenge as she stared straight into the camera. She looked irritated, probably doing the math, figuring how much money she was going to lose before she made bail.

"Her pimp's Baby G," Angie told them. "Mean mother-fucker. Been up for assault, rape, attempted murder—probably ordered a hit on two other guys, but there's no way they can pin it on him." She indicated her mouth, showing her front teeth. "Has a gold grille with crosses cut into them like he's Jesus's own."

Michael asked, "Where does he hang out?"

"At the Homes," she said. "His grandmother lives in the same building as Aleesha."

Trent had tucked his hands into his pockets again, and he was staring at Polaski like she was a Martian from space. His silence was annoying, and he exuded an air of superiority, like he knew more than he was saying and thought it was some kind of joke that they couldn't figure it out.

Michael asked him, "You got anything to add to this?"

"It's your case, Detective," Trent answered. He told Angie, "Thank you for your assistance, ma'am," flashing what might have been a smile on someone less patronizing.

Angie looked at Michael, then Trent, then back at Michael. She lifted an eyebrow, asking a question Michael couldn't answer. "Whatever," she muttered, holding up her hand in the universal sign of dismissal. She turned her back on both of them, and Michael was too pissed to admire the view this time.

He asked Trent, "What's your fucking problem?"

Trent seemed surprised by his tone. "I'm sorry?"

"You gonna just stand there all day or are you here to get your hands dirty?"

"I told you—I'm just here to advise."

"Well, I've got some advice for you, Mr. Here to Advise," Michael said, his fists clenching so hard he could feel his fingernails digging into his palms. "Don't fuck with me."

Trent didn't seem threatened by the warning, but considering Michael had to crane his neck up to give it, this didn't come as a complete surprise.

"All right," Trent said. Then, as if that had settled everything, he asked, "Would you mind going to the Homes again? I'd really like to see the crime scene."

CHAPTER FIVE

Everything Will Trent said and did grated on Michael's nerves, from his "of course" when Michael said he would drive to the way he stared blankly out the car window as they traveled up North Avenue toward the Homes. The GBI agent reminded him of those geeky kids in high school, the ones who kept slide rules in their breast pockets and quoted obscure lines from Monty Python. No matter how many times he watched it, Michael still didn't get Monty Python and he sure as shit didn't get geeks like Trent. There was a reason these guys got the shit beaten out of them in school. There was a reason it was guys like Michael doing the beating.

Michael took a deep breath, then coughed, his lungs still pissed about the cigarette. He thought about Tim, how his son wasn't normal, how this attracted abuse from other kids. There was already a group of bullies at Tim's school who had given him some grief—stealing his hat, flattening his sandwich at the lunch table. The teachers tried to stop it, but they couldn't be everywhere all the time and some of them weren't real happy to begin with about Tim's being mainstreamed into their classrooms. Maybe Will Trent was Michael's karma playing out. He was being tested. Be nice to this freak and maybe Tim would get the same kind of pass.

"Oh," Trent said, pulling a small tape recorder out of his jacket pocket. "I've got the nine-one-one call." He pressed the play button before Michael could comment. A tinny, high-pitched voice bleated from the small speaker, *You gotta come to building nine at the Homes. They's a woman being raped pretty bad.*

Michael drummed his fingers on the steering wheel as he waited for a red light to change. "Play it again."

Trent did as he was told, and Michael strained his ears, trying to hear background noise, to figure out the tone and tenor of the voice. Something was off, but he couldn't put his finger on it.

" 'Raped'," Michael echoed. "Not 'killed'."

Trent added, "The caller doesn't sound frightened."

"No," Michael agreed, accelerating as the light changed.

"I would think," Trent began, "if I were a woman, that I would be frightened if I saw, or even heard, another woman being attacked."

"Maybe not," Michael contradicted. "Maybe if you lived in the Homes, you would've already seen your fill of this kind of violence."

"If that were the case," Trent said, "then why would I report it?" He tried to answer his own question. "Maybe I knew the woman?"

"If you knew her, then you'd sound more upset than that." Michael indicated the recorder. The caller had sounded calm, like she was reporting the weather or the score from a particularly boring game.

"It took over thirty minutes for the unit to come." Trent didn't seem to be making a condemnation when he pointed out, "Grady has the slowest response time in the city."

"Anybody watching the news would know that."

"Or living in the Homes."

"We've checked everybody in the building, did door-to-doors that night. Nobody's popping up with a big sign hanging around his neck."

"No sex offenders in the buildings?"

"One, but he was banged up the whole day being interviewed on another case."

Trent rewound the tape and played it yet another time, letting it run into the emergency operator saying, *Ma'am? Ma'am? Are you there?*

Trent tucked the recorder back into his pocket. "The victim's a little old, too."

"Monroe?" Michael asked, trying to switch gears. Trent was finally talking to him like a cop. "Yeah, if Pete's right, she's probably around my age. Your girls were—what—fourteen? Fifteen?"

"White, too."

"Monroe was black, living in the projects, working the streets."

"The others were white, middle to upper class, came from solid families, doing well in school."

"Maybe he didn't have time to hunt down a new one," Michael suggested, feeling like he was walking on a very thin wire. He got that buzzing in his ears again, that something in his head that told him to shut up, don't trust this new guy, don't let him fool you.

"Could be," Trent allowed, but his tone of voice said he didn't find it likely.

Michael kept his mouth closed as he took a right into Grady Homes. The development looked a hell of a lot better at night, darkness covering the worst of its flaws. It was almost ten o'clock on a Monday morning, but kids were milling around on their bikes like they had been freed for the summer. Michael had done this same thing when he was a kid, straddling his Schwinn as he bullshitted with the other kids on his block. Only, Michael hadn't been passing dime bags out in the open like these kids were doing now, and he sure as hell wouldn't have had the balls to toss a wave at a couple of cops as they cruised through his neighborhood.

The BMW was still parked outside of building nine, two teenagers sitting on the hood with their arms crossed over their chests. They looked about fifteen or sixteen, and Michael felt a cold sweat at the soulless look in their eyes as they watched his car pull into the lot. This was the age that scared him most as a cop. They had something to prove, a quest to fulfill in order to grow from boy into man. Spilling blood was the quickest way to cross over.

Trent was looking at the boys, too. He gave a resigned "Great," and Michael was relieved to see him still thinking like a cop.

The front door to the building banged open and they both reached for their guns at the same time. Neither one drew as a short, fireplug of a man stalked down the broken sidewalk, pounding right past Trent's side of the car without giving them a second look.

The man wasn't wearing a shirt and his broad chest showed hints of thick muscle under jiggling fat, his pecs jerking up and down like tits with each step he took. He had an aluminum bat in one hand, and as he got closer to the boys on the car, he wrapped his other hand around the base, ready to break some balls.

Michael looked at Trent, who said, "Your call," but he was already getting out of the car.

"Shit," Michael hissed, opening his door, getting out just as the fireplug reached the boys.

"Get the hell off my car!" the man screamed, waving the bat in the air. Both teens stood up straight, arms dangling at their sides, mouths slack. "Get on a'fore I beat your asses, you lazy motherfuckers!"

Wisely, the kids bolted.

"Well," Trent said, letting out a breath.

"Stupid motherfuckers," the man repeated. He was looking at Michael and Trent, and Michael was pretty sure he wasn't talking about the boys anymore. "What the fuck you two pigs want?"

"Baby G?" Trent asked.

The man kept the bat up, ready to strike. "Who the fuck's asking?"

Trent took a step forward as if he wasn't scared his head would be knocked into right field at any moment.

Assault, Michael remembered Angie saying when she told them about Baby G. *Rape, attempted murder.*

Trent said, "I'm Special Agent Will Trent, this is Detective Ormewood." Michael waved, glad there was a car between him and the angry pimp. Trent was an idiot if he thought he'd get anything useful out of this thug.

"We're investigating the death of Aleesha Monroe."

"Why the fuck should I talk to you?" Baby G kept the bat in the air; his muscles tensed.

Trent looked back at Michael. "Any ideas?"

Michael shrugged, wondering how he was going to write this up in his report once he got Will Trent to the hospital. *Officer antagonized suspect...* came to mind.

Trent turned back to the pimp, holding his hands out in an open shrug. "Honestly, I'm shocked my good looks and charm aren't enough for you."

Michael felt his jaw drop in surprise. He closed it quickly, let his hand reach down to his gun again so he'd be ready to react when the pimp figured out he was being disrespected.

Two or three seconds passed, then two or three more. Finally, Baby G nodded. "All right." He smiled, showing the gold caps on each tooth, crosses cut through the centers showing the whites, just as Angie had described. "You got ten minutes before Montel comes on."

Trent held out his hand, as if they'd made a deal. "Thank you."

The pimp shook the offered hand, looking Trent up and down, saying, "You sure you a cop?"

Trent reached into his pocket and pulled out his badge.

Baby G glanced at it, then let his eyes do a once-over of Trent again. "You one weird motherfucker."

Trent tucked his badge back into his pocket, ignoring the observation. "You want to talk out here?"

Baby G dropped the bat to his side, leaning on it like it was a cane. "Them's my cousins," he said, indicating the car, obviously meaning the boys he'd chased off. "Up to no good. They should have they asses in school."

"It's nice that you take an interest in their lives," Trent allowed. He had tucked his hands into his pockets again, and was casually leaning against the back of the car like this was some kind of friendly conversation. "When did you last see Aleesha?"

Baby G took his time. "About six last night," he finally answered. "She was going off to work. Wanted a little something before she went out." He lifted his chin, waiting for Trent to ask what the little something was.

Trent obviously knew. He had seen the tracks on the hooker's arms just like Michael. "Did you give it to her?"

Baby G shrugged, which Michael took for a yes.

"Did she have any other suppliers?"

The pimp looked around as if he was checking his audience. He spit on the ground, puffing out his chest in defiance, but he still answered the question. "Hell no. She didn't have no money. Nobody was gonna float that ho for a dime."

"I could run up the street and blow just about anybody for a baggie," Trent pointed out. "No cash involved."

Baby G laughed at the thought. "Yo, bitch, not on my turf."

"I'm sure Aleesha reported all her income," Trent said, more like a question.

"Shit," Baby G grunted, like it was stupid to even suggest such a thing.

Trent asked, "She a good earner?"

"She like that needle in her arm. Do anything you ask to get it."

"Did she have any regulars? Men we should be looking out for?"

"Not sick mothers like what did that," he used the bat to indicate the top floor of the building where Monroe had been found. "I take care of my girls." He kept the bat raised in the air, using it to make his point. "If I'd'a seen this motherfucker, you best be sure he'd be the one going in the ground right now, not my Leesha."

Trent nodded toward the building. "You live here?"

He softened a bit. "With my granny. She gettin' kind of old. I gotta look out for her."

"Were you with her last night?"

"Me an' my boys was out at the Cheetah watching the game."

"Do you mind if we speak with your grandmother?"

"Hell yes, I do. Don't go gettin' my granny mixed up with this shit. She didn't see *nothing,* you hear? She just an old lady."

"All right," Trent acquiesced. He looked back at Michael as if to ask if he had any questions. Michael shook his head and Trent told the pimp, "I know you want to go watch your program. Thank you for your time."

Baby G stood there, unsure of himself. He finally

shrugged them off, repeating, "You just one weird mother-fucker," before walking back into the building.

When the door had banged shut, Trent turned to Michael. "What do you think?"

"I think he's right," Michael said, pushing away from the car. "You're pretty fucking strange."

Trent's cell phone chirped, and Michael felt his earlier irritation spark again as Trent walked a few feet away to take the call.

"Yes, sir," Trent said. "Yes, sir."

Michael looked up at the sky, the dark clouds that were starting to roll in. The way today was going, a storm would break just as they were leaving the scene and he'd end up sloshing through the parking lot, ruining his new shoes.

Trent snapped the phone closed, tucking it into his vest pocket. "You need to go home, Michael."

Michael felt his heart stop in his chest. "What?"

"You need to go home," Trent repeated. "There's been an accident."

ARREST MADE IN FINNEY MURDER

Police announced this morning that an arrest has been made in the murder of fifteen-year-old Mary Alice Finney. The suspect's name has not been released because he is a juvenile, but Police Chief Harold Waller describes the boy as a fifteen-year-old whose name was well known to the City of Decatur Police Department. The arrest was made after several neighbors identified the suspect as the stranger who walked Mary Alice Finney home from the party where she was last seen alive. Waller claims that a full confession is expected in what he has called "the most heinous violation" he has seen in his entire law enforcement career.

The girl's father is Paul Finney, a well-respected member of the bar as well as assistant district attorney for DeKalb County. Mother Sally Finney, a homemaker, has been active in the Women's League as well as a fund-raiser for Agnes Scott College. The couple have no other children. A candlelight vigil for Mary Alice Finney will be held on the Square at 8:30 tonight, and closed services will be held at the Cable Funeral Home tomorrow afternoon. The family asks for donations in lieu of flowers to be made to the Decatur City Library, one of Mary Alice's favorite places.

CHAPTER SIX

Michael drove like the devil, his hands gripping the wheel. Trent sat beside him, stone quiet even as Michael blasted through red lights and ran stop signs. The house was less than twenty minutes away from Grady Homes, but Michael felt like it was taking hours to get there. His heart was in his throat, pumping like a freight train. All he could think about was all the horrible things he had done to his family, how he didn't deserve them, how he would clean up his act, turn his life around, if only Tim was okay.

"Fuck!" Michael twisted the steering wheel hard to the left, narrowly avoiding a Chevy Blazer that had the right of way.

Trent had grabbed the side of the door, but he wasn't stupid enough to say anything about slowing down.

Michael straightened the wheel, making another hard left onto a back road that would take them out of heavy traffic and hopefully get them home sooner. The clutch slipped but quickly caught again as he accelerated. A light was flashing on the dashboard, the engine temperature gauge pushing well into the red. All he needed was for the piece of shit car to get him to the house. That's all Michael needed.

He hit the redial on his cell phone again, listening to the phone ringing at his house for the fiftieth time.

Barbara's cell wasn't picking up and he hadn't been able to find Gina at the hospital.

"God damn it!" Michael screamed, smashing the phone against the dashboard, breaking it to pieces.

Greer had called Will Trent to tell him there was a problem, like Michael was some pansy civilian instead of a seasoned cop. All the lieutenant had said was that there had been some kind of accident involving a kid at Michael's house. Standard fucking procedure—don't tell them on the phone, don't freak them out so they drive their car over a bridge on the way to the scene. When Michael had tried to call Greer back for more details, the fucker had talked to him like he was twelve. "Just get home, Michael," Greer had said. "Everything's going to be okay."

"Bike," Trent said, and Michael saw the cyclist at the last second, nearly clipping the guy as he darted the car into the other lane. There was an oncoming truck, and Michael jerked the wheel back just in time to avoid a head-on collision.

"We're almost there," Michael said, as if Trent had asked. "Shit," he hissed, slamming the heel of his palm into the steering wheel. Tim was always getting into things he shouldn't. He didn't know any better. Barbara was getting old. She was tired most days, didn't have the energy to keep up.

The car fishtailed as he turned onto his street. There were two cruisers in front of his house, one of them parked in the driveway behind Barbara's car. Uniformed cops were milling around on the sidewalk in front of Cynthia and Phil's house. Michael's heart stopped when he saw Barbara sitting on the front porch, head in her hands.

Somehow, Michael got out of the car. He ran to her, bile rushing up his throat as he tried not to be sick. "Where's

Tim?" he asked. She didn't answer quickly enough and he repeated himself, yelling, "Where's my son!"

"In school," she screamed back as if he was crazy. He had grabbed her wrists, dragging her up to standing. She had tears in her eyes.

"Hey," Trent said, a quiet word that held a warning.

Michael looked at his hands, not knowing how they had wrapped themselves around Barbara's wrists. There were red marks where he held her. He made himself let go.

Behind him, a coroner's wagon pulled up, its brakes grinding as it stopped and idled by the mailbox.

He put his hands on Barbara's shoulders, this time to hold himself up. They had said it was a kid. Maybe they got it wrong. Maybe Greer had lied.

"Gina?" Michael asked. Had something happened to Gina?

One of the cops was at the meat wagon. He motioned the driver toward the house next door. "In the backyard."

Michael's feet were moving before he knew it. He slammed open his front door and bolted up the hall. He heard footsteps pounding behind him and knew it was that bastard Trent. Michael didn't care. He threw open the back door and ran into the yard, stopping so fast that Trent bumped into him from behind.

Michael saw the white first, the skimpy robe, the see-through camisole. She was on her stomach, feet tangled up in the broken chain-link fence. Six or seven men stood around her.

Michael managed to walk toward her, his knees giving out when he reached the body. The mole on her shoulder, the birthmark on the back of her arm. He pressed his fingers into the palm of her small hand.

Somebody warned, "Sir, don't touch her."

Michael didn't care. He stroked her soft palm, tears streaming down his face, whispering, "Jesus. Oh, Jesus."

Trent was making noises to the group of cops, words Michael couldn't understand. He could only look at the back of Cynthia's head, see the long strands of her silky blonde hair draping around her shoulders like a scarf. He pulled the robe down, covering her bare bottom, trying to give her some dignity.

"Detective," Trent said. His hand was tucked under Michael's arm, and Trent easily pulled him up to his feet. "You shouldn't touch her."

"It's not her," Michael insisted, trying to kneel back down, wanting to see her face. It was some kind of trick. It couldn't be Cynthia. She was at the mall spending Phil's money, hanging out with her friends.

"I want to see her," Michael said. His body was shaking like he was cold. His knees didn't want to work again, but Trent supported him, keeping him up so he didn't fall back down. "I want to see her face."

One of the men, obviously the medical examiner, said, "I was just about to flip her anyway."

With help from another cop, the doctor gripped her by the shoulders and turned her so that she was facing up.

Cynthia's mouth gaped open, blood spilling out and dribbling down her neck like a slow leak from a faucet. Her beautiful face was marked by a deep cut slashing across her temple. Vacant green eyes stared up at the open sky. Strands of hair were stuck to her face, and he tried to lean down to brush them back but Trent wouldn't let him.

Michael felt hot tears stinging his eyes. Somebody should cover her. She shouldn't be exposed like this for everybody to see.

The medical examiner leaned down, pressing her jaw

open, peering into her empty mouth. He said, "Her tongue is gone."

"Christ," one of the cops whispered. "She's just a kid."

Michael swallowed, feeling like he was choking on his grief. "Fifteen," he said. She'd just had a birthday last week. He'd bought her a stuffed giraffe.

"She's fifteen."

PART II

CHAPTER SEVEN

John Shelley wanted a television. He had been working the same crappy job for the last two months, showing up every day on time, making sure he was the last to leave, doing every nitpicking shit job his boss assigned, and to him it wasn't just a matter of wanting, but *deserving* a television. Nothing fancy for him, just something in color, something with a remote control and something that would pick up the college games.

He wanted to watch his teams play. He wanted to hold the remote in his hand and if Georgia was playing bad, which was highly likely, he wanted to be able to turn the channel and watch Florida getting its ass kicked. He wanted to watch the cheesy halftime shows, hear the stupid commentators, see Tulane at Southern Mississippi, Texas A&M at LSU, Army-freakin'-Navy. Come Thanksgiving, he wanted an orgy of bowl games and then he'd switch to the big dogs: the Patriots, the Raiders, the Eagles, all leading up to that magic moment come February when John Shelley would sit in his crap room in his crap boarding-house and watch the freaking Super Bowl all alone for the first time in his life.

Six days a week for the last two months, he had looked out the bus window and stared longingly at the Atlanta City Rent-All. The sign in the window promised "your job is your credit," but the asterisk, so tiny it could be a squished bug, told otherwise. Thank God he had been too nervous to walk right into the store and make a fool of himself. John had stood outside the front door, his heart shaking in his chest like a dog shitting peach pits, when he noticed the fine print on the poster. Two months, the tiny type said. You had to hold down a steady job for at least two months before they would allow you the honor of paying fifty-two weekly installments of twenty dollars for a television that would retail for around three hundred bucks in a normal store.

But John wasn't a normal person. No matter his new haircut or his close shave or his pressed chinos, people still felt that otherness about him. Even at work, a car wash where mostly transients showed up to wipe down cars and vacuum Cheerios out of the backs of SUVs, they kept their distance.

And now, two months later, John sat on the edge of his chair, trying to keep his leg from bobbing up and down, waiting for his TV. The pimply faced kid who had greeted him at the door was taking his time. He'd gotten John's application and rushed to the back about twenty minutes ago. Application. That was another thing they hadn't put on the sign. Street address, date of birth, social security number, place of employment, everything but his freaking underwear size.

The Atlanta City Rent-All was noisy for a Sunday afternoon. All of the televisions were on, bright images flashing from a wall of tubes, whispered undertones from nature shows, news channels and do-it-yourself programs buzzing in his ears. The noise was getting to him. Too much light was pouring in from the floor-to-ceiling windows. The televisions were too bright.

He shifted in his chair, feeling a bead of sweat roll down

his back. John didn't wear a watch, but there was a big clock on the wall. This represented poor judgment on the store planner's part, considering the fact that all it served to do was remind people they were stuck here waiting for some kid fresh out of high school to tell the lucky customer that they had qualified for the extreme honor of paying five hundred bucks for a Simzitzu DVD player.

"Just a TV," John whispered to himself. "Just a small TV." His leg was bobbing up and down again and he didn't bother to stop it. His hands were clenching and unclenching, and that was bad. He had to stop doing that. People were staring. Parents were keeping their kids close.

"Sir?" Randall, John's own personal sales assistant, stood in front of him. He had a smile plastered onto his face that would have given a Labrador pause. "Sorry to keep you waiting." Randall reached out his hand as if John might need help up.

"It's okay," John said, trying not to mumble as he stood. He started looking around, wondering what was going on. The kid was being too nice to him. Had something happened? Did someone call the police?

"We can show you these sets here," Randall offered, leading him to the back of the store where the big screens were displayed.

John stood in front of a television that looked as huge as a movie screen. The set was almost as tall as him and twice as wide.

Randall picked up a remote control the size of a book. "The Panasonic has advanced real black technology that gives you—"

"Wait a minute." John was walking around the television. It was only a few inches thick. He saw the price tag and laughed. "I told you what I make, man."

Randall flashed him a smile, took a step forward that

made John want to take a step back. He kept his ground, though, and the kid lowered his voice, saying, "We understand when some of our customers have outside income sources they can't list on their credit applications."

"That right?" John asked, recognizing something illicit was happening but not quite sure what.

"Your credit report..." Randall seemed almost embarrassed. "The credit cards came up."

"What credit cards?" John asked. He didn't even have a damn checking account.

"Don't worry about it." Randall patted John on the shoulder like they were old buddies.

"What credit cards?" John repeated, the muscles in his arm aching to slap the kid's hand away. He hated admitting he didn't know something. Being in the dark made you vulnerable.

Randall finally dropped his hand. "Listen, guy," he began. "No big deal, right? Just make the payments and we don't care. We don't report to anybody unless you stop paying."

John crossed his arms over his chest, even though he knew it made him look bigger, more threatening, to other people. "Lookit," he said. "I want that crappy TV up front, the twenty-two-inch with the remote control. That's all I want."

"Dude," Randall said, holding up his hands. "Sure. No problem. I just figured with your credit score—"

John had to ask again. "What score?"

"Your credit score," the kid said, the tone of his voice passing incredulous and settling on plain dumbfounded. "Your credit score's the best I've ever seen here. We get some people in, they're not even breaking three hundred."

"What was mine?"

Randall seemed startled by the question. "We're not allowed to tell you."

John made his voice firm, let some of the gravel come out. "What was mine?"

Randall's pimples turned white, his skin a bright red. He whispered, "Seven-ten," glancing over his shoulder to see if his boss was watching him. "You could go to a real store, Mr. Shelley. You could walk into a Circuit City or a Best Buy—"

"Let me see it."

"Your report?"

John closed some of the space between them. "You said there were credit cards on there. I want to know what cards."

Randall looked over his shoulder again, but he should have been more concerned about what was in front of him.

"Stop looking behind you, kid. Look at me. Answer my question."

Randall's Adam's apple bobbed as he swallowed. "Maybe I put in your social security number wrong. The current address was different—"

"But the name?"

"Same name."

"Same previous address in Garden City?"

"Yes, sir."

He summed it up for the kid. "You think there's another Jonathan Winston Shelley out there with my birth date and my previous address, living in Atlanta, who has a social security number that's close to mine?"

"No—I mean, yes." Sweat had broken out on Randall's upper lip and his voice began to shake. "I'm sorry, mister. I could lose my job if I showed you that. You can get a copy of it yourself for free. I can give you the num—"

"Forget it," John said, feeling like a monster for pushing

the kid. The fear in his eyes cut like a piece of glass. John walked back through the store, past the television he wanted, and left before he said something he would regret.

Instead of going home, John crossed the street and sat on the bench beside the bus stop. He took one of the free community newspapers out of the stand and thumbed through it. The street had four lanes, but was pretty busy. Using the paper as a shield, he watched the store, tracking Randall and his fellow clerks as they talked people who should know better into signing away their lives.

Credit reports, credit cards, scores. Shit, he didn't know anything about this.

A bus came, the driver glancing out the door at John. "You gettin' on?"

"Next one," John said. Then, "Thanks, man." He liked the MARTA bus drivers. They didn't seem to make snap judgments. As long as you paid your fare and didn't make trouble, they assumed you were a good person.

Hot air hissed from the back of the bus as it pulled away. John turned to the next page in the paper, then went back to the front, realizing he hadn't read any of it. He sat at the bus stop for two hours, then three, leaving only once to take a piss behind an abandoned building.

At eight o'clock, Randall the salesboy left the rental store. He got into a rusted Toyota, turning the key and releasing into the otherwise quiet night the most obnoxious music John had ever heard. It had been dark for at least an hour, but Randall wouldn't have noticed John even if it had been bright as day. The kid was probably seventeen or eighteen. He had his own car, a job that paid pretty well, and not a care in the world except for the asshole with good credit who had tried to strong-arm him that afternoon.

The manager came out. At least, John guessed he was the manager: older guy, flap of hair stringing across a bald spot, yellowish skin and a round ass that came from sitting around all day telling people no.

The guy's groan could be heard from across the street as he reached up and pulled down the chain mesh that covered the front windows of the store. He groaned again as he stooped to lock the brace, then groaned a third time as he stood. After stretching his back, he walked over to a taupe Ford Taurus and climbed in behind the wheel.

John waited as the guy slipped on his seat belt, adjusted the rearview mirror, then put the car into reverse. The Taurus backed up, white lights flashing over red, then straightened out and left the parking lot, the engine making a puttering sound like a golf cart.

Ten minutes, fifteen. Thirty minutes. John stood up, giving his own groan from the effort. His knees had popped and his ass hurt from the cold concrete bench.

He looked both ways before crossing the street and walking past the store. The chains guarding the front doors and windows were strong, but John wasn't planning on smashing and grabbing. Instead, he went to the back of the building to the Dumpster.

The security camera behind the rental place was trained on the back door, the Dumpster free and clear. He slid open the steel door, releasing a metallic shriek into the night. The odor coming off the metal container was bad, but John had smelled worse. He started pulling out the small black kitchen garbage bags like the kind he had seen lining the trash cans in the rental store. He was careful, untying the knots instead of ripping the bags open to search them, then tying them back in the same knot before moving to the next one. After thirty minutes of going through the store's trash, he had to laugh at the situation. There was enough information in the trash bags—social security numbers, street addresses, employment histories—to launch a major con.

That wasn't what he was looking for, though. He wasn't a con man and he wasn't a thief. He wanted information, but only his own, and of course he found it in the last bag he opened.

He tilted the credit report so that the security lights made it easier to read.

Same social security number. Same date of birth. Same previous address.

Jonathan Winston Shelley, age thirty-five, had two MasterCards, three Visas and a Shell gas card. His address was a post office box with a 30316 zip code, which meant he lived somewhere in southeast Atlanta—several miles from John's current room at Chez Flop House on Ashby, just down from the Georgia state capitol.

His credit was excellent, his checking account with the local bank in good standing. Obviously, he was a pretty reliable customer and had been for about six years. But for one "slow pay" on the Shell card, all his creditors were satisfied with his prompt payments, which was kind of funny when you thought about it, because for the last twenty years, Jonathan Winston Shelley hadn't gotten out much. The guards at the prison tended to keep a close eye on you when you were serving twenty-two-to-life for raping and killing a fifteen-year-old girl.

CHAPTER EIGHT

John had known Mary Alice Finney all of his life. She was the good girl, the pretty cheerleader, the straight-A student, the person just about everybody in school knew and liked because she was so damn nice. Sure, there were some girls who hated her, but that's what girls did when they felt threatened: they hated. They spread nasty rumors. They were nice to your face and then when you turned around they stuck the knife in as far as it would go and twisted it around for good measure. Even in the real world, find some woman who's doing well for herself, being successful, and there's always going to be a handful of other women standing around saying she's a bitch or she slept her way to the top. That was just how the world worked, and it was no different in the microcosm of Decatur High School.

Actually, John later found that it was a hell of a lot like prison.

The Shelleys lived a couple of streets over from the Finneys in one of Decatur's nicer neighborhoods bordering Agnes Scott College. Their mothers knew each other in that circular world of the upper middle class. They had met the way doctors' and lawyers' wives have always met, at some fund-raiser or charity for the local high school, hospital, college—whatever institution served as an excuse to throw an elaborate party and invite strangers into their beautifully decorated homes.

Richard Shelley was an oncologist, head of the cancer treatment ward at Decatur Hospital. His wife, Emily, had at one point been a real estate agent, but she'd quit that job when Joyce, their first child, was born. John came three years later, and the Shelleys thought their world was complete.

Emily had been one of those mothers who threw herself into parenting. She was active in the PTA, sold the most Girl Scout cookies, and spent the end of most school years sewing costumes for the Quaker Friends School's graduation gala. As her two children grew up and stopped needing her—or wanting her, for that matter—she found herself with a lot of time on her hands. By the time John was in junior high and Joyce was two years away from attending college, she had gone back to the real estate agency part-time just to give herself something to do.

Their lives were perfect except for John.

The lying came early on and seemingly for no reason. John was at home when he had said he would be at football practice. He was at football practice when he said he would be at home. His grades started slipping. He let his hair grow long. Then, there was that smell. It seemed like he wasn't even bathing and his clothes, when Emily would pick them up off the floor of his dank bedroom to throw them in the washer, had an almost chemical feel to them, as if they had been sprayed with Teflon.

Richard worked long hours. His job was emotionally and physically demanding. He didn't have the time or inclination to be concerned about his son. Richard had been sullen when he was John's age. He had secrets when he was a teenager. He got into trouble but he straightened out, right? Time to take him off the tit. Give the boy some space.

Emily was worried about marijuana, so she did not register danger over the powdery residue she found in the front pocket of her son's jeans.

"Aspirin," he told her.

"Why would you put aspirin in your pocket?"

"I've been getting headaches."

As a child, John had put stranger things in his pockets: rocks, paper clips, a frog. She was worried about his health. "Do we need to take you to the doctor?"

"Mom."

He left her standing there in the laundry room, holding his pants.

The Shelleys, like most affluent couples, assumed that their money and privilege protected their children from drugs. What they did not realize was that those two factors helped their kids get *better* drugs. Even without that, Emily Shelley wanted to believe her son was a good boy, so she did. She didn't notice the glazed look he had in the mornings, the eyedrops he was constantly using, the sweet, sickly smell that came from the back shed. For his part, Dr. Richard didn't look across his newspaper at the breakfast table and see that his son's pupils were the size of half-dollars or that his nose bled more often than some of the cancer patients on his ward.

Life came apart in pieces.

A random search at the school yielded a bag of pot tucked into a pair of sneakers at the back of John's locker.

"Not my shoes," John said, and his mother agreed that the shoes didn't look like any she had seen him wear before.

A security guard at the local mall called them to let them know their son had been caught stealing a cassette tape.

"I forgot to pay for it." John shrugged, and his mother

pointed out that he *did* have twenty dollars in his pocket. Why on earth would he steal something he could pay for?

The last piece came undone one Friday night. An intern at the hospital called, waking Richard Shelley to tell him his kid was in the emergency room, having overdosed on coke.

Talk about ripping off the blinders. Medical evidence— something his father could wave under his mother's nose as physical proof of their son's worthlessness.

At night, John would sit in his bedroom and listen to his parents argue about him until his father screamed something along the lines of "and that's final!" and his mother ran into her bedroom, slamming the door behind her. Muffled sobs would come next, and he'd turn up his stereo, Def Leppard screaming from the speakers, until Joyce (studying, of course) pounded on the wall between their bedrooms, screaming, "Turn it down, loser!"

John would bang back, call her a bitch, make enough noise so that his father came into his room, yanking him up by the arm and asking what the hell was wrong with him.

"What are you rebelling against?" Richard would demand. "You have everything you could possibly want!"

"Why?" his mother would ask her boy, tears streaming down her face. "Where did I go wrong?"

John shrugged. That's all he did when they tried to confront him—shrug. He shrugged so much that his father said he must have a neurological disorder. Maybe he should be put on lithium. Maybe he should be put in a mental home.

"How did it start?" his mother wanted to know. There had to be a way she could fix it, make it better, but only if she could find out how it began. "Who got you hooked on this? Tell me who did this to you!"

A shrug from John. A sarcastic comment from his father.

"Are you retarded now? Autistic? Is that what's wrong with you?"

It had started with pot. There was a reason after all that Nancy Reagan told kids to just say no. John's first hit, fittingly, was right after a funeral.

Emily's brother, Barry, had died in a car accident on the expressway. Sudden. Fatal. Life-changing. Barry was a big guy, ate whatever he wanted, smoked cigars like he was Fidel Castro. He was on pills for high blood pressure, taking shots every day for diabetes and generally working his way toward the grave in a slow crawl. That he was killed by a truck driver who had fallen asleep at the wheel was almost a joke.

The funeral was held on a hot spring morning. At the church, John had walked behind the casket, his cousin Woody at his side. He had never seen another guy crying before, and John felt weird watching his tough cousin, four years older and cooler than John could ever hope to be, breaking down in front of him. Barry hadn't even been the guy's real father. Woody's mother was divorced—a shocking event in those days. She had only been married to Barry for two years. John wasn't even sure if the guy was his cousin anymore.

"Come here," Woody had said. They were back at his house, so empty now without Uncle Barry in it. His uncle had been a gregarious man, always there with a joke or a well-timed chuckle to take off the tension in the room. John's dad didn't like him much, and John suspected this was out of snobbery more than anything else. Barry sold tractor trailers. He made a good living, but Richard put the job on par with selling used cars.

"Come on," Woody told John, walking up the stairs to the bedrooms.

John had looked around for his parents, no reason but

the tone in Woody's voice warning him that something bad was about to happen. Still, he followed him to his room, shut the door and locked it when he was told.

"Shit." Woody sighed, sinking into the beanbag chair on the floor. He took out a plastic film canister from behind a couple of books stacked on the shelf behind him, then pulled some rolling papers from under his mattress. John watched as he deftly rolled a joint.

Woody saw him watching, said, "I could use a toke, man. How about you?"

John had never smoked a cigarette before, never taken anything stronger than cough medicine—which his mother kept hidden in her bathroom like it was radioactive—but when Woody offered him the joint, he had said, "Cool."

He watched his cousin suck the smoke into his lungs and hold it, hoping for pointers. Sweat formed on John's upper lip as the joint was handed to him. He was more afraid that he would look stupid in front of his cousin than because he was doing something illegal.

John loved the relief that came from smoking a joint, the way it took the edge off of everything. He no longer cared that his father thought he was a total fuck-up or that his mother was constantly disappointed with him. His sister Joyce's perfection as she followed in their father's footsteps didn't grate as much after a toke, and he actually enjoyed being around his family more when he was high.

When his parents finally realized what was happening, they blamed that age-old culprit, the bad crowd. What they did not realize was that John Shelley *was* the bad crowd. In a few weeks, he'd graduated from gawky nerd to pothead, and he loved the attention his newfound transformation gave him. Thanks to Woody, he was the kid who had the stash. He was the one who knew where the cool parties were, where underage high schoolers were welcome as long as they brought some pretty girls along with them. He was dealing dime bags to his new friends by the time he was fifteen. At a family reunion, Woody gave him his first hit of coke, and after that, there was no looking back.

By seventeen, he was a convicted murderer.

As far as John could remember, Mary Alice Finney was the first friend he'd ever had who wasn't a member of his immediate family. Their mothers had carpooled, taking turns every other week shuttling the kids to school. The kids had sat in the backseat, giggling about stupid things, playing the silly games that you played to make the time go by faster. Through elementary school, they had stayed on pretty much the same path. They were the smart kids, the ones who had all of the advantages. By junior high, everything was different. Uncle Barry was dead. John was the leader of the wrong crowd.

"You've changed," Mary Alice had told him the day he'd cornered her outside the girls' locker room. She had kept her textbooks pressed tight to her chest, covering the front of her Police concert T-shirt as if she felt the need to protect herself. "I don't think I like the person you're choosing to become."

Choosing to become. Like he had a choice. He hadn't chosen his hard-ass father, his ditzy mother who practically invented rose-colored glasses. He hadn't chosen Joyce, the perfect sister, the bitch who set the bar so high all John could ever hope to do was bounce on his toes, trying to touch the edge of the bar but never getting high enough to go over.

He had chosen this? He hadn't had a chance.

"Screw you," he told Mary Alice.

"You wish," she snapped, flipping her hair to the side as she turned on her heel and left him standing there like an idiot.

He had looked in the mirror that night, taken in his greasy long hair, the dark circles under his eyes, the acne spotting his cheeks and forehead. His body hadn't yet caught up with his enormous hands and feet. Even dressed up for church, he looked like a string bean standing on a couple of cardboard boxes. He was an outcast at school, had no real friends left and at the ripe age of fifteen, all of his sexual experience thus far had involved his sister's Jergens hand lotion and an active imagination. Looking in the mirror, John had taken all of this in, then sneaked out to the shed in the backyard and snorted so much coke that he made himself sick.

John hated Mary Alice from that day on. Everything bad in his life was her fault. He spread rumors about her. He made jokes at her expense and within her hearing so she'd know just how much he despised her. At pep rallies, he heckled her as she was leading cheers on the gym floor. Some nights, he would lie awake thinking about her, detesting her, and then he'd find his hand had gone from resting flat on his stomach to reaching down into his shorts and all it took was picturing her at school that day, the way she smiled at other people when she walked down the hallway, the tight sweater she had worn, and he was gone.

"John?" His mother had some sixth sense and always seemed to knock on his bedroom door when he was jerking off. "We need to talk."

Emily wanted to talk about his failing grades, his latest detention, something she had found in the pocket of his jeans. She wanted to talk to the stranger who had kidnapped her son, to beg him to give her her Johnny back. She knew her baby was in there somewhere, and she would not give up. Even at the trial, John had felt her silent support as he sat at the table listening to the lawyers who said he was scum, facing a panel of jurors who wouldn't even look him in the eye.

The only person in that courtroom who still believed in John Shelley was his mother. She would not let go of that boy, that Cub Scout, that model airplane builder, that precious child. She wanted to put her arms around him and make everything better, to press her face to the back of his neck and inhale that odd scent of cookie dough and wet clay he got when he played in the backyard with his friends. She wanted to listen to him tell her about his day, the baseball game he had played, the new friend he had made. She wanted her son. She *ached* for her son.

But he was already gone.

SHELLEY TO BE TRIED AS ADULT IN FINNEY MURDER

District judge Billie Bennett ruled yesterday that fifteen-year-old Jonathan Winston Shelley of Decatur will be tried as an adult in the murder trial of Mary Alice Finney, also of Decatur. Attorneys for the accused argued extenuating circumstances, but speaking from the bench, Bennett said based on the defendant's previous arrests as well as other mitigating factors, she saw no reason why the youth should not be charged as an adult. Prosecutor Lyle Anders has said that his office will seek the death penalty.

Paul Finney, the slain girl's father, told reporters outside the courthouse that he was "pleased" with the judge's ruling. Shelley, charged with felony murder, will be the first teenager in DeKalb County to be tried as an adult. In a separate ruling, Bennett denied a change of venue requested by Shelley's attorney.

Six convicted murderers have been executed by the state of Georgia since the United States Supreme Court upheld the constitutionality of the death penalty in *Gregg v. Georgia* (1976). The youngest offender executed in the state's history was sixteen-year-old Eddie Marsh, who was put to death February 9, 1932, for the murder of a Dougherty County pecan farmer. In March of this year, twenty-eight-year-old John Young, who at eighteen murdered three elderly people in their Bibb County home during the commission of a robbery, was put to death by electrocution at the Georgia Diagnostic and Classification Prison in Jackson.

CHAPTER NINE

John hadn't slept well, which was nothing new for him. In prison, nighttime was always the worst. You heard screams, mostly. Crying. Other things he didn't like to think about. John had been fifteen when he was arrested, sixteen when he was incarcerated. By the age of thirty-five, he had lived in prison more years than he had slept in his parents' home.

As noisy as prison was, you got used to it. Being on the outside was what was hard. Car horns, fire engines, radios blasting from all over. The sun was brighter, the smells more intense. Flowers could bring tears to his eyes and food was almost inedible. There was too much flavor in everything, too many choices for him to feel comfortable going into a restaurant and ordering a meal.

Before John was locked up, you didn't see people jogging in the streets, headphones tucked into their ears, tight spandex shorts clinging to their bodies. Cell phones were in bags like big purses that you carried over your shoulder and only really wealthy people could afford to have them. Rap didn't exist in the mainstream and listening to Mötley Crüe and Poison meant you were cool. CD players were something out of *Star Trek* and even knowing what *Star Trek* was meant you were some kind of nerd.

He didn't know what to do with this new world.

Nothing made sense to him. None of the familiar things were there. His first day out, he had gone into a closet in his mother's home, shut the door and cried like a baby.

"Shelley?" Art yelled. "You gonna work or not?"

John waved his hand at the supervisor, pushing his mouth into a smile. "Sorry, boss."

He walked over to a green Suburban and started wiping water off the side panel. That was another thing that had shocked him. Cars had gotten so huge. In prison, there had been one television that got two channels, and the older inmates got to decide what was playing. The antenna had been ripped off and used to pluck out somebody's eyeball well before John showed up, and the reception sucked. Even when the snow cleared and you could halfway see the picture, there was no sense of scale with the cars on screen. Then you wondered if what you were seeing was real or something just made for a particular show. Maybe the series was really about an alternative world where women wore skirts up to their cooches and men weren't beneath sporting tight leather pants and saying things like, "My father never understood me."

The guys always got a laugh out of that, shouting "pussy" and "faggot" at the set so that it drowned out the actor's next line.

John didn't watch much TV.

"Yo, yo," Ray-Ray said, bending down to sponge silicone onto the Suburban's tires. John looked up to see a police cruiser pulling into the drive of the car wash. Ray-Ray always said things twice, hence the name, and he always alerted John when a cop was around. John returned the favor. The two men had never really talked, let alone exchanged their life stories, but both knew on sight what the other was: an ex-con.

John started cleaning the glass over the driver's door,

taking his time so he could watch the cop in the reflection. He heard the man's police radio first, that constant static of the dispatchers speaking their private code. The officer glanced around, pegging John and Ray-Ray in about two seconds flat, before he hitched up his belt and went inside to pay for the wash. Not that they would charge him, but it was always good to pretend.

The owner of the Suburban was close by, talking on her cell phone, and John closed his eyes as he cleaned the window, listening to her voice, savoring the tones like a precious piece of music. Inside, he had forgotten what it was like to hear a woman's voice, listen to the sort of complaints that only women could have. Bad haircuts. Rude store clerks. Chipped nails. Men wanted to talk about *things:* cars, guns, snatch. They didn't discuss their feelings unless it was anger, and even that didn't last for long because generally they started doing something about it.

Every two weeks, John's mother had made the drive from Decatur down to Garden City to see him, but as glad as John was to see her, that wasn't the kind of woman's voice he wanted to hear. Emily was always positive, happy to see her son, even if he could tell by looking in her eyes that she was tired from the long drive, or sad to see that he'd gotten another tattoo, that his hair was in a ponytail. Aunt Lydia came, but that was because she was his lawyer. Joyce came twice a year with their mother, once at Christmas, once on his birthday. She hated being there. You could smell it on her. Joyce wanted to be out of that place almost more than John did, and whenever she talked to him, he was reminded of the way the black gangbangers and Aryans talked to each other. *You fucking nigger dog. You fuck-eyed white motherfucker. I'll kill you soon as I get the chance.*

His father came to see him twice in all the time he was locked up, but John didn't like to think about that.

"Excuse me?" The woman with the cell phone was beside him. He could smell her perfume. Her upper lip was a little bow tie, gloss making her mouth look wet.

"Hello?" she said, half-laughing.

"Sorry," John managed, shocked that she'd gotten this close to him without him even noticing. In prison, he would be dead right now.

"I said 'thank you,' " she told him. She held a dollar in her hand and he took it, feeling cheap and dirty at the same time.

John made a show of putting the bill in the communal tip box, knowing every eye in the place was watching him. He did the same thing when a customer handed somebody else a tip. No one trusted anybody around here and for good reason. You didn't need a college degree to figure out why a bunch of middle-aged guys were working for minimum wage plus tips at the Gorilla Car Wash.

Art came out of the office, yelling, "First shift, lunch," as he walked over to the cop standing by the vending machine. Shit, John hadn't noticed that, either. The cop had come outside, had been watching him, and he hadn't seen it happen.

John tucked his head down as he went into the back, clocking out and grabbing his lunch off the shelf. He had a soda in the refrigerator, but there was no way he was going back out there until the cop was gone and Art was back behind his desk counting his money.

Chico, one of the other workers, was sitting on the cement wall under the shade of a big magnolia tree that grew in the strip of grass in back of the car wash. John liked to sit there under the tree, enjoyed the solitude and the shade, but Chico had beaten him to it today. This sort of thing wouldn't have happened in the joint. Taking a man's space was like fucking his sister up the ass. Nothing happened in that place that didn't have some kind of price attached to it.

"How's it going?" John said, nodding at Chico as he walked past him to the carport that served as a detail shop. The detail guys went out for lunch. They made enough money to afford the luxury.

John sat on the ground under the canopy. He took off his ball cap and wiped the sweat off his forehead with the back of his hand. November used to mean winter, but now it meant you were lucky if the jacket you put on in the morning didn't have you sweating by noon.

Christ, even the weather had changed without him.

He glanced around before pulling a piece of paper out of his back pocket. The credit report. Part of him had wanted to shove it back in the trash bag last night, just let it go. So some motherfucker was pretending to be him. What did that mean to John Shelley? Obviously, the poser wasn't running some fraud. Why would he pay off the credit cards every month for six years? John had heard about all kinds of scams in prison, and though he hadn't really had access to any computers, he knew that the Internet was the best way to run an identity fraud. This, though. This was nothing like that. You took the money and ran. You didn't stick around and pay your monthly bills on time. It was like that old joke of ordering fifty pizzas to somebody's house, only you paid for them yourself with your credit card.

He folded the report and tucked it back into his pocket. He should leave it be. No good would come out of any of this. What John should do is exactly what his parole officer said: Concentrate on rebuilding your life. Get a steady job. Show people you've changed.

It bothered him, though. Like a splinter that wouldn't come out, he had picked at it all night, trying to see the angle. There had to be an angle. Why else would someone do this? Maybe somebody with a past was using John's vitals as a cover. Could be some escaped ax murderer or blue-collar guy was on the lam and John Shelley seemed like a good cover.

He laughed at this idea, taking a bite of his peanut butter and banana sandwich. You had to be pretty desperate to assume the identity of a convicted murderer and registered sex offender.

The peanut butter caught in his throat and he coughed a couple of times before getting up and going to the coiled hose on the ground. John turned on the spigot and took a drink, watching Ray-Ray talking to some woman over by the vacuums. John could tell the other man was doing his usual jive, trying to work his magic on the woman. Judging by the way she was dressed, Ray-Ray could have saved some time and just given her some money. Most of the guys around the Gorilla availed themselves of the local talent. Straight up Cheshire Bridge Road, you ran into the Colonial Restaurant, a meat-and-potatoes kind of joint with hookers a'plenty trolling the apartments behind them. John had often heard the guys arguing Monday mornings about which was best: get them early when they were fresh and pay more, or go later when they were sloppy and pay less.

Street economics.

"Fuck off, asshole!" the hooker screamed, slamming her hands into Ray-Ray's chest.

Ray-Ray growled something and pushed her back until she fell on her ass.

John's first impulse was to stay exactly where he was. You didn't get involved in other people's shit. That was how you got yourself killed. This was a woman, but she worked the streets. She knew how to take care of herself. At least it seemed that way until Ray-Ray hauled off and punched her square in the face.

"Damn," Chico muttered, ringside at a championship wrestling bout. "Didn't even give her time to stand up."

John looked down at his shoes, which were soaking wet. The hose was still on. He could get into trouble for that. He went back to the spigot, turned it off, forgetting for a minute that it was righty-tighty and turning it lefty-loosey. He coiled the hose back in place. When he looked back up, Ray-Ray's foot was in the air, sailing down toward the hooker's face.

"Hey!" John said, then, "Hey!" again when Ray-Ray's foot made contact.

John must have run over to them. He must have said something else along the way, something loud that called even more attention to the situation. By the time his brain caught up with his actions, John's fist hurt like a hornet had stung him and Ray-Ray was splayed out on the ground.

"What the *fuck*," Art yelled. He barely topped five feet on a good day, but he stopped about two inches from John's chest, screeching up at him, "You fucking *monkey*!"

They both looked down. One of Ray-Ray's teeth was on the sidewalk swimming in a puddle of blood. The guy looked dead, but no one was dropping to check his pulse.

The cop stood in the doorway. Slowly, John let his eyes trace up the man's thick black shoes, following the sharp crease in his pants, skipping past his gunbelt where a large hand was resting on the butt of his gun and forced himself to look the guy in the face. The screw was staring straight back at John as he turned his radio down, the calls from the dispatcher turning to a whisper. "What's going on here?"

It took everything John had in him not to just assume the position right then and there. "I hit him."

"Well, no shit, asshole!" Art barked. "You are so fucking fired." He prodded Ray-Ray with his foot. "Jesus Christ, Shelley. What'd you hit him with, a fucking hammer?"

John's head dropped, and he looked at the ground. Oh, Jesus. He couldn't go back to prison now. Not after all of this. Not after everything he'd been through.

"I'm sorry," John said. "It won't happen again."

"You're damn right it won't," Art snapped. "Christ." He looked at the cop. "This is the thanks I get for giving these guys a second chance."

"I apologize," John offered again.

"Hey!" the hooker yelled. "Somebody wanna give me a hand?"

All of the men looked down, shocked, like they had forgotten her existence. The whore had a hard face, the kind that told her life story in the millions of lines wrinkling her skin. Blood poured from her nose and mouth where Ray-Ray's foot had done its damage. She was propped up on her elbows, a filthy white feather boa wrapped around her scrawny neck, a purple plastic-looking miniskirt and a black tank top that showed the bottom of her sagging breasts barely covering her wasted body.

Nobody wanted to touch her.

"Hey, Knight in Shining Armor All," she said, shaking her hand toward John. "Come on, stallion. Help me the fuck up."

John hesitated, but then he reached down and pulled her up. She smelled of cigarettes and bourbon, and had a hard time standing on the spike heels of her shoes. Her hand dug into his shoulder as she steadied herself. He tried not to shudder in revulsion, thinking about where that hand had been. In the sunlight, her skin was sallow, and he guessed her liver was desperate enough to shit itself out of her navel if it was ever given the opportunity. She could have been thirty, she could have been eighty.

The cop took charge. "You wanna tell me what this is about?"

"He wouldn't pay me," she said, tilting her chin, indicating the prone Ray-Ray. Her voice was like loose rock rolling in a cup of phlegm. What words she didn't slur were probably not worth hearing.

"You gave him one on credit?" the cop asked, not bothering to hide his incredulity. The man had a point. John wouldn't sell Ray-Ray a petrified turd on credit.

"We was in there," she said, meaning the Port-a-John behind the building. "He tried to sweet-talk me, the lousy fucker. Said he was gettin' paid tomorrow."

The cop's eyebrow shot up. "You gotta be shittin' me."

"He followed me out here, trying to make a deal," she continued, clutching John's arm again as she swayed. "Like it's double coupon day at the fucking Kmart. Stupid cocksucker." She lifted a patent-leather heel and kicked Ray-Ray in the arm.

"Hey, hey, now," Ray-Ray said, groaning as he rolled over onto his back. John figured the asshole had been playing possum and wanted to beat him again for causing all of this.

The cop prodded Ray-Ray with his shoe. "You try to get a freebie, you stupid mope?"

Ray-Ray put his hand over his eyes, shielding the sun so he could look up at the cop without being blinded. "No, no, man. That ain't the thing. Ain't the thing at all."

"Get up, you fucking idiot," the cop ordered. "You." He pointed at the whore. "Where's your drag?"

She was busy wiping the concrete off her elbows. "Up by the liquor store."

There was a crash of static from the cop's radio, then, *"Unit fifty-one, fifty-one?"*

The cop clicked the mic, said, "Check," then pointed to John, talking over the information the dispatcher gave but obviously still listening. "You. Prince Charming. Make sure she gets back home safe. You," he pointed to Ray-Ray. "Don't make me tell you one more fucking time to get the fuck up or I will run your ass in so quick your P.O. won't even have time to call you a cab back to the pen." Ray-Ray jumped up and the cop clicked on the radio and said, "Roger, I'm there in ten minutes." As an afterthought, he asked Art, "You okay with all this?"

Art frowned, his forehead sloping into a V. "Yeah, whatever," he finally agreed. "Shelley, take the day off. Come back with your head in the right place tomorrow."

"Thank you," John said, so relieved he could have cried. "Thank you, sir. I won't disappoint you."

The respect brought him some back. "You want me to get rid of this stuttering freak?" Art asked John as he jabbed his thumb at Ray-Ray.

John thought about it for a good second, but he couldn't spend the rest of his life looking over his shoulder for this asshole. "We're fine," he said. "Right, Ray?"

"Yeah, yeah," Ray-Ray said. "We cool. We cool."

"Shut up," Art said. "I don't want to see you back here until Wednesday morning, you got that?"

Ray-Ray nodded. Twice.

Art gave the prostitute a scathing look, then told John, "Get her out of here before we start losing customers."

John didn't think he had a choice. The whore had grabbed on to him again, her bony fingers pressing into his arm just above the elbow. He started walking alongside her because something told him if he didn't, she'd end up face-first in the street.

Traffic whizzed by as they walked up Piedmont Avenue. John saw about a zillion SUVs and sports cars going up and down this road every day. With Buckhead at one end and Ansley Park at the other, the only crappy cars John saw on the road belonged to the maids, landscapers, pool boys and all the other hapless souls who made their living doing the shitwork rich folks didn't have to do.

"Fucking asshole," the pross muttered as they waited for the light. Her bony fingers pressed deeper into his flesh as she tried to steady herself on her ridiculously high heels. "Hold up a minute," she finally relented, keeping her grip on him as she took off one, then the other shoe. "Fucking heels."

"Yeah," John said, because she was obviously expecting an answer.

"It's red," she told him, jerking him into the street as traffic stopped for the light. "Christ, my feet hurt." She looked up at him as they reached the other side of the intersection. "I gotta loose tooth, you know? From where he kicked me."

"Oh," John said, thinking she was either stupid or crazy if she thought he had the extra money to send her to the dentist. "Okay. Yeah. Sorry."

"No, you dumb prick. I'm saying I can use my hands but you can't put it in my mouth."

John didn't realize he was clenching his teeth until his jaw started to ache. "No," he answered. "That's okay."

"Lissen." She stopped, dropped her hand, and started swaying like a raft in the middle of a tsunami. "You can head on back, Romeo. I can make it the rest of the way myself."

"No," he repeated, this time taking her arm in his hand. With his luck, she'd fall into the street and the cop would pin a manslaughter charge on him. "Let's go."

"Whoops," she breathed, her knee buckling as she slipped on a broken section of sidewalk.

"Steady," he told her, thinking she was so thin he could feel the bone in her arm moving against the flesh.

Out of the blue, she told him, "I don't take it up the ass."

John couldn't think of which was worse: the thought of her mouth or the thought of her asshole. A quick glance at the sores on her arms and legs made him taste the peanut butter and banana sandwich from lunch.

"Okay," he said, not knowing why she felt like sharing and wishing to hell she'd stop.

"Makes me shit funny," she told him, giving him a sideways glance. "I thought I should tell you if that's what you were planning."

"I'm just going to make sure you get back," he assured her. "Don't worry about that other stuff."

"Nothin' comes for free," she told him, then laughed. " 'Cept maybe this time. Of course, the walk—now, if you consider that your payment, it ain't exactly free."

"I was going this way anyway," he lied. "I live down here."

"Morningside?" she asked, referring to one of the wealthier neighborhoods backing onto Cheshire Bridge Road.

"Yeah," he said. "Three-story house with a garage." She stumbled again and he kept her from falling on her face. "Come on."

"You don't gotta be rough, you know."

He looked at his hand around her arm, saw immediately how tight he was holding it. When he let go, there were marks where his fingers had been. "I'm sorry about that," he told her, and really meant it. Jesus, he was thinking about women all this time and he didn't even know how to touch one without hurting her. "I'm just going to walk you back, okay?"

"Almost there," she told him, then mercifully fell into

silence as she concentrated on navigating the bumpy path where the sidewalk ended and dirt took over.

John let her take the lead, keeping two steps behind her in case she fell over into the street. He let the enormity of what had just happened wash over him. What had he been thinking? There was no reason to get himself involved in Ray-Ray's troubles, and now he was losing a day's pay so he could take this pross back to her strip, where she'd probably make more money in one hour than he made in three. Christ. He could have lost his job. He could've been thrown back in prison.

Art got a nice stipend from the state for employing a parolee, plus extra tax breaks from the feds. Even with all that—all the so-called incentives that were out there—finding somewhere to work had been almost impossible when John had gotten out. Because of his status, he couldn't work with kids or live within a hundred yards of a school or daycare center. Legally, employers couldn't discriminate against a felon, but they always found a way around the law. John had been on nineteen interviews before finding the car wash. They always started out, "How you doing/we'd love to have you here/just fill this out and we'll get back to you." Then, when he called the next week because he hadn't heard from them, it was always, "We've filled that job/we found a more qualified candidate/sorry, we're cutting back."

"More qualified to pack boxes?" he had asked one of them, the shipping manager at a pie company. "Listen, buddy," the guy had answered. "I've got a teenage daughter, all right? You know why you're not getting this job."

At least he was honest.

The question was standard on every application. "Other than misdemeanor traffic violations, have you ever been convicted of a crime?"

John had to check yes. They always ran a background check and found out anyway.

"Please explain your conviction in the space provided."

He had to explain. They could ask his P.O. They could get a cop to run his file. They could go on the Internet and look him up on the GBI's site under "convicted sex offenders in the Atlanta area." Under Shelley, Jonathan Winston, they'd read that he raped and killed a minor child. The state didn't differentiate between underage offenders and adults, so he came up not as a person who had committed this crime when he was a minor child himself, but as an adult pedophile.

"Hello?" the hooker said. "You in there, handsome?"

John nodded. He'd been zoning out, following her like a puppy. They were in front of the liquor store. Some of the girls were already working, hoping to catch the lunch crowd.

"Hey, Robin," the hooker yelled. "Come on over here."

The woman who must've been Robin came over, doing a better job on her high heels than John's companion had managed.

Robin stopped ten feet away from them. "What the hell happened to you?" She looked at John. "Did you get rough with her, you motherfucker?"

"No," he said, then, because she was digging into her purse for something that would probably bring him a great amount of pain, he said, "Please. I didn't hurt her."

"Aw, he didn't do nothing, baby girl," the hooker soothed. "He saved me from that jackass down at the car wash."

"Which one?" Robin asked, her anger still well above ballistic. The way she was looking at John said she hadn't quite made up her mind about him and her hand was still in her purse, probably wrapped around a can of pepper spray or a hammer.

"Which one? Which one?" the hooker said, a good imitation of Ray-Ray. "That skinny nigger that says everything twice." She looked up at John, batting her eyelashes. "You like 'em a bit younger, don't you, honey?"

John felt his body stiffen.

"No, I don't mean it like that," she said, rubbing his back like she was soothing a child. There was something almost maternal to her now that she was back in her fold. "Lissen, Robin, do me a favor and give 'em a half-and-half. He really saved my ass."

Robin's mouth opened to respond, but John stopped her. He held up his hands, saying, "No, really. That's okay."

"I always pay my debts," the old hooker insisted. "Kindness of strangers or whatever the fuck." She followed a car with her eyes as it pulled into the parking lot. "Shit. That's my regular," she said, using the back of her hand to wipe the blood off from under her nose. She waved at John as she jumped into the man's car, yelling something he couldn't make out.

John watched the car leave, feeling Robin's eyes on him the entire time. She had the same steely stare as a cop: *what the fuck are you up to and where do I have to hit you to bring you to your knees?*

She said, "I'm not her fucking stand-in."

"Don't worry about it," he said, throwing up his hands again. "Really."

"What?" she demanded. "You too good to pay for it?"

"I didn't say that," he countered, feeling his face turn red. There were five or six other hookers openly listening to their conversation and the amused expressions on their faces made him feel like his dick was getting smaller and smaller with every second that ticked by.

He added, "And she didn't say anything about paying for it, anyway." When Robin didn't jump in with something else, he said, "I was just doing her a favor."

"You didn't do *me* any favors."

"Then don't do me any," he said, turning to go.

"Hey!" she screamed. "Don't walk away from me."

Without thinking, he had turned back around when she yelled. She was obviously playing to the crowd. He felt himself shrink another few centimeters.

He tried to moderate his tone, asking, "What?"

"I said don't walk away from me, you stupid prick."

John shook his head, thinking his day couldn't get much worse. "You wanna do this?" he asked, reaching into his pocket. He had saved twenty bucks a week for the last three weeks just to make sure he could swing the payments on the TV. He had fifty bucks in his pocket and seventy tucked into the sole of his shoe. John doubted the girl made even half that during the lunch rush. Hell, he barely made that in a day.

Her chin went up in defiance. They must have picked up the gesture in hooker school or something. She asked, "How much you got?"

"Enough," he said. What the fuck was he doing? His tongue felt thick in his mouth and he had more saliva than he knew what to do with. Flashing the money had worked, though. The peanut gallery had shut up.

Robin stared at him another beat, then nodded once. "All right," she said. "You want dinner and a drink?"

John chewed his lip, trying to figure out how much that would cost him. "I just ate lunch," he told her. "If you want something to drink..."

"God," she groaned, rolling her eyes. "Are you a cop?"

"No," he said, still not following.

"Half-and-half," she told him. "Dinner and a drink."

John looked over at the other women. They were laughing at him again.

"Shut up," Robin barked, and for a minute John thought she meant him. "Come on," she said, grabbing his arm.

For the second time that day, John was being led down the street by a hooker. This one was a hell of a lot better than the last one, though. She looked cleaner, for one. Her skin was probably soft. Even her hair looked good—thick and healthy, not stringy from too many drugs or covered with some cheap wig. She didn't smell like a smoker, either. John's cellmate had been a chain-smoker, lighting one off the last. The guy couldn't even sleep for more than an hour without waking up to have a smoke and there were some days he smelled worse than a wet ashtray.

Robin pulled him into the woods behind the Colonial Restaurant, tossing over her shoulder, "You got enough for a room?"

He didn't answer, couldn't believe this was actually happening. She was holding his hand, walking him through the woods, like they were on a date. He wanted to hear her voice again. The tone was soothing, even though she was obviously in a hurry to get this over with.

She stopped, still holding his hand. "Hey, I asked if you have enough for a room." She indicated the woods. "I don't do it outside like some fucking animal."

He had to clear his throat so he could speak. His heart was pounding so hard in his chest that he could feel his shirt moving. "Yeah."

She didn't move. "You're sweating."

"Sorry," he said, taking back his hand, wiping the palm on the leg of his jeans. He felt a stupid, uncomfortable smile on his lips. "I'm sorry," he repeated.

She was giving him that hard look again, trying to figure

out what he had in mind. Her hand was tucked into her purse. "You okay?"

John looked around, thinking no matter what she carried in her bag, it was a real mistake for her to be taking strange men into the woods. "It's not safe here," he said. "I could be anybody."

"You've never done this before." She wasn't asking a question, just stating the obvious.

He thought of Randall, that kid at the rental store, the way his Adam's apple had bobbed in his throat when John crowded in on him. John could feel his own throat clenching, making it hard for him to talk.

"Hey," she said, rubbing her hand on his arm. "Come on, big boy. It's okay."

John noticed that her voice had changed. He didn't know why, but suddenly, she was talking to him like he was a human being instead of something she had to scrape off the bottom of her shoe.

"I didn't want to do this," he told her, realizing his tone was different, too. Soft. Real soft like he was trusting her, sharing something with her. Without warning, his mouth opened, and out slipped, "Oh, God, you're so pretty," like he was some kind of pathetic freak. He tried to make it better, adding, "I know that sounds stupid, but you are." He scanned her face, trying to come up with something else to say, some proof that he wasn't some kind of freak she should pepper spray.

Her mouth looked soft, the kind of mouth you could kiss forever.

No, he couldn't talk about her mouth. That was too sexual.

Her nose?

No, that was stupid. Nobody talked about pretty noses.

They breathed, they ran sometimes and you blew them. They were just there on your face.

"You okay?" she asked.

"Your eyes," he blurted out, feeling like even more of an idiot than before. He'd said the words so loudly that she'd flinched. "I mean," he began, lowering his voice again. "I'm sorry. I was just thinking that your eyes..." Christ, she was wearing so much makeup it was hard to tell. "I think you have nice eyes."

She stared at him, probably wondering how fast she could get the Mace out of her purse and douse him, maybe wondering if she could snatch his money when he went down. "You know," she finally said, "you don't have to woo me. Just pay me."

He tucked his hand into his pocket.

"Not now, baby," she said, nervous suddenly. He was doing something wrong. There was a way to do this and John didn't know.

"I'm sorry—" he apologized.

"You pay me in the room," she told him, waving for him to follow her. "It's just over here."

He stood in place, his feet refusing to move. Christ, he felt like he was a pimply kid again trying to get to second base.

She finally sounded annoyed. "Come on, big boy. Time is money."

"Let's stay here," he said, and when she started to protest, he talked over her. "No, not like that. Let's just stand here and talk."

"You wanna talk? Get a shrink."

"I'll pay you."

"This some twist for you?" she asked. "I start talking and you jerk yourself off? No way."

She was walking back toward the road and he scrambled

to get the money out of his pocket. Some of the bills flew out of his hand and he dropped to the ground, picking them up. When he looked up, she was still moving away.

He said, "Fifty dollars!" and she froze.

She turned slowly, and he couldn't tell if the offer had made her more annoyed or just plain angry.

"Here," he said, standing up, walking over to her and putting the cash in her hand. There were a lot of ones, a couple of fives—all part of his take from the tip box back at the car wash.

He said, "I'll keep my pants on, okay? No funny stuff."

She tried to give him back the money. "Don't fuck with me, okay?"

"I'm not," he told her, hearing a tinge of desperation in his voice. He was going to scare her away again and this time no amount of money would get her back. "Just talk," he said, pressing the money back on her. "Just tell me something."

She rolled her eyes, but she kept the money. "Tell you what?"

"Anything," he said. "Tell me..." Jesus, he couldn't think of a damn thing. "Tell me..." He stared at her, willing her face to give him a clue—anything that would keep her here a little longer. He looked at her beautiful mouth, the way it was twisted with irritation and maybe something that looked like curiosity. "Your first kiss," he decided. "Tell me about your first kiss."

"You have *got* to be kidding me."

"No," he said. "I'm not." He took a couple of steps away from her, held his hands out to the side so she could see he wasn't going to do himself. "Just tell me about your first kiss."

"What, you want me to say it was with my sister? My father?"

"No," he said, shaking his head. "Please don't lie."

She crossed her arms, her eyes giving him the once-over. "You're giving me fifty bucks to tell you about my first kiss?"

He nodded.

She looked behind her, then looked back at him. She counted the money out, crisp bills tugged from one hand to the other as her lips moved silently. "All right," she finally said, tucking the wad of cash down the front of her shirt. "Stewie Campano."

He laughed at the name.

"Yeah," she said, smiling for the first time. She had perfect, straight teeth. "Real Romeo, our Stewie."

"You went out with him?"

"Hell no," she said, insulted. "He was two years younger than me, one of my little brother's friends. We were playing around one day."

"Playing what?" Her brow furrowed and he quickly said, "No, I'm not looking for that. I just want to know what you were doing."

"Swimming in his pool," she said, hesitant, obviously still trying to see what John's angle was. "That was the only reason I'd go over there with my brother, because Stewie had a swimming pool."

John felt his smile come back.

She had decided to continue the story. "So, like I said, it was late one night, full moon and all that, and we were playing in the pool, just horsing around, and he looked at me and I looked at him and then he just leaned over and kissed me."

"Real kiss or a kid kiss?"

"Kid kiss," she said, a smile working its magic on her face. She was truly beautiful, the kind of dark-haired, olive-skinned woman that poets wrote about.

Her smile turned mischievous. "Then a real kiss."

"Go, Stewie," John said, creating the image in his mind—the backyard, the moon, the various floats and flotsam in a family pool. "How old were you?"

"Thirteen," she admitted.

"So Stewie was—"

"Ten. I know." She held up her hands. "Cradle robber. Guilty."

John was amazed at the kid's bravado. "God, I don't even think I knew what a tongue kiss was when I was ten."

"Yeah, well I was thirteen and I didn't know," she told him. Then she laughed, maybe at the memory or maybe at the absurdity of the situation. John laughed, too, and it was such a sweet release that for the first time in twenty-five years he honest to God felt like he was okay.

"Jesus," Robin said. "I haven't thought about that kid in years."

"What's he doing now, you think?"

"Doctor, probably." She laughed again, a short, sharp sound of pleasure. "Gynecologist."

John was still smiling. He said, "Thank you."

"Yeah." She pressed her lips together. "Hey, what's your name?"

"John."

She laughed like he was joking.

"No, really. John Shelley." He made to offer his hand, and she took a step back from him. "Sorry," he said, dropping his hand. What had he done? How had he ruined this?

"It's okay. I just need to get back." She checked over her shoulder. "My minder's gonna be looking for me soon and I—"

"It's okay," he told her. He had put his hands in his pockets because he didn't know what else to do with them. "I'm sorry if I—"

"No problem," she interrupted.

"I can walk you back."

"I know the way," she said, practically bolting back toward the road.

All he could do was watch her go, wonder what he had said wrong that made her run. Fifty bucks. He could buy a lot with fifty bucks. Food. Rent. Clothes. Laughter. The way her eyes sparkled when she really smiled. That wasn't something you could buy. Yeah, she had taken the money, but that laugh—that had been a real moment between them. She had talked to him, really talked to him, because she wanted to, not because of the fifty bucks.

John stood in the forest, rooted to the spot, eyes closed as he summoned up the memory of her voice, her laugh. She had a brother somewhere. She'd grown up in a neighborhood with a pool. Her parents had spent some money on orthodontics, maybe taken her to ballet lessons so she'd have that lean dancer's body or perhaps she'd been like Joyce, the kind of girl who metabolized food so quickly all she needed to do was walk around the block to keep her figure.

From the road, a car horn sounded and John opened his eyes.

Why hadn't he gone into that hotel room with her? Fifty bucks. That was a good day's work for him. A full day of wiping cars, cleaning up people's shit, waiting for Art to come out and inspect his work, point to some nonexistent smudge on a windshield so the customer thought he was getting his money's worth.

Fifty dollars and for what? The memory of someone else's kiss?

John snapped an overhanging twig as he walked back toward the road, careful to angle his path so he wouldn't end up at the liquor store. He could be holding her right now, making love to her. He stopped, leaning his hand against a tree, his lungs feeling like he'd gotten the breath knocked out of him.

No, he thought. He would be doing the same thing in that room that he was doing now: making a fool of himself. The truth was that John had never really made love to a woman. He had never experienced that intimacy that you read about in books, never had a lover take his hand in her own, stroke the back of his neck, pull his body closer to hers. The last woman he had kissed was, in fact, the only woman he had ever kissed and even then, she wasn't a woman but a girl. John remembered the date like it was seared into his brain: June 15, 1985.

He had kissed Mary Alice Finney, and the next morning, she was dead.

CHAPTER TEN

When John was a little kid, he had loved playing in the dirt, building things with his hands then tearing them apart chunk by chunk. His mother would see him walking up the street, the mud on his pants, the twigs sticking out of his hair, and she'd just laugh and grab the hose, making him strip off his clothes in the backyard so she could squirt him down before letting him into the house.

At night, he slept hard from his busy days. John wasn't the type of kid to do things halfway. He was scrawny for his age, his chest almost concave, but he made up for it with sheer willpower. If there was any kind of game in the street, he was there, and despite his size, he was never picked last for any team. Stickball, baseball, dodgeball—he loved moving. Football was hardly a natural fit for his small frame, but he did all the leagues as soon as he was old enough to qualify. By junior high, he'd grown taller but his body was closer in proportion to a rubber band than a jock's athletic build. Still, the football coach had been impressed with his drive and John's first week of junior high found him on the field sweating his ass off, every muscle in his body screaming with joy at the prospect of playing with the big dogs.

In high school, he found out that you weren't allowed to play football when your grades sucked. He was more upset than he thought he'd be when he got dropped from the team. In a sudden burst of anger, he had thrown his helmet at the wall, punching a large hole into the Sheetrock. He had started walking around the neighborhood after school because he knew if he went home, his mother would ask him why he wasn't at practice. He had trashed the note the coach sent home and paid for the damaged wall with money from his illicit drug sales. He figured his parents would know soon enough what had happened when report cards were in and he wanted to enjoy his freedom as much as he could before Richard came down on him like the wrath of God.

Even after the rest of his life started falling apart, John still liked to walk. That first time he was suspended from school for the pot in his locker, he spent most of the day strolling around the neighborhood. After the cassette tape theft, his father grounded him for six months and except for his mother's kind heart ("Be back in an hour and don't tell your father") John probably would have atrophied in his room. Sometimes, he thought that was just what his dad wanted. Let the bad son fade away on his own; out of sight, out of mind. Dr. Richard still had Joyce, after all. He had one good child left.

John liked being outdoors, seeing the trees sway in the breeze, watching the leaves sail to the ground. He never got high on his jaunts. He didn't want to spoil things. Besides, the allure of coke was quickly fading. The visit to the emergency room, waking up feeling like his head was on fire, blood streaming out of his nose as he puked up the charcoal they had forced into his stomach, had been somewhat of an eye-opener. He had decided then and there to stick to pot. Nothing was worth dying for. Woody would give him shit for it, but John wasn't going to kill himself because he couldn't stand up to his cousin.

The night of the overdose, John's father had come to

the hospital, shirt hastily thrown on, buttons done up wrong. The nurse had left John alone with his dad, thinking they'd have a bonding moment or something.

"What the fuck is wrong with you?" Richard had demanded. He was beyond angry. His voice was strained like it was going through a sieve and John's ears, already buzzing from being sick, could barely comprehend what he was saying.

Richard liked his quotes. He kept some of them taped to the wall of his study, and sometimes when he'd pull John in to talk to him about his son's latest fuckup, he'd just point to one of the sayings. "Stupidity is a learned behavior" was one of his favorites, but that night at the hospital, John knew that the days of his father pointing to faded pieces of paper in the hopes of giving him guidance were over.

"You are not my son," Richard said. "If it weren't for your mother, I would toss your useless ass onto the street so fast your head would spin." He slapped John on the side of the head as some kind of illustration. It wasn't a hard hit, but it was the first time since John was six or seven that his father had raised a hand to him, and he had never, ever hit him anywhere but his bottom.

"Dad—" John tried.

"Don't ever call me that again," Richard commanded. "I *work* here. I have colleagues—I have *friends*—here. Do you know how embarrassing it is to get a phone call in the middle of the night telling you your worthless son is in the ER?" His face was red, and he was leaning over the bed, inches from John's face. His breath smelled of mint, and it occurred to John that his father had taken the time to brush his teeth before coming to the hospital.

"Do you know who does this shit?" his father had asked, pushing away from the bed. "Worthless junkies, that's who." He paced along the length of the small room, hands clenching and unclenching. He turned around and gave a single nod of his head like he had decided something and there was no going back.

John tried again. "Dad—"

"You are not my son," Richard repeated as the door closed behind him.

"He'll get over it," his mother said, but John knew otherwise. He had never seen that look in his father's eyes. Disappointment, yes. Hatred . . . that was something new.

John was thinking about that look as he walked around the neighborhood the day after his father's confrontation in the emergency room.

"Just an hour," his mother had said, but she hadn't added, "Don't tell your father," because they both knew that his father didn't care. As if the hospital scene weren't enough, Richard had come into John's room that morning and told him point-blank that he would feed and clothe him until he was eighteen, and then he wanted John out of his house, out of his life. He rubbed his hands together, then held them palm out to illustrate. "I wash my hands of you."

The breeze picked up and John pulled his jacket around him. Despite nearly dying the night before, he wanted a bump of coke, something to take the edge off. He wasn't going to do it, though. Not for his dad or his mom, but because he was scared. John didn't want to die, and he knew the coke would kill him sooner rather than later. He'd only snorted it a handful of times anyway, right? It shouldn't be hard to quit. Still, no matter how much pot he smoked, the craving ached inside his body like he'd swallowed a razor. God damn Woody and his stupid parties.

"Hey."

John looked up, startled out of his thoughts. Mary

Alice Finney was sitting on one of the swings in the playground.

His hatred of her sparked like a flash fire. "What are you doing here?"

She said, "I didn't know you owned the playground."

"Shouldn't you be in school?"

"I skipped."

"Yeah, right," he said, snorting a laugh that made him taste blood in the back of his throat. "Shit," he said, putting his hand to his nose. Blood was coming out like a faucet had been turned on.

Mary Alice was beside him. She had a tissue in her hand—why did girls always have these things?—and she pressed it under his nose.

"Sit down," she told him, leading him over to the jungle gym. He slumped on the bottom bar, his bony butt feeling the cold through his jeans. "Tilt your head forward."

He had his eyes closed, but he could feel her hands on him: one on the back of his neck, one holding the tissue to his nose. You were supposed to lean back when your nose bled, but he didn't care as long as she was touching him.

She sighed. "John. Why are you doing this to yourself?"

He opened his eyes, watched blood drip onto the sand between his feet. "Did you really skip school?"

"I was supposed to have a doctor's appointment, but my mom forgot to pick me up."

John tried to turn his head, but she wouldn't let him. Mothers didn't miss doctors' appointments. It just didn't happen.

"Yeah," she said, like she could read his mind. "My parents are getting divorced."

John straightened up quickly, seeing stars for a moment.

She was embarrassed. She clutched her hands together,

the bloody tissue between them. "My dad's been seeing this woman at his office." He could see the tight smile on her face. Perfect Mary Alice's parents were splitting up.

She said, "Her name is Mindy. Dad wants me to meet her. He thinks we'll be great friends."

John could hear Paul Finney saying this. The guy was a lawyer and he had the arrogance of most lawyers where he figured anything that came out of his mouth was the God's honest truth.

John stubbed his toe into the sand. "I'm sorry, Mary Alice."

She was crying, and he could see her watching her tears hit the sand just like he had watched his blood a few moments before.

He hated her, right? Only, he wanted to put his arm around her, tell her it was going to be okay.

He had to think of something to say, something to help her feel better. He blurted out, "You wanna go to a party?"

"A party?" she asked, her nose wrinkling at the thought. "What, with all your stoner friends?"

"No," he said, though she was right. "My cousin Woody is having a party Saturday. His mom's out of town."

"Where's his dad?"

"I don't know," John admitted. He'd never really thought about it, but Woody's mom was away so much that the guy practically lived alone. "You could drop by."

"I'm supposed to go to the mall with Susan and Faye."

"Come after."

"I don't really belong with those people," she said. "Besides, I figured you were grounded after what happened."

So, the whole school knew about his trip to the emergency room. John had figured he'd get at least a couple of days before the story leaked out. "No," he said, thinking of his father, the way he had looked at him this morning. It was the same way he had looked at dead Uncle Barry lying in his coffin, thin lips twisted in distaste. Glutton. Womanizer. Used car salesman.

Mary Alice asked, "Where does your cousin live?"

John told her the address, just three streets over. "Come on," he said. "Say you'll go."

She wrinkled her nose again, but this time she was teasing. "Okay," she said, then to give herself an out, "I'll think about it."

CHAPTER ELEVEN

John was lying in bed at the flophouse, half asleep, when a knock came at his door. He rolled over and looked at his clock, squinting his eyes to read the tiny numbers. Six-thirty. He had another hour to sleep before he had to get up.

"Knock-knock," a woman said, and he lay back in bed with a grunt. "Rise and shine, choirboy," Martha Lam sang. The first thing he had found out about his parole officer was that she loved surprise inspections.

"Just a minute," he called back, sitting up in bed, rubbing his eyes.

"Not a minute, cowboy," Ms. Lam insisted, her voice polite but firm. "Open up this door, now, you hear?"

He did as he was told—quickly—because he knew if she got it into her head she could throw him back inside before the day was out.

She stood at the door with one hand on the jamb, a cheerful smile on her face like she was happy to see him. She was dressed up as usual: pressed black shirt, gold lamé vest and tight black leather pants. Between her hoochie-mama shoes and the Glock she wore strapped to her side, she could be the poster girl for a fetish magazine.

She glanced down at the tent in his boxers, then gestured

down the hallway to the bathroom. "Go on and salute your little general. I'll just poke around on my own."

John put his hands over his crotch, feeling fifteen. "I just have to go to the bathroom," he explained.

She gave him that cheerful smile again, her southern drawl making her words sound polite. "Fill me up one'a them cups from the cooler in the hall, why don't you?"

He made his way to the communal bathroom as quickly as possible, peeing as fast as he could, spilling enough into the specimen cup for the random drug screening, then hurried back to his room. Ms. Lam would be going through his stuff now, and even though John knew there was nothing for her to find, he felt guilty, terrified she'd toss him back in prison. Guys back in the joint talked about parole officers, how they planted stuff on you if they didn't like you, how they were especially hard on sex offenders, looking for any excuse to send you back inside.

She was holding a framed photo of his mother when he got back.

"That was taken last year," he said, feeling a lump in his throat. Emily was standing in the visitor's hall at the prison. John had his arm around his mother, the dirty white cinder-block wall behind them serving as a backdrop. It had been his birthday. Joyce had taken the photo because his mother had insisted.

"Nice," Ms. Lam said. John always called her Ms. Lam, never Martha, because she scared him and he wanted to show her that he was capable of respect.

She opened up the back of the frame and checked it for—what? He didn't know, but he felt himself sweating until she put the photo back down on the cardboard box that served as a bedside table.

Next, she went through the paperback books he had borrowed from the library, thumbing through the pages, commenting on the titles. *"Tess of the d'Urbervilles?"* she asked, pausing on the last book.

He shrugged. "I've never read it before." He had been arrested the day after Ms. Rebuck, his English teacher, had announced in class that *Tess* would be their next major paper.

"Hm," she said, giving the book a second, more careful inspection.

She finally replaced the book and put her hands on her hips, surveying the room. John didn't have a chest of drawers so his clothes were folded and stacked in neat piles on top of the red cooler where he stored his food. He could tell she had already gone through the clothes because the shirt on top was folded differently, and he assumed she'd checked out the bananas, bread and jar of peanut butter in the cooler. There was one window in the room, but he had taped construction paper over it to block out the early morning sun. Ms. Lam had peeled back the edges to make sure there was no contraband hidden behind it. A bare lightbulb overhead illuminated the room and he noticed she had turned on the floor lamp beside the bed. The shade was askew. She had checked that as well.

She said, "Lift up your mattress, please," then, as if they were old pals, she explained, "I just had my nails done."

John took two steps into the tiny room and was at the mattress. He picked it up and leaned it against the wall so she could see the dirty box spring underneath. They both saw the back of his mattress at the same time. The bloodstains and some kind of gray circle of grime in the middle made her frown in disgust.

"That, too," she said, pointing to the box spring resting flat on the floor.

He picked this up, and they both jumped back like a

pair of frightened little girls when a cockroach scuttled across the dank brown carpet.

"Bleh," she said. "No luck finding another room?"

He shook his head, dropping the box spring and mattress back into place. He had been fortunate to find this one. As in prison, even flophouses had standards and a lot of them wouldn't take sex offenders, especially if the victims had been young. John was stuck in a house with six other men who were all registered with the state. One of them had a record for going after an eight-year-old girl. Another liked to rape old women.

"Well." Ms. Lam smiled, cheerful again. "I guess the Pedo Arms will do for the time being." She indicated the cardboard box by his bed. "Open this, please."

"There's nothing—" He gave up, knowing there was no use. He took the stack of books off the box and put them on the bed, then placed the photo of his mother on top of them, not wanting the frame to touch the dirty sheets.

He opened the box, showing her it was empty.

She went down her checklist. "Not hiding any Viagra in here, are you?" John shook his head. "Illegal drugs? Porn? Weapons of any kind?"

"No, ma'am," he assured her.

"Still working at the Gorilla?"

"Yes, ma'am."

"Anything changes, you'll tell me about it first, right?"

"Yes, ma'am."

"Well." She had her hands tucked into her hips again. "All righty, then. Clean bill for today."

"Thank you," he said.

She wagged a manicured finger at him. "I'm watching you, John. Don't you forget that."

"No, Ms. Lam. I won't."

She looked at him a moment longer, then shook her

head as if she couldn't understand a thing about him. "You stay out of trouble and we won't have any problems, okay?"

"Okay," he agreed. Stupidly, he added, "Thank you."

"I'll see you around," she said, heading for the door. "Keep your nose clean."

"Yes, ma'am," he agreed. He closed the door behind her, leaving his palm flat against the wood, resting his head on the back of his hand and just trying to breathe.

"Knock-knock," he heard above him. Ms. Lam was in charge of the old-lady rapist, too. John didn't know the guy's name because every time he saw him in the hall, it took all of John's willpower not to deck him.

He turned back to his room, blocking out Ms. Lam's voice as she made her cheery rounds upstairs. John hated people going through his shit. The most important thing he had learned in prison was that you never touched another man's property unless you were willing to die for it.

He picked up his T-shirt, one of the six that he owned, and refolded it. He had a pair of chinos, two pairs of jeans, three pairs of socks and eight pairs of boxers because for some reason his mother had always brought him underwear in prison.

John used his foot to upright one of his sneakers. Ms. Lam had searched them, too. The tongues were pulled out, the inserts crooked. Thirty dollars for a pair of shoes, John thought. He couldn't believe how expensive clothes and shoes had gotten while he was inside.

Upstairs, he heard Ms. Lam say, "Uh-oh!" John froze, knowing she had found something. He heard the rapist mutter a response, then Ms. Lam's voice loud and clear: "Tell it to the judge."

There wasn't much of a scuffle. She had a Glock, after all, and it wasn't like there was anywhere to run in the dilapidated house they all called home. John couldn't resist sticking his head out the door when he heard them making their way down the stairs. Ms. Lam had one hand on the rapist's shoulder, one on the cuffs that were locking his hands behind his back. The guy was still in his underwear, no shirt, no socks, no shoes. They'd have a real nice time with him in the holding cell, as Ms. Lam well knew.

She saw him peering from behind the door. "He messed up, John," she said, as if that wasn't obvious. "Take it as a lesson."

John didn't respond. He closed the door, waiting until he heard a car door slam on the street, an engine turn over, the car pull away.

Still, he checked out the window, pulling back the construction paper in time to see Ms. Lam's red SUV stop at the light at the end of the street.

John dropped to his knees and picked at the edge of the filthy brown carpet. He tried not to think about the roach they had seen or the mouse turds between the carpet and the pad. He found the credit report right where he had left it. Not contraband, but what would Ms. Lam say if she found it? "Uh-oh!" And then he'd be gone.

John slipped on his jeans and shoved his feet into his sneakers. He took the stairs two at a time. There was a phone in the hallway that they could use for local calls, and he picked it up, dialing the number he knew by heart.

"Keener, Rose and Shelley," the receptionist on the other end said. "How can I direct your call?"

John kept his voice low. "Joyce Shelley, please."

"Who can I say is calling?"

He almost gave her a different name, but relented. "John Shelley."

There was a pause, a hesitation that kept him in his place. "Just a moment."

The moment turned into a couple of minutes, and

John could picture his sister's frown when her secretary told her who was on the line. Joyce's life was pretty settled and she seemed to be doing well. She had rebelled against their father in her own way: instead of becoming a doctor, she had dropped out of medical school her second year at Emory and switched to law. Now, she did real estate closings all day, taking a flat fee for getting folks to sign on the dotted line. He couldn't imagine her doing something so boring, but then, Joyce probably got a good laugh out of him wiping soapy water off of cars all day.

"What is it?" his sister whispered, not even bothering with a hello.

"I need to ask you something."

"I'm in the middle of a closing."

"It won't take long," he said, then kept talking because he knew she'd cut him off if he didn't. "What's a credit score?"

She spoke in her normal voice. "Are you an idiot?"

"Yeah, Joyce. You know I am."

She gave a heavy sigh that sounded more labored than usual. He wondered if she had a cold or maybe she'd started smoking again. "All the credit card companies, the banks, anybody who lets you buy anything on credit, report to credit agencies about how well you pay your bills, whether you're on time, whether you're slow, if you make the minimum payment or pay it all off each month or whatever. Those agencies compile your payment histories and come up with a score that tells other companies how good a credit risk you are."

"Is seven hundred ten a good score?"

"John," she said. "I really don't have time for this. What kind of scam are you running?"

"None," he said. "I don't run scams, Joyce. That's not why they sent me to prison."

She was quiet and he knew he had pushed her too far. "I haven't forgotten why they sent you to prison," she said, the edge to her voice telling him she was having a hard time keeping control.

"What if somebody got my information and used it to get credit cards and stuff?"

"Then it'd wreck your score."

"No." He clarified, "What if they were paying off the cards and everything every month?"

She hesitated a moment. "Why would they do that?"

"I don't know, Joyce. That's why I'm asking you."

"Are you for real?" she demanded. "What is this, John? Just ask me what you need to know. I've got work to do."

"I *am* asking you," he said. "It's just that someone…" He let his voice trail off. Would this implicate Joyce in whatever was going on? Could she somehow get in trouble for having knowledge of this? He didn't know how the law worked. Hell, last week he hadn't even known there was such a thing as a credit score.

He didn't know, either, if Ms. Lam tapped the phone.

He finally said, "It's this scam some guys were running in prison."

"Jesus." She was whispering again. "You'd better not be getting involved in it."

"No," he said. "I'm keeping my nose clean."

"You'd better be, John. They will throw your ass back in jail so fast you won't even have time to think."

"You sound like Dad."

"Is that your way of asking how he's doing?"

John realized he was holding his breath. "No."

"Good, because he wouldn't want me telling you anyway."

"I know."

"Christ, John." She sighed again. He was upsetting her.

Why had he called her? Why did he have to bother her with this?

He felt tears in his eyes and pressed his fingers into the corners to try to stop them. He remembered when they were little, how she used to play with him, dress him up in Richard's clothes, pretend she was his mother. They had tea parties and cooked cupcakes in her Easy-Bake Oven.

He asked, "Do you remember that time we melted Mom's present?" John was six, Joyce was nine. They had saved their allowance and bought a bracelet for their mother's birthday. Joyce had suggested they bake it in a cake to surprise her, something she'd read about in a book. They didn't realize the bracelet was costume jewelry, and when they put it in the little oven, turned on the hundred-watt bulb to cook the cake, the bracelet had melted into the rack. The smoke had set off the fire alarm.

"Remember?" he asked.

Joyce sniffed, not answering.

"You okay?" he said. He wanted to know about her life. Was she seeing anybody? She'd never been married, but she was so damn pretty and smart. There had to be somebody in her life, somebody who wanted to take care of her.

"I'm getting a cold," she said.

"You sound like it."

"I gotta go."

He heard the soft click of the phone as she hung up.

The next three days were riddled with storms—the clouds spitting down rain one minute, parting for the sunshine the next—and John was basically out of a job until they cleared. He found himself wishing he hadn't blown fifty dollars on that hooker. But then, sometimes he found himself wishing he had fifty more to give her. What question would he ask her this time? Maybe, what did it feel like to be in love? What did it feel like to hold somebody who wanted to hold you back? He wanted to talk to her again. He wanted to know about her life.

Unfortunately, he couldn't afford it.

Growing up, John hadn't had to worry about how to put food on the table or clothes on his back. His parents took care of everything. There were always fresh sheets on the bed, the toilet was magically clean and whenever he opened the refrigerator, it was filled with all the things he liked to eat. Even in prison, everything was provided for him. They had a strict schedule and firm rules, but as long as you did what you were told, you didn't have to worry about anything.

During a good month at the car wash, John pulled in about a thousand dollars after taxes. Rent for his ten-foot by ten-foot roach-encrusted room was four hundred fifty dollars—a premium, to be certain, but no one else would take him in so his landlord felt entitled. Renting an apartment would have made things cheaper, but John couldn't swing the hefty deposit, let alone the various connection charges and down payments utility companies required. MARTA wasn't cheap, either. The city offered a Monthly Trans Card for unlimited bus and subway rides, but that cost around fifty-two dollars a month. Sometimes, John couldn't afford to pay all that up front and he ended up shelling out a buck seventy-five each way in order to get to and from work.

Food, which mainly consisted of dry cereal, banana and peanut butter sandwiches and the occasional piece of fruit, ran around a hundred twenty dollars a month. John had to buy milk in small containers he could drink right away and stick with nonperishable foods. The cooler in his room was used to keep the roaches out; John couldn't buy a bag of ice every day, especially in the summer when the heat would turn it to water before he could get it home on the bus.

For the privilege of being paroled, he paid the state two hundred thirty dollars a month. Rape and murder wasn't cheap, and if he failed to make a payment, his ass went straight back to prison. The first money order he bought each month was made payable to the state.

This usually left him with a little less than seventy-five dollars each week for things that he needed. That was from a good week, though, and some weeks he pulled in considerably less. John forced himself to save money, skipping meals sometimes, making himself so dizzy from lack of food that he practically fell into bed at night. Once, in desperation, he had gone into one of the millions of cash-until-payday stores spotting the poorer parts of the city, but John couldn't bring himself to pay 480 percent interest on a week-long loan. Even if he had been, they required you to have a checking account so they could wire the money directly to your bank. No bank in the world would give John Shelley a checking account.

Health insurance was a fantastical dream. John lived in terror of getting sick.

After the ill-fated phone call to his sister, John walked through the rain, kicking puddles, wishing he could kick himself for calling Joyce. She had enough trouble without him putting more on her. The truth was, he just wanted to talk to her, wanted to see how she was doing. John called her maybe once a month and she was always as happy to hear from him as she had been this morning.

A MARTA bus squealed to a stop in front of him and John checked the number before getting on. This month had been a good one, so he waved his Trans Card in front of the reader, giving the driver a nod of recognition.

"Getting cold," the driver said.

"Sure is," John agreed, enjoying the simple banter until he realized he'd have to buy a winter jacket. God, how much would that cost?

The bus jerked as it accelerated and John grabbed the back of a seat to steady himself as he walked down the aisle. The bus was packed, and he found a seat by an old black woman who was reading a Bible in her lap. Despite the weather, she was wearing a large pair of black sunglasses over her eyeglasses. She didn't look up when he sat down, but he knew she had read him out of the corner of her eye.

There were scams to make money. There was always a scam, always an angle. Prison was full of men who thought they had discovered the perfect scheme. John knew that some of the guys at the Gorilla would steal receipts out of cars and change them into cash. The big chain stores were the best. All you had to do was walk in and find the same item number as what was printed on the receipt, then hand it to the girl behind the desk and get the cash. Easy money, they all said. Ray-Ray said it twice.

He changed buses at the Lindbergh station, passing the closed car wash on the way. Figuring he was running what amounted to a fool's errand, he took the long route down Cheshire Bridge Road, knowing it would pass the liquor store where he had met Robin. That whole week, he had been thinking about her, wondering what she was up to.

Somehow, he had imagined this kind of life for her, one that mirrored his own. Maybe she had been a little spoiled like Joyce, a daddy's girl. He wondered about her younger brother, friend to Stewie the kisser. What was he like? Did she call him up some days when she was having an especially bad time? Was he as upset to hear from her as Joyce was when John called? John couldn't imagine what it'd be like to have a sister who was a whore. He'd want to kill every freaking man who even looked at her.

The bus passed the liquor store, and he could see three working girls standing under the cover of the awning. One of them was the loudmouth who had fought with Ray-Ray. None of them was Robin.

John sat back in his seat, watching the fancy restaurants go by. The bus stopped at the corner where the movie theater was, and he stood so that the old black woman could get off. He read the marquee, not recognizing any of the movies. He had gone to a movie with his first paycheck, shocked when he got to the ticket counter and saw the prices. Ten bucks! He couldn't believe how much a movie cost. Even a matinee was expensive.

The bus took a right at the intersection and the scenery changed, turning more residential. John stared out the window as the houses got bigger, the yards nicer. Morningside, Virginia Highland, Poncey-Highland. Through Little Five Points, past the new Barnes & Noble, Target, Best Buy. It didn't start to get bad again until they were well down Moreland Avenue. Liquor stores, corner groceries and auto parts stores lined the filthy street. Signs advertised cheap check cashing, low-cost insurance; one proudly proclaimed, "The only place in town selling clothing by the pound."

Men with dirty T-shirts wrapped around their bare shoulders stood at the bus stop, slipping on their shirts at the last minute before they got on. The bus took on a new odor as construction workers started to file in. Mexicans, Asians, blacks. Pretty soon, John was the only white person on the bus.

He got off the bus when the street turned almost pretty. This part of Moreland was bordered by Brownwood and Grant Park. Families had started to move in, reclaiming the in-town area for their own. They took care of their houses, kept their yards trimmed and demanded better treatment, nicer restaurants, safer streets, than the previous inhabitants had. John had learned a long time ago that the reason the middle class had it so good was because they *expected* things to be better. They wouldn't settle for less than they were worth. They'd just get into their shiny cars and go where they were appreciated. Poor people, on the other hand, were used to just taking what was given to them and being grateful for it.

For the moment, the rain had cleared, the sun peeking out from behind dark clouds. John didn't want to go back up Moreland, so he got off the bus and walked into Brownwood Park, cutting through the woods. He had looked up this area in the street atlas he found in the library and was glad to see the roads were much as he expected. New construction was going up all around him, three-story mansions towering over 1950s ranch houses. How much did something like that cost? John wondered. What kind of job did you need in order to be able to buy your own house, raise your kids, maybe drive a nice secondhand car? He couldn't fathom the amount of cash that would take.

He took Taublib Street into East Atlanta Village, surprised to find a couple of nice restaurants and a coffee joint where he had expected abandoned buildings and auto-body repair shops. There were a couple of boutiques, a bakery and a pet store. He looked in the window where a fat orange cat was sunbathing on a bag of dog food. A cat would be nice, some kind of animal to keep him company. The cockroach Ms. Lam had found didn't really count. That would be a luxury for another day. John could barely afford to feed himself.

At Metropolitan Avenue, he took a right, walked down a few blocks and found himself in front of the East Atlanta branch of the post office. John stared at the squat, institutional-looking building. The sign outside showed the same zip code as the credit report: 30316.

The place was packed, cars filling the front and side lot, spilling onto the street even though there were signs warning against it. The driveway to the light blue Victorian house next to the post office was blocked by a large cargo van.

The rain had started again, a light drizzle that darkened the sky. John walked down Metropolitan about fifty feet, then turned around and walked back. He watched people going in and out of the post office, wondering why the hell he had come here.

After thirty minutes of pacing up and down the street, John realized that there was nothing stopping him from actually going inside the building. His local post office was gloomy and smelled of bacon grease for no apparent reason. He bought his money orders for rent and his state fine there because it was only a ten-minute walk from where he lived. There were a lot of immigrants in the neighborhood, and sometimes people would bring in chickens and other small animals to ship to God only knew where. Oftentimes, he'd hear a rooster crowing while he was waiting in line.

The East Atlanta branch was well-lit, clean and just seemed to have a good vibe. Right across from the front door were rows of post office boxes, small ones at the top, large ones at the bottom. To his left was the office where two women were helping customers as quickly as they could. A line of people went out from the lobby all the way to the stamp vending machine by the front door. John pulled a blank envelope out of his back pocket and got in line, trying to act like he belonged. Inch by inch, the line moved forward, and he didn't look back at the mailboxes until he was up close to the glass doors leading into the office.

Box eight-fifty was on the first row about eye level. The

box next to it had an orange sticker pasted to it, the words too faded to read.

"Have a good one," one of the ladies behind the desk called as a customer brushed past John on her way out. He stepped back quickly to get out of the woman's way, mumbling an apology as rain dripped from his hair. When he looked back up, he saw someone heading toward the boxes.

John held his breath, clutching the envelope in his hand as a skinny black woman talking on her cell phone jabbed her key into the lock of box eight-fifty. She was laughing into the phone, saying something derogatory about a family member, when she jerked the key back out, saying, "Shit, girl, I just put my key in the wrong box."

She pushed the key into the lock below eight-fifty, cradling the cell phone with her shoulder as she kept on talking.

"Sir?" the woman behind John said.

The line had moved, but John hadn't. He smiled, saying, "Sorry. Forgot my wallet," and stepped out of line.

What a stupid waste of time. There was no way he could sit on this box all day, and the odds of whoever had taken his name just showing up when John happened to be there were ridiculously low. He'd have better luck buying a lottery ticket.

He pushed open the door, tossing the blank envelope into the trash. The sky had opened up again, sending down a cold deluge. John shivered. A hundred dollars. A good winter coat would be at least a hundred dollars. Where would he get that kind of money? How long would it take to save up for a freaking coat?

He hunched his shoulders as he stood at the bus stop, cursing himself and the rain. He would have to start looking for a new job. Maybe something inside, something that had regular hours and didn't depend on the weather.

Something where they didn't mind if you had a record, and if that record said you were the kind of man who should be put down like a rabid dog to protect the rest of the world from the evil inside of you.

John's job choices were limited to the dangerous ones. Half the guys in prison were there because they'd knocked over a convenience store or a mom-and-pop diner. Most of the guys on death row had gotten their start robbing the local Quickie Mart, ending their criminal careers by putting a bullet in some low-wage worker's head for the sixty bucks in the cash drawer. Before Ms. Lam had hooked him up at the Gorilla, John had almost been desperate enough to try the convenience stores. He knew now that he couldn't keep working at the car wash, not through the winter. He needed a way to find money, and fast.

The bus was late, the driver irritated when he finally pulled up. John's mood matched everybody else's as he sloshed up the stairs and walked to the back, his thirty-dollar sneakers practically disintegrated from the rain. He fell into the empty seat at the back of the bus, half-wishing the lightning zigzagging out of the sky would come through the window and hit him right in the head. He'd end up brain-damaged, a drooling vegetable taking up space in a hospital somewhere. He was beginning to see why so many guys ended up back in prison. He was thirty-five years old. He had never driven a car, never really dated, never really lived. What the hell was the point, John thought, staring glumly out the window as some guy struggled to close an umbrella and get into his car at the same time.

John stood up as the bus pulled away, looking out window, keeping his eyes on the man. How many years had passed? His brain wouldn't let him do the math, but he knew it was him. John was slack-jawed as he watched the man give up on the umbrella and toss it into the parking lot before slamming his car door shut.

Yes. It was him. It was definitely him.

Just as a million raindrops fell from the sky, there existed a million chances that John would go to the post office on the right day at the right time.

A million to one, but he had done it.

He had found the other John Shelley.

CHAPTER TWELVE

John couldn't remember being arrested—not because he was in shock at the time but because he had been semi-conscious. Woody had come by that morning to check on him and hooked him up with some Valium. John had taken enough to tranquilize a horse.

Apparently, the cops had come to his house with an arrest warrant. His father had led them up to John's room and they had found him passed out on his bed. John remembered coming to, his face on fire where his father had slapped him. The cops dragged him out of the house, handcuffs biting into the skin on his wrists. He passed out again on the lawn.

He woke up in the hospital, the familiar taste of charcoal in his mouth. Only, this time, when he tried to move his hand to wipe his face, something clattered against the bed rail. He looked down at his wrist, his eyes blurry, and saw that he was cuffed to the bed.

A cop was sitting by the door reading a newspaper. He scowled at John. "You awake?"

"Yeah." John fell back asleep.

His mother was in the room when he next came around. God, she looked horrible. He wondered how long he had been asleep because Emily looked like twenty years had passed since he had climbed up the stairs to his room, turned Heart down low on the stereo and taken a handful of the little white pills his cousin had given him.

"Baby," she said, rubbing his forearm. "Are you okay?"

His tongue was lolled back in his mouth. His chest hurt like he had been slammed in the sternum with a sledge-hammer. How had he managed to breathe all this time?

"You're going to be okay," she said. "It's all a mistake."

It wasn't though—at least as far as the police were concerned. The district attorney came in an hour or so later, Paul Finney standing behind the man, glaring at John like he was ready to jump onto the bed and throttle him right then and there. The cop must have picked up on this, too, because he was staying close to Mr. Finney, making sure nothing got out of hand.

The DA made the introductions. "I'm Lyle Anders. This is Chief Harold Waller." The cop by Mr. Finney was holding a sheet of paper. He cleared his throat, looking down at it like he was reading from a script.

John looked at his mother. She said, "It's all right, baby."

"Jonathan Winston Shelley," Waller began. "I'm arresting you for the rape and murder of Mary Alice Finney."

John's ears did that thing where he felt like he was underwater. Waller's lips were moving, he was definitely saying something, but John couldn't understand him.

Lyle Anders finally reached over and snapped his fingers in front of John's face. "You understand what's happening, son?"

"No," John said. "I didn't—"

"Don't say anything," his mother shushed, putting her fingers to his lips. Emily Shelley, PTA sponsor, den mother, baker of brownies and master of Halloween disguises, straightened her back and addressed the three men in the room. "If that's all?"

They loomed over his small mother, Paul Finney especially. He was a big man to begin with, but his rage made him larger.

Anders said, "He needs to make a statement."

"No," she said, this woman who was his mother. "Actually, he doesn't."

"It'd be in his best interest."

"My son has been through a horrible ordeal," Emily answered. "He needs rest."

Anders tried to speak directly to John, and even when Emily blocked his way, he still made an attempt. "Son, you need to get on top of this and tell us what happened. I'm sure there's a reason you—"

"He has nothing to say to you," Emily insisted, her voice firm. John had only heard her speak this way once, when Joyce was ten and she'd tried to walk on the railing to the top deck at the house.

One by one, Emily looked them all in the eye. "Please leave."

Paul Finney lunged for John, but the cop caught him. "You son of a bitch," Mr. Finney spat at John. "You'll fry for this!"

Mr. Finney had been an all-state wrestler. Anders and Waller had their hands full trying to keep him off John. In the end, they had to physically pick him up and carry him out of the room. As the door closed, he screamed, "You'll pay for this, you fucker!"

His mother's bottom lip was trembling as she turned back to John. He thought, oddly, that she had been upset by Mr. Finney's language.

He asked, "Where's Dad?" Richard was the one who took care of things, cleaned up the messes. "Mom?" John asked. "Where is he?"

Her throat worked, and she reached out, taking his

hand. "Listen to me," she said, urgent. "They're going to come back any minute and take you to jail. We only have a few seconds."

"Mom—"

"Don't talk," she said, squeezing his hand. "Listen."

He nodded.

"Don't say anything to the police. Don't even tell them your name. Don't tell them where you were that night, don't tell them what you had for dinner."

"Mom—"

"Shush, Jonathan," she ordered, pressing her fingers to his lips. "Don't talk to anyone in jail. No one is your friend in there. They're all looking out for themselves and you should, too. Don't say anything on the phone because they tape the conversations. There are snitches everywhere."

Snitches, John thought. Where had his mother heard that word? How did she know about any of this? She wouldn't even watch *Kojak* because she thought it was too violent.

"I want you to promise me, John," she insisted. "Promise me that you will not talk to anyone until your aunt Lydia shows up."

Aunt Lydia. Barry's wife. She was a lawyer.

"John?" she prompted. "Do you promise? Not a word? Don't even talk about the weather. Do you understand me? This is the most important thing I have ever told you to do and you must obey me. Do not talk to *anyone*. Do you hear me?"

He started crying because she was. "Yes, Mama."

The door opened and Waller was back. He glanced at the scene, mother and child, and John saw part of him soften. He sounded almost kind when he told Emily, "Mrs. Shelley, you're going to have to step outside now."

Her hand tightened around John's. She looked down at

him, tears spilling out of her eyes. For some reason, he had been expecting her to say that she loved him, but instead, she mouthed, *"No one."*

Talk to no one.

Anders let Emily leave before he reached into his pocket and pulled out the keys to the handcuffs. The moment of softness was gone as quickly as it had come.

He told John, "You listen to me, you little bastard. You're gonna get out of that bed, get your clothes on and put your hands behind your back. If you give me a millisecond of trouble, I will come down on you like a ton of bricks. Do you understand me, you murdering piece of shit?"

"Yes," John said, breathless with fear. "Yes, sir."

CHAPTER THIRTEEN

OCTOBER 15, 2005

Coastal State Prison was located near Savannah in a town called Garden City, Georgia. The names sounded beautiful on paper, conjuring up a quaint seaside town you might find on a postcard. Whoever selected the spot for the state correctional department must have gotten a pretty good joke out of the whole thing.

Coastal was a maximum-security facility, only a few years old by the time John got there and remodeled ten years into his sentence to accommodate the influx of violent criminals. Today, the prison consisted of seven housing units with twelve two-man cells and twenty-four four-man cells. There were forty-four segregation cells, thirty disciplinary cells and fifteen protective custody cells. The L-building housed over two hundred men, N had another two hundred and O and Q were open dorms with bunk beds laid out like general military quarters. All told, around sixteen hundred men called it home.

John didn't think he'd ever willingly go back to Coastal, but he had taken off work and boarded the Greyhound bus at six that morning. The ticket had cost him the rest of his television money, but that was hardly the point. He tried to sleep on the bus, leaning his head against the window, but all he could do was think about that first time he had made this trip in handcuffs and shackles. He couldn't go back in. He could not die in prison.

He had brought a book—*Tess of the D'Urbervilles*—and he made himself read it during the nearly five-hour journey. John kept having to backtrack in the book, his mind wandering as each mile ticked past. How had his mother made this drive every two weeks, rain or shine? No wonder she had looked exhausted by the time she got there. No wonder she had looked so defeated that first time she was allowed to visit him. She did it for twenty years, though, and she had only missed three visits during all that time.

Tess had just confided her noble ancestry to Angel when the Greyhound pulled up outside of the state prison. John used his ticket to mark his place, then put the book in the plastic grocery bag he had brought along with him.

At visitor processing, John burned with shame as he was searched and questioned—not because he was above it all, but because he finally knew what his mother had gone through every time she had come to see him. He did the math as they searched his grocery bag, opening the carton of cigarettes, checking the book almost page by page. Over five hundred times she'd made this trip. How had Emily endured this? How could he have brought this humiliation down on his mother? No wonder Joyce had been so livid. John had never hated himself more than at this moment in time.

He sat on one of the plastic chairs as he waited for his name to be called. His knee was bobbing again, but everyone else in the room looked perfectly calm. Mostly, it was women with their children. They had come to see daddy. One kid near John held a crayon drawing of an airplane. Another was crying because they hadn't let her bring her teddy bear in. Something unusual had shown up on the X-ray and the mother had refused to let them inspect it.

"Shelley?" a uniformed woman called. None of the guards had recognized him, but considering the volume of prisoners and visitors they had each week, this shouldn't have come as a surprise.

"Shelley?" she called again.

John stood, clutching his grocery bag to his chest.

"Table three," she said, nodding him in.

He put his bag on the X-ray belt, the third time it had been screened, and walked through the metal detector and into the visitors' room. He stopped at the end of the belt, staring at the room, trying to see it the way his mother had. There were picnic-style metal tables bolted to the floor all around the twenty-by-thirty room. Men sat on one side, their wives or girlfriends or hookers they'd paid to come see them sitting on the other. Kids were running around laughing and screaming and, about every ten feet, there was a guard standing with his back to the wall. Cameras were everywhere, their lenses swinging back and forth in slow disapproval.

Ben Carver sat at one of the back tables, table three. He was dressed in his usual white shirt, white pants and white socks. He had a pair of matching patent-leather slippers that his mother had sent, but Ben seldom wore them outside the cell because he didn't want them to get dirty.

Everybody had a persona in prison, a different personality they adopted that helped them survive. The thugs got meaner, the Aryans more cruel, the gays gayer and the loonies absolutely fucking nuts. Ben fell into this latter category, and he worked it like a master thespian. Not that John thought it was much of a stretch for the man. By the time the GBI caught up with him, Ben had killed six men in the surrounding Atlanta area. His particular twist was to cut off their right nipples for souvenirs. During his arrest at the main branch of the Atlanta post office where Ben had worked as a mail sorter for eighteen years, one of the cops became a little overzealous and slammed Ben to the ground. A piece of tissue—later identified as the right nipple of his last victim—flew out of Ben's mouth where he had been sucking on it like a Lifesaver.

This lurid detail combined with Ben's appropriate last name of Carver had made a big splash in the press. Unlike John, he made the national news, even got his own nickname: the Atlanta Carver. Ben had never been particularly pleased with the moniker, but then he was also angry with Wayne Williams, the man convicted in the Atlanta Child Murders case, for pushing him off the front page a few weeks after his arrest.

"My dear boy," Ben said, smiling his thin smile as he sized up John. His lips were wet, a black stain at the center where he usually kept a cigarette. His teeth were likewise marked, nicotine drawing a bull's-eye right at the center. One of the first things Ben had told John was that he had something of an oral fixation. "Better cigarettes than your right tit, my dear boy." John had never complained about his smoking after that.

"So," Ben said.

John stood at the table, not sure whether he wanted to sit. He told Ben, "You look good."

"Of course I do." He pretended to primp his hair, which was practically nonexistent, winking at someone behind John.

Though Ben was in protective custody, there wasn't really a room set up to accommodate visitors in that wing, so he had to sit with the general population on the rare occasion someone came to see him. Any prisoner from the Level III mental health unit was at his most vulnerable during visitation. He had to rely on his fellow inmates being too distracted by their whores or too respectful of their wives and girlfriends to pull out a shiv and rip open his belly.

John said, "I had to see you."

Ben tsked his tongue, and John tried not to think about what the man would have in his mouth right now if the cops hadn't caught him. "Didn't I tell you not to ever come back to this hellhole?"

"It's good to see you," John said, and he meant it. He hadn't seen a welcoming face since he'd gotten out.

"Well," Ben said, smacking his lips. "What have you brought me?"

John took the carton of unfiltered Camels out of the bag.

"Oh, you shouldn't have!" Ben cradled the carton to his chest. "My sweetness, please do sit. You know I don't like hovering even if it does give me a wonderful view of your package."

John sat, feeling embarrassed by Ben's language. He had forgotten how Ben spoke to him, the way he made you feel dirty even if he was just asking you what time it was. John had to remind himself this was part of Ben's act, the way he got through the day without cutting his own throat open.

Ben confided, "Oprah is doing her favorite things today."

Oprah, the only program the entire cell block could agree on.

"I'm sure it'll be a good one," John said. He didn't add anything else as a guard walked by, lingering near their table for a few minutes before moving on.

"Now," Ben said, "you know I can't stay away from my nicotine for long. What do you desire?"

John leaned in close, keeping his hands flat on the table so the guard could see he wasn't doing anything to break the rules. "I've got a problem."

"I assumed as much."

The guard had moved on. John resisted the urge to look over his shoulder. Ben was scoping out the situation behind him just as John was keeping his eye on everyone behind Ben.

"Precious," Ben said, "let's keep in mind the walls have ears."

The tables, more like. John wasn't sure whether it was true or not, but everyone in the prison believed there were bugs all over the visitors' room—some under the tables, some overhead in the fluorescent lights. The cameras were visible enough, sweeping the room back and forth, zooming in on suspicious visitors. You couldn't trust a priest in here.

In low tones, John told Ben about the television, the credit report, the post office. He told him about the man with the umbrella, careful not to say his name because who knew if the rumors were true.

When he had finished, Ben said, "I see."

John sat back a little. "What should I do?"

Ben's full lips pressed together and he put his finger where the black dot was burned into the flesh. "The question, my love, is not an easy one."

"He's jacking me up for something," John said, then, because he wasn't sure, "Right?"

"Oh, indeed," Ben agreed. "There's no other reason for this type of behavior. No reason at all."

"He's using me as a cover."

"He's framing you, my love."

John shook his head, leaning in close again. "It doesn't make sense. This started six years ago. I was in here six years ago. It's an airtight alibi."

"True, true," Ben agreed, tapping his finger to his lip again. "Did he know you got out?"

John shrugged. "He could find out."

"But did he know?" Ben said. "I must say, my darling, that it came as a surprise even to me when you spoke so eloquently to the parole board. Such a silver tongue."

John nodded. He had surprised himself.

"Let's pose a what-if," Ben suggested. "What if your friend assumed you would rot away here in our little Maison du Feces?"

"Okay."

"And what if, much to his surprise, he found our little darling boy got out?"

"Yeah?"

"And what if he felt threatened by your return?" Ben leaned in closer. "He has something going, obviously."

"Yes," John agreed.

"And he doesn't want you to interfere with this little side thing, does he?"

"Right."

"So, what does he do?"

Both men went quiet, tried to think it to the next step.

"I don't know," John admitted, frustrated. "I need to find him."

"You've tried all the obvious routes?"

"Yeah." He had checked the phone book, but the guy wasn't listed. He'd even tried the computer at the library, feeling like an idiot as he followed the printed directions on how to do an Internet search. Nothing.

John said, "I have to find out what he's up to."

Ben fingered the carton of cigarettes, picking at the edge. John knew he was running out of time. "Of course, I could use the contacts from my previous life to get you this fella's current address."

"You've still got people?" John was surprised Ben was admitting this where he might be heard. There had been "sources close to the case" at the time of Ben's trial who claimed that he had used the post office's intercompany mail to send some of his souvenirs to fellow fetishists.

Ben slapped on a wide smile. "Through rain, sleet and snow . . . but you have yet to tell me the information I need to know."

The name. He needed the name. John glanced around, opened his mouth, but—

"Hush, hush," Ben warned.

Another guard walked by, standing just opposite their table. Both men fell silent again, and John stared at his hands, questioning the logic of coming here. Who else could he talk to? He couldn't get Joyce wrapped up in this. The only people he knew were convicted felons and whores.

The guard moved along and Ben made a funny face. In a lot of ways, this man had been a father to John. How had that happened? How could somebody so evil, so absolutely without any redeeming qualities, be his friend?

There was no explaining it except to say that Ben thought he and John were two of a kind.

"I'll tell you what," Ben said. "I have a car."

"What?"

"It's at my mother's house. I'll call her today and say a friend is going to borrow it."

Ben was smarter at this than him. John was just going step by step, not even thinking it through. So what if he found out the guy's address? It's not like he could follow him around on a MARTA bus.

John asked, "Does it still run?"

"Mother used to drive it to church every Sunday but her gentleman friend, Mr. Propson, takes her now," Ben said. "Beulah Carver. I daresay she's the only one in the book. She'll give you the key, but don't tell her how you know me."

"You've been in jail for almost thirty years. Don't you think she'll figure it out?"

"I kept men's nipples in her refrigerator for three years and told her they were herbal treatments for alopecia. What do you think?"

John conceded the point.

"Okay." Ben's eyes darted somewhere over John's shoulder, and he spoke quickly, dropping the act for a moment. "You need to follow him," he said. "Follow this man and find out what he's doing, where he's going. Everything happens for a reason. Everything." He stood as another guard walked by. "Now go, my love, and thank you for the lovely gift." He tapped the carton of cigarettes.

John stood, too. "Ben—"

"Go," he insisted, throwing his arms around John's shoulders, hugging him close.

The guards converged en masse—physical contact was strictly forbidden—but Ben held on tight, his wet lips brushing just under John's ear. He was laughing like a hyena when they pulled him off, but he had the presence of mind to hold on to the cigarette carton.

"Good-bye, sweet boy!" Ben called as they dragged him to the door.

John waved back, resisting the urge to wipe off Ben's saliva until the man had been taken out of view.

About five years into his sentence, John had asked Ben why the older man never made a pass or tried anything with him. John was bigger then. Just like his mother had always predicted, he had finally grown into his hands and feet. Weights at the gym had bulked him up and he had enough hair on his body to warm a polar bear.

Ben had shrugged. "Don't eat where you shit."

"No," John persisted, not letting him get away with a sarcastic non-answer. "Tell me. I want to know."

Ben had been doing a crossword, and he was annoyed at first, but then he saw John was serious and set the paper aside.

"There's no sport in it," Ben finally said. "I like the seduction of the show, my boy. I am an actor on a stage and you..." He gave his wet smile. "You are a rube."

The rube hadn't done too bad this time, though. In the few seconds Ben's face had been pressed close to his, John had been able to tell him all he needed to know.

CHAPTER FOURTEEN

After the jury returned with his sentence, John had been taken back to his cell at the county jail. They had left the cuffs on but taken away his belt and the laces in his shoes so he wouldn't do anything crazy. They needn't have bothered. He was too stunned to move, let alone figure out a way to kill himself in his tiny five-by-eight cell.

Twenty-two to life. Twenty-two years. He would be thirty before he was eligible for parole. He would be an old man.

"It's good," his mother had said, tears in her eyes. She didn't cry much after he was arrested, but now she let the tears flow. "It's good, baby."

She meant it was good because he had avoided the death penalty. A fourteen-year-old in Massachusetts had just made national headlines for beating another fourteen-year-old to death with a baseball bat. A twenty-eight-year-old in Texas had recently been executed for a crime he committed at the age of seventeen. Juvenile offenders were no longer a novelty. John could have been on his way to death row right now instead of looking at a lifetime behind bars.

"We can appeal," his mother told him. "It won't be long," she said. "We'll appeal."

Behind her, his aunt Lydia looked dubious. Later, he would find out that but for one juror, a father of three boys, one of whom was John's age, everyone else had voted for death. The rest had taken one look at John, then at the supersized photos of Mary Alice's mutilated body, and wanted him to die, too.

In the holding cell, John kept going over and over everything that was said about him during the trial. The state's psychologist had seemed nice enough when they talked a few months ago, but at trial he had told the entire courtroom that John was obviously a delusional psychopath, a cold-blooded killer who showed no remorse. Then, there were the kids from John's school who had stood up during the sentencing phase to talk about what a good girl Mary Alice was and what a horrible person John Shelley had always been. Principal Binder, Coach McCollough... they had all talked about him like he was Charles Manson.

Who was that person they were talking about? John didn't recognize him. Half of those kids hadn't even said two words to him in the last three years, but now they acted as if they knew everything about him. There had been that split when they went from elementary to middle school, and the popular clique had left John behind. If not for sports, he would have been some kind of geek left to hang in the wind. When he was kicked off the football team, none of them would even meet his eye in the hallway. Now, according to these "friends" of his, John was some kind of... monster.

John had been staring at the concrete floor of the cell, following the cracks spreading out like a palm reader trying to divine his future. When he looked up, Paul Finney was standing on the other side of the bars.

Mary Alice's father was smiling.

"Enjoy yourself now, you little piece of shit," he told John. "This is as good as it gets from here on out."

John didn't answer. What would he say?

Mr. Finney leaned closer, hands gripping the bars. "Think about what you did to her," he whispered. "Think about her when you bend over in the shower."

John didn't understand. He was sixteen years old. Even if Mr. Finney had explained it to him in minute detail, John would have probably shaken his head, said it wasn't possible.

But it was.

They kept him at the county jail for the evening, guards strolling by his cell every half hour to make sure he wasn't trying to twist his sheets into a noose. Coastal State Prison was near the Atlantic Ocean, several hundred miles away in a town John had never heard of. The prison's policy was strict about visitors. He would have to be in a full month before they would allow his mother to see him. They said it was a period of acclimation, time to let the prisoner get used to his surroundings and make sure he deserved the privilege of having a guest come to see him. The longest John had ever gone without seeing his family was a week-long church holiday he had spent in Gatlinburg, Tennessee.

They woke him at dawn to get a head start on traffic, and John shuffled onto the prison transport bus, feet shackled, arms handcuffed in front of him. His wrists were so slender that they had borrowed smaller cuffs from the women's jail. He had always been rail thin, and stress made it worse. He'd lost almost twenty pounds during the trial and his ribs were clearly visible under the baggy orange jumper he wore.

There were other men on the bus, and they whistled and hooted when John got on. He smiled because he thought it was some kind of rite of passage.

"Be strong," his mother had said, using more of her tough *Kojak* talk. "Don't let them get to you and don't trust any of them with anything."

One of the guards had slammed his baton on the cage separating the driver's area from the prisoners. He pointed to a seat directly behind the driver, telling John, "Sit."

The bus was not air-conditioned, the ride bumpy. John's chains clanked like Jacob Marley's the whole way. He played games in his head, games he and Joyce used to play when they took family vacations to Florida. How many license plates from out of town could he find? How many cows were on one side of the road? How many on the other?

His bladder was so full by the time they got to the outer limits of Savannah that his eyes were watering with pain. He knew instinctively there was no rest stop on this trip, and he kept his legs squeezed together when the bus pulled through the first gate of the prison, then the second, then the third.

He felt a sharp pain in his bladder when he stood, but he was glad he had the shackles around his ankles because it gave him an excuse to keep his legs together. The guard led the way to the first building, John in the front, the rest of the prisoners towering behind him. One of the men kept kicking at John's heels and he walked faster, his bladder screaming in his gut.

They were all led to an open bathroom with a row of urinals. Slowly, each man was uncuffed, unshackled. John, embarrassed, waited for someone else to go before he did. He could feel eyes on him as he reached down to the fly of his jumper. The uniform was for a grown man, so the crotch had settled somewhere around his knees. Nerves kept him from being able to go at first, but he finally was able to release a thin stream of urine.

"Looks like a little Vienna sausage," the man beside him said. He was staring right at John's penis. When John looked up at him, the man gave a smile that showed a row of crooked teeth. "I'm getting hungry just lookin' at it."

"Shut up," one of the guards ordered. The patch on his uniform read "Everett" and he held a baton between both of his hands like he was blocking a tackle. "Everybody take your clothes off and stand on the black line."

John's face went bright red. Because of his age, he had been kept in isolation at the county jail during his trial. The guards had still searched him plenty of times, but never like this. His entire life, he had never stood naked in front of a bunch of strangers. His hands felt numb as he worked the buttons on his jumper, and he tried not to look down at the other men, though of course he could see. They were huge—all of them. Their bodies were grown men's bodies, hair sprouting everywhere. John was a late bloomer. He shaved his face maybe once a week and then it was out of wishful thinking more than necessity. He looked like a girl next to them, like a frightened little girl.

Everett started going through the rules, listing things they could and could not do. While he was talking, another guard walked behind the prisoners with a flashlight, making each man bend over and hold themselves open for inspection. Another man put on a pair of gloves and stuck his fingers into their mouths to check for contraband or weapons. A third took out a hose and washed them all down, then sprayed powder on them to delouse their bodies.

They were each given a pair of white pants and a white T-shirt. John was given an extra-small shirt but his pants were large enough to fit an elephant. He had to hold them up around his waist as he walked, carrying his pillow and his sheets in one hand, the meager toiletries they had been given precariously balanced on the top.

He moved as if he were in a fog, staring straight ahead, trying not to be sick.

"Shelley," Everett said. His baton was resting on the outside of an open cell door. "In here."

John walked into the cell. It reeked of urine and shit from the stainless steel toilet in the corner. The sink mounted to the wall had been white at some point in its life, but rust and grime had made it dirty gray. There was a desk on the left, two bunk beds stacked on the right. You could touch the opposite walls just by standing in the middle of the cell and holding both your arms out. A guy who looked to be about twenty-five lay on the top bunk and he turned to look at John, smiling.

"You're the bottom," he said.

There were more wolf whistles, but Everett was already moving on, assigning the next cell to the next prisoner.

"Zebra," the guy said, and John guessed that was his name.

"John."

"How old are you?"

"Sixteen."

Zebra smiled. His teeth were black and white, striped like a zebra. "You like it?" he said, pointing to his teeth. "We can do yours that way, too. You want?"

John shook his head. "My mom would kill me."

Zebra laughed; a shocking sound in the concrete building. "Go on and make your bed, Johnny. You like being called Johnny?" he asked. "That what your mommy calls you?"

"Not really," John said. Not since he was a baby, anyway.

"You'll be all right in here, Johnny," he said, reaching out and ruffling John's hair so hard that John had to tilt to the side.

Zebra gave a private chuckle. "I'll take care of you, boy." And he did.

After lights-out, every night like clockwork Zebra was down on the bottom bunk, pressing John's face into the pillow, raping him so hard that the next day blood came out when he sat on the toilet. Crying did not stop him. Screaming only made him ram harder. By the end of the first week, John could barely stand.

Zebra was a predator. Everybody in the prison from the warden to the guards to the guys who came in to take off the trash knew that. He kept John to himself for that first week, then he started trading him out to the other men for cigarettes and contraband. Three weeks later, John was in the prison hospital, his asshole shredded, his eyes swollen shut from crying.

This was the first of two visits Richard Shelley made to visit his son in prison.

He was led back to the hospital by the guard named Everett, whom John hadn't seen since his first day in lockup.

"Here he is," Everett told Richard, stepping back against the wall to give the man some space. "You got ten minutes."

Richard stood at the foot of John's bed. He just stared, for a long time not saying anything.

John stared back, feeling relieved and ashamed at the same time. He wanted to reach out to his dad, to tell him he loved him and that he was sorry for all he had done and that Richard was right, John was worthless. He didn't deserve anything his dad could offer but he wanted it, he *needed* it so bad that his heart felt like it was on fire.

Richard spoke with some effort. "Are you in pain?"

John could only nod.

"Good," his father said, sounding as if some justice had been done. "Now you know how Mary Alice felt."

CHAPTER FIFTEEN

John didn't want to think about his first night in prison, but it kept coming back to him like a waking nightmare. Someone walked behind him at work and he would flinch. A loud noise from the street sent his heart into his throat. He would bend over to get the sponge out of the bucket, put some shine on the wheels of a truck or a sedan, and it would flood into his brain.

After Zebra had passed him around, John had spent a full month in the hospital wing at Coastal, learning how to shit again. When he got out, he found that he'd been transferred into the protective ward with all the serious sex offenders. Maybe they had thought Ben Carver would have a field day with John, finish the work that Zebra had started, but the older man had taken one look at the scrawny sixteen-year-old boy and said with great disappointment, "A brunette! I asked for a blonde!"

John didn't know who was responsible for transferring him into protective custody, but even if he did, John wouldn't know how to thank him. Sometimes he thought it was Everett, the guard, but then sometimes he would be lying in his bunk at night and let his mind play out this fantasy story where it was his dad who had rescued him. Richard stormed into the warden's office. Richard wrote an angry letter to his state senator. Richard demanded fair treatment for his son.

John laughed at his foolish boyhood dreams as he slid his card into the time clock, waiting for the loud chu-chunk as he signed himself out of the car wash for the day. The weather had been good for several weeks, and holiday shoppers had been out getting their cars washed. John hadn't had time to go to Ben's mother's house and pick up the car until yesterday afternoon. He had been working on his learner's permit when Mary Alice had died, but that was a long time ago and he had sweated like a whore in church at the prospect of getting behind the wheel. If he got caught in the car, Martha Lam would throw his ass back in jail. Of course, if he didn't use the car, he might end up back there anyway.

Over the telephone, Ben's elderly mother had been open and friendly, "pleased to talk to a friend of Ben's." When asked, she assured him that the insurance was paid on the car. Mrs. Carver had further explained to John that her Mr. Propson was taking her to a church social over in Warm Springs on Sunday, but could he please remember to return the car with a full tank of gas. John had agreed to everything, but she had kept him on the phone for another fifteen minutes to tell him about her sciatica. Both sets of John's grandparents had died while he was in prison, none of them ever bothering to visit. He had listened intently to her woes, making the right noises at the right times until the pedophile from across the hallway had glared at him and demanded to use the phone.

John had found the dark blue Ford Fairlane parked in the carport as promised. The key was tucked into the visor along with the title and insurance card. What mattered to John most at that moment was that it cranked on the first try. He put the car in gear and rolled into the street, his foot stuttering between the gas and the brake as he practiced up and down the one-lane road running outside Mrs. Carver's house. Praise Jesus it wasn't a manual transmission or he would have left the car where he found it. John had spent most of the afternoon figuring out how to drive the Fairlane and by the time he pulled out onto the two-lane highway his hands were hurting from clutching the wheel.

He could do it, he kept saying, teeth gritted as he drove down I-20 back toward Atlanta. All he needed to do was make sure he looked like he knew what he was doing. Not too slow, not too fast, confidence high, arm out the window. That's all the cops ever looked for: somebody who looked guilty. Their little cop radar went up and they could feel indecision coming off you like a pulse.

John had told himself that he was getting in some more practice when he got into the Fairlane around midnight last night. He couldn't fool himself for long when the car ended up parked across the street from the liquor store on Cheshire Bridge Road. He waited for thirty minutes, but Robin obviously wasn't working. Driving back home, he figured if he'd had a tail it would've been hanging between his legs.

Since gas was another luxury he couldn't afford, John left the car wash on foot, walking up Piedmont, crossing the intersection to Cheshire Bridge. He pretended he was going for a stroll at first, but then decided self-delusion was as stupid as what he had planned for later that night. Ben had finally come through. John had gotten two postcards in the mail this week—the only mail he'd ever gotten at the boardinghouse. The first one was postmarked in Alabama and listed a series of numbers: *185430032*. The second card was from Florida and read, *On our way to Piney Grove. See you when we get back!!!*

John hated puzzles, but he knew enough to go to the library and sit down with the atlas again. After a couple of hours of staring aimlessly out the window, he got it. 30032 was the zip code for Avondale Estates. 1854 Piney Grove Circle bordered Memorial Drive on the edge of Decatur.

"Hey, baby!"

The hookers were out at the liquor store, including the older woman John had rescued at the car wash. He should probably learn her name, but he knew it would only make him sad if he did. Giving her a name meant she had a family somewhere. She had been a kid at some point, gone to school, had hopes and dreams. And now . . : nothing.

One of the women asked, "You wanna date?"

He shook his head, keeping his distance. "I'm looking for Robin."

"She's at the theater," the hooker said, jerking her chin toward the road. "*Star Wars* is playing. She figures the last time any'a them guys saw a pussy was when they was being born out of one."

The girls laughed good-naturedly at the joke.

"Thanks," John said, tossing them a wave before they could offer him more of their wares.

The theater was a pretty good distance from the liquor store, but John had time. He let himself concentrate on breathing the air, even the exhaust from the cars. You couldn't do this in prison. You had to find other ways to get lung cancer.

His hamstrings were aching by the time he reached the movie theater. *Star Wars*. He had seen that when he was a kid, probably six or seven times. Every weekend his mother had driven him and his friends to the theater, dropping them off and coming back a few hours later. This was before the drugs, before John was cool. He had loved that movie, relished the escape.

In prison, Ben had been in charge of everything they did and even as he grew older, John had kept it that way because it was easy. The bad part was that all of John's cultural knowledge was that of a man over thirty years his senior. He didn't know many movies or television shows from the last two decades. No one on his wing visited the main hall on movie night because they weren't stupid enough to mix with the general population. Doris Day, Frank Sinatra, Dean Martin—these were the singers always playing on the small transistor radio Emily had brought John his first Christmas inside. Music had been so important to him as a kid, the sound track to his disaffected life. Now, he couldn't have named a current popular song if someone had put a gun to his head.

John had already convinced himself that Robin wouldn't be at the theater so he was surprised when he nearly bumped into her turning the corner.

"What are you doing here?" she asked, looking pleased, he thought, then nervous.

"The girls told me you were here," he explained. He could see a line of young men snaking around the building. "Busy night?"

"Nah." She waved it off. "Stupid fuckers want to see the movie first. I guess I'll come back later."

"How long's the movie?"

"Jesus, I don't know." She started walking back toward the liquor store and he followed her. She turned around, demanding, "What are you doing?"

"I thought I'd walk you back."

"Lookit," she said. "This ain't no *Pretty Woman.*" She added, "And you sure as shit ain't Richard Gere."

John had no idea what she was talking about. The only Richard Gere movie they'd watched in prison was *Sommersby,* and that was only because it had a kid in it.

She clarified, "We're not going to fall in love and get married and have babies, okay?"

John hadn't thought about it, but maybe that had been his plan.

He told her, "I just wanted to let you know that I'm not going to see you anymore."

"You've only seen me once, you stupid fuck."

"I know," he said. When she started to walk away again, he followed her. "Please stop," he said. "Listen to me."

She crossed her arms over her chest. "All right. Go."

"I've just . . ." God, now that she was listening, he didn't know what to say. "I've been thinking about you," he said. "Not in a sexual way." His face must have shown otherwise because she rolled her eyes. "Okay, maybe sex," he admitted.

"Unless you're here to pay me for your happy junior-jerk, I gotta get back to my drag."

"It's not like that," he said. "Please."

She started walking again and John got in front of her, walking backward because he knew she wouldn't stop.

"I'm mixed up in something," he said.

"Color me shocked."

"I was in prison."

"Am I supposed to be surprised?"

"Please," John said. He stopped walking and she did, too. "I don't want to be mixed up in this, but I am. I have to do something about it. I don't want to go back to prison."

"Somebody blackmailing you?"

He thought about it. "Maybe," he said. "I don't know."

"Go to the cops."

He knew she wasn't being serious. "I just wanted to see you again, to let you know that I couldn't see you anymore. After this, I mean." He paused, trying to make sense. "I don't want you mixed up in it, is what I'm saying. This guy, he's bad. He's really bad, and I don't want you to get hurt."

"You're scaring me here," she said, her bored tone belying the statement. "Who's trying to hurt me?"

"Nobody," John said. "He doesn't even know you exist." He rubbed his face with his hands, letting out something like a groan. "This doesn't mean anything to you," he said. "I'm sorry I bothered you with this. I just wanted to see you one last time."

"Why?"

"Because of what you told me about your first kiss. I just..." He tried a smile. "I was a real loser in school. Girls didn't really want to have anything to do with me."

"I got a news flash, junior. They still don't." Her words were sharp but her tone told him she was teasing.

He said, "I went to jail real early. I was up for twenty years."

"Am I supposed to feel sorry for you?"

He shook his head. He had stopped expecting people to feel sorry for him a long time ago. "I want to thank you for telling me that story about Stewie and all. I've been thinking about it a lot, and it's a really nice story."

She chewed her bottom lip, her eyes searching his. "All right. You told me."

"And I..." His voice trailed off. He'd rehearsed this a hundred times at work, but now nothing was coming to him.

"You what?" she prompted. "You wanna fuck me?"

"Yeah." He couldn't lie. "Yeah, I really do."

"Well, shit, you could've saved me some fucking time just saying that to begin with." She started back up the road, saying, "It's ten for the room, thirty for a half-and-half. No Greek, no hitting or I'll rip your fucking cock off."

She was about ten feet away before she realized he wasn't following her. "What the fuck is wrong with you?"

"Thank you," he repeated. Then, "Good-bye."

CHAPTER SIXTEEN

Look at me," his mother had said, leaning over the table in the visitors' room. It was her first time seeing him since he'd gotten to Coastal, and neither one of them said anything about Zebra, the hospital, the fact that John was having to sit on an inflatable cushion just to talk to her.

"You will *not* waste away in here," she told him. "You *will* do something with your life."

He sat there crying, big tears rolling down his cheeks, his chest shaking as he tried to keep in the sobs.

"You aren't a boy anymore, John. You are a strong man. You will survive this. You will get out of here eventually."

Emily still had hope for the appeals. She believed in the justice system, didn't think the founding fathers had designed this sort of treatment for a sixteen-year-old boy.

"I got you these," she said, indicating the textbooks she'd brought in with her. Math and science, his two favorite subjects back when he actually enjoyed school.

She told him, "You can still get your GED."

John stared blankly. He was wearing a diaper to catch the pus coming out of his ass and his mother was worried about him graduating from high school.

She said, "You'll need it to get into college when you get out."

Education. Emily had always insisted that education

was the only thing that truly enriched your life. As far back as he could remember, his mother had always had a book she was reading, some article she'd clipped from the paper or a magazine that she found interesting and wanted to remember.

"Are you listening to me, Jonathan?"

He couldn't even nod.

"You'll get your GED, and then you'll go to college, okay?" She took his hand in hers. His wrists were still bruised where the men had held him down. One of the guards stepped forward, but didn't break them apart.

"You will not give up in here," she told John, her grip tight, as if she could force some of her strength into him, take the pain away and carry it herself. She had always said that she would rather suffer herself than see her children hurt, and John saw for the first time that it was true. If Emily could, she would trade places with him right now. And he would let her.

"Do you understand me, Jonathan? You will not give up in here."

He hadn't spoken to anyone in four and a half weeks. The taste of his own shit and other men's come was still stuck to the back of his throat like molasses. He was scared to open his mouth, scared his mother would smell it on him and know what he had done.

"Tell me, John," she had said. "Tell me you will do this for me."

His lips were stuck together, chapped, bleeding. He kept his teeth clamped tight, stared at his hands. "Yes."

Two weeks later, she asked him if he had been studying. He lied to her, said he had. John was celled up with Ben by then, not sleeping at night because he was terrified the older man was biding his time, playing out some game as he waited for the right moment to make his move.

"Sweetheart," Ben had finally said. "You flatter yourself if you think you're my type."

In retrospect, John *was* his type: young, dark hair, slim build, straight. Ben had never crossed that line, though, and there were only two times that John had seen him truly angry. The most recent was when the planes had been crashed into the Pentagon and World Trade towers. For days after, Ben had been too livid to speak. The first time he showed his anger was years before, when he had caught John with drugs.

"You will not do this, boy," Ben had ordered, his hand gripped so tightly around John's wrist that the bones felt ready to break. "You hear me?"

John looked into his eyes, knew that the last man who had seen Ben Carver this angry had ended up floating naked and facedown in a shallow pond outside an abandoned church.

"I will turn them loose on you, son. Like a pack of jackals. Do you understand me?"

The protective custody wing had ten cells with two men each. Six of them were pedophiles. Two liked girls, four were stalkers of young boys. At night, John could hear them jerking off, whispering his name as they moaned their release.

"Yes, sir," John had answered. "I promise."

The rest of the offenders in the wing were like Ben. They preyed on adults on the outside, so John felt fairly safe around them. But sex was sex, and on the inside, you took fresh ass where you could get it. He had found out later from Ben that all of them had at separate times offered various trades for a go at the new boy. Prison etiquette dictated that as cellmates, Ben had first dibs. As time wore on and Ben didn't take his due, some of the guys got twitchy; but every last one of them, from the baby-rapers to the child-killers, was afraid of Ben. They thought he was a sick bastard.

Those first few years in lockup, John blocked off every day in his calendar with a big X, counting down until he was released. Aunt Lydia was working on his case, trying to find every angle she could exploit to get him out. Appeal after appeal was rejected. Then, Aunt Lydia came one day with Emily and they both told him that the Georgia Supreme Court had refused to hear his case. Lydia had been his champion, the only other person aside from his mother who had insisted he fight it out in court and not take the plea the state offered.

Her expression said it all. It was the end of the line. There were no other options.

The state plea had been fifteen years no parole. Lydia had told him not to take it, that she would fight for his innocence with every bone in her body. Now he was looking at twenty-two to life.

Aunt Lydia shook with sobs. John ended up being the one to comfort her, trying to soothe her with his words, absolve her from the guilt she felt for not saving him.

"It's okay," he told Lydia. "You did your best. Thank you for doing your best."

When John got back to his cell, he started reading his latest issue of *Popular Mechanics*. He didn't cry. What was the use? Show his emotions so some murdering child rapist in the next cell could get off on his pain? No. John had toughened up by then. Ben had shown him the ropes, how to make it in prison without getting knifed or beaten to death. He kept to himself, never looked anyone in the eye and seldom spoke to anyone but Ben.

What John found out in prison was that he was smart. He didn't come to the realization out of vanity. It was more like an epitaph, a sort of eulogy to the person he could have been. He understood complex formulas, mathematical equations. He liked to study. Sometimes, he could almost feel his brain growing inside of his head, and when he solved a problem, figured out a particularly difficult diagram, he felt like he'd won a marathon.

And then the depression would set in. His father had been right. His teachers were right. His pastor was right. He should have applied himself. He should have—could have—put his brain to work and *done* something with his life. Now, what did he have? Who cared if you were the smartest convicted murderer in prison?

Some nights, John would lie awake in bed thinking about his father, how disgusted Richard had been that one time he'd visited his son. John was learning other things about life while he was incarcerated. As bad as Richard was, he had never hurt John the way some of his fellow inmates had been hurt. His father may have been thoughtless, but he wasn't cruel. He had never tortured him. He had never beaten him so badly that a lung collapsed. He had never put a gun to his son's head and told him to choose between letting some old bastard suck him off so daddy could have a bag of dope or getting a bullet in his brain.

Years passed, and John saw that he had adapted. He could take prison. His days were long and drawn out before him, but he had learned the patience, had built the capacity, to do hard time. The possibility for parole came up for him his tenth year in, and then again every two years after. He was a week away from his sixth parole board hearing and a year and a half away from completing his twenty-two-year sentence when Richard visited his son for the second and last time in prison.

John had been expecting Emily in the visitors' room,

and he'd been staring at the metal detector, waiting to see her come through, when Richard had blocked his view.

"Dad?"

Richard's lip curled in distaste at the word.

John had barely recognized him. Richard's hair was a shock of white, still thick and full, a sharp contrast to his well-tanned face. As always, his body was fit. Richard saw obesity as a sign of laziness and he was a health nut long before it became a national obsession.

Emily had divorced Richard a year after John's conviction, but the two had stopped living together under the same roof the day John was arrested. Richard did not go to the trial, did not pay a dime for his son's defense, refused to testify on his behalf.

"You've finally done it," Richard said, not sitting at the table but looming over John, his disapproval and disgust raining down like a summer shower. "Your mother has end-stage breast cancer. You've finally killed her, too."

A week later, John sat in front of the parole board, looking them each in the eye in turn, telling them how he had finally come to realize that he had no one to blame for his incarceration but himself. He had hated Mary Alice Finney. He was jealous of her popularity, of her friends, her status. He had been a drug addict, but that was not an excuse. The coke had only lowered his inhibitions, his ability to judge between right and wrong. He had followed her home the night of the party. He had broken into her bedroom and brutally raped her. When he started to come down from the coke, he realized what he had done and murdered her in cold blood, mutilating her body to make it seem as if a psychotic stranger had killed her.

His record was remarkably clean. John had been a model inmate with only two infractions on his record, both over a decade old. He had attended every class the prison offered: Victim Impact, Family Violence, Corrective Thinking, Depression Group, Post Traumatic Stress Disorder, Life Issues, Communication Skills, Anger Management, Focus Group and Worry Control. He had finished his GED, completed a bachelor's degree and was in the middle of completing a postsecondary degree when an amendment to the 1994 Crime Bill banned federal education grants to prisoners. John volunteered at the prison hospital where he taught CPR and basic hygiene to the other inmates. He had attended on-the-job training sessions in horticulture and food preparation. A letter penned by John and attached to his file stated that his mother was sick, and he just wanted to go home and be there for her the way she had been there for him all these years.

The official notice granting him parole came on July 22, 2005.

Emily had died two days earlier.

CHAPTER SEVENTEEN

Cousin Woody. The cool one, the popular one. He had a weight machine in the garage and he spent most of his days working out and smoking dope. His chest was ripped, six-pack abs separated by a trail of hair leading down to his privates. Girls climbed all over him like kudzu up a pine. He drove a silver Mustang hatchback, brand-new. He got the kids at the local school to sell some of his stash for him so he always had money burning a hole in his pocket. His widowed mother was on the fast track at her law firm, always working late nights, always leaving her son alone. Mr. "Come Upstairs," Mr. "You Wanna Toke?" Mr. "Just Snort It Up Your Nose."

Cool Cousin Woody.

John had been following Woody for almost two months now, parking the Fairlane at the Inman Park MARTA station because gas was too expensive to use the car for anything but business. That's how John thought about it: business. He was the CEO of Keep John Out of Prison. The fucking chief financial officer, the vice president, the secretary, all rolled up into one.

From the beginning, Woody had made it easy for John to keep tabs on him. He had always been a creature of habit, and his adult life had proven no different. John could set his watch by the guy. He went to work every day, came straight home after, kissed the wife if she was home, tucked in the kid, then planted himself in front of the television for the rest of the evening. He did this every evening the first week, and John was beginning to think he was wasting his time when Sunday rolled around. The kid wasn't there—the wife hadn't brought him back from church and John assumed he had been left with a family member. The wife left around six, dressed for work, leaving her husband all alone in the house.

Woody waited about thirty minutes after she was gone, then he got into his car and drove away. Weeks passed with him doing this, then a month, then another. Every Sunday night, Woody was in that car like clockwork.

With time, John had gotten good at keeping his distance, making sure Woody couldn't see the Fairlane trolling along behind his car. Not that Woody seemed to be looking anywhere except toward the row of women who lined the streets of downtown Atlanta. He'd stop, wave one over, then drive her into an alley or park on an empty street. John would see the woman's head go down for a few minutes, then it'd bob back up for good and she'd get out and Woody would move on down the road, have himself back in front of the TV an hour later.

Then one night, he'd changed the pattern. He took a left out of his street instead of a right, heading east up Highway 78. John had been forced to hang back farther than usual because there weren't many cars on the road. He'd jerked the steering wheel hard at the last moment to take an exit, following Woody up a winding road for about twenty minutes, passing a sign that read, *Welcome to Snellville . . . Where Everybody's Somebody!*

John had parked the car on a residential street, going on foot because that's what Woody was doing. It was cold out, the first week of December, but John was sweating bad because he was smack in the middle of a neighborhood, sleeping kids packed into every house around him. He got so caught up in his fear that he lost sight of his target. He scanned the empty streets, walking down dead-ends, getting so turned around that he couldn't even find the Fairlane.

John was worrying about his own safety now. He hid in the shadows, tensed at every noise, certain some cop would pull up, run his record and wonder what brought a pedophile to this neck of the woods.

Suddenly, in the distance, he saw a man walking with a little girl beside him. Both of them got into Woody's car and drove off. John found the Fairlane five minutes later, cursing himself the whole way back to Atlanta. The next two weeks, he scanned the papers, looking for news of something bad happening in Snellville—an abducted child, a murder. There was nothing, but he knew it was just a matter of time.

The truth was simple: Woody was using John's identity for a reason. He was trying to cover his tracks. John had spent enough time surrounded by criminals to know when he was seeing one in action. It was just a matter of time before whatever Woody was up to landed squarely back on John's shoulders.

John decided then and there that he would kill himself, or find someone else to do it for him, before he would go back into prison. He had already lost twenty years of his life rotting away among pedophiles and monsters. He would not go back to that. He would not put Joyce through that pain and humiliation again. He had been strong on the inside, his will hardened steel, but the outside had made him soft and he knew that he could not take the loss of what little life he had carved for himself. He would put a bullet in his own brain before he did that.

John saw his sister around this time. Just before Christmas, Joyce had called him at the boardinghouse and he had been so surprised to hear her voice that he thought maybe someone was playing a joke on him. Only, who would play a joke? He didn't know anybody, didn't have any friends on the outside.

They met for coffee at a fancy café off of Monroe Drive. John had worn a new shirt and his only good pants, the chinos Joyce had sent to him so he would have something to wear when he left Coastal. The custom was to just give the inmate back the clothes he'd come in with, but John was several sizes larger than that scrawny kid who'd ridden the prison transport down to Savannah.

The night before, he had taken off work early so he could go to the gift shop down the street. John had spent an hour picking out a Christmas card for Joyce, going back and forth between the cheap ones and the nice ones. The weather had made business at the Gorilla sporadic. Art was laying off guys left and right. John had saved as much money as he could during the flush times, but he had finally had to get a winter coat. Even though he told himself he was never going to wear used clothes again, John had no choice but to go to the Goodwill Store. The only coat he could find that halfway fit him was torn at the collar and had a funky smell to it that he couldn't wash out at the Laundromat. It was warm, though, and that was all that mattered.

Joyce was five minutes late to the café, and John was sweating it out over the fact that he'd had to pay three dollars for a cup of coffee just to be able to sit at one of the tables when she rushed in. She looked harried, her sunglasses pushed onto the top of her head, her long brown hair down around her shoulders.

"Sorry I'm late," she said, pulling out a chair and sitting

across from him. She left about six inches between her and
the table, even more space between her and John.

"You want some coffee?" He started to stand to get it
for her but she stopped him with a terse shake of her head.

"I've got to meet some friends in ten minutes." She
hadn't even taken off her coat. "I don't know why I called
you."

"I'm glad you did."

She looked out the windows. There was a movie theater
across the way and she was watching the people who were
standing in line.

John pulled the Christmas card out of his pocket, glad
he had gone for the more expensive one. Three sixty-eight,
but it had glitter on the outside and the inside was folded so
that when you opened it, a snowflake popped up. Joyce had
loved pop-up books when they were little. He could remember her giggling over one that had farm animals jumping off the pages.

He held out the card. "I got you this."

She didn't take it, so he set it on the table, slid it toward
her. He had spent most of last night testing out his
thoughts on notebook paper, not wanting to give her a card
with words scratched out, or worse, to write something stupid that would ruin the card and make him have to buy a
new one. In the end, he had simply signed it, "love, John,"
knowing there was nothing else he could say.

He asked, "What have you been up to?"

She focused back on him as if she had forgotten he was
there. "Work."

"Yeah." He nodded. "Me, too." He tried to make a joke
of it. "Not like what you do, but somebody has to clean
those cars."

She obviously didn't think he was funny.

He stared at his cup, rolling it in his hands. Joyce was

the one who had called him, inviting him to this place where he couldn't even afford a sandwich off the menu, yet he felt like the bad guy.

Maybe he *was* the bad guy.

He asked her, "Do you remember Woody?"

"Who?"

"Cousin Woody, Lydia's son."

She shrugged, but said, "Yeah."

"Do you know what he's up to?"

"Last I heard, he joined the army or something." Her eyes flashed. "You're not going to try to get in touch with him again?"

"No."

She leaned forward, urgent. "You shouldn't, John. He was bad news then and I'm sure he hasn't changed now."

"I won't," he said.

"You'll end up back in jail."

Would she care? he wondered. Would it be better for her if he was back at Coastal instead of living right under her nose? Joyce was the only living person in the entire world who remembered John the way he used to be. She was like a precious box where all his childhood memories were stored, only she had thrown away the key the minute the police had dragged him out the front door.

Joyce sat back in her chair. She looked at her watch. "I really should go."

"Yeah," he said. "Your friends are waiting."

She met his eyes for the first time since she'd walked in. She saw he knew she was lying.

Her tongue darted out and she licked her lips. "I went to see Mom last weekend."

John blinked back sudden tears. In his mind, he saw the cemetery, pictured Joyce standing at his mother's grave. The buses didn't go out there and a cab would cost sixty dollars.

John didn't even know what his mother's headstone looked like, what inscription Joyce had decided on.

"That's why I called you," she told John. "She would've wanted me to see you." She shrugged. "Christmas."

He bit his lip, knowing if he opened his mouth he would start crying.

"She always believed in you," Joyce said. "She never once thought you were guilty."

His chest ached from the effort of reining in his emotions.

"You ruined everything," Joyce told him, almost incredulous. "You ruined our lives, but she wouldn't give up on you."

People were looking, but John didn't care. He had apologized to her for years—in letters, in person. Sorry didn't mean anything to Joyce.

"I can't blame you for hating me," he told her, wiping a tear with the back of his hand. "You have every right."

"I wish I could hate you," she whispered. "I wish it was that easy."

"I would hate you if you had done..."

"Done what?" She was leaning over the table again, an edge of desperation in her voice. "Done what, John? I read what you said to the parole board. I know what you told them. Tell *me*." She slapped her hand on the table. "Tell *me* what happened."

He pulled a napkin from the container on the table and blew his nose.

She wouldn't let up. "Every time you were up in front of the board, every time you spoke to them, you told them you weren't guilty, that you wouldn't say that you had done it just so you could get out."

He took another napkin so he'd have something to do with his hands.

"What changed, John? Was it Mom? You didn't want to disappoint her? Is that what it is, John? Now that Mom's gone, you could finally tell the truth?"

"She wasn't gone when I said it."

"She was wasting away," Joyce hissed. "She was in that hospital bed wasting away and all she could think about was you. 'Look after Johnny,' she kept saying. 'Don't let him be alone in there. We're all he has.' "

John heard himself sob, a bark like a seal that echoed in the restaurant.

"Tell me, John. Just tell me the truth." Her voice was quiet. Like their father, she didn't like to show her feelings. The more upset she got, the lower her tone tended to be.

"Joyce—"

She put her hand on his. She had never touched him before, and he could feel her desperation flowing through her fingertips and needling under his skin. "I don't care anymore," she said, more like a plea. "I don't care if you did it, Johnny. I really don't. I just want to know for myself, for my own sanity. Please—tell me the truth."

Her hands were beautiful, so delicate, with such long fingers. Just like Emily's.

"John, please."

"I love you, Joyce." He reached into his back pocket and took out a folded piece of paper. "Something is going to happen," he said. "Something bad that I don't think I can stop."

She took her hand away, moved back in her chair. "What are you talking about, John? What have you gotten mixed up in?"

"Take this," he said, putting the credit report on top of the Christmas card. "Just take this and know that whatever happens, I love you."

John hadn't brought the Fairlane with him, but he

didn't want Joyce to see him waiting at the bus stop outside the entrance to the mall so he jogged up the street toward Virginia-Highland, catching MARTA there. He didn't want to go home, couldn't face his roach-infested hovel or his fellow rapists in the hallway, so he went to the Inman Park station and picked up the Fairlane.

He didn't normally follow Woody until the evenings on the weekend. John's first two weeks of reconnaissance had proven the guy pretty much stayed inside unless his wife made him take out the trash. John had been thinking, though, that maybe Woody was more clever than he seemed. Maybe he had another car somewhere. It wasn't much of a stretch, considering the post office box and the credit cards. Maybe John Shelley had purchased a car during the last six years.

This close to Christmas, Woody's neighborhood was decked out with colorful lights and decorations. Luminaries made of old milk jugs lined the street. Just the week before, John had watched an old lady walking her dog go around and light each one.

It was a nice neighborhood.

John tucked his car between an SUV and a station wagon parked in the church lot, glancing at the times on the sign outside to check when the services were over. Woody's wife always took the kid to church on Sundays, then spent most of the time with a woman who was probably her mother.

From the church, John walked down a side street that ran parallel to Woody's house, whistling as if he was just a guy taking a walk. He plotted the distance in his head, cutting across a field until he could see what had to be the back of Woody's house. There weren't many trees for cover and John felt exposed. Anybody could come out their back door and see him. He was about to turn around when that very thing happened. A woman came out, standing in the open doorway. John froze because he was right in her line of sight, but she wasn't looking at him. She was turned toward Woody's house next door, her hand held up in a salute as she shielded her eyes from the sun.

John dropped flat to his stomach. The girl's backyard was overgrown with weeds, but anybody who was looking could have seen him lying there. Thankfully, her eyes were following something more interesting. John saw Woody walk across his yard, hopping over a chain-link fence that had been taken down by a tree. He went right to the girl, not even tossing a look in John's direction, picked her up and started kissing her.

John watched as she wrapped her skinny legs around him, their lips locked together as Woody carried her into the house and slammed the door closed.

CHAPTER EIGHTEEN

John waited all night for Mary Alice to show at the party, smoking enough pot to make his lungs ache in his chest. Woody kept catching his eye, giving him the thumbs-up like he was cheering him on. John could have kicked himself for telling his cousin that he'd invited a girl to the party. It was bad enough Mary Alice wasn't here, but looking like an idiot in front of Woody made it a million times worse.

John had already given up hope when around midnight, she walked through the front door. The first thing he noticed was how out of place she looked in her freshly ironed Jordache jeans and high-collared white shirt. She looked beautiful, but everybody else was dressed in varying degrees of black: filthy jeans, stained heavy metal T-shirts, greasy hair.

She was about to turn right around and leave when he grabbed her arm.

"Hey!" She sounded surprised and giddy and wary all rolled into one.

"You look nice," he told her, raising his voice over Poison blaring from the stereo.

"I should go," she said, but she didn't make to leave.

"Come have something to drink."

He could see her thinking it out, wondering what he meant by drink, wondering if she should trust him.

"Woody has soft drinks in the kitchen," he said, thinking he'd never used the words "soft drink" in his life. "Let's go."

She still hesitated, but when John stepped aside so he could walk behind her to the kitchen, blocking her exit, she finally relented.

He saw Woody as they passed the stairs. His cousin was leaning against the banister, his pupils blown, a lazy smile on his face. One of the girls from the only black family in the neighborhood was stuck to him like Velcro, her arms wrapped around his neck, leg snaked around his. They kissed long and deep while John watched. She was gorgeous, with creamy dark skin and exotically braided hair. Leave it to Woody to score with the best-looking girl at the party.

He gave John the thumbs-up again, but this time he wasn't smiling.

The kitchen was filled with smoke and Mary Alice coughed, waving her hand in front of her face. In the corner, a couple was making out, and John found himself stopping to stare because the guy had his hand right down the front of the girl's jeans.

"Cool party," another guy said, bumping into John. His drink spilled over John's hand, and he apologized, passing John the half-full plastic cup as a peace offering. John had already had more than enough alcohol that night, but he took a large gulp from the cup, the liquid burning his throat as it went down.

When John looked around for Mary Alice, she was already heading out the back door.

"Hey," John said, chasing after her.

She stood by a tall oak, looking up at the stars. Her hair was messed up and she looked nervous. Maybe he could hold her hand. Maybe he could kiss her.

She laughed for no reason. "I couldn't breathe in there."

"Sorry."

She saw the cup in his hand. "Give me that."

"I don't know what's in it," he said. "You'd better not."

"You're not my father," she said, taking the drink from him. She kept her eyes on his as she took a healthy swallow of the dark liquid. "Tastes like Coke and something else."

He hoped to God it wasn't something else. Woody was nineteen years old and all of his buddies were a couple of years older than that. Some of them were into hard drugs, stuff John didn't even want to know about. There was no telling what was floating around.

John said, "Sorry about this. I didn't think it would be that wild here."

She took another swig from the cup and gave him a sloppy smile. God, she was so pretty. He had been hating her so long that he'd forgotten she was gorgeous.

She lifted the cup again and he stopped her. "You're going to get sick." He was actually thinking that even if she puked, he would still kiss her.

"Are you stoned?"

"No," he lied. He was so nervous he would have smoked a goat's ass if he thought it'd help calm him down.

She took another swallow and he didn't try to stop her. "I want to get stoned."

He would have been less shocked if she'd said she wanted to fly to the moon. "Mary Alice, come on. Take it easy on that stuff. You don't want to make yourself sick."

"It's good enough for you," she said, draining the cup. She turned it upside down to show him it was empty. "I want another one."

"Let's just stay out here for a while."

"Why?" she asked. She was swaying a little and he reached out to steady her. "I thought you hated me."

He could smell her perfume and the hairspray in her hair. Her skin felt hot under his hand. He could hold her, just pull her into his arms and hold her all night. "I don't hate you."

"You say nasty things to me all the time."

"I don't," he said with such conviction that he almost believed himself.

She pulled away from him. "My parents think I'm at home."

"Mine, too."

"Did you get suspended from school?"

"No."

"They should suspend you," she said. "My dad says you're a total loser."

"Yeah," he said, wishing she hadn't finished the drink. "My dad, too."

She said, "He moved out of the house tonight."

"Your dad?"

"He just packed his bags and left while I was at the mall. My mom said he was moving in with that woman from work." She hiccupped softly. "She wouldn't stop crying."

Mary Alice was crying, too, but he was still at a loss as to how to comfort her. Finally, he said, "I'm sorry."

"I called him at the number he left," she told John. "Some girl answered."

John's tongue wouldn't move in his mouth. What should he say?

"He said he'd see me on the weekends. He says Mindy will take me shopping."

John repeated, "I'm sorry."

"Why do you hang around with that jerk?" Mary Alice asked.

"Who?" John turned around, following her gaze to Woody. His cousin practically fell off the back stairs as he walked toward them. He laughed at his lack of coordination, so John laughed, too.

"Wet your whistle," Woody said, handing John another drink.

John took a sip, trying to pace himself because his head was already swimming.

"Hey, girlie," Woody said, leaning against John as he stared at Mary Alice. "What took you so long? I was beginning to think my cousin here made you up."

John started to make introductions, but something stopped him. He didn't like the way Woody was looking at her, the open lust in his eyes. The guy already had Alicia back in the house ready to do whatever he wanted and now he was going after Mary Alice. It wasn't fair.

"We were just going," John said, taking Mary Alice's hand as if she belonged to him.

"So soon?" Woody asked, and John realized he was blocking their way. "Come on back inside with your old cousin Wood. I got something for you."

"I don't think so." John threw the empty cup into the yard. "I should take her home. Her mom will be looking for her."

"Just a little hit," Woody insisted. "Or another, I guess I should say." He winked at Mary Alice. "Think you can handle a drink, sweetheart? Might help dry those pretty blue eyes of yours."

Mary Alice looked odd. She was smiling, almost flirting. "I wasn't crying."

"Sure, babydoll."

"Woody," John began, but Woody put his hand over John's mouth to stop him, telling Mary Alice, "This one likes to talk too much."

She laughed, and John felt his anger spark up. She was laughing with Woody. She was laughing at *him*.

Woody asked, "You think you can handle a little drink, little girl?"

Her lips went into this sexy kind of half-smile. "I can handle it."

"Mary Alice," John said.

Woody had taken away his hand and wrapped his arm around Mary Alice's shoulders. He licked his lips as he looked down her shirt, telling John, "Shut up, Cousin."

Mary Alice laughed. "Yeah, John, shut up."

Woody pulled her closer in and she tilted up her head. He kept his eyes locked on John's as he pressed his open mouth to Mary Alice's.

She started to kiss him back and John felt like somebody had ripped his heart out of his chest. He stood helpless as Woody's hand went down Mary Alice's blouse, cupped her breast like groping her was something he did every day. His mouth got wider against Mary Alice's and she jerked away, coming to her senses a second later than she should have.

She yelled, "Stop it!" as she tumbled toward John.

John caught her, holding her up. The button had ripped off her shirt where Woody's hand had reached inside.

"You're disgusting," she told Woody, clasping the blouse closed, tears springing into her eyes.

Woody was smiling. "Come on, baby. Don't be like that."

"I can't believe you," she cried. "Your tongue is disgusting."

His smile became more sinister. "Watch it now."

She curled in closer to John, crying, "Please, take me home."

John started to lead her away, his eyes on Woody, not liking the way his cousin was staring at them.

"Get back here," Woody ordered, reaching out for her again.

"Leave her alone!" John yelled, fists clenched. Woody had about a hundred pounds on him but John firmly believed he could and would kick his ass if he so much as touched another hair on Mary Alice's head.

"Whoa." Woody held up his hands, taking a step back. "Didn't know you'd already claimed her, little man. Go on. Take her home to her mommy."

"Stay away from her," John warned. "I mean it."

"No hard feelings," Woody said, but he was still leering at Mary Alice like a lion who had been denied its prey. "Best man wins."

"Damn straight."

"Here," Woody said, digging into his front pocket. "Parting gift." He tossed a bag of powder to John. "No hard feelings, right, Cousin?"

CHAPTER NINETEEN

FEBRUARY 6, 2006

John had found out about the news story by accident. He had been vacuuming out the cargo space of a mud-splattered Subaru Forrester. He picked up a stack of newspapers to throw in the trash and the whole pile fell from his hand like playing cards scattered on a table. He bent down to gather up the pages and saw two words he had never noticed before: Local Edition.

The Subaru's owner was from Clayton County, but John knew if there was a special insert for one town, there had to be one for the others.

He had told Art he was having stomach problems so he could leave work early and headed straight downtown to the main branch of the Fulton County Public Library. The newspaper's online archive required a credit card for access, so instead he requested microfiche of the Gwinnett County local editions going back the last three months. Two hours later, he'd found what he was looking for. The story was dated December 4, 2005.

SNELLVILLE GIRL ABDUCTED
FROM LOCAL NEIGHBORHOOD.

There weren't any details. No name was mentioned, just the age—fourteen—and that she had been walking from her home to visit an aunt down the street. Obviously, the family wasn't talking to the press and there was no mention of suspects or leads the police were following. John scanned the next few weeks and found only one more story. This one added the detail that the girl had been found hiding in a ditch the next day.

John's heart had been in his throat from the moment he'd found the article. Slowly, he put the pieces of the puzzle together. Ben's game of what-if kept coming back to mind. What if Woody had been using John's identity to cover his tracks for the last six years? What if Woody had assumed John would never get out of prison? What if Woody found out John was walking among the free and had decided to do something about it?

The car behind beeped its horn and John sped up, taking the first side street he came to and pulling up behind a parked cable truck. His heart was pounding so hard that he felt dizzy. Vomit swirled in the back of his throat, threatening to come up in a hot rush of panic and fear.

He put his head on the steering wheel, playing out the night before. Sunday. Super Bowl Sunday. The fucking Falcons were playing that night and John didn't want to watch it on TV, didn't want to hear the game on the radio. He wanted to see what Woody was doing, wanted to watch him like he could stop what had happened from happening again. And again.

The wife had gone to work and Woody had waited thirty minutes before heading out. He had taken his usual route into Atlanta, but this time he'd turned into Grady Homes. John had followed him, so tense he'd forgotten to keep back, a couple of times thinking for sure Woody had seen him, that he'd been caught.

A white guy driving a dark blue Ford Fairlane through the projects on a late Sunday afternoon was too conspicuous, but John had followed him in anyway. When Woody had stopped in front of a row of hookers, John had driven past him, thinking he'd be better served keeping an eye on his cousin in the rearview mirror. Nothing ever worked out as planned, though, and when Woody drove with the hooker to the back of the complex, John got out of his car and followed on foot.

Now, John broke into a cold sweat when he thought about what had happened next, what he had seen. He could still hear it, those piercing screams, the primal fight for life.

John got out of the car, nodding to the guy in the cable truck. Casual. Cool. He belonged here.

He tucked his hands into his pockets as he walked down Woody's tree-lined street, trying to convey the image that he was just a normal guy going for a stroll, even though having his hands in his pockets made him uncomfortable; they didn't allow pockets in prison.

The woman John guessed was the grandmother took the kid to school Monday mornings. She did some shopping after, sometimes had coffee with her friends. She stayed out of the house for at least an hour and that was all John needed.

He took the same route behind the houses, head up, whistling like he didn't have a care in the world. He trudged through the backyards, keeping a careful eye on the houses, figuring that in a working-class neighborhood like this most people were either at work or too busy to look out their back windows.

The chain-link fence was still broken. John hopped over it, heading straight for the back door as he slipped on a pair of latex gloves he had stolen from the guys in the detail shop. Woody didn't have a dog, but there was a dog door cut into the bottom panel of the back door. John was too big to fit through, but he reached his arm in, feeling blindly for the lock. His fingers grazed the knob and he twisted the catch.

He stood back up, looking around to make sure he wasn't being watched, then opened the door. John tensed as he waited for an alarm to go off. He wasn't an experienced burglar, but he assumed Woody was too arrogant to spend money on an alarm system.

He was a cop, for Chrissakes.

John bypassed the kitchen and went straight to the family room. He went to the desk in the corner, ignoring the big-screen TV, the digital equipment lying around the house that screamed out that Woody made a good living, that he could afford to buy an expensive pair of shoes or a nice meal whenever he wanted. Hell, he could afford a lot of things, couldn't he? Two identities, to begin with. What else was he up to?

Woody was too smart to leave anything incriminating in the obvious places. His checkbook with the joint account he shared with his wife was right out in the open, their bills stacked neatly in an in-tray. They owed a lot, but they made what to John seemed like a fortune. Thousands of dollars a month in and out, a brand-new car for the wife, expensive school for the kid. It was almost too much to grasp.

In the garage, there was every tool you could imagine, though from what John had observed, Woody spent most of his time holding down the couch. There was a kid who came sometimes to mow the yard, so why Woody needed an enormous riding lawn mower with a freaking cup holder was a mystery. What angered John the most was the pool table in the middle of the garage. The thought of Woody out here with his kid, maybe some neighbors or the guys from work, drinking beers and playing pool, made John more livid than anything else he had found.

John went through the drawers of the workbench, careful not to move anything out of place. He found a stack of porn mags under the tray in the toolbox, all the headlines promising "barely legal action" and "cum shots galore." He flipped through the pages one by one, looking for clues, trying not to stare at the young girls—children, some of them—spread out for the world to see. Maybe something inside of John had been turned off in prison, but all he could think about when he saw their soulless gazes was Joyce, and how insecure and vulnerable she had been at that age. He put the magazines back under the tray, wishing he hadn't seen them.

Woody's bedroom was next, a huge master suite with a king-sized bed where the fucker probably made love to his wife every night. The bathroom was enormous, bigger than John's room back at the hovel. Even the kid's room was large, a race car for a bed, toys spilling out of the chest under the window. John felt odd being in the kid's room. The little bed would be changed for a big one soon. The kid would start growing up, wanting his privacy more. He'd go to school, meet a girl, take her to the prom. It was just too depressing to be in there, so John backed into the hall again.

He returned to the master bedroom, certain he had missed something. He tried to think like his parole officer, Ms. Lam, looking for contraband. He checked under the mattress, felt the pillows for hard lumps. He went through the shoes in the closet and the shirts in the drawer.

Shirts. All designer labels. Soft cottons, some silk. Woody's underwear was Calvin Klein, his pajamas Nautica.

"Christ," John whispered, so caught up in hating Woody that he couldn't breathe. "Think," he said, like that would make it happen. "Think."

Two bottles of men's cologne were on the dresser. John wasn't interested in the brands, but what had been placed in front of them. A large folding knife. Woody had carried this same knife when they were teenagers. He said it was because he dealt with some badass motherfuckers in his drug dealings, and John had believed him, imagining tense stand-offs and risky drug deals as his cousin brandished the sharp, serrated blade.

Woody carried a knife. How had he forgotten that?

"Who are you?"

John spun around, shocked to see the next-door neighbor standing in the doorway to the bedroom. She was wearing a silky white nightgown with a robe. The outfit hung from her child's body like a wet sack on a pitchfork. Her voice was a little girl's, high-pitched, almost squeaky.

"What are you doing here?" she demanded, but he could tell she was scared.

"I might ask you the same thing," he said, palming the knife, trying to call up the authoritative tone adults used when they spoke to kids.

"This isn't your house."

"It's not yours, either," John pointed out. "You live next door."

"How do you know that?"

"Woody told me."

She glanced down at his hands, the latex gloves, the knife. "Who's Woody?"

The question tripped him up, and she must have sensed his hesitation, because she bolted down the hall.

"Hey!" John called, chasing after her through the living room, the kitchen. "Hold up," he yelled, but she had already flown through the open door and into the yard.

She chanced a look over her shoulder as she made for the fence. He remembered that he still had Woody's knife in his hand, realized how that must look to her, and stopped. She hesitated again, but her body was still moving. Moving forward.

He watched her fall in slow motion, her bare foot catching on the broken fence, her head slamming into the ground. John waited. She didn't get up. He waited some more. She still did not move.

Slowly, he stepped into the backyard, the grass soft under his feet. He remembered how it had felt when he got out of Coastal to walk on grass for the first time in twenty years. His feet were used to solid concrete or red Georgia clay packed hard as brick from thousands of men pacing it every day. The grass in the cemetery had felt so soft, like he was stepping on clouds as he followed his mother's coffin toward her grave.

Twenty years and he had forgotten what grass felt like. Twenty years of loneliness, of isolation. Twenty years of Emily suffering the bimonthly degradation of visiting her son. Twenty years of Joyce being eaten up inside by the knowledge of what kind of monster her brother was.

Twenty years of Woody living on the outside, getting a good job, marrying, having a kid, making a life.

John stepped carefully over the fence. He realized he still had Woody's folding knife in his hand, and he put it on the ground beside him as he knelt by the girl. He had learned how to check a pulse at the prison hospital. She didn't have one. Even without that evidence, he could see from the way her skull was broken that she had probably died the minute her head had slammed against a large rock on the other side of the fence. Her blood was smeared across the quartz, pieces of long blonde hair sticking into the wet.

He sat back on his heels, his mind going over the last time he had seen Mary Alice. Her eyes. He would never forget her eyes, the way she had stared into nowhere. Her body told the real story, though. She had endured horrible things, unspeakable things. In his mind, he could still recall the blown-up pictures from his trial, the photographs showing Mary Alice Finney's violated body splayed out for the world to see. He remembered his aunt pacing back and forth in front of the jury, and how he'd thought at the time that Lydia's pacing was bad because all it did was draw their attention to the pictures that were right behind her.

"It's okay," John had told Lydia when she'd come to Coastal and explained that their appeals were exhausted, that he would more than likely die in prison. "I know you did everything you could."

Lydia had told him not to talk about drugs with the police, not to mention Woody because bringing her son into it would open up John's past drug abuse and they didn't want that, did they? If Woody was put on the stand, he'd tell the truth.

They didn't want Woody telling the truth, did they?

That night at the party, Woody had said, "No hard feelings," tossing him the baggie. Was that when he had decided to hurt Mary Alice?

No hard feelings. John didn't have any feelings left—just rage that burned like he'd swallowed gasoline and lit a match.

He looked down at the girl. She was a child, but she was also a messenger.

John's stomach clenched as he slid his gloved fingers into her mouth, pinched her tongue between his thumb and forefinger.

Woody had brought all of this to John's door. John would put it right back on his. The most important thing he learned in prison was that you never touched another man's property unless you were willing to die for it.

"Woody," he had called him, but that was a boy's name and Woody wasn't a boy anymore. Like John, he was a man. He should be called by a man's name.

Michael Ormewood.

John picked up the knife.

CHAPTER TWENTY

You need to walk it off," John told Mary Alice. "You can't go home like this."

"Have you ever kissed a girl?"

He blushed and she laughed.

"Mark Reed," she told him. "He thinks he's my boyfriend because he kissed me after the game."

John kept quiet, saying a silent prayer of death for Mark Reed, quarterback of the football team, driver of a red Corvette, and proud owner of much body hair, which the fucker liked to show off around the locker room like he was working at freaking Chippendale's.

"You didn't answer me," Mary Alice said, and John thought about Woody's bag of white powder in his pocket.

She could read his mind. "Let me try it."

"No way."

"I want to."

"No you don't."

"Come on." She reached into his pocket and her hand brushed against him. John sucked in air so hard he was surprised his lungs didn't explode.

Mary Alice was holding the bag up to the streetlight. "What's so good about it?"

John couldn't answer. He had more pressing matters requiring his attention.

She opened the bag.

He came to his senses. "Don't do that."

"Why not? You do."

"I'm a loser," he said. "Isn't that what you told me?"

There was a noise behind them and they both turned to look.

"Cat," Mary Alice guessed. "Come on."

She had taken his hand and John let her lead him down the street toward her house. John stayed quiet as she took him through her backyard. He knew her bedroom was on the bottom floor, but he hadn't been expecting her to open the window and climb in.

"What are you doing?"

"Shh."

A twig snapped behind him. He turned again, but all he could see was shadows.

Mary Alice said, "Come on."

He climbed up, stopping halfway over the sill, whispering, "Your mom will kill me if she finds me in here."

"I don't care," she whispered back, turning on a Hello Kitty lamp that cast a thin halo of light.

"You sleep with a night-light?"

She playfully slapped his shoulder. "Just get in."

John landed softly. Her bed was pushed up underneath the window. They were both sitting on her bed. Mary Alice's bed. John felt his erection return with a vengeance.

If Mary Alice noticed, she didn't say. "Show me how to do it," she asked, handing him the bag of coke.

"I'm not going to."

"I know you want to."

He did. God, he did. Anything that would give him the ability to get past his own idiotic personality and kiss her.

"Show me," she repeated.

He unknotted the bag and used his finger to scoop some out.

"You snort it," he said. "Like this."

John coughed, almost a gag, as the powder hit the back of his throat. It tasted bitter, metallic. He tried to get enough spit to swallow but his mouth was too dry. His heart did something funny, like a flop, then he felt as if a knife had slammed into it.

Mary Alice looked scared. "Are you—"

The coke hit his brain. Two seconds, tops, and he was so fucked up he couldn't keep his eyes open. He saw stars— actual stars—and he fell forward, right into Mary Alice. She put her hands on his face to steady him and he tilted his chin up, his lips meeting hers.

The next thing he remembered was waking up with the worst headache he'd ever had in his life. There were shooting pains in his chest and he felt cold, though sweat covered his body. He rolled over, his skin sticking to the sheets. He was thinking that his mother was going to kill him for wetting the bed when he felt her body beside him.

Mary Alice was completely naked. Her neck was twisted to the side, her mouth open and filled with blood. He saw bruises on her legs and other parts of her. Patches of her pubic hair had been ripped out. Bite marks were all over her small breasts.

John was too freaked out to make any noise. He was panting, his bladder pressing for release as he pushed himself back away from her body. The open window was behind him. He reached up, his fingers sliding against the frame. Blood. He had blood all over his hand. He had lain in it all night, his clothes soaking it up like a sponge.

He heard a noise, a "huh-huh-huh," but it was coming from him. Her face. He couldn't stop looking at her face. So much blood. His bladder released, a warm, wet liquid flooding down his leg.

He had to get out of here. He had to leave.

John pressed himself against the wall, using his legs to push himself up over the window ledge. He fell through the open window and into the backyard flat on his back, the air puffing out of his lungs in a sharp cough.

He looked up at the sky. It wasn't yet morning, the sun making the trees gray shadows against black. His legs shook, but he managed to stand, his pants sticking to his thighs, his bloody shirt like a second skin on his back where he had lain beside Mary Alice all night.

John ran, his heart pulsing in his throat.

He had to get out of there.

He had to get home.

DECATUR CITY OBSERVER
· JUNE 18, 1995

THE FINNEY MURDER: TEN YEARS LATER

Ten years have passed since fifteen-year-old Mary Alice Finney was found raped and murdered in her parents' Decatur home, though the crime that rocked the small Atlanta suburb is still fresh in the minds of longtime residents. "It changed everything," claims Elizabeth Reed, whose son was dating Finney at the time of her death. "We went from being an open community to locking our doors at night."

Police were at first baffled by the murder of the young girl, a cheerleader and class president at Decatur High School. "She was just a normal girl living a normal life," says Reed. That all changed on June 16, 1985, as neighbors woke to a woman's screams. Sally Finney had gone to wake her daughter for church and instead found carnage.

"It was a difficult scene to process," retired police chief Harold Waller admits. "There was blood everywhere. We had never seen anything like it. We thought we were looking at the work of a psychopath... and of course, we were."

Court psychiatrists agreed with Waller's appraisal of the cold-blooded killer, saying that the boy's drug-fueled rage revealed an underlying psychosis. Although the killer claimed only "recreational" drug use, friends revealed a much darker side. Coach Vic McCollough, testifying about Shelley's violent temper on the football field, said that he finally had to suspend the boy from the team. A close friend who asked not to be named said at the time that Shelley had developed a fixation on Mary Alice Finney and seemed to "burn with hatred" for the honor student.

In addition to being brutally raped, the body had several deep bite wounds about the breasts and thighs. The teenage killer further defiled the young girl's body by urinating on it. This, however, was not the most jarring discovery. During testimony at the trial, Waller revealed that the girl's tongue had been removed with a serrated knife.

Few in the neighborhood were surprised when local boy Jonathan Shelley was arrested for the crime. According to police, the fifteen-year-old had a history of drug abuse and petty theft. Principal Don Binder stated during trial that Finney was a known drug dealer on campus with a "serious problem." Found at the murder scene was a bag containing a mixture of cocaine and heroin, known in street terms as a "speedball." Shelley's bloody fingerprints were on the bag as well as in several key areas of the girl's room.

"We didn't lack for evidence," Waller says. "His bloody prints were all over the place." The defense pointed out during trial that there were several unidentified fingerprints found at the scene, but could not explain the most damning evidence: the six-inch serrated kitchen knife later found hidden in the closet of the boy's bedroom. The knife, one of a set from the Shelley kitchen, had been thoroughly cleaned, but traces of human blood were found embedded in the wooden handle. Emily Shelley, the boy's mother, testified at trial that she had cut herself using the knife, claiming the blood was her own. On cross-examination, she could not explain how or why the knife had found its way to the back of her son's bedroom closet.

"I have never believed for a moment that John Shelley is innocent," says state senator Paul Finney (R-Fulton). "He chose to go on a drug-addled rage and my daughter paid the heavy price for it." Sally Finney has never spoken on the record about the loss of Mary Alice, her only child. Neighbors say the mother refused to return to her home on St. Patrick Drive and that she filed for divorce from her husband during the trial. "This violence has torn my family apart," Paul Finney stated at the time. The twice-divorced senator is a known advocate for victims' rights and has coauthored or sponsored several Georgia State bills to make it tougher for violent criminals to make parole.

Fitting, as Shelley's first parole hearing was scheduled last Friday. Standing in front of the board, Shelley read from a prepared statement. "I did not commit this crime," he told the packed room. "I will not admit to something I did not do."

Says still-grieving father Paul Finney, "John Shelley is exactly where he deserves to be."

PART III

CHAPTER TWENTY-ONE

Will Trent was brushing his dog when the doorbell rang. Betty started barking, her body nearly skittering off the table from the force. He shushed her and was rewarded with a curious look. Will had never told the dog no.

A full minute passed. Will and Betty waited, hoping whoever was at the door would go away, but the doorbell rang again, then three more times in rapid succession.

The dog started barking in earnest. Will sighed, put down the brush and rolled down his shirtsleeves. He scooped up the dog in his hand. The doorbell rang again—six times in a row—as he walked to the front door.

"What the fuck took you so long?"

He looked into the street to see if she was alone. "I've been plagued by Jehovah's Witnesses lately."

"Might be a good way for you to meet women." Angie wrinkled her nose. "God, that is one ugly dog."

Will followed Angie into his house, holding the dog close to his chest, feeling the slight even if the animal hadn't. Angie was still dressed for work and he remarked, "You look like a prostitute."

"You look like a corpse in a coffin."

He pressed his hand to the tie. "You don't like the suit?"

"What happened to those jeans I bought you?" She flopped onto his couch and let out a sigh of relief, not waiting for his answer. "These fucking shoes," she complained, sliding out of the six-inch heels and letting them hit the rug. She unpinned her long brown hair and shook it out so it fell around her shoulders. "I am so sick of this fucking job."

Will put Betty down on the floor. The Chihuahua's nails clicked across the hardwood as she headed toward the kitchen. He heard her drink some water, then nibble on what was left of her supper. The dog was an unwelcome and, hopefully, temporary companion. Two weeks ago, Will had come back from his morning run to find his elderly neighbor being loaded into an ambulance. The woman had some sort of speech impediment and, judging from the timbre of her voice, a five-pack-a-day habit.

"Watch Betty!" she had screamed across the front lawn, though Will had heard it as *Wash Betty*!

"What do I do with her?" he had asked, somewhat horrified at the prospect. The woman just glared, so he pointed to the tiny Chihuahua standing on her front porch. "The dog. What about the dog?"

"Brush her!" the woman had screeched, and the ambulance doors had slammed shut.

Will didn't know the neighbor's name. Other than her love of listening to *The Price Is Right* at full volume, he knew little about her. He had no idea where the ambulance had taken her or if she had any family or, for that matter, if she was ever coming back. The only reason he knew the dog's name was because the woman had a habit of yelling at it.

"Betty!" he would hear in the middle of the night, her voice a deeper baritone than any man's. "Betty, I told you not to do that!"

Angie had her arms crossed over her chest as she stared

up at Will. "You realize you look absolutely ridiculous carrying that little dog around."

Will sat across from her, leaning back in his chair. He picked up the remote control for the stereo and stopped the audio book he had been listening to. Two very long years had passed since he had talked to Angie Polaski, and now here she was back in his living room like they hadn't missed a day. She had always been like that, ever since they were children. Pretend nothing was surprising and you would never be surprised.

He said, "Thanks for helping me with the vending machine this morning," leaving out that he'd almost had a heart attack when he saw her standing in the hallway at City Hall East today.

"What were you doing with Michael Ormewood, anyway?" Again, she didn't let him answer. "Jesus, I can't believe that about his neighbor. How weird is that?"

He tried to settle on one topic at a time. "He pulled a case that interested me. How do you know him?"

"Used to work Vice," she told him. "Do you have anything to snack on?"

Will got up to check the refrigerator, Betty close on his heels. He ate most of his meals out, but the dog liked cheese and he kept some on hand for her.

Angie had followed him into the kitchen. He asked, "When did Ormewood get transferred to Homicide?"

"About six months ago."

Will had been living in north Georgia six months ago, exiled to busting abandoned chicken farms that had been turned into methamphetamine labs while his boss decided what to do with him.

"Vice was his first big assignment when he got his gold shield," she said. "He worked it about ten years."

Will figured she was trying to tell him something. "Why did he leave?"

"Me." She pulled out a chair and sat at the table. "I told him he had to leave or I'd report him."

"For?"

"He was diddling some of the girls."

Will put the cheese down on the counter. "That's interesting."

"I thought it was pretty fucking disgusting, but to each his own."

Will mulled this over a moment, his picture of Michael Ormewood changing yet again. The man was certainly hard to pin down. "Was he doing this the whole ten years he worked Vice?"

"I only worked on his team for a few months. If I had to guess, I'd say yeah."

He asked, "Is that common?"

She shrugged. "Happens sometimes, especially with the married guys. Free pussy, who's gonna say no?"

Will turned to get a plate out of the cabinet so she couldn't read his expression, but Angie had known him since he was eight years old and she laughed anyway.

She said, "You're such a prude, William."

"Not much has changed in two years."

She didn't take the bait. Two years and a handful of months was more like it. They had been in this same kitchen, Angie screaming at him and Will looking down at his shoes while he waited for her to stop. She *had* stopped finally, only it was when she slammed the door on the way out.

He cubed the cheese with the knife, trying to ignore the expectant look Betty gave him. "What did you hear about what happened this afternoon?"

"Michael's neighbor?" Angie clarified. "Not much. Just that it's probably connected to the Monroe case."

"The neighbor's tongue was severed. They haven't found it yet."

"Why would someone go after Michael's neighbor?"

"That's what I was wondering."

"Do you think it's random?"

He leaned his back against the counter and looked at her. "Doesn't seem likely. Does Ormewood have many enemies?"

"I'm not his best friend, but from what I can tell, the guys like him. He hangs around with that asshole Leo Donnelly a lot, so there's no explaining his taste."

"Were there any cases you heard about where he might have angered somebody?"

"You mean pissed them off?" She shrugged again, a new habit she'd picked up since he had last seen her. "Nothing spectacular. You really think it's connected to Monroe?"

"The coroner's report on the girl will be ready tomorrow. From what I could see, there were some differences." He paused, recalling the scene in his head. "The top of her foot was scratched. She had obviously tripped over the fence. There was a wound here." He touched his temple. "She hit a rock when she fell, pretty hard from the look of it. And the blood." He paused again. "There wasn't enough blood. With Monroe, the mouth filled with blood pretty quickly, enough to choke her. This kid was facedown, of course, but there wasn't much blood on the ground. If I had to guess, I'd say her heart had stopped beating before the tongue was removed."

"Was she raped?"

"There was bruising on her thighs, but we won't know for certain until they get her on the table."

"Pete Hanson's handling this?"

"Yeah. The murder was in DeKalb County, but I asked them to let him handle the body just for continuity." He provided, "Hanson did Aleesha Monroe this morning. He seems like a good man." Will thought of something the doctor had raised during autopsy. "Do condoms with spermicide and lubricant cost that much more than the ones without?"

She stared at him. "Do I look like an expert?"

He knew that she probably was but did not want to have that particular discussion right now. "Monroe's killer used a condom that had lubricant and spermicide on it. I was just curious if they cost more."

Angie made the obvious conclusion. "He didn't want to leave his DNA."

"Ormewood thinks it means he didn't intend to kill her."

"That's bullshit," Angie countered. "The johns don't bring rubbers with them. They're not exactly worried about the girls they're banging. You know what they call all that extra skin around the vagina? A woman." She added, "Michael Ormewood of all people should know that."

"Then that brings me back to the original question. Are they more expensive?"

Angie studied him for a few seconds. She knew he had never bought a condom in his life. "The girls are just like everybody else in the world: they think if something costs a little bit more then it's better. They'll spend the extra thirty, forty cents if they think it'll stop hep C."

"They're not more worried about AIDS?"

"AIDS you can usually hide. Hepatitis turns you yellow. Leesha was one of the smart ones. She took whatever precautions she could."

Angie looked at her hands as if she was checking her

nail polish. She seldom let the job get to her—she would probably end up an alcoholic in the street if she did—but Will could see that she was struggling with this one. As much as she hated working Vice, she had a sort of kinship with the girls. They shared similar backgrounds of abuse and abandonment. She could have just as easily been one of them.

"I liked her," Angie finally said. "Monroe. We locked her up about six times in a row last year. She was sweet. Got into the game for the usual reasons, didn't know how to get out. I tried to get her into treatment, but you know how it is. Can't make someone do it unless they want to."

He tried to think of something nice to say about the dead hooker, knowing it would comfort Angie in some way. He settled on, "She was pretty."

"Yeah, she was." Angie stood up and walked over to Will. He kept perfectly still, foolishly expecting her to do something, but she only took a few cubes of cheese and sat back down. "I asked Michael about her this morning. He didn't even remember her."

"Was Monroe one of the prostitutes he interfered with?"

"No idea," Angie admitted. "It was mostly a rumor going around with the girls. 'There's some cop who'll give you a slide for some action.' That sort of thing. I didn't really believe it but one of them told me his name. It's not like Ormewood's a common name, right? I asked him about it and he didn't deny it, so I said, 'Lookit, either transfer out or this goes to the lieutenant.' He took door number one."

Will turned back around, crossing his arms over his chest. "What kind of guy is he?"

"An okay cop." She took a bite of cheese. "For what that's worth anymore." She chewed, obviously thinking through his question. "Truth is, I never liked him. He was always sniffing around me, offering to show me the ropes. I told him to fuck off."

"In your usual ladylike manner." He tossed Betty some cheese.

"You shouldn't feed her that," Angie warned. "She'll get corked up and then you'll be sorry."

"Moderation."

"Don't come crying to me when the little rat starts farting the 'Copacabana.'"

Will tossed Betty another piece of cheese, though he usually limited her to one a night. "Tell me more about Ormewood."

Angie shrugged. "I didn't really see how much he annoyed me until he was gone. Always acting like he was the big man on campus, you know? He's a war veteran—"

"He told me."

"Yeah, he likes to make sure people know that about him." She looked down at Betty suspiciously, as if the dog had already started to ferment. "Even after he transferred, he kept coming back to Vice like it was old home week. Once a week at least he was down there sniffing around, telling us about the big cases he'd caught, like being on the murder squad made his dick bigger."

"He has a pretty good clearance rate."

"Better than yours?"

Will asked, "Do you think he kept poking around because he was worried you'd change your mind about his extracurricular activities?"

"I think he just couldn't let it go that I'd gotten the upper hand with him." She smiled that sweet smile that meant she was going to push him. "Come on, baby. Your clearance rate is bigger than his, right?"

"Let's talk about Ormewood."

She pretended to pout, but couldn't hold it for long. "I just told you—Michael likes to be in control."

"He seemed all right to me."

"Guys don't see it, but it's there, right under the surface. Trust me, ask any woman and she'll tell you after spending ten minutes with him that he's a control freak."

"All right." This wasn't an unusual trait for a policeman and Will ran into it often. "I did notice that he's pretty competitive."

"That's an understatement," she told him. "He took the transfer, but he just couldn't let go of it that I'd beat him. He'd always come around at the end of my shift, right after I'd typed all my DD-fives."

"Did he go through them?"

"I would've ripped his fucking cock off if he did." She tossed another cube of cheese into her mouth. "But I think if I'd left him alone for two seconds, he would've turned my desk upside down."

"He got a temper?"

"No more than the rest of us."

Will wondered what she meant by that, but didn't press it. "Sounds like he's making sure you're not banging him up."

"Could be." She chewed some more, keeping her thoughts to herself.

Will studied her for a moment, trying to guess what she was hiding. With Angie, there was always something she kept in reserve. Even after all these years, Will wasn't certain whether or not she did this on purpose or if it was just a protection mechanism. There was lying and then there was what he thought of as survival instinct. He was the last person on earth who could fault her for that.

Will said, "Ormewood seemed very upset about his neighbor this afternoon."

"He really likes kids," she told him. "His son's got some mental problem, but I met him once and he's super sweet. The wife is pretty cold, but I would be too if I had to bang that prick every night." She explained, "I met them at a retirement dinner for his partner. Ken Wozniak, black guy but another Polack. I thought I'd go and support the home team."

"Nice of you."

"I doubt he's long for this world. Had some kind of stroke right in the middle of the squad. Half his body's gone."

"He got any family?"

"Nope."

They were both quiet for a while.

Angie opened her mouth to speak, then changed her mind. Will knew better than to prompt her, and sure enough she finally told him, "The thing about Michael is, he's not his own person."

"Which means?"

"He's always trying to fit in, but it just doesn't work for him."

Will thought the same thing could be said about himself. "Is that a bad thing?"

She stopped a few seconds to think before explaining, "Like with Wozniak. We weren't close, but I'd seen him around. Big guy, has a gut out to here." She held out her hand several inches in front of her stomach. "But he's a real lady's man, right? Always has a comment about what I'm wearing, 'Can I have some fries with that shake,' and that kind of bullshit, but he's an older guy, a real teddy bear, so it's funny and maybe kind of flattering instead of being creepy."

"Okay," Will said, not really understanding the line but

knowing the important part was that the man hadn't crossed it.

She continued, "Ken has these sayings. Like, he hands a civilian his card and says, 'Something to wipe your ass on,' and it's kind of disarming, and they laugh, but they keep the card, you know? He may be a freaking cop, but they know he's a cool guy."

"Right," Will agreed. Cops had all kinds of tricks they used to connect with potential witnesses. Everybody had a different bag they pulled from, but they all needed the same magic if they were going to get anything done on the street.

"So, Ken's in the hospital, right? Laid out on his ass. I mean, frankly, the guy's not gonna make it."

"That's too bad."

"Yeah," she waved her hand, dismissing his words. "The point is, a couple of weeks later, I'm on my strip with the girls and Michael drops by. The girls know he's a cop because . . . well, fuck, he's a cop. They can smell it, right?" She sat back in the chair, and Will could see she was getting angry at the memory. "So Michael goes up and down the line, cock-of-the-walk, gives me a fucking wink like what he's doing is funny and not stupid and risking my fucking cover, and he asks the girls if they've seen this guy hanging around, says he's one bad motherfucker and to stay clear of him. Then he hands out his card and says . . . ?"

Will guessed, "Something to wipe your ass on?"

"Right," she said. "He's always like that, always trying so hard to be the cool guy, to fit in, but the thing is, he doesn't know how so he has to mimic other people."

"Like guys who copy lines from movies."

She did a perfect Austin Powers, *"Yeah, baby."*

Will thought it through, considered the brief time he had spent with Michael Ormewood before they had found the dead girl in the detective's backyard. Angie had obviously given a lot of thought to the man's personality, but Will wasn't totally buying her conclusion. "I didn't pick up on that."

"No," she said. "But you think there's something off about him. Your radar went up."

Her words cut straight to the core of their relationship. Twenty-five years ago, they had met each other in a state children's home. Will was eight, Angie was eleven. They had both already spent a lifetime honing their instincts; both learned the hard way to listen to their gut when it said that just because someone was wearing a white hat, that didn't make them one of the good guys.

"Yeah," Will admitted. "I didn't get a good read on him. I assumed that was because he was irritated with me. Nobody likes to be forced to play well with others."

"There's more to it than that," she insisted. "And you know it just as well as I do."

"Maybe." He picked up Betty to give her a scratch behind her ears.

Angie stood up. "I need you to look up a name for me."

"What name?"

She walked back into the living room to get her purse. Will followed, holding Betty to his chest. The dog's tiny frame was so fragile that sometimes he felt as if he was holding a bird.

"Here." Angie held up a pink Post-it note with block letters neatly printed across the middle. "He said he was mixed up in something. It sounded bad, but I just got this feeling..." She shrugged off the rest of the sentence. "I think he's in trouble."

Will hadn't taken the note. He tried to sound like he was kidding. "Since when do you save people?"

"You wanna help me with this or you wanna stand there with your ass clenched, petting your little dog?"

"Can I do both?"

Her lips twisted in a smile. "His parole sheet only listed the highlights and the complete file is too old to be on the computer. You think you can work your GBI magic and get me a copy out of archives?"

He realized this was why she had really come tonight, and tried not to show his disappointment. He took the note, glancing at the words, which were little more than a blur across the page. Will had never been able to see his letters right, especially when he was upset or frustrated.

"Will?"

He warned, "It might take a while to find it if it's archived."

"No rush," she said. "I'll probably never see him again."

He felt relieved, which must have meant he had felt jealous before.

She was already opening the door to leave. "It's got two *e*'s. Can you read that okay?"

"What?"

She sounded annoyed, as if he hadn't been listening. "The name, Will. The one on the note. It's Shelley with two *e*'s."

CHAPTER TWENTY-TWO

Angie lived less than five miles from Will's house. She drove away with the radio down low, letting her mind wander as she turned down familiar roads. He looked the same as always, maybe a little thinner, and God knows what he had done to his hair. Angie had always cut it for him, and she assumed he'd gotten an electric shaver to avoid going to a hairdresser who might see the scar on the back of his head and ask him who had tried to kill him.

She knew that Will had been living in the north Georgia mountains for the last two years. Maybe he hadn't gotten out much while he was up there. Will had always let his dyslexia limit his life. He didn't like going to new restaurants because he couldn't understand the menus. He bought food at the grocery store based on the familiar colors of the labels or the identifiable photographs on the packages. He would rather starve than ask for help. Angie vividly recalled the first time he had gone shopping on his own. He had returned with a can of Crisco shortening, thinking the fried chicken on the label indicated the contents.

Turning into her driveway, Angie tried to remember how many times she had left Will Trent. She counted them off by the names of the men she had left with. George was the first one, way back in the mid-eighties. He'd been a punk rock enthusiast with a closet heroin addiction. Number two and number eight were Rogers, different men, but both with the same shitty character flaws; as Will often pointed out, Angie was only attracted to guys who were going to hurt her.

Mark was number six. He was a real winner. It had taken Angie five months to figure out he was running up debt on her credit cards. The idiot had been so shocked when she'd called a buddy from Fraud and had him arrested that she still laughed when she thought about the stupid expression on his face. Paul, Nick, Danny, Julian, Darren... there had even been a Horatio, though that one only lasted a week. All told, none of them had ever lasted, and she always found herself back on Will's doorstep, ruining his life again until she found another man who might take her away from him.

Angie parked the car in the driveway. The engine kept knocking even after she'd taken out the key and she thought for the millionth time that she should have the poor thing serviced. The car was leaking like an old lady and the muffler was hanging on by a thread, but she couldn't bring herself to let some strange man work on the engine that Will had restored with his own two hands. It took him about six hours to read the morning newspaper, but he could take apart an engine and put it back together blindfolded. Whether it was a pocket watch or a piano, he could repair just about anything that had moving pieces. He looked at cases the same way—how the pieces were put together to make a crime work—and he was one of the best agents the bureau had. If only he could turn that razor-sharp mind on his own life.

The security lights came on as she walked to the back door and slid her key into the lock. Rob. How had she forgotten about Rob, with his carrot-colored hair and sweet smile and gambling addiction? That made eleven men, eleven times she had left Will and eleven times he had taken her back.

Shit, that didn't even include the women.

Angie turned on the kitchen lights and pressed the keys on the alarm pad. Will did love her. She was certain of that. Even when they fought, they were careful not to go too far, not to say that one thing that would cut too deep, hurt too much, and make it all final. They knew everything about each other—or everything that mattered. If someone held a gun to her head and asked her to explain why she and Will always ended up together again, Angie would have died not knowing the answer. Not being one for introspection, Will would probably suffer the same fate.

She took a bottle of water out of the refrigerator and walked to the back of the house, trying unsuccessfully not to think about Will anymore. Angie checked the machine for messages as she started to undress. Half of her had been expecting him to call, but the other half knew he wouldn't. Calling her would have been impulsive, and Will was not impulsive. He liked routine. Spontaneity was something for people in movies.

Angie turned on the shower, staring at her reflection in the mirror as she took off her clothes. She could not look at her body without thinking of Will's. She'd had her share of abuse at the hands of various foster parents and stepfathers, but all of her scars were on the inside. Unlike Will, she did not have the scar down her face, the cigarette burns and gashes where drunken bullies had decided to take out their anger on a defenseless child. She didn't have a jagged scar ripping up her leg where an open fracture had led to six operations. Neither did she have the still-pink line slicing up her forearm where a razor blade had opened the flesh, draining her blood and nearly costing her life.

The first time they had met was at the Atlanta Children's Home, which for all intents and purposes was an orphanage. The state tried to place the kids with foster families, but more often than not they came back with new bruises, new stories to tell. Ms. Flannery ran the home, and there were three assistants who took care of the hundred or so children who lived there at any given time. Unlike the Dickensian image this conjured up, the staff were as devoted to their charges as they could be considering the fact that they were understaffed and underpaid. There was never any abuse there that Angie knew of, and for the most part, her happiest childhood memories were from her time spent under Ms. Flannery's care. Not that the woman was particularly maternal or caring, but she made sure that there were clean sheets on the beds, meals on the table and clothes on their backs. For most of the children living at ACH, this was the only stability any of them had ever known.

Angie always told people that her parents had died when she was a child, but the truth was she had no idea who her father was and her mother, Deidre Polaski, was currently a vegetable living in a state home. Speed had been Deidre's drug of choice, and an overdose had finally put her into an irreversible coma. Angie had been eleven when she found Deidre in the bathroom, slumped over the toilet, the needle still in her arm. She had stayed with her mother for two days, not eating, barely sleeping. Sometime around midnight on the second day, one of her mother's suppliers had come by. He had raped Angie before calling an ambulance to come get her mother.

She got into the shower, let the water cascade down on her and wash off some of the day's grime.

Rusty.

That was his name.

"I'll kill you if you tell anyone," he had warned, his hand wrapped around her throat so tight that she could barely breathe. His pants were still down at his knees, and she remembered looking at his flaccid penis, the curly, dark hairs sprouting along his thighs. "I'll find you and kill you."

He wasn't the first. By that time, Angie was already sexually experienced thanks to a never-ending line of her mother's boyfriends. Some had been nice, but others had been cruel, menacing animals who had doped up Angie's mother just so they could get at her girl. In all honesty, by the time Angie reached Ms. Flannery and the children's home, she could feel only relief.

Will's story wasn't exactly the same but it was close enough. His body served as a map to pain, whether it was the long, thin scars on his back where the skin had been rent by a whip or the rough patch of flesh on his thigh where they had made a graft to close the electrical burns. His right hand had been crushed twice, his left leg broken in three places. He had once been punched in the face so hard and so repeatedly that his upper lip had split open like a peeled banana. Every time Angie kissed him, she felt the scar against her lips and was reminded of what he'd been through.

That was the one thing about the older kids at the orphanage: they all had a similar history. They were all unwanted. They had all been damaged. The younger ones never stayed for long, but by around the age of six or seven, there was basically no hope that you'd ever be part of a family. For most of them, that was a good thing. They had seen what families were like and preferred the alternative. At least, most of them did.

Will never gave up, though. On visiting day, he'd stand at the mirror, carefully combing his hair, smoothing down his cowlick, trying to make himself look like the kind of kid you'd want to take home with you. She'd wanted to kick him in the teeth, to shake him hard and explain that he wasn't ever going to be adopted, that no one would want him. One time, she had actually started to do this, but there was something in his expression, a kind of hopefulness mixed with the expectation of failure, that stopped her. Instead of punching him, she had guided him back to the mirror and helped him comb his hair.

Angie turned off the shower and wrapped herself in a towel. She smiled, letting herself remember the first time she had seen Will in the common area. He was eight years old with curly blond hair and a little cupid's bow of a mouth. He'd always had his nose in a book. At first, Angie had assumed he was a nerd but she later figured out that Will was staring at the words, trying to get them to make sense. The irony was that he loved words, adored books and stories and anything else that might take him out of his surroundings. In a rare moment of candor, he had once told her that being in a library was like sitting down at a table laid with all his favorite foods but not being able to eat any of them. And he hated himself for it.

Even now, he would not accept that his dyslexia was anything but his own personal failure. No matter how much Angie prodded and even begged, he would not get help. By the time she met him, Will had learned all kinds of tricks to hide his problem and Angie doubted his teachers thought of him as anything but slow. His current job was no different. He used colored folders so that he could find cases by sight, and different types of paper so that he could locate them by texture.

In school, Angie was the one who wrote out his term papers, taking dictation on subjects she had no desire to understand. She was the one who had to hear his tape recorder going night after night as he listened to books, memorizing whole passages so that he could contribute in class the next day. By graduation, he had worked ten times as hard as anyone else and still barely passed by the skin of his teeth. And then he went to college.

Angie had never understood why all of this mattered so much to him. With his height and good looks, Will should have grown into the kind of heartbreaker that Angie was always running off with. Instead, he was quiet, shy, the sort of man who would fall in love with the first girl who let him fuck her. Not that Will was in love with Angie; sure, he loved her, but being *in* love and loving someone were two different things. He wanted her for her familiarity in the same way that he wanted to go to the same restaurants and buy the same groceries. She was a known quantity, a safe bet. Their relationship was more along the lines of an overprotective brother and sister who happened to be having sex with each other.

Not that sex had ever been an easy thing between them. God knew Will had the equipment—before she had gone on the pill, Angie's diaphragm had been the size of a dinner plate—but there was a big difference between holding a hammer and knowing how to hit the nail on the head every time. Over the years, they had gone backward from that first awkward time in the upstairs janitor's closet at the children's home, so that now when they had sex, it was like a couple of bumbling kids sneaking around behind their parents' backs instead of two grown adults making love. They always had the lights off and most of their clothes on, as if sex was a shameful secret between them. The three-piece suit Will was wearing this afternoon shouldn't have surprised her a bit. The more clothes he could wear to cover his body, the happier Will was.

This was some kind of cosmic joke, because Angie knew that underneath his clothes, he had a beautiful body.

She could feel the muscles in his back when he tensed, her hands wrapped around the curve of his ass, her feet cupping his strong calves as she pushed up to meet him.

Yet, he was ashamed of his body, as if the scars said something bad about him instead of the people who had caused them. She hadn't seen him fully undressed in at least twelve years. That was what their last fight was about. They had been in his kitchen just as they were tonight. Will was leaning against the counter and Angie was sitting at the table, yelling at him.

"Do you realize," she had said, "that I have no idea what you look like?"

He'd tried to act confused. "You see me every day."

Angie had slammed her fist on the table and he'd jumped. Will hated loud noises, took them as a signal that he was about to get hurt despite the fact that he was more than capable of defending himself.

The clock in the living room had ticked audibly in the ensuing silence. Finally, he'd started nodding, then said, "Okay," as he unbuttoned his shirt. He was wearing an undershirt, of course, and she had stepped forward, put her hands over his, as he started to pull it off.

It was her. She was the one who couldn't look at him, who couldn't bear to see the reminders of what he had been through. His scars were not his own, they were souvenirs from their childhood, symbols of the men who had abused her, the mother who had chosen a needle over her own daughter. Angie could writhe naked in the backseat of a car with a total stranger but she could not bring herself to look at the body of the man she loved.

"No," she had told him. "I can't do this anymore."

"Who's the guy?" he had asked. There was always a guy. The next day, she had called his boss, Amanda Wagner, and told the woman to look for the tape recorder Will kept in his pocket so he could record all of their conversations.

"And here I was thinking you were his friend," Amanda had said. Angie had given some crass response, but she knew in her heart that this was the right thing to do, the right thing for Will. The only way he would ever have a chance at a real life, at any kind of happiness, would be on his own. Still, she had burst into tears the moment she put down the phone. Maybe he had been fine up in his mountain enclave, but Angie had missed him like hell. The truth was that she had longed for him like a stupid schoolgirl.

And then the bitch had transferred him back to Atlanta. He was too good at his job to waste away in the hills, Amanda claimed. Besides, she liked Will too much to keep him away. For his part, she was the closest thing to a mother that Will had ever had. They pretended to hate each other, two tomcats sizing up each other for a fight, but Angie knew that in their own dysfunctional way they were a team. She recognized the signs.

To her credit, Amanda had given Angie a courtesy call to let her know about the transfer. "Your boyfriend's back."

Angie had finished the song, her smart-ass on autopilot. "Hey-la, hey-la."

Even though Angie had known for weeks that Will's new office was in the building, had prepared herself for running into him, she had felt blindsided when Will had gotten off the elevator this morning. Seeing him with that prick Michael Ormewood had been like a punch in the stomach. After that, Angie had spent most of the day trying to think of a reason to go see him. She knew he would go straight home after work. He didn't date and as far as Angie knew, except for a hand job from another little slut at the children's home, he had never been with another woman.

As the day wore on, she'd felt almost sick from wanting

to see him. After arresting three johns who had the bad fortune of choosing "Robin" from the line of working girls in front of the liquor store, Angie had swiped a pad of pink notepaper from the fruit who worked across from her, knowing the bright background somehow helped Will read words more easily. In careful block letters, she had written out John Shelley's name, then driven straight to Will's house before she could think about it too much and stop herself. His face was so easy for her to read, and she had known from his expression exactly what he was thinking when she handed him the note: *so this is the guy, the next one you're going to leave me for.*

Angie wiped the steam off the bathroom mirror, caught her reflection and did not like what she saw. John had said she was pretty, but he was only looking at the surface. Underneath, she was a hag, a miserable old witch who brought misery to everyone she met.

Will was worried about John Shelley, but he could not have been more wrong if he'd tried. It was only a matter of time before Will figured out the truth. He could barely read a book, but he could read the signs clearly enough. One of the biggest regrets in Angie's life wasn't the eleven men or her comatose mother or even the hell she routinely put Will through. Her biggest regret was that she had slept with that asshole Michael Ormewood.

CHAPTER TWENTY-THREE

Will looked at his cell phone, the digital numbers telling him the time. He always took lateness as being rude. It said to the other person that their time was more valuable than yours. Amanda Wagner was totally aware of this. She had never been on time for an appointment in her life.

"Get you anything?" Caroline asked. Amanda's secretary was a pretty young woman, ultraefficient and seemingly impervious to her boss's sharp tongue. As far as Will knew, Caroline was the only woman who had ever worked with Amanda Wagner for more than an hour.

He said, "I'm fine, thank you, but—" Caroline waited as Will pulled the pink Post-it note from his pocket. "Could you run down this man's record for me? Under the radar, if that's okay."

She understood instantly he meant for her to keep the trace from Amanda. Caroline's eyes lit up at the prospect. "When do you need it?"

"Sooner rather than later."

She saluted him, returning to her desk. Will looked at the empty doorway. He wanted to call back Caroline, tell her to forget about it. Angie was right about gut feelings, and even though Will had never met Jonathan Shelley in his life, just the sight of the man's name sent up an alarm. Maybe Will was being jealous. Maybe he was just tired.

Angie had been right again, this time about the perils of giving a dog too much cheese. Will had found out the hard way that it's nearly impossible to go to sleep with a flatulent Chihuahua sharing your pillow.

Will sat in one of the two chairs across from Amanda's desk. Like its usual occupant, the desk was uncluttered. Stacks of papers were neatly filed in the in- and out-boxes. Phone messages were stuck to the blotter in a straight line.

The office walls had framed news clippings of Amanda's exploits: Atlanta's mayor giving her a medal. Bill Clinton shaking her hand. Some south Georgia chief of police she had saved during a hostage situation. There were various plaques for faithful service as well as a shelf devoted to her shooting trophies.

After twenty years at the GBI working with tactical negotiations, Amanda Wagner had wanted a change. The brass had given her her choice of assignments. Typically, she had taken it into her head that she wanted to shake things up, and in a year, she was heading up a new division of her own making, the criminal apprehension team. Special Criminal Apprehension Team. Never was an acronym more appropriate for the group she put together.

For the most part, the ten men Amanda had chosen to work under her were all like Will: young agents who had been on the job awhile and proven that they didn't exactly get along with others. Their superiors had rated them as difficult, but there was never anything they did that merited a formal warning, let alone firing. They were good cops, though, the kinds of men who as adults tried to correct the wrongs they could not control as children. Amanda had an uncanny eye for broken people, the ones who had something in their past that made them fall easy prey to her pseudo-mothering. Will could imagine Amanda presenting her carefully culled list of potential recruits to Susan

Richardson, her chief at headquarters. Susan must have looked at the list the way you look at a cat when it brings you a dead bird. "Yes, thank you, please excuse my dry heaves."

Will shifted in his chair, looking at his phone again for the time. He wore a watch on his wrist, but only as a cheat to help him differentiate between left and right. Growing up, he had learned all kinds of tricks to hide his problem. Angie gave him constant grief about it, saying he shouldn't be ashamed. Will wasn't ashamed. He just didn't want to have one more thing that made him different from everybody else. He sure as hell didn't want to give Amanda Wagner more ammunition. She had been trying to get into his head as long as he had known her and this particular bit of information was tantamount to baring your neck to a hungry wolf.

He looked out the window, watching birds gliding along with the wind. Amanda had been working out of the Marietta building when Will had been thrown to the meth freaks up in the mountains. She had moved to City Hall East a little over a year ago, her corner office affording her a panoramic view of downtown Atlanta. She was right by the elevator, which let her keep a finger in every pie the building cooked up. Caroline was in the outer office, but Amanda never closed the door between them. He could hear the secretary typing on her computer now. If she had any self-respect, she was working on her résumé.

"Hello, Will." Amanda had sneaked up on him while he was staring out the window. She pressed her hand to his shoulder as she walked past him.

"Dr. Wagner."

She sat behind her desk, saying, "Sorry I'm late," the same automatic and meaningless way people say, "excuse me" when they bump into you.

He watched as she reviewed her phone messages, showing him the top of her carefully coiffed salt-and-pepper hair. Amanda was probably in her mid-fifties, a small woman, maybe five-three on a good day. Her attitude filled the room, and she walked with a swagger that rivaled a bullfighter's. She wore a simple diamond ring on her wedding finger, though Will knew she wasn't currently married. She had no children, or perhaps she had eaten them when they were young. Amanda was extremely private with her personal life—a luxury she didn't afford others. Will thought of her time away from work the way he used to think of his schoolteachers crawling into their caves under the school building at night, lulling themselves to sleep with dreams of torturing their students the next day. Will imagined Amanda getting ready for work in the mornings; shaving her chest, tucking her tail, slipping her cloven hooves into her dainty size-six pumps.

"I suppose I should call you Dr. Trent now?" she said, not looking up from her messages.

Will had made himself busy during his mountain exile, knowing without a doubt that Amanda would eventually pull him from the Epworth office and put him back under her thumb. The correspondence school in Florida let him do the work online at his own pace, and the state recognized the criminology degree despite its dubious origins.

He told her the truth. "I was trying to make my pay grade too rich for your budget."

"You don't say," she said, taking out a gold fountain pen and making a note on one of the messages.

Will glanced at the scar on his hand where Amanda had shot him with a nail gun. He told her, "Nice pen."

She raised an eyebrow, sitting back in her chair. Almost a full minute passed before she asked, "Where is Two Egg, Florida, exactly?"

He fought a smile. He had chosen the school primarily for its ridiculous location. "I believe it's near the picturesque Withlacoochee River, ma'am."

She obviously didn't believe a word he was saying. "Of course it is."

Will was silent, a lobster being appraised in the tank.

She capped the gold fountain pen and placed it perpendicular to the blotter. "You're not taping this, are you?"

"Not today, ma'am." Will had a hard enough time reading typewritten documents, but his own handwriting was the kind of backward scrawl you'd find on the walls at the local kindergarten. Amanda was prone to giving out long lists of tasks. The only way Will could keep up with them was to record her so that he could take his time transcribing her words onto the computer. Two years ago, she had caught him red-handed in a meeting. Amanda hadn't liked being taped without her permission and of course she had assumed Will was doing it for nefarious reasons. He would be damned if he told her about his reading problem, and even if he'd been inclined, Amanda had transferred him to the North Pole before he could get his snowshoes on.

"All right," she said. "Tell me about your case."

Will gave her a briefing on what little he had. He ran through the case files of the three girls he had found, said he believed two of them were connected. He told her he had read about Aleesha Monroe, the slain prostitute, on the GBI's daily report that highlighted crimes around the state. Following protocol, he had asked Lieutenant Ted Greer to be let in on the case and been assigned to Michael Ormewood, the lead detective. When he got to the part about Ormewood's dead neighbor, Amanda stopped him.

"The tongue was bitten off?"

"I'm not certain how it was removed," Will told her. "Perhaps if I had known you were going to be late this morning, I could have taken the time to discuss this with the coroner so that I would be better informed for this briefing."

"Don't whine, Dr. Trent. It doesn't suit you." Her tone was soft, conciliatory, but he could tell from her smile that he had been given a point in her scorebook. That he was even playing the game meant she had already won.

Amanda went back to the case. "The tongues weren't taken from the scene in the previous crimes?"

"No, ma'am," Will told her. "The first girl's tongue wasn't completely severed. The second was holding it in her hand when they found her, but it was too late to do anything about it. Monroe's tongue was left on the stairs. Spit out, most likely. Cynthia Barrett's tongue was not found at the scene."

"Did you search the Barrett house?"

"The DeKalb PD did," Will told her. "From what I gathered, they didn't find anything unusual."

"From what you gathered?" she echoed.

"I didn't want to step on their toes."

"Probably wise," Amanda admitted. DeKalb County was still tightly controlled by a handful of men who didn't like the state—or anyone, for that matter—messing in their business. Six years ago, DeKalb sheriff-elect Derwin Brown had been assassinated in his own driveway while he was carrying in some Christmas packages from his car. He was three days away from being sworn into office, and Sidney Dorsey, the outgoing sheriff, hadn't taken the defeat well.

Amanda took a file out of the top drawer of her desk and opened it to the first page. "What do you think of this Michael Timothy Ormewood?"

"I haven't yet formed an opinion," Will answered, thinking that if she had pulled Ormewood's personnel file, she already knew more than Will did.

She read aloud as she traced down the page with her finger. "Army man. Sixteen years Atlanta PD. Worked his way up from foot beat to his gold shield. Accused in ninety-eight of excessive use of force." She made a jerking-off motion with her fist, dismissing the complaint. "He moved up pretty quickly. Narcotics—not for long, probably got bored—Vice, and now Homicide. No college education." She glanced up at Will. "Do try not to lord your fancy Two Egg degree over him, Dr. Trent."

"Yes, ma'am."

She turned the page. "Commendation for saving a civilian. Even you have one of those. They hand them out like candy." She closed the file. "Nothing to shout home about. Wears beige and keeps quiet." This was a general phrase she used for cops who did their jobs and waited out their pensions. It was not a compliment.

"Anything else?" Will asked, knowing full well there was.

She smiled. "I put in a call to a friend in uniform." Amanda always had friends. Considering her personality, Will wondered about the nature of these relationships, and if by friend she meant someone she gripped by the short hairs. "Ormewood worked in supply when he was over in Kuwait. Never made it past the rank of private."

Will was mildly surprised. "Is that so?"

"He was honorably discharged, which is all the Atlanta PD would have known—or cared—about. My guy says he was wounded his second week overseas, and that they never did find out who shot him."

"The wound was self-inflicted?"

She shrugged. "Wouldn't you shoot yourself in the leg to get out of that hellhole?"

Will would have shot himself in the leg to get out of Amanda's office.

"So." Amanda pressed her palms together as she leaned back in the chair. "Plan of action?"

"I need to talk to Ormewood. It can't be a fluke that this has happened in his own backyard."

"Do you think he might have gotten too close to the doer in the Monroe case?"

"Cynthia Barrett's body was fresh when we got there, probably no more than an hour old. I was with Ormewood the whole morning and I didn't see that we made any great strides toward breaking the case, let alone pushed someone so hard that they jumped in their car, went to his house and mutilated his next-door neighbor."

Amanda nodded for him to continue.

"We talked to Monroe's pimp. He didn't strike me as the type to cut off a good source of income, but obviously I'll go back at him today."

"And?"

"And as I said, I'll talk to Ormewood about this, ask if he saw or did anything unusual the night of the Monroe murder."

"Is he in today or did he take compassionate leave?"

"I have no idea," Will answered. "Wherever he is, I'll find him."

She picked up one of her messages. "A Leo Donnelly was trying to get your personnel file."

"I'm not surprised."

"I sealed it," she said. "No one needs to smell your dirty laundry."

"No one but you," Will corrected. He looked at his watch as he stood. "If that's all, Dr. Wagner?"

She held her hands out in an open gesture. "By all means, Dr. Trent. Go forth and conquer."

CHAPTER TWENTY-FOUR

8:56 AM

John had been forced to get rid of his shoes. He wasn't sure if he had left any footprints at the scene, but he wasn't taking any chances. When he got back to the flophouse, he had cut at the soles with a kitchen knife, altering the waffle pattern. Not trusting his luck, he had then gotten on the bus, paying cash so his Trans Card wouldn't track him, and ridden to Cobb Parkway all the way up in Marietta. There he had walked around for an hour, dragging his feet on the hot asphalt, scoring the soles some more.

At the Target, he'd bought a new pair of sneakers—twenty-six dollars he could ill-afford—then tossed his old shoes into a Dumpster behind a shady-looking Chinese restaurant. His stomach had rumbled at the smells coming from the kitchen. Twenty-six dollars. He could have bought a nice meal, had a waitress bring him food, keep his glass filled with iced tea, talked to her about the crazy weather.

All the tea in the world wasn't worth going back to prison.

God, he was in such a fucking mess. He shuddered, thinking how that girl's tongue had felt when he'd pinched it between his thumb and forefinger. Even through the latex glove, he could feel the texture of the thing, the warmness to it from being in her mouth. John put his hand to his own mouth, trying not to vomit. She'd been an innocent, just a little girl who had been too curious, too easily swayed.

John's only consolation was the thought of Michael Ormewood's face when he went into his garage in search of the porn he kept in the bottom of his toolbox and found his trusty knife sitting beside his teenage victim's tongue.

"Shelley!" Art yelled. John bolted up. He had been kneeling beside a sedan, rubbing bug guts off the front bumper.

"Sir?"

"Visitor." Art jerked his head toward the back of the building. "Make sure you're off the clock."

John stood frozen in place. A visitor. No one visited him. He didn't know anybody.

"Yo, yo," Ray-Ray mumbled. They had worked out an uneasy peace since the hooker incident.

"Yeah?"

"It's a girl." Not a cop, was what he meant.

A girl, John thought, his mind reeling. The only girl he knew was Robin.

He told Ray-Ray, "Thanks, man," tucking in his shirt as he headed to the back of the car wash. As John punched out, he caught his reflection in the mirror over the clock. Despite the chill in the air, sweat had plastered his hair to his head. Jesus, he probably smelled, too.

John ran his fingers through his hair as he opened the back door. His first thought was that the girl who stood there wasn't Robin, then that the girl wasn't really a girl. It was a woman. It was Joyce.

He felt more nervous than if it had actually been the prostitute come to see him, and ashamed by the cheap clothes he was wearing. Joyce was in a nice suit jacket with matching slacks that she sure as shit hadn't bought at a discount store. The sun was picking out auburn highlights in her hair and he wondered if it was streaked or something she'd always had. He remembered the way Joyce's face used to twist up when she got angry with him, the smile on her mouth when she gave him an Indian burn and the sneer she'd give when she slapped him for pulling one of her braids. He didn't, however, remember the color of her hair when they were children.

She greeted him with a demand. "What are you mixed up in, John?"

"When did you start back smoking?"

She took a long drag on the cigarette in her hand and tossed it to the ground. He watched her press the toe of her shoe into it, grinding the butt, probably wishing she was grinding his head in its place.

She let out a stream of smoke. "Answer my question."

He looked back over his shoulder, though he knew they were alone. "You shouldn't be here, Joyce."

"Why won't you answer my question?"

"Because I don't want you involved."

"You don't want me *involved*?" she repeated, incredulous. "My *life* is involved, John. Whether I like it or not, you *are* my brother."

He could feel her anger like a heat radiating from her body. Part of him wished she would just haul off and hit him, beat him to a bloody pulp until her fists were broken and her rage was spent.

She said, "How can you have credit cards when you're in prison?"

"I don't know."

"Is it allowed?"

"I..." He hadn't even considered the question, though it was a good one. "I suppose. You can't have cash, but..."

He tried to think it through. You could get a warning or even thrown into solitary for having cash in prison. Everything you bought at the canteen was debited through your account and you weren't allowed to order anything through the mail.

"I don't know."

"You realize if Paul Finney finds out any of this, he'll sue you in civil court for every dime you have."

"There's nothing to get," John said. His mother's will had left everything to Joyce for this very reason. Under the victim's compensation act, if John ever had more than two pennies to rub together, Mary Alice's family could get it. Mr. Finney was like a circling shark waiting for a drop of John's blood in the water.

Joyce said, "You own a house in Tennessee."

He could only stare.

She took a folded sheet of paper out of her coat pocket. "Twenty-nine Elton Road in Ducktown, Tennessee."

He took the page, which was a Xerox of an original. Across the top were the words, "Official Certificate of Title." His name was listed above the property address as the owner. "I don't understand."

"You own this house free and clear," she told him. "You paid it off in five years."

He had never owned anything in his life except a bicycle, and Richard had taken that away from him after his first arrest. "How much did it cost?"

"Thirty-two thousand dollars."

John choked on the amount. "Where would I get that kind of money?"

"How the hell do I know?" She yelled this so loudly that he stepped back.

"Joyce—"

She jabbed her finger in his face, saying, "I'm only going to ask you this one more time, and I swear to God, John, I swear on Mama's grave, if you lie to me I will cut you out of my life so quick you won't know what hit you."

"You sound just like Dad."

"That's it." She started to walk away.

"Wait," he said, and she stopped but didn't turn around. "Joyce—someone's stolen my identity."

Her shoulders sagged. When she finally looked at him, he could read every horrible thing he was ever involved in etched into the lines of her face. She was quiet now, anger spent. "Why would someone steal your identity?"

"To cover himself. Cover his tracks."

"For what reason? And why you?"

"Because he didn't think I would get out. He thought I'd be in prison for the rest of my life, that he could use my identity to keep from getting caught."

"Who thought this? Who's doing this to you?"

John felt the name stick like a piece of glass in his throat. "The same guy who hurt Mary Alice."

Joyce visibly flinched at the girl's name. They were both quiet, nothing but the swish of water through the car wash and the buzz of the vacuums interrupting the silence.

John forced himself to close some of the space between them. "The person who framed me for killing Mary Alice is trying to do it again."

She had tears in her eyes.

"I didn't do it, Joyce. I didn't hurt her."

Her chin trembled as she struggled to contain her emotions.

"It wasn't me."

Her throat worked as she swallowed. "Okay," she said.

"Okay." She sniffled, taking a deep breath. "I need to get back to work."

"Joyce—"

"Take care of yourself, John."

"Joyce, please—"

"Good-bye."

CHAPTER TWENTY-FIVE

Will watched Pete Hanson's hands as the medical examiner deftly sewed together Cynthia Barrett's abdomen and chest. Her skin tugged up as the doctor pulled the baseball stitch through the Y-incision he'd made at the beginning of the autopsy. During the procedure, Will had concentrated on the parts of the body rather than the whole, but now there was no avoiding the fact that Cynthia Barrett was a human being, little more than a child. With her slim build and delicate features, she had an almost elfin quality about her. How a man could hurt this girl was beyond him.

"It's a sad thing," Pete said, as if he could read Will's mind.

"Yes." Will had been gritting his teeth from the moment he entered the morgue. In his law-enforcement career, Will had seen all kinds of damage done to people, but he still found himself shocked when he saw a child victimized. He always thought about Angie, the horrible things that had been done to her when she was just a little girl. It made his stomach hurt.

The doors opened and Michael Ormewood walked in. There were dark circles under his eyes and he still had a piece of tissue stuck to his chin where he had apparently cut himself shaving.

"Sorry I'm late," Michael apologized.

Will looked at his watch; the movement was reflexive, but when he looked back up, he could see Michael's irritation.

"That's fine," Will said, realizing too late that he had said the wrong thing. He tried, "Dr. Hanson was just finishing up. You didn't miss anything."

Michael kept silent, and Pete broke the tension, saying, "I'm so sorry for your loss, Detective."

After a few seconds, Michael nodded his head. He wiped his mouth, rolling the tissue off his chin. He looked surprised at the bloody paper between his fingers and threw it in the trashcan. "It's been a little hard at home."

"I can imagine." Pete patted him on the shoulder. "My condolences."

"Yes," Will agreed, not knowing what else to say.

"She was just a neighbor, but still..." The smile on Michael's face seemed forced, as if he was having trouble keeping his emotions in. "It eats you up when something bad happens to an innocent kid like that." Will saw his gaze settle onto the body, noticed the flash of despair in the other man's eyes. Michael reached out as if to touch the blonde hair, then pulled his hand back. Will remembered how Michael had acted this same way the day before when they had first seen the body. It was as if Cynthia was the man's own child instead of a neighbor's.

"Poor baby," Michael whispered.

"Yes," Pete concurred.

"I'm sorry, guys," Michael apologized. He cleared his throat a few times, seemed to try to get himself together. "What have you got, Pete?"

"I was just about to do my summary report with Agent Trent." Pete started to roll back the sheet covering the lower half of the body.

Michael flinched visibly. "Just give me the highlights, okay?"

Pete rolled the sheet back up, stopping just under the girl's neck, telling them, "I believe she tripped and hit her head. The force from the fall shattered her skull above the left temporal lobe. Her neck twisted on impact, snapping the spinal cord at C-2. Death was instantaneous. An unfortunate accident, but for the missing tongue."

Michael asked, "Did they locate it yet?"

"No," Will answered, then asked Pete, "Could you go over the differences between the two murders?"

"Of course," Pete replied. "Unlike your prostitute, this girl's tongue was not bitten off, but cut. Most likely a serrated knife was used. A lesser man might not notice, but I'm certain it's different."

Michael asked, "How can you tell?"

"The cut is not clean, like your biter." The doctor snapped his teeth together to illustrate, the sound echoing in the tiled room. "What's more, I would expect a crescent pattern, because the teeth are not in a straight line in the mouth, but curved. If you look…" He had been about to open the girl's mouth, but seemed to change his mind. "There are several test marks where whoever removed her tongue obviously had difficulty getting a grip on it. The tongue slid and the blade caught. Your guy was determined, though. He accomplished the task on the third or fourth try."

"It was slick?" Will asked. "From blood? Saliva?"

"There would have been little blood because she was already dead by the time the mutilation occurred. I would assume his grip was compromised because the tongue is so small. Further, a grown man would have difficulty reaching his hand into her mouth. It's very narrow."

Michael was nodding, but he didn't seem to be listening to Pete. His eyes were still locked on the girl and a single tear rolled down his cheek. He looked away for just a second, using the back of his hand to wipe the tear, pretending to be rubbing his nose.

"And of course the missing tongue is interesting," Pete opined. "In the other cases, the tongue was always left with the victim. Perhaps your perpetrator has graduated to taking souvenirs?"

"That's common with serial killers," Will told them, trying to draw Michael out. Maybe the man was back too soon. Angie had said that he loved children. Perhaps, like Will, this was harder on him because of the girl's age. And, Barrett was his neighbor, so Michael had probably watched her grow up. That kind of thing would be hard on anyone, even without a trip to the morgue to see her cut open.

Michael cleared his throat twice, finally asking, "Was she raped?"

Pete equivocated, and Will waited to see how he would answer, and how that answer would affect Michael. "There are definitely signs of forcible entry, but it's difficult to say whether the act was consensual or not." Pete shrugged. "Of course, if the rape was postmortem, then there wouldn't be signs of vaginal trauma because the force reflex would be gone."

There was a tight smile on Michael's face, the kind you gave when you were anything but pleased.

Will reminded, "You said that she's sexually experienced. Maybe we should find out if there's a boyfriend in her life."

"I asked Gina about that last night," Michael offered, explaining, "Gina's my wife." Will nodded and he continued, "Cynthia wasn't dating anybody. She was a really good kid. Phil never had a moment's trouble with her."

Will knew the father was a traveling salesman who had been on the other side of the country when his daughter was murdered. "When will he be back?"

"This afternoon at the latest," Michael answered. "I'd like to knock off early so I can go check on him." He turned to Will. "I'll let you know if he has anything useful."

Will nodded, understanding the message: Michael would talk to the father alone. Part of Will was glad he was being spared the task.

Michael asked Pete, "Did you get any DNA?"

"Some."

"I'll run it upstairs for you."

"Thank you," Pete said, walking over to the counter by the door. He handed Michael a sealed paper bag containing Cynthia Barrett's rape kit.

Will asked Michael, "Do you think there's a connection between these cases and the ones I showed you yesterday?"

The other man's gaze was back on Cynthia's face. "No question about it," he answered. "He's obviously escalating."

Will asked, "Is there anyone you've come across since the Monroe murder who might look good for this?"

The detective shook his head. "That's all I thought about last night. There's nobody I can think of who would do this." He paused a second before suggesting, "I figure it's somebody who was watching the Monroe crime scene when I showed up. I went straight home after. They probably followed me. Jesus!" He put his hand to his forehead. "They could have gotten Tim. My wife..." He dropped his hand. "I've moved my family out of the house. They're not safe with this maniac out there."

"That's probably best," Pete said. He put his hand on Michael's arm. "I'm so sorry, Detective. I'm so sorry that this has happened to you."

Michael nodded, and Will saw that he had tears in his eyes again. "She was a good kid," Michael managed. "Nobody deserves this kind of thing, but Cynthia..." He shook his head. "We've got to catch this guy. I won't feel safe until the warden's putting the needle in this fucker's arm." He looked right at Will, repeating himself. "I won't feel safe."

Will leaned against Michael Ormewood's car, waiting for the detective to join him. He flipped open his cell phone and stared at the screen, wanting to call Angie. There was something she was not telling him. He had known her long enough to figure out when she was hiding something. Maybe he could ring her up and ask if she'd remembered anything else about Michael. Angie had worked with the detective. She knew about his extracurricular activities. She had to know more than she was letting on.

"Shit," Will whispered, snapping the phone closed. What an idiot. She had probably slept with the man. He was just her type: a married, unavailable asshole who was bound to use her, then walk away.

Will inhaled and let out a long sigh of breath, feeling his own stupidity overwhelm him. He had been worried about John Shelley when Michael Ormewood was the latest jerk in her life. Will wondered if she was still seeing him. They had been standing pretty close together when he'd found them in the hallway yesterday. Though, last night, Angie had been brutal about Ormewood when Will had asked her about him. If she was still sleeping with him, Will was certain she would have said so then. Or maybe not. Two years had passed. This was the longest he and Angie had ever gone without talking to each other. Things might have changed.

No, nothing ever changed.

"Shit," Will repeated. He put his hands on the roof of the car and pressed his forehead against them. What could he do? Go confront her? Demand she tell him what she'd been doing for the last two years?

Will dropped his hands and turned as the stair door banged open. Ormewood was walking across the parking lot, one hand in his pocket, a half-smile on his face. He didn't look tired anymore. The man actually looked pleased. He'd probably dropped by Angie's desk on his way to delivering the rape kit to the lab. He might have even grabbed a quickie in the supply closet for all Will knew.

"Sorry I took so long," Michael said as he unlocked the car doors. "Had to see a man about a dog."

"Right," Will mumbled, sliding into the passenger's seat. He looked out the window, waiting for Michael to get in and start the car. If he clenched his jaw any harder, his back teeth were going to break.

Michael put his arm along the back of Will's seat as he reversed out of the parking space. He shifted into drive and headed out of the garage, saluting the guard at the gate as they passed.

"What a shitty day," he said, slipping on a pair of dark sunglasses. "You got kids?"

"No," Will said, thinking this was the second time Michael Ormewood had asked him that question. Maybe Angie had told him Will wouldn't have kids. He had a mental image of her and Ormewood splayed out in bed, post-coital bliss turning into a game of telling secrets. Would Angie do that? Would she betray Will like that?

"I can't imagine what Phil's thinking right now," Michael said. "If something ever happened to Tim, I'd feel like my heart had been ripped out of my chest. He's a part of me, you know?"

"I can see that."

"What about a wife?" Michael asked. "You married?"

Will turned to look at him, trying to figure out where he was going with these questions. "No," he said.

"Seeing somebody?"

Will bristled, but he tried to control it. "No."

"Gina," Michael said, oblivious. "She works at Piedmont in the ER. What's that they always say about cops? They either marry nurses or hookers?"

Considering Michael had left his last assignment under such a dark cloud, Will thought it was pretty dangerous for him to be joking about prostitutes.

Will began, "That Polaski woman . . ." He tried to think of something an asshole would say about a woman. All he could come up with was, "She's pretty attractive."

Michael looked surprised, like he might not have considered Will had a penis. "Yeah," he said. "Listen—man to man—I'd stay away from that one."

"Why's that?"

"She's got a temper. Know what I mean? She looks real sweet, but inside, she's a class-A ball-breaker."

Will leaned his elbow on the door, stared out the side window.

So, he *had* slept with her.

Michael changed the subject. "I'm sorry I kind of lost my shit yesterday when I saw Cynthia. I've been doing Homicide for a while now, but you never expect something like that to happen, to actually know the person."

Will counted the telephone poles, saw the billboards and street signs in a blur of letters that would never make sense at this speed. "Yeah."

"I've gotta tell you, I'll never be able to do this job the same way again. Notify people, I mean. Puts it in a whole new light when you know the person involved, know the victim and the parent and all."

"I imagine so."

"Did you get a chance to look at that Monroe file?"

"I skimmed through it," Will lied, relying on what Angie had told him about the prostitute. "You arrested her a few times when you were in Vice."

Michael finally seemed to feel the tension in the air. He gave Will a sideways glance. "Yeah," he admitted. "Polaski told me that yesterday. I'd forgotten all about it. Those sweeps. You ever work Vice?" Will managed to shake his head. "You can go through a hundred of 'em in a week. It's all chasing your tail, no pun intended. You lock 'em up and they're out on the street an hour later."

"You never dealt with her pimp before? Baby G?"

Michael shrugged. "Not that I remember. These guys grow up so fast. One minute they're a little kid skipping school, the next they're toting a nine-mil and running everything from pussy to meth." He shrugged again. Maybe that was where Angie picked up the gesture. "Baby G might know me from before, but he didn't let on if he did. You think he's got something to do with the murders? I never checked his alibi for Sunday night."

"He was with us when Cynthia was killed," Will reminded him.

"I'm sure he's got plenty of soldiers to do his dirty work."

Will nodded.

"I need to look through my Vice files. I'll take them home tonight."

Will felt the need to offer, "I can help, if you like."

"No." His tone had been sharp, but he softened it with an explanation. "You know how it is. You only put down half the information in the reports. The rest you keep in your head so they can't trap you when you're on the stand, say you wrote one thing when you meant another."

"Right." Will stole another glance at Michael Ormewood. He was not as tall as Will but he had the usual dark good looks and a solid build Angie was always attracted to. He obviously didn't work out as much as Will, but he hadn't gone to seed, either. Maybe he had played football in high school. Will had loved football, but he'd been too ashamed to join any team sports that would require him to strip down in the locker room. Ormewood had probably been some kind of all-star, the captain of the team, the one all the other guys looked up to.

Will took another deep breath and let it out slowly.

This was really great. One stray thought about Angie sleeping with Ormewood and suddenly Will was reliving his failed high school sports dreams. Will knew that Angie would never tell any man much about anything. Meeting new conquests was a game she played, a game where she got to reinvent herself. Telling them the truth about her past would spoil her fun. If she wanted to be with someone serious, someone who knew her inside and out, she would stay with Will.

Michael tapped his fingers on the steering wheel. "Greer told me I could take some personal time. I don't know. Sitting on my hands isn't something I'm good at. I'd never forgive myself if I missed something and this guy took another life. He could be out there right now looking for a new victim."

"Yeah," Will agreed, realizing that in his personal quest to emasculate himself he'd failed to notice that Michael was talking to him as an equal rather than an adversary.

Michael drove through the Homes, passing the same

teenagers on their bikes that Will had noticed the day be-fore.

"We should bust them up," Michael said. "They should be in school."

"Why wasn't Cynthia in school?" Will questioned.

"I dunno. Maybe she wasn't feeling well."

"What's her attendance record like?"

"What's that got to do with anything?"

"Her father was out of town most of the time. She was alone a lot without parental supervision."

"Gina and I did the best we could looking out for her." He had taken Will's words as a condemnation.

"Did your mother-in-law often see her at home during the day?"

"You'd have to ask Barbara that," Michael said, parking the car in front of building nine.

"Do you mind if I do?"

"Barbara and I are pretty close, and she never men-tioned anything to me about Cynthia being home. I'll ask her, okay? But I think that's a dead end. Cyn was a good kid. She got great grades in school, never got in trouble. Phil always said she was an angel."

"You seem to know a lot about her."

Michael looked at his hands on the steering wheel. When he spoke, it seemed he was confiding in Will. "We tried to look out for her. Phil was never home. His wife ran off with some loser about six years ago, never looked back. He did his best, but I dunno..." He turned to Will. "Your best isn't good enough when you have a kid—you have to do better. You change your priorities, don't drive a new car every two years, don't wear expensive suits and go out to dinner and movies all the time. You sacrifice."

"Phil didn't do that?"

"I think I've said enough," Michael told him, taking the key out of the ignition. "He's got enough in his life right now without his friends talking about him behind his back."

Michael opened the car door. He said, "The BMW's gone," meaning the pimp was probably not home.

Will followed him to the grandmother's flat, which was on the bottom floor. They knocked several times but even though they could hear a television blaring inside and the old woman laughing along with the studio audience, no one answered.

Will asked, "Monroe's apartment is on the top floor?"

"Yeah," Michael said. "I wouldn't take the elevator if I were you."

Will followed Michael up the stairs. Except for the grandmother's apartment, the building was quiet. People were either at work or sleeping off last night, and the only sound was their footsteps making scuffing noises against the stairs.

Toward the top, Will slowed his pace, stopping where Aleesha Monroe's body had been found. Blood stained the stairs, despite the fact that someone had obviously tried to clean up the marks.

"She died here," Michael told him, stopping on the landing to catch his breath.

Will knelt to look at the pattern, the bloody ghost of the handprint climbing the stairs. The crime scene photos were bad enough, but there was something eerie about being in this place where the woman had died.

"I don't think he meant for her to die," Michael said.

Will looked up, thinking the man had said this at least twice before. "Why is that?"

"She rolled onto her back." He indicated the outline

where Monroe had lain. "The blood must have pooled and she choked to death." He waited a second, looking down at the bloody stairs. "It's sad, but it happens."

Will didn't think he'd ever had a case where this had happened before, but he nodded as if people accidentally died this way all of the time. He asked, "What do you think happened?"

Michael squinted up the stairs as if he could see it all unfolding. "I'm guessing they were in the apartment when some kind of dispute broke out. The john left and maybe she didn't want him to. They scuffled here," he indicated the steps, "then it went bad."

"Was the door locked or unlocked when the first cop got here?"

"Unlocked."

Will played the scene in his mind, thinking Michael's scenario was as likely as any. "Do you have the key?"

"Yep." Michael took a plastic bag out of his pocket. He unrolled it and showed Will a key with a red tag. "It was in her purse."

"Did you find anything else?"

"Makeup, couple of dollars and some lint."

"Let's go," Will said, continuing up the stairs. He could feel the hair on the back of his neck standing up as they got closer to the top. Will had never been one to believe in ghosts and goblins, but there was no denying that a murder scene had a certain feel to it, an energy that told you violent death had occurred.

"Here we go," Michael said, slicing the yellow police tape with the edge of the key. He unlocked the door. "After you."

Aleesha Monroe had obviously not been rich, but from the looks of her apartment, she had taken great care of her few nice things. Besides the small bathroom, there were only two rooms in the apartment, a bedroom in one and a kitchen/living room space in the other. What struck Will was that the place was surprisingly clean. No dirty dishes were decaying in the sink and the same stink that hung out in the hall didn't seem to permeate the walls.

Will asked Michael, "This is how it looked when you got here?"

"Yep."

Michael's team had already tossed the place two nights ago. The fact that he now stood back by the door, leaning against the frame, indicated clearly that he thought this was a waste of time.

Will ignored this message as he walked carefully around the room, looking for anything unusual. The kitchen was an efficiency with a single cabinet and only two drawers for storage. One was used for silverware, the other contained the usual household items that found their way into the junk drawer: a couple of pens, an array of receipts and a ring of keys that probably had outlived the doors they opened.

He stopped at a plant by the window. The soil was bone dry; the plant was dead. The glass table by the couch was sparkling clean, the matching coffee table just as pristine. There was a neat stack of magazines beside an ashtray that had obviously been wiped out. There didn't seem to be any dust on the floor or for that matter any indication that an addict had lived here. Will had been into many a junkie's home and knew how they lived. Heroin was especially bad. Smack heads were like sick animals who had stopped grooming, and their surroundings generally reflected this.

Will saw telltale signs of black dusting powder on the doorjambs and windowsills, but he still asked, "Did you find many fingerprints?"

"About sixty thousand," Michael said.

"Not on the glass tables?"

Michael was looking out into the hall as if he'd heard a noise. "She must'a brought her johns up here. There was enough DNA on the sheets to clone an entire village."

Will walked into the bedroom, making a mental note to follow up on the question. He checked the drawers, noting that the clothes hadn't been rifled through. The closet was packed with clothes, an old Hoover tucked in between boxes of shoes. The vacuum's bag was empty. The scene-of-crime techs had removed it for closer examination. They had probably taken the sheets off the bed, too. Monroe's mattress was bare, a bloodstain flowering out from the center.

Michael stood in the bedroom door. He obviously thought he could anticipate Will's next question. "Menstrual blood, Pete says. She must have been on the rag."

Will was silent, continuing his search in the bedroom, still thinking about the clean glass tables. He could hear Michael walking around in the other room, impatient. Will followed the black dusting powder where the crime scene techs had looked for fingerprints on all the usual surfaces: the edge of the nightstand, the doorknobs, the small chest that held mostly T-shirts and jeans. They must have checked the tables in the other room. The absence of dust indicated that the glass had been clean of prints.

Michael asked, "Did you see the story in the paper this morning?"

"No," Will admitted. For obvious reasons, he got most of his news from the television.

"Monroe was the second story after some scandal over at the hospital."

Will got on his hands and knees, checking under the bed. "Did you release her name yet?"

"Can't until we find next of kin." Michael added, "We're holding back on the tongue thing, too."

Will sat back on his heels, looking around the room. "She didn't list her parents on any of her arrests?"

"Just Baby G."

He opened the drawer in the bedside table. Empty. "No address book?"

"She didn't have a telephone—no landline, no cell."

"That's odd."

"Everything costs money. Either you got it or you don't." Michael was still watching Will. "Mind if I ask you what you think you're gonna find?"

"I just want a feel of the place," Will answered, though he was getting plenty more than that. Either Aleesha Monroe was the Mr. Clean of hookers or someone had taken great care to scrub down her apartment.

Will stood and walked back into the main room. Michael was at the front door again, arms folded across his chest. Why hadn't he noticed that the apartment had been cleaned? Even an armchair detective with nothing but television cop shows for training would have picked up on this detail.

Will said, "Sink's been scrubbed clean." The sponge was still damp and when he held it to his nose, he caught the strong odor of bleach.

"You sniffing that for a reason?" Michael asked. He was watching Will carefully, no longer casually leaning against the doorjamb.

Will dropped the sponge back in the sink. "She have any money stashed in here?" he asked, purposefully avoiding Michael's question.

"It's in the log."

Will hadn't had time to decipher the scene-of-crime log, so he said, "Run it down for me."

Michael was obviously irritated by the request, but he still provided, "She had some cash in a sock shoved down the back of the couch. There was about eight bucks in it. Her kit was in a metal box on the kitchen counter. Syringes, foil, a lighter, the usual."

"No drugs?"

"Residue in the bottom of the tin, but nothing we found."

"So, she had to work."

"Yeah," Michael said. "She didn't have a choice."

Will turned back to the bathroom. The shower curtain was a spotless dark blue, as were the matching rug on the floor and cover on the toilet seat. He lifted the rug, noting that the linoleum floor had been swept.

Thirty-two minutes for a cruiser to show up. The killer had counted on the slow response time, taken advantage of it so he could clean up after himself. There was no sign of panic here, no rush to cover his tracks and get out. The guy knew what he was doing.

"Well?" Michael asked. He was standing outside the bathroom, watching Will.

"She kept a clean house," Will said, opening the medicine cabinet. Besides the usual Tylenol and toothpaste, it was pretty much as he would have expected. He said, "No condoms here."

"I thought we'd established that the perp brought them."

"Maybe," Will answered, thinking that he trusted Angie more on the matter. He stopped in the doorway because the detective was blocking his way. "Is something wrong?"

"No." Michael took a step back. "I just get the feeling you're checking my work."

"I told you I'm not," Will said, though being honest, he

was beginning to question Michael's skills as a detective. A blind man could see the apartment had been scrubbed top to bottom.

Will asked, "Did you already call in the cleaners?"

"What?"

"I saw the stairs had been scrubbed," Will told him. "I assumed you called in a crew to clean up."

"Must have been one of the tenants," Michael answered, walking toward the door. "Tape wasn't cut and I didn't call anybody. I can ask Leo."

"That's fine. I was just curious." Will pulled the door closed. He was twisting the key in the lock just as a loud bang rang through the stairwell, followed by a child's scream.

Will passed Michael on the stairs, grabbing the banister as he swung across the landing. He could hear more screaming, a second child yelling, "Help!" as he bolted down the last set of stairs and threw open the door.

"Help!" a small boy screamed as he ran across the parking lot, a girl chasing him.

"Oh, for fuck..." Michael breathed. He was panting from the run. "Jesus Christ," he exhaled, bending at the waist.

The boy darted onto a small patch of grass that had the mailboxes for the building. He circled once before the girl caught up with him. She was sitting on his back by the time Will reached them.

"You give that back!" she demanded, delivering a sharp kidney punch to her captive.

"Jazz!" the boy screamed.

"Hold up," Will said. "Come on." Gently, he took the girl's arm.

She jerked away from him, snapping, "This ain't none of your business, fool."

"All right," Will said, kneeling down to talk to the boy. "You all right?"

The boy rolled onto his back. Will guessed the wind had been knocked out of him. He helped the boy sit up, knowing that would help. The kid was probably nine or ten, but the clothes he was wearing seemed better suited for a grown man. Even his shoes were too large for his feet.

Will asked the girl, "Tell me what happened here."

"He took my—" She stopped as Michael joined them, her mouth open, eyes wide with fear as she stared at Michael.

"It's all right," Michael told her, holding out his hands. The girl hadn't pegged Will but Michael might as well have worn a sign around his neck that read "cop." She had probably been taught at her mother's knee that you don't talk to the police.

She stepped back, reaching for her brother and yanking him up by one arm. "You get away from us. We ain't got nothing to say to you."

Michael indicated the boy. "This your brother?" He smiled at the boy. "What's your name, buddy? I've got a son about your age."

"Don't talk to him," the girl cautioned.

"We're not here to bang you up," Will assured her. She looked about thirteen or fourteen, but the way her little fists were balled up told him he didn't want to be sitting on the ground if she got angry enough to start swinging.

He told her, "We're looking into something bad that happened here Sunday night."

"Leesha," the boy said, just as the girl clamped her hand around his mouth. He squirmed impatiently. Obviously, the boy had something to say that his sister did not want them to hear.

"What's your name?" Michael asked.

"We ain't got nothing to say," the girl repeated. "We didn't see nothing on Sunday night. We didn't see nothing. Ain't that right, Cedric?"

"You said—" the boy tried, but his mouth was covered again before he could get anything else out.

Michael lowered his voice, asking Will, "Which one do you want?"

Will offered, "Your choice."

"You sure?"

Will nodded.

"All right." Michael raised his voice. "Girl, this is the last time I'm going to ask this. What's your name?"

She stood defiant, but answered, "Jasmine."

"That's a pretty name," Michael tried. When she didn't soften, his voice became authoritative again. "Come with me."

"The fuck you say."

Michael exchanged a look with Will. "That's quite a mouth you've got on you, little girl."

"I ain't your little girl!"

"Sweetheart, do you really want to make this hard?" Michael put his hands on his hips. The gesture would have been almost feminine if not for the fact that his jacket swung open, revealing his holstered nine-millimeter. Typical cop move: scare them early and scare them often. It worked. Fear flashed in her eyes, and she looked down at the ground, all of the fight gone out of her.

Michael actually winked at Will, as if to say, "That's how you do it." He asked Jasmine, "Is your mother inside?"

"She at work."

"Who's watching you?"

She mumbled something.

"What's that?"

She glanced at the boy. "I asked if Cedric gonna be okay."

"He's your brother?" Michael asked.

She hesitated, then nodded.

"He's going to be fine once you and I figure out who's supposed to be watching you and why you aren't in school." He put his hand on the girl's shoulder and led her back toward the building. "You shouldn't be running around screaming like that."

She mumbled something again that Will couldn't hear. Michael laughed, then told her, "We'll see about that."

Will watched them go into the building, then turned back to the boy. "Cedric?" he asked. "That's your name, right?"

The boy nodded.

"Come with me." He held out his hand but the child gave an ugly frown.

"I ain't no kid, bitch."

Will sighed. He leaned against the mailboxes, tried to make this go a little easier. "I just need to ask you some questions."

Cedric echoed his sister. "I ain't got nothing to say to you." His lower lip went out in an exaggerated pout and he crossed his stick-thin arms over his chest in an imitation of a gangster. Will would have laughed but for the fact that the kid probably had more access to weapons than most cops did.

"Hey," Will began, trying another tactic. "What did the number zero say to the number eight?"

Cedric shrugged, but Will could tell he was curious.

" 'Nice belt.' "

Cedric's mouth went up in a smile before he caught himself. "That was lame, man."

"I know," Will admitted. "I'm just trying to get you to talk to me."

"Nothin' to talk about."

"Did you know Aleesha?"

His bony shoulders went up in another shrug, but he was still a child and hadn't yet mastered the ability to hide his emotions.

"Aleesha was a friend of yours?" Will guessed. "Maybe she looked out for you?"

Again, the shoulders went up.

"I asked around about her, you know? Asked some friends about her. Seemed to me that she was a really nice lady."

Cedric stubbed his toe against the concrete. "Maybe."

"Did she look out for you?"

"My granny told me to keep away because of what Leesha did."

"Yeah," Will said. "I guess Aleesha didn't have a very good job. But she was nice to you, wasn't she?"

This time, he nodded.

"It's hard to lose a friend."

"My cousin Ali died last year. Got shot in his bed."

Will knelt down in front of the boy. "Did you see something that night, Cedric?"

His eyes were red with tears he obviously didn't want to fall.

"You can tell me, Cedric. I'm not going to hurt you. I'm not going to get you into any trouble downtown. All I care about is finding out who killed Aleesha, because she was a good lady. You know she was a good lady. She looked out for you and now it's time you looked out for her."

"I can't tell you nothing."

Will parsed the sentence. "Can't or won't?" He thought of something. "Did somebody threaten you? Maybe Baby G?"

Cedric shook his head.

"I'm just trying to find out who hurt your friend." Will tried, "You can trust me."

The child's gaze turned hard, and the gangster face came back. "Trust ain't a word I know."

Will hadn't grown up in the Homes, but as a kid, he had confided in plenty of adults who wouldn't—or couldn't—help him. There was no telling who was good or bad. A shiny badge did not necessarily help point the way.

"You see this?" Will asked, putting his finger to the side of his face, touching the scar that twisted its way down his neck. "This is what I got once for telling on somebody. I wasn't that much older than you."

Cedric tilted his head, looked at the scar. "Did it hurt?"

"At first," Will admitted. "But then I couldn't feel it anymore, and when I woke up, I was in a hospital."

"Were you sick?"

"I lost a lot of blood."

"Were you going to die?"

Will had wanted to, but he had told the story to draw out Cedric, not confess his darkest secrets. "The doctors took care of me."

The boy stared at the scar a moment longer before he nodded his approval. On the streets, a near-death experience was a badge of honor, especially if it came by dangerous means.

Will reached into his pocket and took out a business card. "This is my cell phone number, okay? You think of anything, or just need to talk, you call me. All right? It doesn't even have to be about Aleesha."

Cedric glanced at Will's scar again, then quickly palmed the card in case anyone was watching. "Can I go now?"

"Yeah," Will said. "But you call me, okay? Call me day or night."

"Right." He darted off, his hand trailing down the row of mailboxes as he headed for the street.

Will straightened, turning around to see Michael walking across the parking lot again, this time without Jasmine. As the other man got closer, Will saw that he had a scratch down the side of his face. Blood was trickling into his collar.

Will looked back at the building, then at Michael. "You okay?"

"She hit me. Can you believe that? What is she, twelve?" He shook his head, more shocked than angry. "I was following her up the stairs and before I knew it, she bolted. I went after her, grabbed her leg, and the little thing turned around and whapped me across the face with her fist." He slung out his own fist to illustrate. "Good thing she punched me like a girl, huh?" Will had never understood that phrase. He'd only ever had one woman punch him, and Angie always put her shoulder into it.

Michael was staring back up at the building. A curtain twitched, and he said, "That's her place. Third floor up."

"Is her mother home?"

"Shit," he said, his tone asking if Will was actually that stupid. Michael touched the gash on his cheek then looked at the blood on the tips of his fingers. "I guess her fingernail caught me or something. Does it look bad?"

"Not too bad," Will lied. He took out his handkerchief and offered it to Michael. "Do you want to go get her or something?"

"What? Throw the cuffs on her and get my picture on the nightly news for roughing up a child? No thank you. Besides, she wouldn't talk to us now if her hair was on fire." He sat on the curb with a groan. Will didn't know what else to do but join him.

Michael laughed again. "Christ, she got me." He looked at the dots of blood on the handkerchief. "I should've let you handle her. Maybe she would have responded to a softer touch." He realized what he'd said. "Hey, no offense—"

"Don't worry about it."

"Still," Michael said, folding the handkerchief in two, then pressing it to his cheek again. He said, "I didn't know people still carried these."

"Old habit," Will admitted. Ms. Flannery had made all the boys in the state home carry handkerchiefs in their pockets. Will had never questioned the practice, just assumed that it was something normal boys did.

Michael asked, "You get anything from her brother?"

"Cedric's not talking."

"You think he knows anything?"

Will did, but for some reason he felt the need to lie. "No. He doesn't know anything."

"You sure?"

"Positive," Will said. "He's got a big mouth. He would've talked."

"You're lucky he didn't kick you in the balls or something." Michael folded the handkerchief again and started to hand it back to Will. "Sorry," he said, taking it back. "I'll get my wife to clean this for you."

"That's okay." Will took the cloth, feeling uncomfortable at the prospect of Michael Ormewood's wife doing his laundry.

"Man," Michael said, resting his elbows on his knees, dropping his head. "I gotta say, the girl reminds me a lot of Cynthia. Got that same fire in her eyes, you know?"

"That so?" Will asked, thinking Michael was painting a very different picture of the neighbor than the one he had offered before.

"Cyn was a good kid, don't get me wrong about that. It's just she had that rebellious streak, too. Your parents divorced?"

Will was caught off-guard by the question. His face must have shown it.

"None of my business, right?" Michael rubbed the back of his neck, looking up at the building again. "My father died when I was about her age. Maybe that's why I kind of took care of her."

Will wasn't sure which girl the man was talking about now.

"I was just thinking that you get a little rebellious streak when you're a teenager and that it gets worse if your parents split up at the same time. You start to push things, right? Trying to test the limits, see how far you can go before they pull you back. My mom yanked me back by the collar— we're talking Wile E. Coyote yanked. She was always looking out for me, always using the heavy hand. Kids today, their parents don't do that. They don't want to be the bad guy."

Will guessed, "Cynthia was a little wilder than Phil knew?"

"Maybe a little wilder than I knew," he admitted. "Or than I wanted to know."

"That sounds like an honest mistake."

Michael smiled at Will. "There was this girl I knew back in high school. God, she was gorgeous. Wouldn't give me the time of day. My cousin hooked her. He was just this scrawny-ass kid, didn't have a hair anywhere on his body except for his head." Michael glanced at him. "You know the type I'm talking about?"

Will nodded because it seemed expected of him.

"Total pud puller," Michael continued. "And he ends up with this beautiful girl. Not just that, but she's letting him touch her, going to let him do her." His laugh was different this time. "I was usually the one who scored, you know? Not him." He turned, facing Will. "I'm thinking I shouldn't have chased her."

Will was confused. "Jasmine?"

Michael turned back, looking at the building. "I should've just let her go, but there was this second where... you know how when your brain thinks of about a billion things at the same time? I kept thinking about Cynthia running, and how she tripped over that fence. I should've fixed that fence last year. I should have fucking fixed that fence." He put his fists to his eyes. "Oh, God."

Will was at a loss. An hour ago, he had wanted to pummel this man to the ground for sleeping with Angie. Now he just felt sorry for him.

Michael continued, "That's what I was thinking about when Jasmine ran—Cynthia running across our yard. And without even thinking, I grabbed her foot to stop her. You know—so she wouldn't get hurt like Cynthia did." He turned to Will. "I think I need that time off Greer was talking about. This is hitting me harder than I thought it would. Do you mind?"

Will was surprised by the question, but readily agreed. "It's fine."

"I'm sorry to let you down like this. I sound like a freaking woman. Hell, I'm acting like one, too. All this crazy talk; you must think I'm some kind of psycho or something." He shook his head again. "I think a couple of days is what I need. Just some time to get over this, come to terms with what happened."

"It's okay," Will said, thinking he was glad that Michael had come to this conclusion on his own. It was clear now that the other man had been fighting to hold it together all morning. "You do what you need to do."

"I just need to be kept in the loop. I need to know what's going on. Would you mind that? I don't want to step on your toes, buddy. I just can't be out there cut off from everything. I know you're gonna catch this fucker, but I need to know what's going on with the case."

Will wasn't happy about it, but he offered, "Call whenever you want."

"Thank you," Michael said. Will heard the relief in the other man's voice, read the gratitude in his eyes. "Thank you."

CHAPTER TWENTY-SIX

John was so exhausted that he almost missed his bus stop. He bolted up from the seat, calling, "Wait!" as the driver started to close the door.

He practically fell onto the sidewalk, his body feeling as if his muscles had been jackhammered. Art had asked for a volunteer to work late and John had gladly raised his hand, thinking he'd be better off having something to occupy his mind other than Joyce and the mess he had gotten himself caught up in. He couldn't even close his eyes without thinking about that little blonde girl in Michael's backyard. Last night, he had been shivering so hard that he woke himself up. Sweat covered his body and he had started keening like a child, rocking himself back and forth until he fell back into a fitful sleep.

Art's overtime job was the kind of shitwork you wouldn't ask your worst enemy to do: cleaning out a clog in the main canister of the vacuum system. The tank was buried underground and designed to hold what seemed like a million gallons of carpet fuzz, Cheerios and what smelled like sour candy gone bad—all the debris they vacuumed out of cars before sending them through the washer. John had barely fit through the opening, and when he had gotten inside, he'd guessed the tank was maybe ten feet wide and eight feet round, more like a coffin than he wanted to think about.

Art had given him a flashlight and a pair of rubber gloves. The battery in the light had lasted about thirty minutes. The gloves had stuck together before he uncovered the intake. John had stuck his bare hand up into the grimy pipe and pulled out a chunk of what felt like human hair. He thought about the flecks of skin and snot that the average body sloughed off on a daily basis and gagged up his banana sandwich before he could make it back to fresh air.

"You are some kind of trooper," Art had told him. The man had looked at John's ashen face, seen the vomit on his shirt and shoved a fifty in his hand. Fifty dollars for less than two hours' work. John would have jumped back into his own vomit if Art had offered to double it.

The fresh air felt good as he walked back to his room at the flophouse. There was always a smell on the street, no matter the weather or the time of day. John had come to associate the odor with poverty. His lungs were probably absorbing it, carcinogens clinging to the insides like the hair clinging to a vacuum tank.

"Hey, cowboy."

John looked up to find Martha Lam sitting on the front stoop of the house. She was in head-to-toe black leather and her makeup was heavier than usual. He wanted to ask the parole officer something flip, like if a date had stood her up, but he said instead, "Hello, Ms. Lam."

She stood, holding her arms out at her sides as she did a little turn. "I'm all dressed up for your random inspection."

He didn't know what to say. "You look nice" seemed forward, something that might be construed as flirting.

He settled on "Yes, ma'am," opening the door and standing aside so she could go in first.

"Got Mr. George back in Bosticks this morning," she told him.

"Who?"

"Your buddy from upstairs."

John didn't know who she was talking about. Then he did. "He's not my buddy," he told her, and she gave him a look that said he had better check his tone. "I'm sorry," he apologized. "It's been a long day. I didn't expect you to be here."

"That's why they call them random."

There were thirteen stairs up to his floor, and John felt like he had to practically drag himself up each one. The truth was that he hadn't really slept since he had followed Michael to Grady Homes two days ago and found out what his cousin was doing. The black woman's terrified screams still echoed in his head. John was reminded of his own screams when Zebra started going at him that first night at Coastal. They were almost exactly the same.

John unlocked the dead bolt and pushed open his door. The first thing he noticed was that the window was cracked open about six inches, the construction-paper shade ripped at the bottom. The other thing he noticed was the smell. It took him a couple of seconds to realize the odor was coming off of his own body. It was fear.

"You've changed the place around." Ms. Lam looped her purse around the doorknob so she could free her hands. "Like what you've done with it." She started going through his clothes, but John could only stare at his bed, the way it had been angled out from the corner instead of left flat against the wall like he always had it.

Whoever had broken in wanted John to know he'd been here.

Ms. Lam was lifting up the cooler, checking inside. She said, "Your urine test came back okay."

John could not answer. The photograph of his mother

was altered. Someone had ripped it down the center, taken John out of the picture.

"John?"

His head snapped around to look at her.

"It was clean," she said, then pointed to the bed. "Want to lift that for me?"

He leaned down to lift his mattress. His fingertips made contact with something solid, something cold.

John froze, one hand under the mattress, the other on top.

"John?" Ms. Lam asked. She clapped her hands together to spur him on. "Let's go, sweetheart. I don't have all night."

Saliva fell out of his open mouth. His chest constricted. He started to shake.

"John?" Ms. Lam was beside him, her hand on his back. "Come on, cowboy. What's going on?"

"S-s-sick," he stuttered, tremors wracking his body. He felt his bowels loosen and was terrified they would let go.

"Let's just sit you down," she soothed, guiding him to sit down on the bed. She pressed the back of her hand to his forehead. "You feel real clammy. You're not getting sick on me, are you, boy?"

"I'm ..." John couldn't form a sentence. "I'm ..." He looked at the open window, the six inches of space.

"You want some water?"

He nodded, quick up and down jerks of his head.

"I've got some bottled water in my purse."

She turned her back to him to get her purse off the door and in one desperate motion he pulled the knife out from under the mattress and tossed it toward the six inches of open space.

Ms. Lam turned back toward him as if in slow motion.

He held his breath, his peripheral vision catching a glint of metal as the folding knife sailed toward the window.

Instinctively, he coughed, leaning over, hoping to muffle the sound when the knife hit the window sash and fell back into the room.

"Here you go," Ms. Lam said, twisting the bottle open. "Take a couple of drinks."

John did as he was told, then chanced a look down as he wiped his brow, scanning the carpet below the window. Empty. The space was empty.

"That's good, now," Ms. Lam said, patting his back. "You just had a bad spell, didn't you?"

He nodded, unable to answer.

"Let's look under the mattress now." She shook her head when he offered her the water. "You keep that. I've got plenty more in my car."

John stood up, his legs still shaky. He looked again at the window, the empty space on the carpet beneath it. The knife had to have gone out the window. There was no other explanation.

When John had propped the mattress against the wall, Ms. Lam requested, "Box spring, too."

There was no roach under the bed this time, but the carpet was still caked with grime. John was so nervous about the knife that he could have fallen to the floor.

"Go on and put it back." She thumbed through the books on the table beside his bed. If she saw the torn photograph of his mother, she didn't say. "You finish your book? *Tess of the D'Urbervilles?*"

"Uh," John said, surprised by the question. "Yes, ma'am."

"Tell me, John, who christened Tess's baby?"

He stared at her expertly made-up eyes. She blinked. "John?"

It was a trick question. She was trying to trick him. "Tess did," he finally said, and even though he knew he was right, he was terrified of being wrong. "The priest wouldn't do it, so she did it herself."

"Good." She smiled, then looked around the room again. "No luck finding another place?"

She had asked this once before. "Should I be looking?"

Ms. Lam tucked her hands into her narrow hips. "I don't know, John. Looks like you've outgrown this place."

"Well, I—"

"There's a house over on Dugdale. A Mr. Applebaum runs it. I'll put in a call for you tonight if you like."

"Yeah," he said. She hadn't offered to help him before and he was worried that she was now. Still, he said, "Thank you," and, "that'd be nice."

"You move real soon now, hear? As in tomorrow."

He didn't understand the rush, but he said, "Okay."

She pulled her purse over her shoulder, digging inside for her keys. "And John?"

"Yes, ma'am?"

"Whatever you just threw out the window when my back was turned?" She looked up from her purse, flashing him a cat's smile. "Make sure it doesn't follow you to your new place."

He opened his mouth but she shook her head to stop him.

"I don't like it when somebody tries to set up one of my charges," she told him. "When you go back in—and trust me, sixty-five percent of your fellow parolees tell me that you will—it's gonna be because *you* screwed it up, not because some dipshit, Barney Fife, Atlanta cop has a hard-on for you."

His heart was in his throat. Michael had called her. He

had found what John had left in the bottom of his toolbox and decided to do something about it. The only reason John wasn't in jail right now was because Ms. Lam played by the rules.

"Watch yourself, John." She pointed at him with her car keys. "And remember, hon, I'll be watching you, too."

CHAPTER TWENTY-SEVEN

8:48 PM

Betty's toenails clicked along the road as Will took her for her evening walk. He had tried to take the dog running their first day together, but ended up having to carry her most of the way. It had unnerved him the way she had adapted to the up and down jogging of her body, tongue lolling out, back legs tucked neatly into the palm of Will's hand, body pressed close to his chest as he tried to ignore the strange looks people were giving him.

Poncey-Highlands was a middle-of-the-road kind of neighborhood with its mixture of struggling artists, gay men and the occasional homeless person. From his back porch, Will could see the Carter Center, which housed President Carter's library, and Piedmont Park was a short jog away. On the weekends, Ponce de Leon took him straight up to Stone Mountain Park, where he rode his bike, hiked the trails or just sat back and enjoyed the sunrise as it peered over the largest chunk of exposed granite in North America.

As beautiful as the north Georgia mountains had been, Will had missed the familiarity of home, knowing instinctively where everything was, the areas that were safe, the restaurants that looked shady on the outside but had the best food and service in the city. He loved the diversity, the fact that there was a Mennonite church across from a rainbow-colored hippie commune at the end of his street. The way the homeless people went through your trash and yelled at you if there wasn't anything good inside. Atlanta had always been his town, and if Amanda Wagner knew how happy he was to be back, she would have jerked him up to the hills faster than he could say, "chicken-fried steak."

"Hiya." A passing jogger flirted, his cut chest glistening in the evening moonlight. Having lived in a city with a large gay population for his entire life, Will had learned to take these casual passes as flattering rather than a challenge to his manhood. Of course, walking a six-pound dog on a hot pink leash (it was the only one he could find that was long enough) was asking for attention no matter where you lived.

Will smiled to himself at the thought of how ridiculous he must look, but his smile didn't last long as his brain returned to the topic that had been plaguing his thoughts for most of the day.

He was stalled in the case and the more he thought about it, the more his initial bad feelings about Michael Ormewood were amplified. The detective came off as an okay guy when he was right in front of you, but closer examination showed some flaws, the biggest being that he had used his job to force women to have sex with him. That was the one detail Will could not get past. Prostitutes weren't walking the streets for the great sex and stimulating conversation. They took money, and Will guessed you could construe that as consent, but there hadn't been any money exchanged when Michael had done it. He had used the power the badge gave him to control the women. That was rape in Will's mind.

Yet Will was having a hard time thinking of the guy he'd

spent most of the last two days with as a rapist. Father, husband, seemingly a well-respected cop, sure. But rapist? There were definitely two sides to the man, and the more Will thought about it, the less he was certain about either one of them.

Working with the GBI, most of Will's time was consumed with chasing down horrendous criminals, but if his stint in the mountains had taught him one thing, it was that people were very seldom either really good or really bad. In Blue Ridge, where poverty and plant closings and a strike at the local mine had practically crippled the small mountain community, the line between right and wrong had been blurred. Will had learned a lot up there, not just about human nature but about himself.

Region eight of the Georgia Bureau of Investigation was the largest district in the state, serving fourteen counties and stretching all the way to the Tennessee as well as North Carolina state line. The men Will met at the northwest Georgia field office were pretty callous about the locals, as if they were above the people they were meant to be serving. Will's chief was called "Yip" Gomez for reasons Will had never been able to determine, and the man had jokingly told Will the first time they met to give up on trying to enjoy any of the local talent. "I've already had all the ladies who still have their own teeth," he had laughed. "Slim pickin's, my boy. Slim pickin's."

Will's face must have betrayed his thoughts—Angie always said he had more estrogen than was good for him— because Yip had given Will every crap assignment in the district after that. He'd been totally excluded from the sting operation that resulted in the biggest bust in the office's history. Working with the locals, Yip had helped break up a cock-fighting enterprise that reached into three different states and twelve counties. The case had implicated a neighboring town's mayor, who'd had his own La-Z-Boy ringside so he wouldn't miss any of the action. Even though the tip-off had come from a bunch of angry wives who were pissed off at their husbands for gambling away their paychecks, that still did not take away from the glory of the sting operation. Yip and the boys had celebrated at the Blue Havana on 515 that night while Will had been stuck in his car, casing an abandoned chicken farm that had reportedly been turned into a meth lab. Not that he wanted to drink with these men, but the point was he hadn't been invited.

Though he was always left out of the more glamorous busts, Will liked to think that what he did up in the mountains was important work. Meth was a nasty drug. It turned people into subhumans, made them leave their kids on the side of the road, open their legs for anything that would get them high. Will had seen plenty of lives ruined by meth well before he got to Blue Ridge. He didn't need a primer to help him want to break apart every lab in his jurisdiction. The work was dangerous. The so-called chemists who made the compound were taking their lives into their own hands. A single spark could ignite the whole building. Dust from the manufacturing process could clog up your lungs like Play-Doh. Haz Mat had to be called in to clear the area before Will could go in and collect any evidence. The cleanup on these labs alone was bankrupting the local police and sheriff's departments and the state wasn't about to lend a helping hand.

Will sometimes thought that for a certain type of mountain dweller, meth was the new moonshine, a product they trafficked in to keep their kids clothed and fed. He had a hard time reconciling the junkies he saw on the streets of Atlanta with some of the everyday people brewing meth up in the hills. Not that Will was saying they were angels.

Some of them were awful, just plain trash doing whatever they could to finance their habit. Others weren't so black and white. Will would see them in the grocery store or at the local pizza place or coming out of church with their kids on Sundays. They generally didn't partake of the product. It was a job for them, a way—to some, the only way they saw—to make money. People were dying, lives were being ruined, but that wasn't their business.

Will didn't know how they could section things off so neatly, but in Michael Ormewood, he saw the same tendency. The detective did his job—by all accounts he did it well—but then there was this other part of him that made him hurt the very people he was supposed to be helping.

Betty made some business under a bush and Will leaned down, using a baggie to scoop it up. He dropped the bag into a trashcan as he made his way back toward the house. Will caught himself glancing into his neighbor's windows as he passed, wondering when the old woman would be back. As if she sensed his thoughts, Betty pulled at her leash, tugging him toward the driveway.

"All right," he soothed, using his key to open the front door. He knelt to unsnap her leash, and she skittered across the room, jumping onto the couch and ensconcing herself on the pillows. Every morning before he left for work, he propped the pillows up on the back of the couch and every evening Betty had managed to push them down to make herself a bed. He could have called it a throne, but that was an embarrassing thought for a grown man to have about a little dog.

Will went to his room and took off his jacket. He was unbuttoning his vest when the phone rang. At first, he didn't recognize the high-pitched voice on the phone.

"Slow down," Will said. "Who is this?"

"It's Cedric," the boy cried. "Jasmine's gone."

*   *   *

Cedric must have been waiting for Will, because the front door opened and the boy ran out of building nine as soon as Will pulled his car into the lot.

"You gotta do something," the boy demanded. His face was puffy from crying. Gone was the wannabe gangster from that morning. He was a scared little kid who was worried about his sister.

"It's going to be okay," Will told him, knowing the words meant nothing but feeling compelled to say them.

"Come on." Cedric took his hand and dragged him toward the building.

Will followed the boy up the three flights of stairs. On the landing, he was about to ask Cedric what was going on, but then he saw the old woman standing in the doorway.

She was in a faded purple housedress with matching socks that slouched down around her thick ankles. A cane was in one hand, a cordless telephone in the other. She wore glasses with black plastic rims and her hair stood out in disarray. A frown creased her face.

"Cedric," she said, her deep tone resonating through the long hallway. "What are you doing with that man?"

"He a cop, Granny. He gonna help."

"He *is* a cop," the old woman corrected, sounding like a schoolteacher. "And I doubt that very seriously."

Will was still holding Cedric's hand, but he used his other one to find the badge in his pocket. He took a step forward to show it to the woman. "Cedric told me that your granddaughter is missing."

She scrutinized the badge and the identification underneath. "You don't look much like a cop."

"No," Will admitted, tucking his ID back into his pocket. "I'm trying to learn to take that as a compliment."

"Cedric," the woman snapped. "Go clean your room."

"But, Gran—" She stopped him with a sharp look that sent him running.

The old woman opened the door wider and Will saw that her apartment was an exact duplicate of Aleesha Monroe's. The couch obviously served as a bed; a pillow, sheets and a blanket were neatly folded on the end. Two wingback chairs flanked the couch, slipcovers hiding obvious flaws underneath. The kitchen was clean but cluttered, dishes drying on a rack. Several pairs of underclothes hung from a laundry stand that was tucked into the corner. The bathroom door was open but the bedroom door was closed, a large poster of SpongeBob SquarePants taped to the outside.

"I'm Eleanor Allison," she informed him, hobbling toward the chair by the window. "I suppose you want to sit down?"

Will realized that his mouth had dropped open. Books were everywhere—some packed into flimsy-looking cases that looked ready to fall over, more stacked around the floor in neat piles.

"Are you surprised that a black woman can read?"

"No, I just—"

"You like to read yourself?"

"Yes," Will answered, thinking he was only telling a partial lie. For every three audiobooks he listened to, he made himself read at least one complete book. It was a miserable task that took weeks, but he made himself do it to prove that he could.

Eleanor was watching him, and Will tried to mend things. He guessed. "You were a teacher?"

"History," she told him. She rested her cane beside her leg and propped her foot on a small stool in front of the chair. He saw that her ankles were wrapped in bandages.

She explained, "Arthritis. Had it since I was eighteen years old."

"I'm sorry."

"Not your fault, is it?" She motioned him toward the chair opposite but he did not take a seat. "Tell me something, Mr. Trent. Since when does a special agent from the Georgia Bureau of Investigation give a hill of beans about a missing black girl?"

He was getting annoyed with her assumptions. "There weren't any white ones missing today, so we drew straws."

She gave him a sharp look. "You're not funny, young man."

"I'm not a racist pig, either."

She locked eyes with him for a moment, then nodded as if she'd made up her mind about him. "For goodness' sake, sit."

Will finally did as he was told, sinking so low into the old chair that his knees were practically around his ears.

He tried to get to the point. "Cedric called me."

"And how do you know Cedric?"

"I met him this morning. I was out here with a detective from the Atlanta Police Department investigating the death of the young woman who lived upstairs."

"Young woman?" she echoed. "She was forty if she was a day."

Will had heard Pete Hanson say as much during the autopsy, but hearing the old woman say it now somehow gave it more resonance. Aleesha Monroe had been at least twenty-five years older than the other victims. What had made the killer break from his usual target group?

Eleanor asked, "Why is the GBI mixed up in the death of a drug-addicted prostitute?"

"I'm with a division that reaches out to local law enforcement when help is needed."

"That's a very fine response, young man, but you've not really answered my question."

"You're right," he admitted. "Tell me when you realized that Jasmine was missing."

She studied him, her gaze steely, lips pursed. He forced himself not to look away, wondering how she had been in the classroom, if she was one of the types who let the dumb kids sit in the back or if she would have dragged him by the ear to the front row, yelling at him for not knowing the answer to the question on the board.

"All right," Eleanor decided. "I assumed Jasmine was in her room doing homework. When I called her for supper, she didn't come. I looked in the room and she wasn't there."

"What time was this?"

"Around five o'clock."

Will glanced at his watch, but the digital clock on the TV told him the actual time. "So, to your knowledge, she's been gone about five hours?"

"Are you going to tell me I need to wait another day before it matters?"

"I wouldn't drive all the way down here to tell you that, Ms. Allison. I would just call you on the phone."

"You think she's just another black girl run off with a man, but I'm telling you, I know that girl."

"She wasn't in school today," Will reminded her.

The old woman looked down. Will saw that her hands were like claws in her lap, arthritis twisting them into unusable lumps. "She was suspended for back-talking a teacher."

"Cedric, too?"

"This is turning adversarial," she noted, but she still kept talking. "I don't get around very easily, especially since they took my Vioxx away. Their mother has been incarcerated for more than half of Cedric's life. She's a heroin addict, just like Aleesha Monroe. The only difference is that my Glory got caught."

Will knew better than to interrupt.

"I laid down the law with Glory. Stayed up nights, followed her whenever she left the house. I was that child's *skin,* I was so close to her. She hated every minute of it—still hates me now—but I was her mother and that's what I was going to do. Same with them." With difficulty, she lifted a hand, indicating the closed bedroom door. Will saw a shadow move underneath and guessed that Cedric was listening.

Eleanor continued, "Glory pretty much let those two run wild. She didn't care what they did so long as she didn't get into trouble and could still keep putting that needle in her veins." The woman sighed, lost in her own memories. "Jasmine's as wild as Glory was, and I can't keep up with her. It took me five minutes to walk to that doorway tonight to see what Cedric was running on about."

Will wanted to say that he was sorry, but knew she would only correct him, remind him that her condition, the miserable way she must have spent her life trying to do the right thing while the walls fell in around her, was not his fault.

Eleanor told him, "Cedric was a baby when Glory lost custody." She managed to lean forward. "He's a smart boy, Mr. Trent. A smart boy with a future if I can keep him out of this mess long enough for him to grow." She pressed her lips together. "There's something he's not telling me. He loves his sister and she loves him—loves him like a mother because that's what she had to be when Glory was busy shooting that trash into her system." She paused. "I think I have more influence on him. And there's no denying Jasmine loves him. She doesn't want him mixed up in the life around here, the thugs and the gangbangers and the hoodlums. She embraces it, but she knows her baby brother can do better."

Will asked, "Has Jasmine run away before?"

"Twice, but always because there was a fight. We didn't fight yesterday. We haven't fought all week, for a change. Jasmine wasn't angry with me, or at least no more angry than any teenager is at the person in charge."

"Does she have a boyfriend?"

"Boy? He's fifteen years older than she is."

"What's his name?"

"Luther Morrison. He lives on Basil Avenue, about three miles from here, in the Manderley Arms. I already called him. He says she's not there." She explained, "Each time she ran away before, I called him. Both times he told me she was there. Luther pretends that he believes Jasmine is seventeen, but he knows that child's age just as sure as I'm sitting here and he'll do anything I say to keep me from calling the cops on him."

Will had to ask, "Why haven't you called the police on him? She's thirteen, he's almost thirty. That's statutory rape."

"Because I learned with her mother that a girl who's set on destroying herself will not be stopped. If I get this one arrested, she'll just go to the next one, and he'll be even worse than this Morrison, if that's possible."

"Gran?" Cedric asked. He was still in the bedroom, peeking around the edge of the door. "I finished cleaning the room."

"Come here, child." She reached out her arm for him and he came. She told Will, "I called the police as soon as I realized Jasmine was missing. I'm sure you can guess their response."

"They told you to give it twenty-four hours, maybe forty-eight if they know she's run away before."

"Correct."

Will addressed his words to Cedric. "You sounded pretty upset when you called me. Can you tell me why?"

Cedric looked at his grandmother, then back at Will. His shoulders went up into a shrug.

The old woman stirred, reaching into the front pocket of her housedress. "Walk Mr. Trent out and check the mail for me, baby. Mr. Trent?" Will struggled to get out of the chair. "Thank you for your concern."

"Please don't bother," he said, noticing that she was trying to stand. "I'll let you know what I find out." He reached out to shake her hand, remembering at the last moment that the arthritis would make it too painful. She grabbed his hand before he could stop her, and he was surprised by the intensity of her grip. "Please," she begged. "Please find her, Mr. Trent."

"Yes, ma'am," he said, knowing that she was proud and that it took everything she had to ask him for help.

He followed Cedric down the stairs and out into the parking lot. The overhead lights cast a strange glow over everything and Will realized that it was only a few hours past the time that Aleesha Monroe had been murdered on Sunday night. Cedric walked to the grassy area by the mailboxes where Jasmine had jumped him this morning.

Will watched the boy slip his key into the lock, waiting until he'd retrieved the mail to tell him, "This is serious, Cedric."

"I know."

"You've got to tell me what you know about Jasmine. Why did she tell you not to talk to the cops?"

"She said y'all are bad."

That was a sentiment shared by pretty much everyone within a five-mile radius. "Tell me what happened on Sunday."

"Nothing."

"That's not going to work this time, Cedric. Jasmine's gone, and you heard your granny in there. I know you were listening at the door. I saw your shadow underneath."

Cedric licked his lips, sorting through the mail.

Will knelt down in front of him, put both his hands on Cedric's shoulders. "Tell me."

"There was a man," Cedric finally admitted, his grammar improved now that his guard was down. "He paid Jazz some money to make a phone call. That's all."

"What kind of phone call?"

"To the police. To say Leesha was being hurt."

Will looked over his shoulder at the pay phone. The booth was dark, the overhead light busted out. "He told her to call from the pay phone?"

Cedric nodded. "Didn't make no sense. She could'a used her cell. Everybody knows y'all can't trace a cell."

"Did he pay her?" Will guessed.

"Twenty bucks," Cedric admitted. "And then he gave her a dime for the phone."

Will dropped his hands and sat back on his heels. "What's that phone cost, about fifty cents?"

"Yeah," Cedric answered. "Jazz told him that a dime don't buy shit, and then he got all nervous and gave her two quarters."

Will wondered what the odds were that they'd find two quarters in the coin box that had the murderer's fingerprints on them. Then he wondered if it was Aleesha's murderer who had paid the girl to make the call. Why would the killer pay someone to report his own crime?

Will asked, "Did you recognize the man?"

The boy went back to shuffling the mail in his hands.

"Do you think you'd remember him if you saw a picture of him?"

"He was white," Cedric said. "I didn't see him too good. I was over here."

Will turned back to the phone booth. The lights around the parking lot and the mailboxes were strong enough to blind a grown man, but none of them would have illuminated the pay phone.

He asked Cedric, "What do you think happened?"

He didn't answer right away. Instead, he started shuffling the mail again. "She always told me before," he said. "When she was going off with Luther, she always told me so I wouldn't worry."

"After Jasmine made the call, which way did the man go when he left?"

Cedric pointed up the street toward the exit.

"He didn't have a car?"

"Don't know," the boy admitted. "We was out here on our way to Freddy's, and then he hollered us over. Jazz told me to go on and see Freddy, but I stayed around to make sure she was okay."

Will wondered at the girl going up to a strange man in the dark. Maybe she was heading down that wrong path faster than her grandmother thought.

He asked, "Where's Freddy's?"

Cedric pointed across the street to another building.

"Did Jasmine go with you after she made the call?"

"After, yeah."

"And the man left up the street, toward the main road?"

Cedric nodded, chewing his bottom lip like he had more to say. Will gave him some time, and eventually, the boy said, "Jazz say she heard screaming in the stairs. Leesha was yelling."

"What was she yelling?"

"Jazz don't know. She was just yelling like she was being hurt, but she done that before, you know? Leesha takes up men sometimes and they kind of mean, but she say she don't mind."

"Cedric," Will said, putting his hands back on the boy's shoulders. "I need you to be straight with me now. Did Jasmine see who was hurting Aleesha? Did anyone talk to her, say anything to her?"

Cedric shook his head. "She told me she didn't see nothing, didn't hear nothing."

"Was she saying it like she did today, where if you thought about it awhile, you might think that what she was really saying was that maybe she *did* hear something, but she just wasn't going to tell anybody?"

"No," Cedric insisted. "She would'a told me."

Will didn't know if that was true or not. Jasmine wanted to protect her brother. She wouldn't have told him something that might put him in danger.

Cedric reached into his pocket and took out a twenty-dollar bill. "This is what she wanted," he told Will. "I took the money he gave her for making the phone call. That's why she was chasing me." He was trying to give Will the money.

"Hold on to it for me," Will said, knowing he couldn't do anything with the bill. "Jasmine didn't leave because you took the money, Cedric. You know that, right?"

The boy shrugged, and the mail slipped from his hands. Will bent down to help pick it up. From the colors, he gathered they were mostly bills with about ten pieces of junk mail thrown in. Will probably had the same limited-time offers waiting for him back home.

He looked up at the mailboxes. "Cedric?"

"Yeah?"

"Did Aleesha have a mailbox here?"

"Yeah," Cedric answered, pointing to one of the higher boxes.

Will stood, making note of the number. "Let's get you back inside, okay?"

"I'm all right."

"I need to check something in Aleesha's apartment. Let me walk you up."

Cedric was slow going up the stairs. He used his key to get into his grandmother's apartment, but didn't go inside. Instead, he watched Will continue up to Aleesha Monroe's place. Will felt the boy's silent disapproval burning into his back: *Where are you going? You promised you'd help.*

Will still had the key in his vest pocket from earlier. He slipped it into the lock and turned it to the side, hearing the bolt engage. He tried the knob but the door did not open. Will was the first person to admit—at least to himself— that he had trouble with left and right, and God knows it got worse when he was tired, but even he had opened enough locks to know which direction to turn a key in order to open it. He slid the key back into the lock and tried the other way, hearing the bolt click again. This time, the door opened.

The apartment still had that same feel to it, like something bad had happened. He stood in the doorway with only the light from the hall illuminating the room. Will saw a drop of blood on the floor and knelt beside it. Without thinking, he put his fingers to the drop to check whether or not it was dry.

His fingers came back clean, but Will hadn't noticed the drop the first time he had come into the apartment. He flipped on the lights, thinking about the lock. This morning, Jasmine and Cedric had been making a racket when Will was locking the door. Michael and Will had run down the stairs at full speed. Maybe Will hadn't locked the door all the way. He'd certainly been in a hurry.

But Will remembered locking that door, hearing the bolt catch.

He checked the apartment, making sure nothing was missing. Because of his reading problem, Will doubted he had a photographic memory, but he could memorize scenes. He remembered where things went and he knew when they were out of place.

Still, something was off. The room just *felt* different.

The junk drawer looked the same, the ring of keys still tucked into the corner under a couple of store receipts. Will checked through them until he found a smaller key like the one Cedric had. Every cop who came into this building had to pass those mailboxes. Will had, too, though, and he hadn't asked if Monroe had any mail. Then again, Will wasn't the lead detective on the case. With Michael on leave, the inimitable Leo Donnelly was now in charge.

Will made sure to lock the door, checking it twice before heading back down the stairs. As with every other surface in the Homes, the mailboxes were sprayed with graffiti, and Will identified Aleesha's by the obscene drawing that pointed up to it. He slid in the key and turned the lock with some difficulty. He found the problem when the door swung open. The small compartment was packed with mail. Will took out the envelopes in clumps, noting the colors and the bright logos adorning the outsides. There was a plain white envelope in with the rest. A bulge was in the bottom corner, and he felt it with his fingers, guessing something metal was inside. From the shape, he thought it might be a cross. Someone had addressed the envelope by hand in a looping cursive that Will could not begin to decipher.

He looked at his watch, really looked at it like he never did, until he could make out the time. It was almost midnight. Angie would probably be getting home from work soon.

Will sat on Angie's front porch, the hard concrete making his bottom numb. He had no idea where she was and his cell phone battery had finally died, so he wasn't even sure of the time.

He had put the phone to good use before it had quit on him, calling a contact at the Atlanta police, making sure the report on Jasmine Allison wasn't filed away like the thousands of other missing persons reports the city collected each year. They had put out an APB on Jasmine, and Luther Morrison had found a highly annoyed cop knocking at his front door. The patrolman had searched the house and discovered an underage girl there, but it wasn't the underage girl they were looking for.

Will had a bad feeling about Jasmine's disappearance. According to Cedric, Jasmine had seen something, talked to someone who was connected to the murder. That made her either valuable or expendable, depending on who you talked to, but as far as the city of Atlanta was concerned, Will's bad feeling didn't warrant an all-out manhunt.

This train of thought had persuaded Will to break down and call Michael Ormewood to find out if the girl had said anything to him before she'd escaped up the stairs. Michael could have been the last person to see her. Unfortunately, the detective either wasn't home or wasn't picking up the phone.

Angie's black Monte Carlo SS pulled into her driveway. The engine sounded like it was running on gravel, and he couldn't help but wince at the knocking that continued when she turned off the ignition. Will had spent a year restoring that car for her. Nights, weekends, a whole vacation.

He had been on a mission to give her something nice, prove that he could build something with his hands without being told by a stupid manual that bolt A matches with nut C. The fresh oil stains on the driveway were like a kick in the face.

Angie threw open the car door and demanded, "What the fuck are you doing here?"

He couldn't help but notice that she was dressed for work. The way she sat in the car gave him and everyone else on this side of the street a clear view right up her short skirt.

Will asked, "What did you do to the car?"

"Drove it." She got out and slammed the door so hard the car shook.

"There's oil all over the driveway."

"You don't say."

"Did you even get it serviced?"

"Where would I do that?"

"There are ten billion garages around here. You can't throw a rock without hitting one."

"If I was going to throw a rock, it'd be at your head, you stupid shit." She pushed him away from the front door so that she could open it. "I'm tired and I'm pissed off and I just want to get to bed." She tossed him a look over her shoulder, like she was just waiting for him to say something about joining her.

He said, "I need to talk to you."

"Will, why didn't you use your key?" She didn't have to crane her neck to look at him and he realized she was still wearing her high heels. She said, "You still have your key. Why did you sit out here in the cold?"

He smelled alcohol on her breath. "Have you been drinking?"

She sighed, giving him another whiff of what had to be whiskey. "Come in," she said, shoving her key into the lock.

"My neighbors get enough of a show with me flashing my cootch every time I get out of the fucking car."

Will followed her inside and closed the door behind him.

She kicked off the stilettos by the couch and slid into a pair of pink flip-flops. Angie hated going barefoot.

"You don't need to be here." She flipped on the hall lights, talking and undressing as she walked toward the bedroom. "I've had the shittiest day of my life. All the girls are freaked out about Aleesha and they just kept fucking crying all night, as if my day wasn't bad enough already." He saw her naked back, the slope down her spine that disappeared into her pink panties, right before she slammed her bedroom door. "Three o'clock, I got a call from Lieutenant Canton," she continued, her voice muffled through the door. "He made me come in early and work with that fucker Ormewood all afternoon to find some stupid files from back when he was in Vice."

Will remembered that Michael had said he'd go through the files, but he was surprised the man had followed through, considering the state he was in the last time Will had seen him.

"I had to spend two hours sitting in this God damn skirt"—he heard something thump against the wall and assumed it was the skirt—"with that asshole breathing down my neck, joking with me like he was my best fucking friend."

Will had used his key about an hour earlier to put Aleesha Monroe's mail on the coffee table so he didn't have to hold it all night. He sat down on the couch now and went through it, stacking the letters into neat piles for Angie.

"I swear to God, Will," Angie began, coming back up the hallway. "Some days I look at those girls and think they gct better treatment from their pimps than I do from these cocksuckers I have to work with."

The flip-flops slapped against her heels as she walked into the kitchen. He heard the refrigerator door open, then ice hitting a glass. She opened a bottle and poured something, then slammed the refrigerator again. Seconds later, she sat on the couch beside him, kicked off the shoes, and took a healthy swig from the glass.

Will couldn't help it. His spine straightened like a Catholic schoolgirl's. "Are you going to drink that in front of me?"

She pushed her bare foot against his leg, saying, "Just until you start to look pretty."

"Don't do that."

"Don't do what?" she teased, nudging him again.

He turned to look at her, which was exactly what she had been waiting for. Angie was lying back on the couch, her foot still pressed against his leg. She had put on a short black robe and nothing else. The belt was tied loosely around her waist and he could see a tuft of hair between the folds.

Will felt his throat tighten. His mouth was so full of saliva that he pressed his lips together to keep from drooling.

She said, "I guess you found out my guy's a pedophile."

Will stood up so quickly he got a head rush. "What?"

"Shelley," she said matter-of-factly. "I'm assuming you pulled his sheet?"

Will put his hand to his eyes, like taking away his ability to see her would change what he had just heard. "He's a pedophile?"

She gave him a funny smile. "You realize you're yelling?"

Will lowered his voice. "You asked me to check up on a

pedophile for you?" He walked to the fireplace, wanting to punch his fist through the brick. "What the hell are you thinking? Is that who you're seeing now? Jesus, I was worried about Ormewood and now you're—"

"What did he say?"

Her tone had changed, and the air in the room seemed to turn cold along with it.

He asked, "What did who say?"

She sat up on the couch, crossing her legs, covering herself with the robe. "You know damn well what I'm talking about."

"No," he countered. "I don't."

She put her glass on the table by the mail. "What's this?"

"I know you slept with him."

"Real gentleman, that Michael Ormewood. Told you all the details, did he?" She gave a dry laugh as she thumbed through one of the stacks of mail he'd brought. "What fun it must have been for y'all to compare notes. No wonder the fucker was so happy this afternoon."

"He didn't tell me anything," Will said. "I figured it out on my own."

"Give the detective a gold star." She lifted her glass as if to toast him, then took a long drink. He watched her throat work as she swallowed and swallowed until the glass was empty.

Will turned his back to her, looking at the painting over the mantel. It was a triptych, three canvases hinged together to make one image when it was open, another image when it was closed. He had always assumed she liked the duplicity of the piece. It was just like Angie, one thing inside, another out. Just like Michael Ormewood, come to think of it. What a perfect pair.

"Aleesha's mail," Angie finally noticed. "Did you just find this?"

He nodded.

"Why didn't Michael's team check for it before?"

Will cleared his throat. "I don't know."

"Junk, junk, bill, bill." He heard the envelopes slapping the table as she rifled through them one by one. "What's this?"

Will didn't answer, but then she wasn't really asking him.

He heard her open the envelope, take out the letter. "Nice cross," she said. "I remember seeing Aleesha wear it sometimes."

He looked up at the painting, wishing it was a mirror that would show him what was inside of her. Maybe it was. Two abstract images, neither one of them making a bit of sense.

Will felt her behind him, her hand snaking into his jacket pocket. She took out his digital recorder. "This is new." She was standing so close that he could feel the heat from her body.

He heard her fiddling with the machine and turned around. "It's the orange button."

She held out the recorder. Will saw that her finger was already on the button. He gently pressed his thumb against her index finger and the recorder came on.

"Thanks."

Will couldn't look at her. He turned back around, leaning on the mantel again. She returned to the couch and sat down. The ice in the glass made a noise. She'd probably forgotten it was empty.

" 'Dear Mama,' " Angie finally read. " 'I know you think that I am writing to ask for money, but I just want to tell you that I don't want anything from you anymore. You always blamed me for leaving but you were the one who left us. You were the one who made me the pariah. The Bible tells us that the sins of the parent are visited on the child. I am the outcast, the untouchable who can only live with the other pariah, because of your sins.' " Angie told him, "She spells her name differently when she signs it: A-L-I-C-I-A instead of A-L-E-E-S-H-A."

Will made a disgusted sound in the back of his throat. She had to know that she might as well be speaking Chinese to him.

"She spells her name correctly—the more common way—when she signs it. She probably changed the spelling when she hit the streets." Angie kept talking and he couldn't stop listening. "Postmark says she mailed it two weeks ago. There's a stamp that says they returned the letter because she didn't put enough postage on it. I guess the cross probably put it over the weight limit or maybe it got caught in one of the machines." She paused. "Are you going to talk to the mother? This zip code isn't far from here, probably about ten miles. I wonder if she even knows her daughter is dead."

Will turned around. Angie held the envelope in her hand, flipped it over to make sure she didn't miss anything on the back. She looked up, saw him staring at her, and asked, "Will?"

He told her, "If I could snap my fingers and make it like I'd never even met you, I'd do it."

She put down the envelope. "I wish you could, too."

"What are you doing with a guy like that?"

"He can be charming when he wants to."

She meant Michael. "Was it before or after you found out he was using the girls?"

"Before, you asshole."

He gave her a sharp look. "I don't think you've got a right to be angry at me right now."

She gave in. "Yeah, you're right."

"So Shelley's a pedophile?"

She smiled, like it was funny. "And a murderer."

"You think this is some kind of joke?"

She leaned her elbows on her knees, giving that coy smile that said she was open to anything. "Don't be mad at me, baby."

"Don't put sex in the way of this."

"It's the only way I know how to communicate with people," she joked, something a psychiatrist had once told her. Will wasn't sure whether or not Angie had slept with the woman, but the observation was dead-on.

"Angie, please."

"I told you this was a bad night for you to be here." She stood up and put the envelope in his hand. "Come on, Willy," she said, pulling him toward the door. "You need to go home."

CHAPTER TWENTY-EIGHT

Angie remembered Gina Ormewood from Ken's retirement party. She was a mousy woman who seemed oblivious to the fact that heavy makeup made acne worse and a hairstylist who charged less than ten dollars wasn't exactly doing you a favor. If Angie hadn't fucked the woman's husband the same night, she probably wouldn't remember a thing about her. As it was, she knew that Gina worked at Piedmont Hospital, which in a roundabout kind of way you could say was on the way to Angie's work—if that was what you could call the strip in front of the liquor store on Cheshire Bridge Road.

She had called the hospital to make sure Gina Ormewood would be there. The woman's shift started in twenty minutes, but Angie didn't have anything better to do than wait. When she got to the hospital, she was glad she'd come early. Cars were backed up into the street and parking space on the deck seemed to be unavailable. After a while, Angie gave up. She flashed her badge to the rent-a-cop standing outside the ER and parked in a handicapped space.

There were a dozen people standing around the entrance of the ER, all with cigarettes dangling out of their mouths. Angie held her breath as she passed through the smoke. She hated cigarettes because they always reminded her of the burns on Will's body. Someone had spent hours searing the flesh around the angles of his shoulder blades, creating obscene patterns along the lines of his ribs.

She shuddered at the thought.

The man behind the counter didn't even look up when Angie stood in front of him. "Sign in, take a seat."

She slid her badge under his nose and he still didn't give her the courtesy of making eye contact. "You need to talk to the hospital administrator if you want records."

She looked at his name badge. "No records, Tank. I'm here for Gina Ormewood."

He looked up then. "What do you want Gina for?"

"It's about her husband."

"I hope the bastard's dead."

"Get in line." Her words were automatic, but she didn't lose sight of the fact that the man obviously hated Michael.

Tank stood, taking her in with his eyes. Angie was dressed for work, which meant she looked like a whore. She was still a cop, though, and this guy wasn't an idiot.

She asked, "When do you think Gina will be in?"

"You're not going to mess with her." He wasn't asking a question.

"I'm going to talk to her," Angie told him.

He kept his eyes locked on hers, as if he could tell just by looking at her whether she was going to be trouble. Working at a place like this, he probably had the instincts. "Give her another ten minutes," he said. "She's always early."

"Thank you." Angie dropped her badge back into her purse and took the only seat available in the crowded waiting room.

There was an older man and woman across from her who had probably been Angie's age when they came in. The woman gave Angie a look of disgust. The man gave Angie one of interest. Jesus, the guy had to be eighty and he was probably wondering how much money he had in his wallet. His wife blew her nose into a well-worn tissue. She looked ready to fall over. Angie spread her legs wide and the man blanched. The wife looked like she was about to have a heart attack.

Before they could move away, Angie stood up and went to the magazine rack. God, this place was depressing. The waiting room was a cesspit of germs and disease. Anybody who thought America didn't have socialized medicine should spend a couple of hours in their local ER. Someone was paying for the uninsured and indigent to see a doctor, and it sure as shit wasn't the uninsured and indigent. Hell, you were better off without insurance these days. You got the same crappy care but you paid less.

She skimmed a *Field & Stream* then a *Ladies' Home Journal* from the Christmas before last as she waited for Gina Ormewood to show up. Michael had gone too far yesterday. He'd grinned at her like a monkey while they worked through his Vice records and now she knew why. It was one thing to fuck with Angie—hell, she probably deserved it—but the fact that he'd gotten Will upset was unforgivable. Michael must have said something, let a few words slip that told Will he'd banged Angie. She worked with men all day, arrested the fuckers, even, and she knew how their little minds worked. A second couldn't go by without them either thinking about sex or talking about it, and the fact that Michael had fucked Angie was very good gossip. He'd probably even told that turdball Leo Donnelly. The whole squad must know by now. No wonder Will felt humiliated.

God, she had to stop listening to the girls so much. No one hated men as much as a prostitute. They spent hours talking about what low-life scum men were, and then they had to go off with the first asshole who flashed a little green in their face. Angie had enough issues with men without starting to think about them like a whore.

The doors opened and she glanced up as a couple of guys came in. She looked back at the magazine, not really seeing the fruitcake recipe. Her head hurt with thoughts of Ormewood, the disappointment on Will's face, the way he had looked at her the night before when she'd gently pushed him out the front door. He must have been seething when Michael started bragging about it, telling the intimate details of his conquest.

Angie flipped to a different page, a different recipe. If Michael was going to screw around with the one person Angie cared about, then she was going to give it right back to him. Nothing distracted a man more than trouble at home.

"Robin?"

Angie turned to the next page. Mother and daughter sweaters. How fucking adorable.

"Robin? Is that you?"

Shit. She looked up. John Shelley stood in front of her. He was beside a black guy whose hand was wrapped in a bloody bandage.

Tank called, "Sign in, please."

"I'll be back," John told her. He took the black guy to the counter. Obviously, profuse bleeding moved you up the list because Tank took the guy right back.

John was staring at Angie. "What are you doing here?"

"Routine maintenance," she said, indicating her lower half. "What's up with that guy?"

"Ray-Ray," John told her, the asshole who wanted one on credit. "He cut his hand on a piece of metal sticking out of a car. Art asked me to bring him up."

"He gonna be okay?"

"If Art doesn't kill him first," John said. He seemed at a loss for words, and blurted out, "You look nice."

She looked like a whore, but a compliment was a compliment. "I thought you were gonna stay away from me."

"Oh." His face fell, and for a split second, she was reminded of Will—the way he could never hide his emotions from her, the way he sometimes wore his shame and disappointment on his sleeve.

"Come here," she said, taking John's arm and leading him out into the hall. They stood just inside the front door. Angie could see the smokers on the other side.

She asked John, "You doing okay?"

He was smiling now, almost hopeful. "Yeah. How about you?"

"No," she insisted. "Last time I saw you, you were in some trouble."

He nodded, looked down at his feet. Why did she always end up talking to men who looked at their feet?

"It's good to see you," he said. "I know I said I was going to stay away, but it's really nice seeing you."

"You hardly know me."

He smiled again. God, he had such a sweet smile. "I know about Stewie."

He knew lies, she thought. The first of many, if history told her anything.

"You really look nice."

"You already said that."

John laughed. "I'm trying to think of something else to say." He laughed again, not so much uncomfortable as really enjoying himself and her company. He looked down at his shoes again, and she saw that he had the prettiest eyelashes she had ever seen on a man. They were a soft, delicate brown. John was a big guy, almost as tall as Will, with a broader chest and a hell of a lot more self-confidence.

Despite the cold weather, his face was tanned and there were golden streaks in his hair from working outside all day.

She said, "You look nice, too."

He smiled, and again she got the feeling that there was nothing more he wanted to do than stand there and talk to her all day.

What lies would she tell him? How long before she ended up taking John to a broom closet or a bathroom and screwing him, then hating him because he had fucked her? How long before she messed up his life, too?

She asked, "What were you in for, John?"

His smile dropped. His shoulders dropped, too.

Angie had already read his parole sheet, but that had only told her the charges, not the details of the crime. "Tell me what you did."

"You don't want to know."

"I had an aluminum siding salesman last night who wanted me to suck his toes and call him daddy," she said. "You think you're going to come up with something that shocks me?"

"I made some mistakes."

"We've all made mistakes."

He shook his head. "I don't want to talk about this."

"You were in a long time," she noted. "Did you kill somebody?"

He licked his lips, nervous. He was so much like Will that they could have been brothers. Hell, considering Will's slutty mother, maybe they *were* brothers.

John told her, "I should get back with Ray-Ray, make sure he's not talking himself into any trouble."

Angie looked out the glass doors. Gina Ormewood was standing with the smokers, her blue nurse's scrubs a stark contrast to the cigarette she was sucking on.

John said, "It was real good seeing you."

"Take care of yourself."

He started to walk away, then stopped. "When this is over," he said, spreading his hands out like there was a tangible thing between them. "When what's going on is over," he said, still being obtuse, "maybe we can go out to dinner or something? See a movie?"

"John," she began. "Do you think that's really gonna happen?"

He shook his head, but he still told her, "I'm going to hope it does, Robin. That's what's going to keep me going. I'm going to think about seeing a movie with you, buying you some popcorn, maybe holding your hand during the scary parts."

"It'd be cheaper if you just gave me the money to hold your scary parts."

He took her hand in his. She stood dumbstruck as he brought his lips to the back of her hand and gently kissed it. "Think about a movie you want to see," he told her. "Something really scary."

Then he was gone.

Angie leaned against the wall. She let out a stream of breath. Here was another perfectly sweet man she was ruining. Okay, he was a perfectly sweet pedophile and murderer, but glass houses and all that.

Gina Ormewood passed through the sliding doors. She did a double take when she saw Angie, but kept walking toward the ER.

"Hey," Angie said. "Wait up."

Gina stopped but didn't turn around. She said, "I just want to be left alone."

Angie walked around the woman to get a good look at her. Gina's lip was split. Her left eye had a bruise that was painful to look at. No wonder the guy at the desk hated Michael.

Angie asked, "What the hell happened to you?"

"I fell down," Gina told her. She tried to walk away, but Angie blocked her path.

"Did he hit you?"

"What do you think?"

"Christ."

Gina narrowed her eyes, finally recognizing Angie. "You fucked my husband."

"Yeah, well." Angie knew better than to lie. "If it's any consolation, I've had much better."

Gina laughed, then winced as her lip split open again. She put her hand to her mouth and looked at the blood on her fingers. "God," she groaned. "Let's go in here."

She pushed open the door to the women's restroom and Angie followed. Gina was petite, maybe five-three in her sneakers and around a hundred pounds. Michael had at least eighty pounds on her. This was like kicking a puppy.

"I met him when I was fifteen," Gina said. She was leaning over the sink basin, looking at her split lip in the mirror. "He was interested in my cousin. She was a year younger than me. I thought I was protecting her."

Angie knew to let her talk.

"He was so sweet," Gina said. "I'd get these letters from him when he was in the Gulf, talking about how much he loved me, that he wanted to take care of me." Her eyes met Angie's in the mirror. "This is how he takes care of me now."

Angie rummaged in her purse. "They're all sweet at first."

"You know that for a fact?"

"Even got the bloodstained T-shirt."

Gina took a tissue from the dispenser and wet it under the faucet. "After Tim was born," she began, "things changed. He started getting angry about everything. He didn't want to touch me anymore. He'd leave the house at night, stay out for hours at a time." She dabbed the tissue at her bloody lip. "Sometimes, he'd go away for the whole weekend. I'd check the odometer and he'd put five, sometimes six hundred miles on the car."

Angie found what she was looking for in her purse. "Where was he going?"

"You get punched in the face enough times, you stop asking questions."

Angie told her, "Turn around." She dabbed some foundation onto the sponge and patted it around Gina's black eye. "This is Clinique," she said. "If you go a little lighter than your usual shade, do a little blending with your finger, it helps soften the bruise."

"Did he hit you, too?"

"No," Angie answered, concentrating on hiding the bruise. The truth was, Angie had been too drunk to remember exactly what Michael had done. All she knew was that she had woken up the next morning in the backseat of her car with a deep bite mark on her breast and a pain between her legs that took a couple of weeks to go away.

It wasn't like this was the first time something bad like that had happened, but it was the first time it had happened with a guy from work.

Gina said, "He told me he was with Ken."

"Wozniak?" Angie asked. Michael's partner in Homicide. "What was he doing with Ken?"

"He said they went fishing up in the mountains together."

Angie pressed her lips together, holding back comment. She couldn't picture Ken with a fishing pole, and even if she could, Ken wasn't exactly Michael's kind of guy.

Gina's voice dropped to almost a whisper. "Was he rough with you?"

Angie nodded. She used her fingers to tilt up Gina's chin so she could check her handiwork in the light.

"He's a bastard," Gina said, still whispering. "I just want to get away."

Angie added some more foundation. "You left him?"

"Two days ago."

"Where are you staying now?"

"With my mother," she answered. "He told me he'd come get me."

Angie checked her again. Perfect. "Did you file a report?"

She laughed. "You're a cop. You know how useless that would be."

"That's bullshit," Angie told her. "You go to DeKalb County and file a report. They don't give a shit if he's a cop. They'll take one look at you and run him in."

"And then what?" Gina asked. "What happens when he gets out?"

"File a restraining order."

"Look at my face," the woman said. "Do you think a restraining order is going to stop him?"

She had a point. Angie remembered her days in uniform, recalled vividly how she had once peeled a bloody restraining order from the hand of a woman who had been beaten to death by her husband. He had used a hammer. Their kids were watching.

Gina washed her hands at the sink. "Why are you here?"

"I wanted you to send Michael a message."

She turned off the faucet and grabbed a towel to wipe her hands. "You think he'll listen to me?"

"No," Angie admitted. She took one of her cards out of her purse. "I want to give you my phone number. Call me if he does anything to you."

Gina didn't take the card. "He's going to do whatever he wants. A phone call isn't going to save me." She checked herself in the mirror, smoothed her hair. "Thanks for the makeup. Clinique?" Angie nodded. "I'll get some at lunch today. If Michael finds out I talked to you, I'm probably going to need it."

"I won't tell him."

Gina leaned against the door, propping it open. "He'll find out," she said. "He always finds out about everything."

Angie stayed in the bathroom a few minutes, trying to regain her composure. She wanted to talk to Will, but what could she say? I went to the hospital to threaten Michael's wife? He beats the crap out of her and, oh, by the way, he was so rough with me that one night we spent together that I couldn't pee straight for a month? Like every other emotion in his life, Will had learned to control his sharp temper. Angie knew it was still there, though, right at the surface waiting for something to set it off. If Angie ever told him what had really happened with Michael Ormewood, Will would kill him.

A young girl came into the bathroom, saw Angie and quickly left. Well, that was a real spirit booster. Angie looked at her reflection, the heavy makeup, the white vinyl crotch-dusting skirt and the hot pink haltertop that barely hid her breasts. No wonder people were scared of her.

She went into the hallway, glancing back toward the doors of the emergency room. Tank held both Gina's hands in his as he talked to her. Angie couldn't hear what he was saying, but she could guess. Suddenly, Gina started crying, and the man wrapped his arms around her. Angie watched them for a moment, feeling like an intruder but unable to look away.

A therapist had once told Angie that she looked for men who would abuse her because that was all she had ever known. This same therapist had also suggested that the reason Angie kept hurting Will was because she wanted to make him angry, to bring him to the point where he finally hauled off and hit her; then Angie could finally open herself up to him. Then she could really love him.

Of course, Angie had lied to the therapist about her relationships, about Will. She wasn't about to tell a complete stranger the truth. Hell, she had told so many lies by now that she wouldn't know the truth if it bit her on the ass.

CHAPTER TWENTY-NINE

Will sat at his desk, listening to his recording of Angie reading the letter Monroe had written to her mother. He'd heard it enough times by now that he knew it by heart, but he wanted to hear her voice, catch her inflections. Sometimes, he'd look at the letter while he listened to the words, trying to follow along. Angie hated reading aloud and her tone showed it. Will thought if he could read as well as she could he would read out loud all of the time.

He slipped the headphones out of his ears and went back to the diagram he had been drawing in his mind. Will saw things in images, like a storyboard for a movie. Jasmine Allison's face came to mind. She was still missing. The Atlanta PD was looking, but Will wasn't certain they were taking this as seriously as he needed them to. Even if they did, where would they look? There were a million places you could stash a little girl—a million more if she didn't need to breathe while you were doing it.

Aleesha Monroe's mother wasn't home; he had called several times that morning until the maid had finally picked up and told him Ms. Monroe wasn't expected back until noon. Will had put in a call to DeKalb and found out that there was nothing new on the Cynthia Barrett case. He had even sent a forensic team back to the Homes to go over the pay phone. There were only seven quarters in the coin box, and none of them had usable prints.

No leads, no clues to follow up on. All he had was the letter and the slim hope that Miriam Monroe would know something.

Leo Donnelly knocked on Will's office door as he opened it. "Hey, man."

Will slid the recorder and headphones into his desk drawer. "What's going on?"

"You got a minute?"

"Sure."

Leo closed the door and sat in the chair beside Will's desk. He looked around the room, obviously nervous. "Nice place you got here."

Will glanced around, wondering if the detective was being sarcastic. The office was so small that Will had pushed one side of the desk up against the wall so that he didn't have to climb over it to get out.

Leo rubbed his palms on his cheap trousers as he stared out the window. The man seemed to be in a state of shock.

Will repeated, "What's going on?"

"I just talked with Greer. He's my lou, right?"

"Yeah." Will had met the lieutenant on Monday when he'd asked to be let in on the Monroe case.

Leo's tone was still incredulous. "He just got a courtesy call from DeKalb PD. Gina filed a restraining order on Mike."

"Gina Ormewood?" Will sat up in his chair. "What did she list as cause?"

"Her broken face." Leo propped his elbow on the desk and leaned his head in his hand. "Greer didn't see the pictures or nothing, but the cop who took the report said she was pretty banged up."

The detective was obviously shaken. Will had guessed that except for Michael, Leo didn't have many friends in the squad. Even if he was close to some of them, you didn't rat out your friends. That still did not explain why he'd come to Will.

Leo rubbed his chin with his thumb. "My old man used to haul off on my ma. Used to watch it when I was a kid."

"I'm sorry to hear that."

"I thought I knew the guy," Leo said, meaning Ormewood. "This is out of left field, you know? At first, I thought maybe the bitch was making it up, but then I called Michael and..." His voice trailed off. "He tried to laugh it off, said it was a big misunderstanding, that she was withdrawing the order, had just made it up to get back at him for working so much." Leo's mouth twisted to the side, like the explanation still didn't sit right with him. The man had been a cop for much longer than Will and he had probably heard that same excuse from many an abusive husband.

Leo continued, "Then I started pushing him about it, asking what was going on. Gina's a good girl, you know? Smart as a whip. I don't see her putting his nuts in a vise just for shits and giggles." Leo glanced at Will, then back out the window. "He told me to mind my own fucking business."

Leo had obviously taken that as an admission of guilt. Will took it as proof that Michael was answering his phone only when the caller ID told him it was somebody he wanted to talk to.

"Anyway," Leo turned back to Will, his knees banging the desk. He cursed a few times before saying, "I thought I'd come in and catch you up on the Monroe case."

"Anything new?"

"Her pimp was shot this morning."

"Baby G?"

"Two in the gut, one in the head. Doctors say it's just a matter of time before he's gone. No brain activity."

"They catch the doer?"

"Two of his cousins, both of them fifteen. G's grandmother saw the whole thing from her front window." Leo gave a half-shrug of his shoulder. "Not that she's saying shit. Both of 'em confessed, though, so it's not like we need her. Still, you'd think she'd be a little more upset that her grandson is dead."

Will thought of Cedric. "Did anyone else get hurt?"

"No, this was a gang thing. They said G dissed 'em the other day, didn't give them respect." Leo rubbed his chin again. "Shit, since when did they start handing out respect without you having to do anything to earn it?"

"You're sure this isn't related to Monroe?"

"Doesn't seem to be," Leo said. "They're sharing a lawyer, some pro-bono fucker from Buckhead who gets his jollies helping the poor. Both of 'em will be out in ten years, tops."

"Maybe," Will said, thinking Leo was more than likely right. "Did you get that memo I sent around about Jasmine Allison?"

"Missing black girl?" he confirmed. "Stick a blonde wig on her, maybe she'll get in the papers."

Will didn't acknowledge the sarcasm. He had thought of something else. "Can you pull the list of recently released sex offenders for me?"

"How recent?"

Four months ago, fifteen-year-old Julie Cooper had been brutally raped, her tongue bitten in two. There was no telling how long her attacker had been operating under the radar. He told Leo, "Let's go back at least eight months."

"Just Atlanta or metro area, too?"

"Metro," Will said, knowing that he'd just tripled the work.

"They don't exactly keep that list up-to-date," Leo pointed out. "I'll have to do some cross-checking, mark off the ones that went back in, moved away, whatever."

"I appreciate it." Will felt the need to add, "I know this is a needle in a haystack, but we don't have much more to go on."

"I'm with you, man." Leo stood up. "Shouldn't take more than a day or so to get them together. You want me to leave them on your desk?"

"That'd be great."

"I'll take the first half," Leo offered. "We're working this together, right?"

"Right," Will echoed, though he didn't exactly count Donnelly as an ally.

Will took out his cell phone as Leo shut the door. He dialed Angie's number, listened to the rings as he waited for her to answer.

She must have recognized his number on the caller ID. "What's up?"

"Why would Michael's wife file a restraining order against him?"

She exhaled slowly, taking her time with the answer. "Because he beats her."

Will felt as if he had been beaten himself.

She asked, "You there?"

He didn't think he could form the words. "Did he hit you, Angie?"

"What you should be asking is how long they've been married."

"Did he ever hit you?"

"No, Will. He never hit me."

"Are you lying to me?"

Her laugh was that strange, disaffected laugh she gave when she needed to distance herself from something. "Why would I lie to you, baby?"

"Aleesha's pimp got shot this morning."

"It wasn't me."

"Can you be serious for just one minute?"

"What do you want me to say, Will?"

"There's a missing girl," he told her. "Her name is Jasmine Allison. She lives three floors down from Aleesha's place. Sunday night, somebody paid her twenty bucks to make a phone call to the police to report that Aleesha was being attacked. Now, she's missing."

Angie's tone changed. "When was she last seen?"

"Yesterday afternoon."

"Do you have any leads?"

"None."

"How old is she?"

"Fourteen."

Angie let out a soft breath. "Is anyone downtown taking this seriously?"

"Yeah, they're bending over backward to help the GBI."

She tried to take up for them. "They've got a lot of work to do down there."

"I'm not saying they don't."

"Has she run away before?"

"Twice."

"It's not something I'd put at the top of my roster if I was working in missing persons. Teenage girls run away all the time. We both know that. They've probably got hotter cases right now."

"Her home situation's not that bad."

"People run away for other reasons." Angie would

know. She'd run away so many times that even Will had lost count.

He looked at the copy he'd made of the letter Aleesha had written to her mother. She'd used pencil on lined paper, so the reproduction wasn't that good. He tried to pick out some words but his eyes couldn't focus. Aleesha had probably run away from home, too.

Angie offered, "I'll talk to some people I know downtown and see if I can light a fire under them. They might take it better from me than some cocksucker from the GBI."

"Thank you."

Will closed the phone and looked at the display.

It was time to pay Aleesha Monroe's mother a visit.

Will seldom drove his car to work unless he knew that he would be on his own that day. Most of the time, he took his motorcycle in so that whoever he was partnered with had to drive. Unless he was going to one of his usual haunts—the grocery store, the local Cuban restaurant, the movies— putting him behind the wheel of a car was an invitation to get lost. He could read street signs eventually, but only at the expense of the other cars behind him. Maps, with their tiny print that skipped across the page, might as well have been written in Swahili and when he got frustrated, which tended to happen when the horns started blaring, Will quickly forgot how to tell left from right.

Driving to Miriam Monroe's house was an exercise in patience. Will ignored the angry stares and nasty shouts as he slowly made his way up DeKalb Avenue. The Monroes lived in Decatur near Agnes Scott College, a pricey little area with old Victorians and the sorts of houses most people could only dream about. Fortunately, the neighborhood wasn't large and with a little trial and error, he would find her house before the sun went down.

Will tapped his foot on the brake as he followed the fork across the railroad tracks and onto College Avenue. He tried not to take it personally when a skinny old woman in a powder blue Cadillac sped past him, her fist shaking in the air.

With great effort, Will had managed to push Angie from his mind. He needed to work the case from the beginning to see if there was anything he had missed. There had to be some detail, some clue, that he just wasn't picking up on.

Thirty-two Paisley Avenue was a grand old home with a wraparound porch and a massive weeping willow draping its branches across the front yard. The house was sandblasted brick on the bottom and darkly painted shingles along the top. The tile roof was covered with pine needles, and Will imagined with the large number of trees in the yard, the Monroes had a constant battle on their hands just keeping the gutters clean.

He parked his car on the street and double checked the mailbox, making out the name MONROE in bold black letters. Still, he checked the street number against the address from the envelope.

The doorbell was the old-fashioned kind that was an actual bell mounted to the center of the heavy front door. Will twisted the bow-tie piece of metal and could hear the shrill ring echoing in the house.

Footsteps clicked on tile; a woman's as well as a dog's. "Hello?"

Will assumed a wary eye was pressed to the peephole in the door. This was a nice neighborhood, but they were still close enough to Atlanta to make the residents careful about opening their doors to strangers.

"I'm Agent Will Trent with the Georgia Bureau of Investigation," Will said, holding up his identification. "I'm looking for Miriam Monroe."

There was a hesitation, maybe a sigh, then the bolt was turned and the door opened.

Miriam Monroe looked just like her daughter. At least, her daughter would have looked like this had she lived a different life. Where Aleesha had been malnourished, almost skeletal, her mother was a robust woman, with long curly hair and an open way about her that seemed to invite people in. There was a glow in her cheeks, a sparkle in her eyes, and even though her mouth was pursed as she stared at Will, her expression guarded as she waited for him to speak, he could tell that she was the sort of woman who sought out the positive in life.

He looked down at the black poodle standing at her feet, then back up at the woman. "I've come about your daughter."

Her hand went to her chest. She grabbed the door to steady herself. "Ashley...?"

"No," he assured her, reaching out to hold the woman up. He'd never considered she had more than one daughter. "Aleesha," he told her. "I've come about Aleesha."

She blinked several times, looking confused. "What?"

Will had a confused feeling himself. Had he read the mailbox wrong? Was he on the wrong street? "You're Miriam Monroe?"

She nodded. The dog barked, sensing trouble.

"I'm sorry," Will apologized to the woman. "I was told you had a daughter named Aleesha."

"I did have a daughter," she agreed. Her voice was far-away, as if she had lost her child long ago, which by her next words was exactly how she felt. "Aleesha left us when she was a teenager, Officer. We haven't seen her in nearly twenty years."

Will wasn't sure what to say. "May I come in?"

She smiled, stepping back from the door, gently moving the dog with her foot. "I've forgotten my manners."

"It's fine," Will assured her, thinking that no matter how many times he did this, he would never be able to predict how a parent would react to news of their child being lost.

She suggested, "Shall we go into the parlor?"

Will was trying not to gawk at the foyer, which was the largest he had ever seen in a private home. A huge staircase spiraled up to the top floor and a chandelier that looked as if it belonged in an opera house dangled above his head.

"We got it in Bologna," Miriam explained, leading him into the adjoining room. "My husband, Tobias, is an amateur collector."

"Oh," Will said, as if that made perfect sense. He thought about the homes he had visited over the last few days, Aleesha's shabby two rooms, the cramped apartment where Eleanor Allison raised her grandchildren. This was a mansion, plain and simple. From the thick rugs on the floors to the colorful African folk art on the walls, this was the type of place you lived in when money wasn't a concern.

Miriam sat back in a comfortable-looking chair as the dog settled at her feet. "Would you like some lemonade?"

"No, thank you," Will told her, sitting on the couch. The cushions were hard and he guessed they didn't use this room much. He wondered if the grand piano tucked under the bay window was just for show. He also wondered what the hell he was doing. Will had learned a long time ago that giving a parent the news that their child was dead should be done quickly. Dragging it out only made it harder when the information finally came. Will wasn't Miriam Monroe's best friend; his job was simply to tell her the truth, then leave.

So, why wasn't he?

Maybe it was because there was something soothing about the woman's voice, her presence. Her face could have been the illustration dictionaries used for "mother." When Will was a kid, he had assumed that black kids were more loved than whites for the simple reason that of the hundred or so kids at the Atlanta Children's Home, there were only ever two African-Americans. Funny how stereotypes got stuck in your head when you were little.

"How can I help you?" she prompted. Her voice was very cultured, and she managed to glance at her watch without looking impatient.

"I'm sorry I frightened you. I assumed the woman I talked to on the phone earlier told you that I called."

"She mentioned someone called, but I wasn't expecting a policeman on my doorstep."

"I'm sorry," Will repeated, taking out a spiral notebook and a pen. He used this for show, mostly to let people know he was paying attention. He had clicked on his recorder when he'd taken the pen out of his breast pocket.

He said, "You don't seem surprised that I'm here about Aleesha."

"I suppose I'm not. Aleesha chose a life for herself that her father and I did not agree with. I'm sure you won't be surprised to know that you're not the first police officer to knock on our door." She smiled, but there was something more guarded about her manner. "If you think we can lead you to her, I'm sorry to say that we cannot."

Despite, or maybe because of, the woman's poise, Will knew that this was not going to be easy. "Where is your husband now?"

"He's giving a lecture in New York," she explained. "He specializes in health issues affecting women."

Will scribbled something in his notebook. "I see."

"You think it's ironic that a man who has devoted his life to helping women has a daughter who is a prostitute and a drug addict."

"Yes," Will admitted. "I do."

She sat back in the chair, seemingly relieved that they had gotten that out of the way. "We did everything we could to try to help our daughter."

"I'm sure you did."

"Are you really?" she asked, as if she wanted to catch him off guard. "We spent thousands of dollars on treatments, family therapy, individual therapy. Anything we thought would help her, we did." She clasped her hands in her lap. "The simple fact was that Aleesha did not want help. She started running away before she turned thirteen."

Will echoed something that Angie had said about the girl. "You can't help somebody who doesn't want to be helped."

"That's true," the mother agreed. "Do you have children?"

"No, ma'am. I don't have any children."

"It's the most wonderful blessing God has given us, our ability to bring a child into the world." She held out her hands, cradling an imaginary infant. "You hold them in your arms that first time, and they are more precious than gold. Every breath you take after that is only for your child. Do you understand what I'm saying?"

Will nodded, his chest feeling as empty as her arms. He figured even if his own mother had held him, she obviously had no problem handing him off to somebody else shortly after.

Miriam continued, "Aleesha got mixed up with this

boy." He could see tears wetting her eyelashes. "I grew up poor, as did Dr. Monroe. We both knew the value of a good education, though, and we worked very hard to take advantage of the opportunities that other folks had fought, even died, for."

He tried to compliment her. "Obviously, you've succeeded."

She gave him a glance that said they both knew that material things were hardly a measure of success. "We thought raising our children here in this neighborhood would protect them. Decatur has always been a little oasis."

"Drugs have a way of getting into any community."

"I suppose that's true," she allowed. "We wanted so much more for her. You live through your children. You ache for them, hurt for them, breathe for them when you can." She told Will, "She ran off with some man she met at the treatment facility. She was arrested a few weeks later on a drug charge. Aleesha went to jail and the man disappeared, probably found himself another silly girl."

When Will started with the GBI, he had been amazed to find how many women ended up in jail because their boyfriends had sent them out on a deal, convincing the women that cops were more lenient with the fairer sex. Prison was full of young girls who thought they were in love.

Miriam interrupted his thoughts. "Dr. Monroe and I realized very gradually that drug addiction is a terminal disease. It is a cancer that eats families alive." She stood up and walked across the room to the grand piano, saying, "You get to a point where you look around and you ask yourself, 'What is this doing to the rest of my family? What harm am I doing to my *other* children by concentrating all of my energy on rescuing this one child who will not be saved?' "

Framed photographs lined the piano, and she held her

hand over each of them in turn. "Aleesha was the last girl. We called her our middle child because she was such a handful." She went to another frame, another child. "Ashley is the oldest. She's a gynecologist, like her father." She indicated yet another photograph. "Clinton is an orthopedist. Gerald is a psychiatrist. Harley is a classical pianist. Mason..." She picked up a small frame shaped like a dog and laughed. "He's a dog groomer, God love him." She was extra careful as she put the frame back in place and Will wondered if Mason was his mother's favorite.

Six children. A comfortable house. Plenty of clothes and food and parents who took care of you. What would it be like to grow up in a family like that? Why had Aleesha turned her back on all of this?

Of course, Will had been in law enforcement too long to take all of this on face value. He knew from experience that drug addicts didn't generally start out as the happiest people on earth. They turned to drugs for a reason, whether it was the desire to fit in or the need to tune out. The absent father could be some kind of sadist. The brothers could have looked no farther than the hallway for their first sexual forays. The older sister could have been an overachiever who cast the kind of shadow in which nothing could grow.

But Will was not here to rattle the skeletons in the Monroe family closet. He was here to tell this woman that her daughter, lost so long ago, was finally lost forever.

He asked, "You haven't seen your daughter in twenty years?"

"At least."

"No phone calls? No cards or letters?"

Miriam recalled, "A few years ago we got a call. She was in jail. She wanted money."

Michael had said that Aleesha listed only Baby G as a contact when she'd been arrested, but the duty officer would have made a notation of who she called while she was inside, who visited her if she was kept more than a day.

He asked, "Were you the one who spoke to her?"

"Yes," she answered. "The conversation didn't last more than a minute. I told my daughter that I was not going to give her any money and she slammed the phone down on me." Miriam explained, "That was the last time we heard from her. I don't even know where she lives now."

"Do you have any idea who she associated with? Who her friends were?"

She shook her head. "I'm sorry, Officer. I warned you I would be little help in finding her." She looked down at her hand, which was still resting on the piano. "Could you tell me what she's done? She hasn't..." She glanced up at Will, then back down again. "She hasn't harmed someone, has she?"

Will felt a lump rise in his throat. "Do your other children live close by?"

"Not close enough," she told him, a smile playing at her lips. "Mason is just down the street, but that's never close enough when you're a grandmother with three grandbabies to spoil."

"Maybe you should give him a call."

Her smile faltered. "Why would I need to do that?"

"Mrs. Monroe, I really wish you would call your son, or somebody who could maybe come and sit with you."

She sagged against the piano much as she had done at the front door. The dog gave a low growl as Will stood up.

Miriam's throat worked. "I suppose you're going to tell me that she finally took too much."

"No, ma'am." Again, he indicated the couch. "Would you please sit down?"

"I'm not going to faint," she told him, though her

chocolate complexion was a marked shade lighter. "Tell me what happened to my daughter."

Will should have just told her and left her with her grief, but he couldn't. To his surprise, when he spoke, he sounded as if he was begging. "Mrs. Monroe, please, sit down."

She let him lead her over to the couch and sit beside her. He should take her hand, do something to soothe her, but Will didn't feel equipped to comfort her. He did know that prolonging the inevitable was one of the most selfish things he had ever done in his life.

He said, "Aleesha was murdered Sunday night in the stairway to her apartment."

Miriam's mouth opened as she gasped for air. "Murdered?"

"Someone killed her," Will provided. "I think she probably knew her attacker. I think that she followed him out into the stairway and he injured her..." He faltered. "He injured her in such a way that it led to her death."

" 'Such a way,' " Miriam echoed. "What does that mean? Did she suffer?"

He was supposed to lie—it did no harm telling a mother her child had died quickly—but he could not. "I don't think there's any way to know if she was aware of what was happening to her. I hope she wasn't—" He stopped. "I hope there were enough drugs in her body so that she had no idea what was going on."

She gasped suddenly. "I saw it in the paper. A woman was murdered at Grady Homes. They didn't list her name, but... I never thought, I just assumed..."

"I'm sorry," Will told the poor woman, thinking he'd said that phrase more times in the last few days than he had in his entire life. He took out the photocopy of Aleesha's letter. "We found this in her mailbox. It was returned because there wasn't enough postage."

The mother grabbed the letter like it was a lifeline. Tears fell down her cheeks as she stared at the words. She must have read it a dozen times before she murmured, "The pariah."

"Can you tell me what she was talking about?"

Miriam held the letter in her lap, her hands trembling. "There was this house across the street—three doors down and a world away." She stared out the window as if she could see it. "We were the only black family in the neighborhood back then. Tobias and I laughed about people saying, 'There goes the neighborhood' when they already had the devil living in their own backyard."

"Does the family still live there?"

She shook her head. "There's been about ten different families in that house since the Carsons moved out. It's been added onto, turned into some kind of palace, but back then, it was just this little house where bad things happened. Every neighborhood has that, don't they? That one bad house with that one bad kid?"

"Yes, ma'am."

She looked back out the window. "Parties every weekend. Cars racing up and down the road. That boy was poison to everybody he came into contact with. We called him the Pariah of Paisley Street."

Will thought of the letter, the way Aleesha had referred to herself as a pariah.

Miriam continued, "His mother was never home. She was a lawyer, if you can believe that." She turned back to Will. "I suppose I could blame her until I was blue in the face, but the fact was that she was just as incapable of controlling her child as we were."

"Aleesha ran off with this boy?"

"No," the woman said. "She ran off with a thirty-nine-year-old man named Marcus Keith. He was one of the advisors in her treatment program. We found out later he had already served time for interfering with a minor." She gave a humorless laugh. "They might as well put a revolving door on every prison in America."

Will tried to tread carefully. "In the letter, she seems to be blaming you for something."

Miriam gave a tight smile. "When Aleesha was eleven years old, I left my family. There was a man. Like mother, like child, I suppose." She held up the letter. "Or, 'the sins of the parent,' as my daughter so eloquently put it."

"Obviously, you came back."

"Tobias and I worked it out, but things were very rocky for a long while. Aleesha got lost in the shuffle, and then she fell in with that boy up the street." She put her hand to her collar, pulling at a small cross that hung from a gold chain around her neck.

Will reached into his pocket and took out the cross from Aleesha's letter. "We found this, too."

Miriam looked at the cross but did not take it. "All my children have one."

He did not want to tell her that Aleesha had sent it back. The letter was bad enough. Still, he had to ask, "Is there any significance to the cross?"

"Tobias bought them when I returned home. We all gathered around the table and he passed them out one by one. It signified our unity, our faith that we could be a family again."

Will put the cross in her hand and folded her fingers around it. "I'm sure she'd want you to have this."

He left her alone in the room, walking down the hall, past the artwork, the photographs, everything Miriam and Tobias Monroe had accumulated over the years to turn their house into a home. There was a tall table by the door, and Will was leaving her one of his cards when he heard her speaking in the other room. Her tone was muffled by distance and grief. She was obviously on the telephone.

"It's Mama," she told one of her many children. "I need you."

CHAPTER THIRTY

9:16 PM

Angie was dead tired by the time she finished her shift.
Thanks to her hard work, a pair of visiting propane sales-
men, a truck driver and an unemployed father of three were
sitting in jail right now, trying to figure out how they were
going to explain to their wives that they had been arrested
for soliciting a prostitute. If their explanations were anything like the ones they gave Angie—*My wife doesn't understand me . . . I get lonely on the road . . . my kids hate me*—they
were looking at a long night in a cold cell.

In the scheme of things, Angie figured what she did
every day was a pointless endeavor. The johns still kept
coming back, the girls still kept going out. No one was interested in getting to the root of the problem. Angie had
spent the last six years getting to know these women. They
all had the same stories of sexual abuse and neglect in their
pasts; they all had run away from something. It didn't take a
Harvard economist to figure out that it'd be a hell of a lot
cheaper spending money on helping keep kids safe when
they were younger than it was to put them in jail when they
were older. That was the American way, though. Spend a
million dollars rescuing some kid who's fallen down a well,
but God forbid you spend a hundred bucks up front to cap
the well so the kid never falls down it in the first place.

Jasmine Allison was probably one of those lost kids who

would never be found. She'd end up on the street with a new name, new attitude, new addictions that a pimp could use to control her. Angie could tell from the way Will talked about the girl that he was worried. He had good reason, considering Jasmine had been paid to make that phone call the night Aleesha was murdered. Angie also knew that there could have been a million other little things that chased the girl from her home. Still, she'd called a couple of guys downtown and asked them to look into the case.

Angie looked at the directions she'd scrawled on the page she'd torn from the phone book. Ken Wozniak was living at a nursing home on Lawrenceville Highway. The charge nurse who had given Angie directions had sounded excited to hear the man was going to have a visitor. Angie had only met Ken a couple of times. She doubted he would even remember her.

Visiting hours were over at ten. Judging from the empty parking lot, Ken wasn't the only person who didn't get many guests. The lobby was sparse but clean, with the usual white tiles and fluorescent lights. Some fake flowers were on a table in the small waiting area and a water cooler burped as she walked to the receptionist's desk.

The man leaned back in his chair, a knowing smile on his face as he looked Angie up and down, taking in every inch of her whore's outfit with the kind of sneer that said he knew exactly what she was and how much she should cost. He laced his fingers behind his head, making his shirt ride up so that she could see his bloated, hairy belly.

He licked his lips, asked, "How much?"

Angie reached into her purse and pulled out her badge.

The guy literally fell out of his chair. He scrambled to stand back up, mumbling, "I was just—"

"I'm here to see Ken Wozniak."

"Oh, God." His voice shook as he tried to right the chair. "I need this job."

She wondered if he needed it so he could diddle the old ladies while they slept in their beds. "Take a pill, Cletus, I'm not here to bang you up."

"I just—"

"Wozniak," she repeated. "Where is he?"

His hands trembled as he tapped something into the computer keyboard. "Up the hall and to the left. Room three-ten. Jesus, lady, I'm sorry, okay? I've never done this before."

"Yeah, right. Me, either."

Angie's spiked heels clicked as she walked up the hallway. She could still see the way the prick receptionist had leered at her when she walked in the front door. That knowing look on his face like she was just a hole he was going to fuck. By the time she got to room three-ten, she felt about two feet tall.

"Hello?" she called, knocking on the door. Over the blare of the television, she heard a pleasant kind of grunt that she took as an invitation to come in.

"Ehn," Ken said when he saw her, his mouth curved up on one side as he tried to smile. He had lost about sixty pounds sitting in his wheelchair, and she wondered how he managed to wake up every morning knowing this was the life he had to look forward to.

"Remember me?" Angie asked.

He gave a deep, knowing laugh, as if to say, "How could I forget?"

Angie pulled a chair over and sat across from him. Ken fumbled with the remote in his lap, trying to mute the television. She hated nursing homes almost as much as she hated hospitals, and here she was visiting both in the same day. The chemical stench of disinfectant, the white sheets and flickering lights, reminded her of the first time she had seen her mother after the overdose. Deidre had been lying in bed, her body completely still, her mouth hanging open as if she had been surprised to find herself here. Irreversible coma. Angie was only a kid, but between *General Hospital* and *Days of Our Lives,* she knew exactly what that meant: baby, you are fucked.

"Deh," Ken said. He had finally managed to mute the television.

Angie tried to sound cheerful. "How you been?"

One shoulder went up. He'd certainly been better.

"Stupid question, huh?"

Ken allowed a smile on the side of his face that he could control.

"You can't talk well?"

"S'bad," he admitted.

"I'm here about Michael Ormewood."

He looked at the silent television for a couple of minutes. Finally, he blew out a puff of air.

Angie cut to the chase. "I know he's an asshole, so you don't have to bother telling me that."

Ken nodded.

"Did you know he beats his wife?"

Shock flickered in his eyes.

"Guess not," Angie said. "I saw her this morning. She looks like he took a bat to her."

His jaw set and his good hand clenched in his lap. Still a cop, even though he probably couldn't go to the toilet without someone there to wipe his ass.

Angie leaned forward, resting her elbows on her knees. "I know you didn't like him. Why? What was it about him that you didn't like?"

He blew out a noisy stream of air in answer.

Angie shook her head. "I'm not following."

He blew out some more air.

"Oh," she said, finally getting it. "Hot air. He's full of hot air."

Ken nodded, excited, and she felt like she was playing a painful game of charades.

Still, she couldn't stop now. "When Michael worked Vice," she confided, "he was taking advantage of the girls."

Ken shrugged.

"Is that a 'what do you expect' shrug or an 'I'm not surprised' shrug?"

He looked at his hand in his lap, the index and middle fingers slowly pointing up to show it was the second choice. *I'm not surprised.*

"I told him to leave or I'd report him, so he left."

"An ah ga..." His mouth closed. She could see he hated trying to talk. "Ah gah hih."

"Yeah," she said. Michael had been assigned as Ken's partner. "You got him."

They both sat there, Ken's mouth working but no noises coming out. Angie tried to keep her face blank, tried not to let on how hard it was seeing him like this.

Finally, he said, "You," clear enough for anyone to understand him.

"You what?"

He just stared, and Angie realized he was looking straight down her shirt. She straightened up, laughing. "Jesus, Wozniak. You old poon hound."

"Nah." He waved her off with his hand. "Nah dah." He glanced around the room as if he needed a prop. Finally, he looked back at his hands. She watched as he forced his right index finger straight out, then made a circle with his left thumb and index finger. He slid the circle up and down the finger.

Angie crossed her arms. "What the hell is wrong with you?"

"Nah," he insisted. *No.*

"Yeah," she snapped, duplicating the fucking gesture with her own hands. "I got you, Ken. I know exactly what you're saying and I gotta say I'm impressed you still got it, but no way in hell is it gonna happen."

"You!" he yelled back, jabbing an angry finger at her. "Ma-ahl." He made the sign again.

"Ohhhh." She drew out the word, his meaning finally sinking in. *You and Michael.*

She asked, "You knew about that?"

Ken raised his eyebrows. *Who doesn't?*

"Yeah," she admitted. "I fucked him."

"He . . . old . . . me."

"I bet he did." Jesus, they all knew.

"Eh," Ken said. *Hey.*

She looked up. He held out his hand in an open shrug, asking her what else.

"One of my girls was killed."

He pointed to the television. "Home." He had obviously seen the story on the news.

"Yeah, she lived at Grady Homes," Angie told him. "Her tongue was bitten off. She choked to death on her own blood."

"Ma-ahl?"

For a minute, Angie thought he was asking if Michael had killed her. Then she realized what he was asking.

"I don't know if Aleesha was one of the girls who went with him to get out of a bust," Angie admitted. "I stopped working the Homes about the same time he partnered up with you. My cover was blown."

"Who?"

Angie laughed at herself. She'd never even considered

the question, just assumed that there was only a certain number of times you could take a john out and not come back with him before people started realizing you were a cop.

"I guess Michael could have outed me," she allowed. "He might have thought he was getting me in trouble, but they just moved me to a different strip. New girls. New johns." She thought about one John in particular. "Michael came to my new drag a few months ago," she told Ken. "I thought he was just being an asshole, but he told us to look out for this guy who'd just been paroled, said he was a bad motherfucker."

Ken snorted. He had obviously had the pleasure of being on the receiving end of Michael's trash-talking.

"Yeah, I didn't think anything about it, either," she admitted. "Then I ran into the guy he'd warned us about. His name is John Shelley."

Ken shrugged. *Never heard of him.*

"Anyway," Angie said, knowing she was talking in circles. "The day after Aleesha Monroe died, Michael's next-door neighbor was found dead in her backyard."

"Huhn?"

"Yeah," Angie agreed. She told him the things he wouldn't have heard on the news. Angie herself would not have known the details but for Will. "The neighbor's tongue was cut out. Monroe's was bitten off, but still..."

Ken sat there. Angie felt bad. The old fucker was confused enough without her pouring her heart out to him.

"I shouldn't be bugging you with this."

"Mo." Ken made a circling motion with his hand. He wanted to hear more.

"Michael's neighbor was just fifteen." Angie stopped. Hadn't Gina Ormewood said she was fifteen when Michael met her?

She asked, "When was the Gulf War? Ninety? Ninety-one?"

Ken held up one finger.

"How old do you think Michael is? He's forty, right? They had some kind of party for him last year. I remember there were black balloons everywhere."

Ken nodded.

Angie sucked at math. Will would have figured all of this in his head, but she needed something to write on. She found a scrap of paper in her purse and scribbled the numbers down with her eyeliner pencil, muttering, "Michael was born in sixty-six, minus two thousand six." She checked the numbers, making sure she had it right. Slowly, she looked up at Ken. "Gina was fifteen when she met him. She said at first he was interested in her cousin, who was a year younger."

She held up the sheet for Ken to see. "He was twenty-five. What's a twenty-five-year-old man doing with a fifteen-year-old girl?"

Ken made a suggestive sound, the meaning loud and clear.

"Tell me something," she began. "You ever go fishing with Michael up in the mountains?"

The expression on his face was as clear as if he had spoken the words. *Hell no.*

Angie drove right past her house, her mind still trying to grasp what she had figured out while she talked to Ken. The fact that Michael Ormewood had pursued and married a teenage girl almost fifteen years ago wasn't exactly evidence that he was involved in something now, but the coincidence was still there and Angie had been a cop too long to believe in coincidences.

She worked a scenario in her head as she made a U-turn at the end of her street, passing by her house again and heading down Piedmont. She took a left at the light, then another left onto Ponce de Leon, as she let the possibilities play out. Michael was still using the girls, pulling rank for freebies. Baby G had figured this out. Maybe Aleesha Monroe had been one of the girls Michael used and G hadn't liked the cut in his income. He had killed Monroe, then killed Michael's next-door neighbor as a lesson.

But why would Baby G kill Cynthia Barrett? Even if Michael did have a thing for teenage girls, that didn't mean he was screwing his neighbor. And it wasn't like that kind of lechery was unusual in a man of forty. All you had to do was look at a fashion magazine or go to the local cinema to find images of scantily clad girls hanging on to men who were old enough to be their fathers. Hell, you couldn't walk through the local shopping mall without seeing a bunch of twelve-year-olds wearing T-shirts up to their nipples and jeans down to their hooches. And their mothers were usually wearing the same thing.

Angie passed City Hall East, then took a right into Poncey-Highlands. She slowed the car, checking to make sure Will's motorcycle was out front before she parked on the street.

She got out of the car, not giving herself time to change her mind. She used her fist to knock on his door, then pushed the bell a couple of times for good measure.

He took his sweet time opening the door. She saw he had rolled down his sleeves but not buttoned the cuffs. He was still wearing his vest and that stupid little dog was scooped into his left hand like a bag of candy.

She demanded, "Why do you always take so long to answer the fucking door?"

"What's wrong?"

She dropped her purse by the door and walked past him into the house. An audiobook was playing in the background and a pocket watch was laid out on the worktable where he had taken it apart to repair it. She looked at the tiny springs and gears he had stuck into a piece of cork, the various instruments he used to repair the winding mechanism. Angie had always been shocked by the fact that Will could figure out how a watch worked in about ten seconds but it took him half an hour to understand a page in a book.

Will put the dog on the floor. She trotted off into the kitchen. Angie heard her drinking some water.

"What's wrong?" Will repeated, muting the stereo.

"You need to talk to Aleesha's pimp."

"Baby G?" Will asked. "He's dead."

"What?"

"He died this afternoon," Will told her. "His cousins got sick of being pushed around."

"Slow down," she said, though she was the one with the racing heart. "Tell me what happened."

He narrowed his eyes, but still told her. "The day that Michael and I talked to Baby G, there were two kids sitting on the hood of his BMW. G said they were his cousins."

Angie sat on the couch. "Okay."

"He chased them off with a bat. I guess they didn't like it. They ambushed him, shot him three times."

"Sit down," Angie told him. She hated when he hovered over her. "Are you sure that's what happened? The cousins shot him?"

"As sure as you can be when you're dealing with these thugs." Will sat beside her. "I talked to the arresting officer this afternoon. The kids will probably be tried as adults. One's already flipped on the other. He's got a record, a drug bust, an assault. This would be his third strike. He's trying to talk his way out of a life sentence."

"Are you sure they're not involved in the case?"

"Neither one of them even knew Aleesha."

Angie nodded, letting him know that she had heard him. She was too shocked to talk. Whatever Baby G knew about Michael Ormewood would be taken to his grave.

Will said, "You look bad."

"Thanks."

"I mean it," he said. "What's wrong with you?"

"I had a really hard day," she told him, suddenly feeling everything catch up with her. "I had to go to the hospital."

He sat up, took her hand. "Are you okay?"

"Not for me." She lied because it was easier than dealing with his anger if he found out she'd gone to Piedmont this morning to put the fear of Jesus into Ormewood's wife. "I took one of the girls in. It wasn't anything bad. Women stuff."

Will nodded, and she knew he wouldn't press her.

Christ, what a mess. She had things to tell him but didn't know where to begin. What could she say? That the night of Ken's party, Michael was rough with her? That Michael was the kind of guy you couldn't change your mind with? That with him, once things got started, there was no such thing as stopping?

She could still remember how much it hurt the next day, the bruises on her thighs, the feeling that something deep inside her had been torn. Shit, she'd been drunk out of her mind, but the marks on her skin were clear enough to tell the story.

"You okay?" Will tucked her hair behind her ear. The gentle gesture was something new. He never touched her like that, or maybe she never let him.

She said, "It was hard being there," not telling him exactly where "there" was. "I kept thinking about my mom."

Will stroked her hair and she wanted to close her eyes, put her head on his shoulder. Angie had taken him to see her mother a couple of times. Going to her mother's grave would have been easier for Angie than seeing Deidre lying in that hospital bed, not knowing if somewhere behind those closed eyes she was screaming for help. Why did Angie love the one person she should hate the most?

"Come here," Will said, pulling her close, putting his arms around her. He leaned back on the couch, taking her with him. "Just stay like this for a while."

Angie wanted to cry, but she couldn't let herself break down in front of Will. She pressed her face to his shoulder, smelling the detergent he used and the soy sauce that had dripped onto his tie. If she could stay like this, if she could just let him hold her, then maybe things would get better. Maybe they could make each other whole.

She turned her face toward him and kissed his neck. His skin reacted, and she kissed his Adam's apple as he swallowed.

He said, "We don't have to . . ."

She cupped her hand around his neck and put her lips to his. Will was reluctant, but she teased the passion out of him, using her teeth and tongue until he started kissing her in earnest. His arms tensed as he gently lifted her up and laid her back on the couch. He kept his weight on his left elbow, his hand brushing her face as he kissed her neck.

The cuff of his shirt had slipped back, and Angie saw the angry pink scar on the inside of his wrist. She had taken him to the hospital that night, stayed by his bed as she waited for him to wake up and realize that it hadn't worked, that he was still alive.

Tentatively, she touched his wrist, tracing her finger

along the same path the razor blade had taken as it had flayed open his skin.

Will jerked away, staring at her in shock.

"I'm sorry," she apologized.

He tried to sit up, but she grabbed his vest in her fists, pulling him back. "I said I'm sorry."

"Angie—" He tried to pull away again, but she wouldn't let him. They struggled but Will would never use his full strength against her. She managed to pull him down, pressing her lips firmly to his. She arced up into him and he stopped resisting. Angie kissed him deeper, rougher than usual, and to her surprise he returned it with the same intensity.

She felt her breath quicken, her mind blur. The weight of him on top of her was enough to bring tears to her eyes, and she slid her hand down into the waist of his pants, needing for this to go quickly before she lost herself.

"Christ," she mumbled, pulling open his vest, tugging his shirt out of his pants, then his undershirt, so that there was room enough for her hand.

He had pushed up her shirt, his mouth finding her bare breast. When she wrapped her hand around him, he lost his rhythm. She took over, using her free hand to slide down her panties. Angie guided him inside her before he could stop her.

His breath caught as she thrust up to him, tightening herself around him, trying to make him come.

"No," he whispered, struggling to slow down. His eyes were squeezed shut and he shook from the effort of restraining himself. She licked her tongue in his ear, bit the lobe, did everything in her power to force his release. He groaned loudly as he gave in, shuddering in climax.

"Oh, God," he breathed. "Angie . . ."

She let him kiss her some more, stopping him when his

mouth started to move down on her. "No," she told him, pulling him back up to her face. "I need to go."

He was sweating, his breathing hard as he kissed her breasts. "Let me taste you."

The raw growl of his voice sent a tingle through her body. She bit her bottom lip, trying not to think about how good his mouth would feel down lower as his lips grazed her stomach.

"No," she managed, gently pulling him back up. "I need to go."

"Stay with me."

Somehow, the begging quality to his voice made it easier for her to leave. "I've got work tomorrow."

"So do I."

She pushed him away more firmly this time. "Will."

He rolled off her and fell against the back of the couch with another groan, but this one was far from an expression of pleasure.

She pulled her underwear back on as she stood. Her shirt was still crooked and she leaned over as she adjusted it.

He wrapped his hand around her leg. "Why do you do this?"

She stepped out of his reach, finding her purse on the table by the front door. "Why do you let me?"

CHAPTER THIRTY-ONE

Martha Lam had apparently made not one but several phone calls. John had gotten a full refund on the rent he had paid at the flophouse and the room at Mr. Applebaum's was almost thirty dollars cheaper a month. Combined with the fifty bucks John had gotten for crawling through the vacuum tank, he might actually be able to eat this month.

"Damn," Ray-Ray said. He was looking at a woman who had just pulled up with a Toyota Camry full of screaming kids. "She cain't help that she ugly, but the least she could do is stay at home."

John gave him a sideways glance. "When'd you learn to speak in complete sentences?"

"They's a lot more to a brother than what you see," Ray-Ray told him.

He left John at the dryer and went to help wipe down one of the cars. John's uneasy peace with Ray-Ray had settled into some kind of friendliness on the other man's part since he'd taken him to the hospital. John wasn't sure what had brought about this transformation, but he wasn't about to complain. He had enough people after him right now. Anything that got Ray-Ray off his back was all right with him.

The hospital visit had been a good thing for John, too. He still felt his heart skip in his chest when he thought about seeing Robin in the waiting room. She'd been wearing her work attire, but he couldn't help seeing past that to her soft skin, her full lips. The way she stood with her weight shifted to one leg, her hip jutting out. What would it be like to run his hand along that hip, pull her close to him? These were the kinds of thoughts that kept a man awake at night.

Robin wasn't the reason John had gotten in to work early this morning, showing up even before Art. Moving from one place to the other wasn't a big deal. John had tossed his clothes into the cooler and used it as a suitcase as he walked the six blocks over to Mr. Applebaum's house. Once John was settled in, he went back to Ashby Street one more time and dug up the knife where he had buried it under a tree for safekeeping. He'd sweated all the way on the bus, scared he'd be caught with a weapon. At the car wash, John had dropped it in the vacuum canister and sat on the retaining wall under the magnolia tree until Art had driven up in his Cadillac, asking, "What's with you, Shelley? You bucking for a promotion?" as he locked his car door.

John was trying to think logically, figure out what to do next, but as much as he tried to concentrate, all he could feel was a burning anger. Michael had put that knife under his mattress in the flophouse just like he'd stashed the kitchen knife, the so-called murder weapon, in John's closet all those years ago. What the hell did the guy have against him? What did John ever do to Michael to bring this down on his head? Not just John's head, but on his entire family.

It was one thing to set up John all those years ago, but to keep it up, to use his identity while he was locked away in prison . . . that was some kind of sick obsession. Michael hated him. You didn't hold on to another man's name for all these years unless you really fucking hated the guy. And the prick had obviously used his position on the police force to reach out to Ms. Lam, trying to get her to throw John back into Coastal with the pedophiles and rapists. It wasn't enough to frame him. He wanted John to suffer.

John had adjusted to his loss of freedom over the years, letting himself believe on some level that he belonged with men like Ben Carver. He had been a bad kid, a bad son. Richard Shelley could have testified to that. Even without his father's damning testimony, in John's own court of opinion, he did not come out completely blameless in Mary Alice's murder. He had invited her to the party. He had been stoned. He had given her the alcoholic drink. He had gone back to her house, sneaked into her bedroom. He had snorted the speedball that knocked him on his ass. He had let it all happen.

But knowing it was Michael, his own cousin Woody, who had butchered Mary Alice made John sick with rage. He couldn't be angry for his own sake, but he could be angry for Mary Alice, livid as hell that Michael had not just raped the girl, not just killed her, but ravaged her like a rabid animal.

The crime scene photographs in the courtroom had been shocking, but John had been there, had seen her body with his own two eyes. The bite marks on her small breasts. The dark bruises and deep lacerations on her inner thighs. The way her eyes were still open, staring at the door like she thought her mother would walk through at any minute and wake her for church. Her mouth had been brimming with her own blood, her hair stuck to the pillow with it.

That fucking bastard. That God damn sick bastard.

It didn't stop with Mary Alice, though. Michael was still out there, still doing whatever the hell he wanted to do in John's name. And he was a cop. A cop! He could jam up John anytime, was probably sitting on his ass right now thinking of yet another way to put John in the frame for his own sick crimes. The thought of last night, the tips of John's fingers touching the folding knife, almost getting caught with a weapon in his hands, made him break out into a cold sweat. Michael could do anything. He could arrest John right now and there was nothing John could do about it.

And maybe John deserved it. Maybe after what he had done to Michael's neighbor, he deserved to be tossed back in jail with all the other sick bastards. He had mutilated a child. He had used his own hands to defile that girl. It didn't seem right that he should get away with such a thing.

The way things were looking, he probably wouldn't.

The dryer stopped and John started folding the towels, piling them up in a rolling sixty-drum trashcan so they could move them around the cars as they worked. He needed to talk to Ben again. John had grown up in prison, but he thought like a prisoner, not a criminal. He needed someone to tell him what to do.

"Are you John?"

The woman in front of him was slim, about five-eight or -nine. Her black hair was in a pixie cut and she wore a close-fit cropped jacket over her tight blue jeans.

"Can I help you?" he asked, looking for the telltale bulge under her jacket. She didn't look like a cop to him, her jacket was too nice, but John had never been good at spotting the bad guys.

"You're John Shelley?" she asked.

He glanced over her shoulder. Ray-Ray was sucking on a lollipop, but John could see his eyes were taking in the scene.

John asked, "Do I know you?"

"You moved," she said. "I thought you lived on Ashby Street."

He tried to smile when what he really wanted to do was drop the towels and run. "What's going on?"

She had her hands on her hips, and he thought about Ms. Lam. He couldn't help himself. He looked right at the metal cap screwed onto the vacuum tank.

"I'm Kathy Keenan," she said. "A friend of your sister's."

He dropped the towels. "Is Joyce—"

"She's fine," the woman assured him. "You just need to talk to her."

"I . . ." He looked down at the pile of towels, then back up at the woman. He didn't know who she was or why she was here, but she was crazy if she thought she could make Joyce do anything she didn't want to do.

John knelt down to scoop up the towels. "She doesn't want to talk to me."

"I know she doesn't," Kathy said. "But she needs to."

"Who are you?"

"I told you. I'm a friend of hers."

"You can't know her very well if you think this will work."

"I've shared her bed for the last twelve years, John. I think I pretty much know her better than anyone on earth."

So, Joyce was gay. John wondered what Richard thought about that. One child a convicted rapist and murderer, the other queer as a three-dollar bill. John couldn't help but smile at the probable magnitude of Richard's disappointment.

Kathy had asked, "Does it bother you that your sister's a lesbian?"

"I really don't think I have room to talk," John had

admitted, all the while thinking, God, Richard must have been livid when he found out. His perfect Joyce was batting for the other team.

Kathy drove a black Porsche, the kind of car John could only see from his hands and knees as he cleaned the trash out of it. She had driven him straight up Piedmont Road, taking a right on Sidney Marcus and ending up parked in front of a small building on Lenox Road right up from the interstate. The sign outside read Keener, Rose and Shelley in fancy gold script. The car beside them, a graphite gray BMW, was parked in the space reserved for Joyce Shelley.

Joyce worked less than two miles from the Gorilla. She might have even passed him every day on her drive in.

"She's handling a closing right now," Kathy said. "She won't be long."

John's knees popped as he rolled himself out of the low-lying car. Time and again, he had to remind himself that he was almost forty years old. For some reason, he still felt fifteen, like Coastal had happened to another John, his mind going there while his body stayed on the outside, not aging, waiting for him to come back and claim it.

"We'll wait in her office," Kathy suggested, leading him through the building. The receptionist's eyes followed John as he walked past her desk, and he imagined that but for the janitor, she wasn't used to seeing his kind strolling through these pristine corridors.

"Back here." Kathy had grabbed some notes from a cubbyhole with her name on it, and she read through these as they walked down the hall.

Joyce's office was nice, exactly as John would have imagined if he let himself think about his sister and her life outside of him. The Persian carpet on the floor had deep blues and burgundies and the curtains were a thin linen that let in the sunlight. The paint on the wall was a kind of chocolate beige. The colors were masculine, but there was something really feminine to the way Joyce had used them. Or maybe a designer had done the office, some pricey chick from Buckhead who got paid to spend rich people's money. There were a couple of Oriental-looking paintings that weren't to John's taste, but the pictures on the credenza under the windows made his heart hurt in his chest.

A young Joyce and John on the log ride at Six Flags. Baby John in Richard's lap as he gave him a bottle. Ten-year-old Joyce on the beach in her two-piece bathing suit, a Popsicle in each hand. There were more recent photographs, too. Kathy and Joyce at the zoo. Kathy on a horse with a mountain view behind her. Two Labrador retrievers rolling around on the grass.

The photo that stopped him was of his mother. Emily with a scarf around her head, her eyes sunken, cheeks hollow. She was smiling, though. His mother had always had the most beautiful smile. John had gotten through so many nights thinking about that smile, the easy way she bestowed it, the genuine kindness behind it. Tears fell from his eyes at the sight of her, and he felt a physical ache knowing he would never see her again.

Kathy said, "Emily was a wonderful person."

John made himself put the frame back where it belonged. He used the back of his hand to wipe his eyes. "You knew her?"

"Yes," Kathy said. "She was very close to Joyce. It was hard on all of us when she got sick."

"I don't..." John didn't know how to say this. "I don't remember seeing you at the funeral."

"I was there," she said, and he saw tension around her eyes. "Your father isn't very accepting of Joyce's relationship with me."

"No," John said. "He wouldn't be." Richard had always

been certain that he knew the difference between right and wrong, good and bad. Whoever crossed that line was as easily cut out of his life as the cancerous tumors he removed in the operating room.

John felt the need to say, "I'm sorry about that. He's always loved Joyce."

Kathy gave him a careful look. "Are you trying to defend your father?"

"I guess it helps me if I try to understand his side of things, why he thinks the way he does."

She walked across the room and opened a door. John assumed it led to the bathroom, but he could see now that it was a walk-in closet lined with three filing cabinets. Spiral notebooks, probably fifty in all, were stacked in neat piles on top of each one.

"These are all your court transcripts from your preliminary hearing, to the change of venue denial, to the last appeal." She had pointed to different drawers as she said this. "This is your medical stuff." She rested her hand on the top drawer of the cabinet nearest John. "Your first overdose in the ER, your admit after they arrested you, and..." Her mouth opened, but she had stopped. She still looked him in the eye, though. "Information from the Coastal infirmary."

John swallowed. Zebra. They knew about Zebra.

"This is mostly parole board reports," Kathy said, opening a drawer that contained six or seven thick files. "Joyce got the copy of your last one about a month ago."

"Why?" John said, thinking about the volumes of files Joyce had kept for over twenty years. "Why would she have this?"

"It was your mother's," Kathy told him. "These notebooks." She took one off the pile. "These are all her notes. She knew your case backward and forward."

John opened the notebook, stared at his mother's neat cursive without really seeing it. When Emily was growing up, penmanship had mattered. Her writing was beautiful, flowing across the page like perfect flowers.

The words, however, weren't so pretty.

Speedball = heroin + cocaine + ??? Why the bradycardia? Why the apnea? John turned the page. *Bite marks around breasts match dental impressions?* And, *No semen recovered. Where is condom???*

Kathy said, "She was trying to get the physical evidence from the county at the end."

"Why?"

"She wanted to do a DNA test on the knife to prove that it was her blood, but the sample was so small they could only do a mitochondrial panel." When he shook his head, Kathy explained, "Mitochondrial DNA comes from the mother, so even if it was Emily's blood, there's no way to rule out that it couldn't be yours, too. Or Joyce's for that matter, but that still wouldn't have helped the case."

" 'Bite marks'?" he read.

"She thought they could show your teeth didn't match the bite marks, but there was a case, a Supreme Court case, where bite-mark evidence was ruled inadmissible." She added, "But she thought that might help with the . . . the severing."

"What?"

"The state's odontologist was never called to the stand. About three years before she died, Emily petitioned for all your evidence, all the files. She was determined to start over, see if she missed anything. She found a report where the state's dental expert said that he thought the tongue was . . . that it was bitten off, not cut off."

"Bitten off?" John echoed. His mind flashed on Cynthia Barrett, the sickening slickness of her tongue when he'd gripped it between his thumb and forefinger. Cutting was hard enough, but biting? What kind of monster bit off a girl's tongue?

"John?"

He cleared his throat, made himself speak. "The knife was their key piece of evidence. They had an expert who said it was used to cut out her tongue. It proved premeditation."

"Right. Emily was going for prosecutorial misconduct. They claim they handed over the doctor's report about the bite to Lydia during pretrial discovery, but Emily couldn't find any record of it. It could have been grounds for an appeal."

He fanned through the pages, looked at the dates. "Mom was working on this when she was sick."

"She couldn't stop," Kathy told him. "She wanted to get you out."

He couldn't get over the volume of notes she had taken. Pages and pages filled with all sorts of horrible details his mother should have never even heard about. For the second time that day, he was crying in front of his sister's lover. "Why?" he asked. "Why did she do this? The appeals were over."

"There was still a slim chance," Kathy answered. "She didn't want to give that up."

"She was too sick," he said, flipping to the back of the notebook, seeing that the last entry was a week before she went into the hospital for the last time. "She shouldn't have been doing this. She should've been focusing on getting stronger, getting better."

"Emily knew she wasn't going to get better," Kathy told him. "She spent the last days of her life doing exactly what she wanted to do."

He was really crying now—big, fat tears as he thought

about his mother poring over all this information every night, trying to find something, anything, that would get him out.

"She never told me," John said. "She never told me she was doing this."

"She didn't want to get your hopes up," Joyce said.

He swung around, wondering how long his sister had been standing behind him.

Joyce didn't look angry when she said, "Kathy, what are you doing?"

"Interfering," the other woman answered, smiling the way someone smiles when they've done something wrong but they know you'll forgive them.

Kathy said, "I'll leave you two alone." She squeezed Joyce's hand as she walked past her, then pulled the door closed.

John was still holding the notebook, Emily's life's work. "Your office is nice," he said. "And Kathy . . ."

"How about that?" she said, wryly. "A bona fide homo in the Shelley clan."

"I bet Dad was proud."

She snorted a laugh. "Yeah. So happy that he changed his will."

John clenched his jaw. He didn't know what he was supposed to say.

"Mama made me promise not to throw those out," Joyce told him, waving her hand toward the closet. "I wanted to. I wanted to dump them all out in the yard and have a big bonfire. I almost did." She gave a humorless bark of a laugh, as if she was still surprised she hadn't torched everything. "I should have. I should have at least put them in a storage place or buried them somewhere." She let out a heavy sigh. "But I didn't."

"Why?"

"Because it's her. All of those files, all of those stupid notebooks. Did you know she never went anywhere without one?" Joyce added wryly, "Of course you didn't. She never took them inside when she visited you, but she worked on them, thought about them, the whole way down and the whole way back. Sometimes she'd call me in the middle of the night and ask me to look into some obscure law she found, something she thought might wrangle a new trial for you." Joyce looked back at the filing cabinets, the notebooks. "It's like they're tiny little pieces of her heart, her soul, and if I throw them out now, then I'm throwing her out, too."

John smoothed his hand along the cover of the notebook. His mother had given her life to him, dedicated her every waking moment to getting him out of Coastal.

All because of Michael Ormewood.

Michael might as well have killed Emily after he finished with Mary Alice. He should have reached into Joyce's chest and squeezed the life out of her heart. Oh, God, John wanted to kill him. He wanted to beat him senseless, then wrap his hands around Michael's neck and watch the other man's eyes as he realized he was going to die. John would loosen his hands, taking him to the edge then bringing him back just to watch the fear, the absolute fucking terror, as Michael realized he was completely helpless. Then, John would just leave him. He'd leave him alone in the middle of nowhere and let him die all by himself.

"John?" Joyce said. She had always been intuitive, always known when something was bothering him.

He opened the notebook again, skimmed his mother's writing. "What's this?" he asked. "Bradycardia. What does that mean?"

Joyce walked over to the closet and opened one of the

file drawers. "When they arrested you," she said, "you were too weak to stand on your own."

"Yeah." He had been terrified.

"They took you to the hospital. Mom kept insisting something was wrong with you." She searched through the files. "She made them do an EKG, an EEG, bloodwork, MRI."

John had a vague recollection of this. "Why?"

"Because she knew that something was wrong." Joyce finally found what she was looking for. "Here."

He took the medical report, carefully reading the words while Joyce waited. The numbers on the tests made no sense to him, but John had worked at the prison infirmary. He knew the section to look for. He read aloud from the handwritten doctor's notes under the box labeled "conclusions."

" 'Resting heart rate below sixty, ataxic breathing and general physical condition indicate drug toxicity.' " He looked back at Joyce. "I took drugs, Joyce. I never said I didn't."

"No." She shook her head. "Read the rest."

John read to himself this time. The doctor had indicated that John's symptoms were not consistent with an overdose of cocaine and heroin. He suspected another drug was involved. Further blood tests were inconclusive, but testing was recommended on the powdered substance found at the scene.

The powdered substance. Michael had given him the baggie. John had never done heroin in his life. He had assumed good old Woody was trying to do him a favor, when in fact he had been trying to knock him out. Not just knock him out. Maybe there had been something else in that bag besides cocaine and heroin. John knew from prison talk that the labs could only find what they were specifically looking for. Michael could have spiked the speedball with something even more potent, something that would finish the job in case the volatile mixture didn't.

"What?" Joyce asked.

John's surprise must have registered on his face. He had been focusing on Mary Alice all this time. Had Michael meant to kill John, too? Had he thought to make it easier for himself to do whatever he wanted with Mary Alice and leave the blame at the foot of John's grave?

Two days after Mary Alice's body had been found, Michael and his mother had come by to visit. John was laid up in his room, feeling like shit, hiding behind a story he told to his mother about having a bad cold when in fact he could barely breathe every time he thought about Mary Alice's body lying beside him in her bed.

Michael had been the same as always, at least as far as John could recall. His cousin had stayed with him in his room, talking about—what?—John couldn't remember now. Something stupid, he was sure. John had fallen asleep. Was it then that Michael had planted the knife in his closet? Was it then that Michael had formed his plan? Or had somebody else worked it out from the beginning, sent Michael upstairs with the knife, told him to put it in John's closet so that there would be something concrete that tied him to Mary Alice's bedroom?

"Johnny?" Joyce said. She hadn't called him that since they were kids. "What is it?"

He closed the folder. "What do you remember about Aunt Lydia?"

"She was your lawyer." Joyce added, "She quit criminal law and went over to corporate after what happened to you. She said she lost her stomach for it. She never forgave herself for not being able to help you."

"I'll bet."

Joyce was obviously taken aback by the hatred in his tone. "I'm serious, John. She came to see Mom at the hospital."

"When was this?"

"I guess it was the day before Mom passed away. They had just put the tube down her throat so she could breathe." Joyce paused, collecting herself. "She was in a lot of pain. They had her on a morphine drip. I'm not even sure she knew Kathy and I were there, let alone Lydia."

"What did Lydia say to her?"

"I have no idea. We left them alone." She added, "She looked really bad. Aunt Lydia, I mean. She hadn't seen Mom in years but she couldn't stop crying. I never thought they were close, but maybe during the trial . . . I don't know. I was so upset back then that I wasn't paying much attention to anybody."

"You didn't hear anything?"

"No," Joyce said. "Well, just at the end. I came back too soon, I guess. Lydia was holding Mom's hand. We'd told her the doctors said she didn't have long, maybe a day at the most." Joyce paused, probably thinking back on the scene. "Mom's eyes were closed—I don't even think she was aware that Lydia was there." She tilted her head. "But Lydia was sobbing. Really sobbing, John, like her heart was broken. She was shaking, and she kept saying, 'I'm so sorry, Emily. I'm so sorry.'" Joyce concluded, "She never forgave herself. She never got over losing your case."

Right, John thought. Aunt Lydia was probably plenty over it now. Nothing like unburdening your sins to someone who wouldn't live to tell them.

He asked, "How was Mom after she left?"

"Still out of it," Joyce answered. "She slept all of the time. It was hard for her to keep her eyes open."

"Did she say anything?"

"She couldn't, John. She had the tube down her throat."

John nodded. It was all making sense now. The first thing Aunt Lydia had done as his lawyer was sit John down and make him tell her everything about that night, everything that had happened. John had been terrified. He had told her the absolute truth, fuck whatever code of honor you were supposed to have about ratting out other kids. He told her about Michael tossing him the bag of what John thought was coke, about walking Mary Alice home and climbing through the window into her bedroom. He told her about the kiss, the way his brain had exploded like a rocket had gone off in his head. He told her about waking up the next morning lying in a pool of Mary Alice's blood.

When John had finished telling her the story, Aunt Lydia had tears in her eyes. She took his hand—grabbed it, actually—so hard that it hurt.

"Don't worry, John," she had said. "I'll take care of everything."

And she did. The bitch certainly did.

Joyce was still looking at him, waiting. He could tell she was tired, maybe exhausted. Makeup couldn't hide the dark circles under her eyes. Her shoulders were slumped in defeat. Still, John could not help but notice that she had stood here in her office talking to him for around thirty minutes without once yelling at him or accusing him of anything.

He asked, "Did they ever test the drugs? The white powder?"

"Of course. Lydia sent it to a private lab. Mom was on pins and needles for a week. They didn't come up with anything unusual, though. It was cocaine and heroin."

John felt a stabbing pain in his jaw. He had been clenching his teeth again.

"Johnny," Joyce said, sounding tired. So tired. "Tell me."

He closed his mother's notebook, the last notebook she had used on his case, the last thing she had ever held in her hands that connected her to her son.

"Get Kathy back in here," John said. "I think she needs to hear this, too."

CHAPTER THIRTY-TWO

9:22 PM

Will sat in his office, trying not to twiddle his thumbs. He had paid a visit to Luther Morrison, Jasmine Allison's... what? What did you call a thirty-year-old man who was having sex with a fourteen-year-old girl? Sick God damn bastard was what Will had decided on, and it had taken everything in him not to punch the animal in the face.

After that pleasant visit, Will had returned to City Hall East and caught up Amanda Wagner on the case. She hadn't offered any staggering insight but neither had she taken him to task for not having a lot to say. Amanda could be demanding, but she knew a difficult case when she saw one.

The one thing she had told him was to not focus so much on the missing girl. Will's case was the murder of Aleesha Monroe and how it connected to the other girls, not a runaway named Jasmine Allison. All he had was a ten-year-old boy's story and a bad feeling, and while Amanda respected his gut instinct, she wasn't about to waste time and resources based on either. She summed it up for him with her usual heart-warming pragmatism: the girl had a history of running away. She was dating a man who was twice her age. Her mother was in prison, her father was who knows where and most days, her grandmother couldn't get out of a chair without assistance.

The only way this would be news is if she *hadn't* run away.

The DeKalb cops hadn't moved an inch on Cynthia Barrett's case and they weren't keen to share their notes with Will. The DNA obtained from the vaginal swab Pete had taken was too contaminated to test. Toxicology had not yet come back, but Will wasn't holding his breath for a miraculous revelation.

As for Aleesha Monroe, Forensics had reported nothing more earthshattering about her apartment than what Will had seen for himself: the place was remarkably clean. He'd even sent back the techs to test the spot he'd found in Monroe's doorway the night Jasmine was reported missing. There had not been enough of a sample to determine anything other than the spot was human blood.

All Will had to follow now was the stack of papers Leo Donnelly had left on his desk. Will had counted out the pages so that he would know what was ahead of him. About sixty rap sheets, two or three pages each, all detailing the lurid crimes of the metro area's recently released sex offenders.

He wasn't that desperate yet.

Will opened the fluorescent pink folder on his desk and found a recordable DVD in the back pocket. He slid this into the tray on his computer and clicked play.

The monitor showed two women and a man sitting at a table with a teenage girl. The man spoke first, identifying himself as Detective Dave Sanders of the Tucker police department, then giving the names of the two women before saying, "This is the statement of Julie Renee Cooper. Case number sixteen-forty-three-seven. Today is December ninth, two-thousand-five."

Julie Cooper leaned toward the microphone. The camera

angle was wide and Will could see the girl's feet swinging back and forth over the floor.

"I went to the movies," the girl began, her words difficult to understand. Will knew that when the recording had been made, her severed tongue had only recently been reattached. "There was a man in the alley." Will had watched the teenager's statement so many times that he could almost recite the story along with her. He knew when she paused to cry, her head down on the table, and the point where she got so upset that the recording had to be stopped.

Her abductor had dragged her into the alley. Julie had been too frightened to scream. He was wearing a black mask with holes for the mouth and eyes. She tasted blood when he put his mouth over hers, shoved his tongue past her lips. When she tried to turn her head away, he punched her in the face.

"Kiss me," he kept saying. "Kiss me."

Will jumped at the sound of his phone ringing. He picked up the receiver, said, "Will Trent."

There was a pause on the other end, but no words.

"Hello?" Will asked, turning down the volume on the computer speakers.

"Hey, man," Michael Ormewood said. "Didn't think you'd be there this late."

Will sat back in his chair, wondering why Michael had called if he'd thought Will wasn't going to be there. "Why didn't you try my cell?"

"Couldn't find the number," Michael explained, though how that was possible, Will did not know. He'd given all his numbers—even his home—on every message he'd left for Michael since Monday night. At first, Will had just wanted to talk to the man about Jasmine; now, he wanted to know why Michael had been avoiding his calls.

Will asked, "Everything okay?"

"Yeah. Thanks for asking." Will heard the click of a lighter. Michael inhaled, then said, "Been making myself useful around here. Knocked out some of those chores Gina's been ragging me about."

"Good." Will was quiet, knowing Michael would fill in the silence.

The detective said, "I talked to Barbara like you asked. My mother-in-law? She says she never saw Cynthia skipping school. Maybe the kid just wasn't feeling good that day?"

"Makes sense," Will allowed. He wasn't used to talking to people like Michael unless he was interrogating them, and Will struggled not to let his hatred come through. That's what it was—hatred. The man beat his wife. To Will's thinking, he raped prostitutes. God only knew what he had done to Angie.

Will asked, "How's your family?"

Michael hesitated. "What?"

"You said the other day you didn't feel safe. I was just wondering if they were doing okay."

"Yeah," Michael answered. "I got them over at my mother-in-law's, like I said." He chuckled. "Tell you what, she spoils Tim. There's gonna be a major adjustment when he gets back home."

Will thought about Miriam Monroe, the huge difference between the loving way she talked about her children and the way Michael talked about Tim. Michael was just giving it lip service, saying the words he thought a good father should say. The man beat his wife. Did he hurt his mentally retarded son, too?

Michael said, "You still there, man?"

"Yes."

"I said, DeKalb PD is shutting me out." He paused,

probably to give Will room to respond. When he didn't, Michael asked, "You hear anything from them?"

He was fishing about the restraining order. Will gave him a non-answer. "They don't exactly have a reputation for flashing their cards around the table."

"Right, right," Michael agreed. He blew out a stream of smoke. "Phil's real broken up about this. I tried to see if there was anything he knew, but the guy's just shattered, you know?"

"I appreciate your trying." Will decided to take a risk. "Detective Polaski told me she helped you go through some of your Vice files."

Michael was silent for a beat too long. "Right, she did. Great chick. You hook up with her?"

"Did you find anything in the files?"

Michael paused, blew out some more smoke. "Nothing. I ran her in a few times, like Polaski said."

"Aleesha?"

"Yeah. Couple of times, maybe three. I wrote down the dates. You want me to get them? She was part of the sweeps we did, just like I told you. Twenty, thirty girls at a time. I'm not surprised I didn't remember her."

"How about Baby G?"

"Nothing on him. He's pretty new at the Homes. I could'a met him before, but there's nothing in my files about it and I sure as shit don't remember. Maybe we should go at him again? Bring him down to the station and see what he knows?"

Will wondered if he knew the pimp was dead.

"So," Michael continued. "How's it going? Anything on Aleesha?"

"Nothing big," Will answered. "Tell me about Jasmine."

"Is that one of the girls?"

"She's the kid who took some skin off your face."

"Oh, that one." Michael's laugh sounded strained. "Yeah. Little hellfire."

"Did she say anything to you before she ran up the stairs?"

"Nothing I want to repeat in front of my wife."

"Your wife's there with you?"

He gave that laugh again. "Where else would she be?"

There was a long stretch of silence. Michael had said less than a minute ago that his family was staying with his mother-in-law. Why was he lying?

"Anyway," Michael said. "The girl—what's her name? She didn't say anything. You think she saw something the night Aleesha was killed?"

"I don't know." Was he embarrassed? Is that why he lied?

"I'd bring her into the station if you're gonna question her, man. I'm not trying to tell you how to do your job or anything, but you don't want some black brat bringing a charge against you. I was lucky I got away with a slap."

"I'll keep that in mind." Will wondered if Michael had already found out that Jasmine was missing. If he'd lie about one thing, he'd certainly have no problem lying about another. "I've been thinking, Michael, how strange it is that Aleesha is so much older than the other victims."

"How's that?"

"She's a grown woman. The other girls were teenagers. Then there's the tongue. Your neighbor's was cut out, the rest of the girls had theirs bitten."

"Yeah," Michael allowed, his tone measured. "Come to think of it, that is kind of strange."

Will watched Julie Cooper giving her statement on his computer screen. She was about to ask the detectives to turn off the camera for a minute so she could collect herself. How did a young girl survive that kind of thing? How did she manage to go to school, do her homework like every other teenager, with the knowledge of what she had endured always lurking in her mind?

Michael suggested, "Maybe he's been visiting the hookers to blow off some steam in between stalking these girls." He paused. "I remember when I was in Vice how these girls used to talk themselves into trouble with the johns. Sometimes they'd get in the middle of things and go up on the price. Sometimes they'd negotiate certain acts, positions, whatever, just to get the guy to go back to their place, then they'd change the rules, say they weren't going to do it or they wanted more money."

Will hadn't considered that angle, but it was actually a good avenue to follow. That still didn't explain Cynthia Barrett, though.

He asked, "Are you sure you didn't piss somebody off, Michael? Maybe piss them off enough for them to do some kind of copycat thing with Cynthia, bring it to your back door?"

Michael laughed. "Are you being serious?"

"You tell me."

"That's fucking crazy, man."

"How's that?"

"They'd have to know a hell of a lot about the case," Michael pointed out. "We didn't release the detail about Monroe's tongue to the press. The only people who knew about that were cops." Michael muffled the phone, but Will heard him say, "Yeah, baby, I'll be right there." He said to Will, "Listen, Gina needs my help with Tim. Can I call you back in about ten minutes?"

"No," Will told him. "I don't need anything else."

"Just call if you do."

Will hung up the phone. He leaned back in his chair as he stared out the window. It had been dark out for some time, but the streetlights cast an unnatural spotlight on the abandoned rail yard next to the building. Will had gotten used to the depressing view.

The computer tooted like a steam train and Will closed the DVD program and opened his e-mail. The state computer wasn't very sophisticated—the dictionary was extremely limited and the spell-check didn't know half the words the average law enforcement officer used every day. Even if Will had asked, he knew they wouldn't let him put any outside programs on the hard drive, so he was stuck with it. Still, like most computers, there was a reading option.

He scrolled through some spam before finding a new e-mail from Pete Hanson. He highlighted the text, clicked the menu bar, then selected "speak." A stilted voice read him Pete's message. The toxicology report had come back on Cynthia Barrett. Her last meal had been eggs and toast. There was a high level of nicotine in her system. There were also traces of alcohol and cocaine in her bloodstream.

Another dead end.

Will took out the copy he'd made of Aleesha Monroe's letter to her mother, and he spread it out on the desk, pressing the folds open so it would lie flat. Her looping cursive was a nightmare but Will had already memorized the letter, so it was easier to read than if he'd come to it cold. Now, he went line-by-line, checking each sentence against his memory. Except for Monroe's tendency to capitalize when it suited her, Will didn't find anything new.

He folded up the letter and tucked it into his pocket. He glanced at the parole forms Leo had culled. A photograph was stapled to the corner of every profile, each inmate looking into the camera as he held up a black signboard that gave his vitals: name, crime, date of conviction, date of parole.

Reluctantly, Will slid open the top drawer to his desk. He found the staple remover and detached the photograph from the first offender profile. His office door was closed, the lights in the hall turned off. Still, he kept his voice to little above a whisper as he sounded out the first name.

After about an hour of this, he'd barely made a dent in the pile. His head was pounding and he dry-swallowed a handful of aspirin, thinking he would rather die of aspirin poisoning than from the headache hammering behind his eyes. Leo Donnelly had taken half the stack. He'd probably finished reading through his group in under an hour.

Will stood up and put on his jacket, thinking the task was probably a pointless one. If there was an offender in the database who had a habit of biting off tongues, Will would have pulled it when he first read about Monroe's case and did a keyword search in the computer. Leo's offender reports were from different districts and sometimes different states, so there was no uniformity in the description of the crimes. Some of the arresting officers had listed little more than the offense and age of the victim, others went into lurid detail, intimately describing the convict's predatory actions. Unless one of the photos had a guy standing with a severed tongue in his hand, Will was pretty much looking for a needle in a haystack.

Still, he grabbed the files before he took the elevator down to the garage. The reports sat on the passenger seat as he drove home, and Will found himself glancing down at them every so often as if he could not quite understand why they were there. He parked in the driveway behind his motorcycle, Betty's barks greeting him before he even made it up the porch. The little dog rushed out the door as soon as he opened it. Will snatched up the leash, prepared to track her down, but she did what she needed to do right on the front lawn and darted back inside before he could make it down the porch steps.

He turned around to find her enshrined on the couch pillows.

"Good evening to you, too," he told her, shutting the door. He stopped it before it caught and went back out to the car to fetch the files. Will dropped them on his desk, glancing at the answering machine. The message light was solid, but he picked up the phone just to make sure it was working.

The dial tone buzzed in his ear.

Supper was the same as breakfast, a bowl of cereal he ate standing over the sink. All he really wanted to do was lie down on the couch and fall asleep watching television. The files were stopping him, though. A man who could read well would have finished those summaries hours ago. A cop who was doing his job would've scanned them over lunch, knowing he was probably wasting his time but also knowing that good police work meant exhausting every lead you had.

Will could not abandon the work halfway through.

He took off his jacket and draped it over the back of his swivel chair. This shouldn't take too long, maybe three more hours at the most. Will wasn't going to quit just because it was hard and he sure as hell was not going to show up at work tomorrow knowing that he had left something undone. He should have come home earlier and tackled the reports in earnest. There were certain things he could not do at work without giving himself away.

The staple remover was in his coat pocket and he put it beside the stack of reports on his desk. He took two rulers out of his desk drawer and adjusted the shade on the desk lamp so that the bulb faced the wall, casting little more than a sliver of light onto the work surface.

"All right, handsome," Will mumbled, looking at the photograph stapled to the top of the next report. The guy had about three teeth and the kind of greasy, thin hair that you only ever found in your lesser trailer parks.

Will removed the photograph and set it aside. He put the two rulers on top of the page and isolated the first line of text. Using the tips of his index fingers, he blocked out individual words so that he could examine them one-by-one. His tendency was to read backward, and separating words with his fingers kept his eyes from darting where they shouldn't go. Oddly, long words were easiest. Will was always seeing something simple, like "never" and turning it into "very" so that the sentence made absolutely no sense by the time he got to the end.

He picked out the three words at the top of the page, reading the name aloud so that he could better comprehend it. "Carter, Isaiah Henry." It didn't come out that easy, though. First, he said Cash, then Ford, probably because of the "car" part at the beginning of the last name. Isaiah was easy. Henry was another matter.

Christ, he was stupid.

Will looked up at the blank computer monitor in front of him, blinked to clear his vision. He turned on the computer just to buy some time while his mind played out the usual taunts, telling him he was probably retarded, that maybe he had something wrong with his brain that no one had ever bothered to figure out. God knew he had been beaten in the head enough times to knock something loose. At the end of the day, none of the possible reasons for his problem mattered and none of it changed the fact that there were kids in third grade who could read better than Will. And he was talking about the stupid ones who sat in the back.

The computer booted up, the fan whirring like the

propeller on a model plane. Will clicked open his e-mail
program and stared at the in-box for a couple of minutes
before deleting an offer to extend the warranty on an appli-
ance he did not even own. There was nothing else to distract him.

He returned to the stack of offenders, trying to make a
game of it. The photograph was of a guy in his sixties. His
white hair was combed in a neat part and his deep blue eyes
made his ordinary face look more interesting. Put a hat on
him and he could be a traveling salesman. Give him a Bible
and he could be a deacon at the local church.

Slowly, Will slid the rulers down the page, reading line
by line. A feed supply salesman by occupation, the man was
a rapist who enjoyed torturing his victims. He had been
sentenced for twelve years but gotten out in seven for good
behavior. What exactly constituted good behavior for a
man who pulled the fingernails off the hands of a twenty-
two-year-old college student, Will was uncertain.

Another photo came off, another sheet of paper was put
under the rulers. Will kept at it for hours, reading all the
horrifying details of the sexual predators who had served
their time and been paroled for good behavior. None of
them did their full time, all but a handful looked like the
sort of man you would smile at if you saw him walking
down the street. Time crawled by, but Will did not look up
until he was three rap sheets away from being finished.

Will stretched back, feeling his spine adjust against the
hard edge of the chair. His knee bumped the desk, and the
computer monitor flickered on.

It was past midnight. He might as well take a break and
check his e-mail before he deciphered the details of the last
three offenders.

There was a new mail from Amanda in his in-box, but
he had no desire to read it. There were two requests from

Caroline, Amanda's secretary, asking about evidence in a case. Will opened his speech program and used the microphone to dictate a response, then did spell-check and had the computer read it back. When he was satisfied the words made sense, he highlighted the text and pasted it into the body of an e-mail, then did another spell-check before sending it off.

A hot stock tip had come in while he was doing this and Will clicked it into the trash. Next, he went into the trash folder and deleted all the crap he had sent there.

Will figured if there was an Olympic medal in wasting time, he was at least qualified enough to be an alternate. Surely there was more he could do, though. He opened up his spam folder, highlighted everything and slid the cursor over to delete. A message popped up and judging by the shape of it, Will assumed it was asking him if he was sure he wanted to do this. Will clicked the blue button that meant okay, then watched the junk e-mails drain off the list.

He scrolled back into his unread mail, thinking he might take a moment to check out what Amanda had to say. A new e-mail from Caroline had come in. She was probably just making a joke about both of them working so late, but at this point, Will would have opened an herbal Viagra offer to postpone reading reports for even a second.

There was a jpeg file attached to Caroline's e-mail, and he clicked on download before highlighting the text of the e-mail so he could copy it into his speech program. Betty stirred on the couch, giving a muffled bark, and he turned around to make sure she was okay. The little dog was on her back with her skinny legs kicking in the air as she dreamed about...whatever it was little dogs dreamed about. Cheese?

Will turned back around, the grin on his face dropping when he saw what was on his monitor. The photo had finished downloading. The boy was probably sixteen, his hair long to his collar, his mouth in a half-smile that came automatically from having a camera stuck in your face at every holiday or family outing. He held a signboard in front of his narrow chest, the skin of his fingertips ragged where he'd bitten his nails down to the quick. Will did not try to read the sign; he knew it told a name, a date of conviction, a charge. The eyes were what gave the boy away. A lot could change from fifteen to thirty-five, but the eyes were constant: the almond shape of the opening, the variation of color in the iris, the long, long lashes that were almost like a girl's.

The photo from the rap sheet Will had been about to read was still at his elbow. He held it up, thinking that there was no mistaking that the boy on the screen had grown up to be the felon in the photo.

Will pasted Caroline's mail into the speech program. He turned up the sound to his speakers, then clicked the menu bar and scrolled down to speak. The words were slow and metallic, their content enough to make him feel like he had been punched in the gut.

The program finished. Will did not need to hear it a second time.

He grabbed his car keys.

Angie's lieutenant had told Will she was at a liquor store on Cheshire Bridge Road. Will found the store easily enough, but Angie was not among the prostitutes leaning against the building.

He said, "I'm looking for someone."

"Me, too, handsome."

"No," Will said. He knew Angie didn't go by her real name when she did this, but she had never told him her chosen alias. "She's about five-eight. Brown hair, brown eyes. Olive skin."

"Sounds like me, sweetheart." This came from a short platinum blonde with a gap between her front teeth so pronounced that she whistled when she talked.

Another one said, "You looking for Robin, baby?"

"I don't know," he admitted, turning to the older woman. She had a black eye that was made worse by the makeup she had spackled over it.

"I'm Lola." She pushed herself away from the wall. "You her brother?"

"Yes," Will managed, not bothering to explain. "I need to talk to her."

"Give it a minute, honey," Lola soothed him. "She went back to the pokey with a date about ten minutes ago. She should be finishing up about now."

"Thank you," Will said. He tucked his hands into his pockets, realizing it was cold. He had been in such a hurry to leave the house that he hadn't even brought his coat.

Behind him, a car door slammed. A woman got out and while Will was watching, she reached between her legs, wiped herself and shook out her hand. She saw Will, then glanced back at the other girls, a question in her eyes.

Lola provided, "He's Robin's brother."

The woman walked her hooker's stroll past Will, giving him the once-over. "I had a brother like that, I would'a never left home."

Will glanced at his watch. He started to pace to try to work out the tension that was coiling every muscle he had into a tight ball, but each second that passed with Angie not showing her face only served to make it worse.

She always did this. She always put herself right in the middle of trouble and did not give a damn that Will suffered the consequences. As long as he had known her, Angie had pushed people as hard as she could, constantly testing their limits. It was a game that would get her killed one day, and then Will would be the one sitting on the couch, some other cop the unlucky bastard who had to hold his hand and tell him that she had been found strangled, beaten, raped, murdered.

The girls had been trash-talking, but Will noticed they'd turned quiet. He heard a rustling from the woods and Angie came out, flashlight in her hand.

She looked at Will, then the girls, then back at Will. Her mouth was set, her eyes lit with fury. She turned on her heel, heading back into the woods, and Will followed her.

"Stop," he said, trying to keep up. "Would you just stop?"

She wouldn't listen. All he could do was follow the beam of her flashlight.

About twenty feet into the woods, she turned on him. "What the fuck are you doing here?" Her tone was sharp as a knife.

"I'm just your brother paying you a call."

Angie looked over his shoulder and Will followed suit. He could clearly see the girls standing in front of the liquor store. They made no attempt to hide their interest.

She whispered hoarsely, trying to keep her voice down. "This is the wrong fucking place for this, Will. Lola already thinks something's up."

He shoved John Shelley's rap sheet in her face. She did a double take when she saw the photograph, and he could have sworn her eyes softened.

"Read it," he ordered. "Read it to me so that I know I've got it right."

Angie shined the flashlight on the first page. He saw her eyes moving, reading the words. She looked up, said, "Will," like he was being unreasonable.

"Read it."

She held the flashlight under her arm, training the beam on the first page, then flipping to the second and third.

Finally, she looked up again. "So?"

He wanted to shake her. "Did you read what it says?"

Taking her time, she turned back to the first page and read aloud in a bored tone, " 'Jonathan Winston Shelley, six-one, one hundred ninety-five pounds, brown hair, brown eyes. Prior record: theft by taking. Received May 10, 1986, Coastal State Prison, maximum security, special offender's wing, age sixteen. Paroled July 22, 2005, age thirty-five. Registered sexual offender, pedophile.' " She looked back up, repeated, "So?"

"Read the last page," he said, meaning the part he'd printed out from Caroline's e-mail. Shelley's rap sheet had been brief, just listing the highlights of his crimes, but the records Caroline had found filled in all the blanks in horrid detail.

"Read it," he demanded.

She didn't want to. He could tell that from the steely way she glared at him.

He asked, "You want me to read it for you?"

"I only get an hour break for supper."

He snatched the pages from her hand, tried to find the right section. He was so angry that the words kept reversing on the page, their shapes morphing one into the other. He tried, "Ca..." Will felt a knife-sharp pain in the front of his temple. God damnit, he knew at least two of the words. "Jonathan Shelley." He tried to pick out another one. "Drain. No, he—dead. He killed—"

Angie put her hand over his. She tried to take the report but he wouldn't let go. "Come on," she coaxed, gently, pulling the pages from his grasp.

Will clenched his fists as he stared at the ground. Christ. No wonder she couldn't stand to be with him.

She spoke softly. "I'm sorry."

He wanted to sink into the ground, just magically to somewhere else.

"I'm sorry."

"I read it before."

"I know you did," she told him, taking his hand again. "Look at me, Will. I'm sorry."

He could not look at her.

"You want me to read it out loud?"

"I don't care what you do."

"Will."

He knew he was sounding petulant, but couldn't stop. "I really don't."

The flashlight had fallen to the ground and she reached down to pick it up, still holding on to him. She shined the light on the pages and read, " 'On June 15, 1985, Shelley sexually assaulted Mary Alice Finney, a fifteen-year-old white female, then removed her tongue with a serrated kitchen knife, resulting in her death. In addition, Shelley made several deep bite marks in the victim's flesh and urinated on the body. Shelley's bloody fingerprints were found at the scene and on the body. The murder weapon was found in Shelley's bedroom closet. Known drug addictions: heroin, cocaine.' "

"Angie," was all he could say.

She was silent, letting a couple of cars pass before she said, "Remember I told you that Michael Ormewood came by here that one time?"

He was sick of hearing about Ormewood. If he never heard the man's name again, Will would die a happy man.

Angie said, "He told us to look out for a recently released sex offender named John Shelley. He said he was really a bad guy and to stay away from him." She looked down at the rap sheet. "Michael went to Decatur High School. He must have grown up in the area."

"Did you manage to ask him about his childhood years while you were going down on him?"

"Do you want me to go down on you, too, Will? Is that what this is about?"

He slapped her hand away. "Stop it."

She told him, "I read his personnel file."

"You're real interested in Michael for some reason. Why is he different? What makes him so special?"

"You're not listening to what I'm saying." She was talking to him like he was a child and he did not like it. "Michael went to Decatur High School, so he must have lived in the area. He was a few years older than John, but he would have heard about the crime. He would have known the details about the tongue. Why didn't he mention it to you? Why didn't he say, 'Hey, this reminds me of something that happened about twenty years ago right down the street from me.' "

Will was too upset to even consider the question.

She said, "John told me that someone was blackmailing him."

Will laughed. "You think that Michael Ormewood knows there's a guy out there raping and murdering women, taking out their tongues, but instead of arresting the doer, Michael's blackmailing him? For what? What could John Shelley possibly have that Michael Ormewood would want?"

"How do you explain Michael telling me to look out for John Shelley? How do you explain his not mentioning this same thing happening to a girl in the same neighborhood where he grew up?"

Will tried to make her see reason. "How do you explain the other girls?"

"What other girls?"

"Last year, two girls were sexually assaulted by a man wearing a black ski mask. Both of them had their tongues bitten off."

Her lips parted in surprise.

"John Shelley's been out seven months," Will told her. "Both girls lived thirty, forty minutes away from here." She was silent, so he added, "Julie Cooper's fifteen. The other girl was only fourteen. What do these crimes have in common? What's the link here?"

Angie said, "You know perps have their way of doing things. Why would he deviate? Why would he cut off some and bite off the others? Why would he go from little girls to a grown woman?"

Will recalled Michael's answer to this question, but he did not share it with Angie.

She asked, "Why didn't you tell me about the other cases before?"

"When, Angie? Over dinner? Maybe when we were holding hands, taking a long stroll in the park?"

"You could have told me."

"Why?" he asked. "Who knew you'd end up screwing around with a convicted pedophile?"

Her head jerked up. "I haven't slept with him."

"Yet."

Angie gave a heavy sigh.

"Here's an indisputable fact: Shelley raped and killed a fifteen-year-old girl. He cut out her tongue."

"He's not..." She looked back at Shelley's photograph. "Whatever he did, he's not that guy anymore."

"Julie Cooper was fifteen," Will told her. "He raped her in an alley behind a movie theater. He bit off her tongue."

Angie shook her head.

"Anna Linder was fourteen. They found her in Stone Mountain Park the next day. She was holding her tongue in her hand like a security blanket. They had to pry it from her fingers."

Angie still did not respond.

"Cynthia Barrett, Angie. Cynthia Barrett was fifteen."

"Michael's neighbor."

Will shrugged. "So what?"

"Tell me this: How do they know each other? How did Michael know to warn me off him in the first place?" She indicated the liquor store with an angry wave of her hand. "You weren't there when he did it. There's something between them. Michael hates the guy."

"What else am I missing here?" Will asked. "Because what it sounds like to me is that you're so pissed at Michael Ormewood that you can't see straight. Why is that, Angie? Why can't you get this asshole out of your system?"

He could see the fury in her eyes, knew she was remembering the millions of times he had asked her this before.

Her voice was eerily calm when she said, "Did you ask Michael how old his wife was when he met her?" She didn't let him respond. "She was fifteen, Will. He was twenty-five."

"Did he rape her and bite out her tongue?" Will asked. "Because, unless he did, I don't see why that makes a bit of difference."

"I'm telling you, John didn't do this."

"I'll ask him myself when I bring him in."

"No." She grabbed his arm as if she could physically stop him. "I'll do it."

Will could only stare at her. "You've got to be kidding me."

"The minute you put those cuffs on him, he's shutting down."

"You don't know that."

"He's a con. Of course he'll shut down. He won't so much as fart until his lawyer shows up, and then the lawyer will tell you to go fuck yourself."

"You're not going to control this."

"What's the charge? Jaywalking?" She raised her eyebrows, as if she expected an answer. "You can bring him in for questioning, but what do you have? You can search his place, but what are you going to tell the judge when you ask for the warrant? 'He did it twenty years ago, Your Honor, so maybe, probably, possibly he could have done it again now?'" Angie crossed her arms. "Last time I checked, unless you're the president of the United States, you need some kind of evidence to throw a guy in jail."

Will did not answer because he knew that she was right.

"Do you have John's fingerprints on anything? Any witnesses? Anybody who saw anything?"

Jasmine, Will thought. Maybe she saw something. If she did, she was probably at the bottom of a lake right now.

Angie summed it up: "No forensic evidence, no witnesses and no case. You're right, Will. Let's go out and arrest him right now, why don't we?"

"He could be stalking his next victim," Will said, not adding that Angie could very well be the next woman he set his sights on.

"If you arrest him now, you'll have to kick him in twenty-four hours, and if it *is* Shelley who's doing this, then he'll know you're onto him and he'll go so deep underground that you'll never find him again."

"What do you propose I do? Wait until another girl is raped? Maybe murdered?" Will pointed out, "He could already have his next victim right now, Angie. What if he's got Jasmine? Am I supposed to sit around while she's counting down the minutes left in her life?"

"He'll talk to me. He doesn't know I'm a cop."

"What is it with this guy, Angie? Why won't you see him for what he is?"

"Maybe it's a good thing I don't judge men based on what they've done in their past."

"Is that supposed to hurt me?"

"Let me talk to him," she pleaded. "You can watch his house until morning, make sure he doesn't go out. If he's got that little girl, then he won't touch her without you knowing. I'll go to the car wash tomorrow morning and sit him down and talk to him."

"You think he's going to confide in you?"

"If he's innocent..." She nodded. "Yeah. I can make him talk."

"And if he's not?"

"Then you'll be there." She actually tried to tease him. "You'll protect me, won't you, Willy?"

"This isn't anything to joke about."

"I know." She was looking over his shoulder again, watching the girls. "I need to get back to work."

"I don't like this," he said. "I don't like any of this and I don't want to do it."

"That's nothing new for either of us, is it?" She put her hand to his cheek, brushed her lips against his. "Go away, Will."

"I don't want to leave you."

"You don't have a choice."

CHAPTER THIRTY-THREE

John sat on a stool at the counter of the Empire Diner. He had walked in the door ravenously hungry, but for some reason when his food came, he could only bring himself to take a few bites. Nerves had his stomach in a death grip as he waited for his life to begin.

He had spent most of the night with Kathy and Joyce, trying to come up with a plan of action. Kathy wanted to go to the police, but if there was one thing the Shelley children could agree upon, it was that you could not trust the police. Michael would never talk. He was too smart to leave himself open. John's credit report might raise some questions, but the answers could very well come back and bite John in the ass. In the end, they had decided that Joyce would use her contacts at the county records department to try to find out where Aunt Lydia was living. Uncle Barry had only been married to her for a few years before he died, and they hadn't been able to find anything under the Carson family name. There had to be a trail somewhere. Once they found it, the Shelley children would confront Lydia about her role in framing John. She had obviously confessed her sins once before. They would not give her a moment's peace until she confessed them again—this time on the record.

As far as John's own confession went, he had not told

his sister and her lover everything that had happened. He'd been as honest as possible up to a point. He had not told them about Michael's next-door neighbor. The thought of what he had done, the depths to which he had sunk, made him sick. All this time, John had believed Michael was the animal, but in that one moment when the opportunity had presented itself, John had been just as sadistic, just as vengeful as his cousin. Was this what Emily had fought for? Was this why his mother had spent hour upon hour writing in her notebooks, so that her little Johnny could get out of jail and mutilate a fifteen-year-old girl? For the first time in his life, John was glad his mother was gone, glad that he would never have to look into her beautiful eyes and know that she was looking at someone who was capable of such atrocities.

"Top you off?" the waitress asked, but she was already filling John's mug with coffee.

"Thanks," he mumbled.

The door opened and he glanced up into the mirror behind the counter to see Robin standing with her hands on her hips, looking around for a table. The restaurant was fairly busy, so she didn't notice him staring.

John fought the urge to turn around. He wanted to call her over, point to the empty stool beside him and listen to her talk. Too much was going on now, though. He had blood on his hands, guilt in his heart. He looked back down at his mug, staring into the murky liquid, wishing it could show him his future. Would there ever be a woman in his life? Would he ever find someone who knew what had happened to him, what he had done, and not run away screaming?

"Hey, you." Robin slipped onto the stool beside him. She was dressed differently. Her hair was in a ponytail and she was wearing jeans and a T-shirt instead of her usual hooker garb.

"Hey," John returned. "Off the clock?"

"Yeah," she said, turning over her coffee cup and signaling for the waitress.

Something else was different about her, but John couldn't pinpoint exactly what that was. It had nothing to do with the way she was dressed or the fact that she wasn't wearing a pound of makeup. If he knew her better, he might say that she was nervous.

She said, "You ever think that you just hate your job? That maybe you should just run away from home and never look back?"

He smiled. He had considered running away from home the whole time he was at Coastal. "You okay?"

She nodded, then gave him a sly smile. "Are you stalking me? First the hospital and now this."

He looked around. "You own this place or something?"

"This is my regular breakfast hangout."

"Sorry," he apologized. "Just looked like a good place to sit awhile." He'd had money in his pocket for the first time in forever and he'd wanted to treat himself.

She said, "I lied to you."

"About what?"

"My first kiss," she said. "It wasn't my little brother's best friend."

He tried to make a joke of it, even though his feelings were hurt. "Please tell me it wasn't your little brother."

She smiled, poured some cream into her coffee. "My parents were speed freaks," she said. "At least my mom and whoever it was she was banging were." Robin picked up her spoon and stirred the coffee. "The state took me away from her when I was a kid."

John didn't know what to say. He settled on, "I'm sorry to hear that."

"Yeah," she said. "I was in and out of foster care for a

while. Met a lot of foster dads who were real happy to have a little girl living under their roof."

John was silent, watching her stir her coffee. She had the smallest hands. Why was it that women's hands were so much more attractive than men's?

"What about you?" she asked. "Did you come from a broken home, too?"

She had said the words sarcastically. John had met plenty of felons who claimed they were victims of circumstance, their dysfunctional families forcing them into a life of crime. The way they told their stories, you wouldn't think they had a choice in the matter.

"No," he told her. "I came from a perfectly normal home. Wonderful, cookie-baking, scout-leading mom. Kind of distant father, but he was home every night and he took an interest in what I was doing." He thought about Joyce. She was probably on the phone right now working her magic. He didn't know whether or not Aunt Lydia would do the right thing, but John thought he could live the rest of his life in peace just knowing that for the first time in twenty years, Joyce believed in him.

Robin tapped her spoon twice against the mug, then put it on the counter. "So, what happened to you, John? How'd you end up in jail?"

He shrugged. "Wrong crowd."

She laughed, but obviously didn't think it was funny. "I guess you were innocent?"

She had asked this two days ago at the hospital, and he gave her the stock answer. "Everybody in prison is innocent."

Robin was silent, staring at the mirror behind the counter.

"So," he said, wanting to change the subject. "Who *was* your first kiss?"

"My first real kiss?" she asked. "The first guy I kissed who I really wanted to kiss?" She seemed to think about it. "I met him at the state home," she finally said. "We were together for twenty-five years."

John blew on his coffee, took a sip. "That's a long time."

"Yeah, well." She picked up her spoon again. "I fucked around on him a lot."

John choked on his coffee.

She smiled, but it was more for her own sake. "We broke up two years ago."

"Why?"

"Because when you know somebody that long, when you grow up with somebody like that, you're just too..." She searched for a word. "Raw," she decided. "Too vulnerable. I know everything about him and he knows everything about me. You can't really love somebody like that. I mean, sure, you can love them—he's like a part of me, part of my heart. But you can never be with them the way you want to. Not love them like a lover." She shrugged. "If I really cared about him, I'd leave him so that he could get on with his life."

John wasn't sure how to respond. "He's crazy to let you go."

"Well, there's more to it than my side of the story," she admitted. "I'm a real bitch, in case you hadn't noticed. What about you?"

John gave a startled "Me?"

"You have a girlfriend?"

He laughed. "Are you kidding me? I went in when I was sixteen. The only woman I ever saw was my mother."

"What about..." Her voice trailed off. "You were a kid, right? When you got to prison?"

John felt his jaw work. He nodded without looking at

her, trying not to let his mind conjure up the image of Zebra, those black-and-white teeth, those hands clamping down on the back of his neck.

If she saw his acknowledgment, she didn't comment. Instead, she blew on her coffee and finally took a sip, saying, "Damn, it's cold."

John signaled for the waitress.

"How y'all doing here?" the woman asked.

"Fine, thank you," John told her, letting her fill his cup with more coffee. He wasn't used to so much caffeine in the morning and his hands were sweating. Or maybe he was just nervous because Robin was here. She was talking to him like they knew each other. John couldn't remember if there had ever been a time in his life when he'd had a conversation like this.

The waitress said, "Y'all let me know if you need anything."

Robin waited for the woman to leave before asking, "So, John, what have you been doing since you got out?"

"Reconnecting with my family," he answered. He couldn't help but add, "I've been looking for my cousin. There's some things we need to talk about."

Robin looked over his shoulder at a man sitting alone in the corner booth. John checked the guy's reflection in the mirror, wondering if he was one of her johns. The man was wearing a three-piece suit. He was probably a lawyer or a doctor with a family at home.

"John?" He looked back at Robin. She surprised him by asking, "What kind of trouble are you in?"

"No kind of trouble."

"You said somebody was blackmailing you."

He nodded. "I did."

"Who?"

John put his hands on either side of his cup. He wanted

to answer her, to tell her everything that had happened, but Robin had enough in her life without him adding to the burden. What's more, he didn't have Joyce's optimism about Aunt Lydia doing the right thing. Michael was still her son, even if he was a sadistic murderer. There was no telling what he was capable of doing. John wouldn't be able to live with himself if something bad came down on Robin because of him.

He told her, "I can't get you caught up in all of this."

Her hand went to his thigh. "What if I want to be involved?" John's breath caught as she moved her hand higher. "I know you're a good guy."

His mouth opened so that he could breathe. "Maybe you shouldn't..."

"I know you don't have anybody to talk to," she said, her hand firm on his leg. "I just want you to know that you can talk to me."

He shook his head, whispering, "Robin..."

She rubbed her hand back and forth. "It's been a long time, huh?"

Never, John thought. It's been never.

"You wanna go somewhere and talk?"

"I don't..." He couldn't think. "I don't have any money to—"

She moved closer to him. "I told you. I'm off the clock."

If her hand went any higher, he was going to have to ask the waitress for a towel. He squeezed his eyes shut, trying to find some strength.

He put his hand over hers. "I can't."

"You don't want me?"

"There's not a man alive who doesn't want you," he said, thinking there were no truer words ever spoken. "I care about you, Robin. I know that's stupid. I know I don't even know you. But I can't get you involved in my problems, okay? There's already been too many people hurt. If something happened to you, if you got hurt, too..." He shook his head. He couldn't think about it. "When this is over," he said. "When this is over, I'll find you."

Robin had taken her hand away. She held her cup up to her mouth and repeated the question. "Who's blackmailing you, John?"

Her tone had changed. He couldn't exactly pinpoint how, but it reminded him of the guards in prison, the way they asked a question knowing that you had to answer them or they'd throw you in the hole.

He said, "It'll all be settled soon."

"How's that?"

"I'm just taking care of it," he told her. "I can't say anything else about it right now."

"You're not going to tell me anything?"

"Nope," he told her.

"Are you sure, John?"

She was so serious. He gave her a questioning smile, said, "Let's talk about something else."

"I need you to talk to me," she said. "I need to know what's going on."

"What's this all about?"

"It's about your life, John. Can't you be up-front with me?"

The hairs on the back of his neck went up. "I don't like where this is going."

Robin put down her mug. She stood up, her expression turning hard. "I tried to help you. Remember that."

"Come on," he said, not knowing what he'd done wrong. "Robin—"

He felt a hand on his shoulder and looked up to see the man in the three-piece suit standing behind him.

John said, "What's going on?"

The man looked at Robin, so John did, too.

"I'm sorry, John," she said, and she really seemed to be, but he did not know why. She reached into her purse and pulled out her wallet. Stupidly, he thought she was going to pay the bill. He opened his mouth to tell her not to worry about it, but by then he caught the glint of gold as she flipped open her badge.

As if he couldn't see for himself, she told him, "I'm a cop."

"Robin—"

"It's Angie, actually." The man behind him tightened his hand on John's shoulder. "Let's do this outside."

"No..." John could feel his body starting to shake, his muscles turning to liquid.

"Outside," she ordered, her hand digging up under his arm, making him stand.

He walked like an invalid, leaning against her as the man opened the door. The Decatur cops had done the same thing to him when they had dragged him out of his bedroom. They had taken him down the stairs, into the front yard, and cuffed him in front of the whole neighborhood. Somebody had screamed, and when he looked behind him, he realized it was his mother. Emily had fallen to her knees, Richard not even trying to hold her up, as she sobbed.

The sun in the parking lot outside the diner was brutal, and John blinked. He realized he was panting. Jail. They were taking him to jail. They'd take away his clothes, strip-search him, fingerprint him, throw him in a cell with a bunch of other men who were just waiting for John to show back up, waiting to show him exactly what they thought about a child-raping con who couldn't make it on the outside.

"Will." She was talking to the man behind John. "Don't."

John saw the silver cuffs the man held in his hand.

"Please..." John managed. He couldn't breathe. His knees buckled. The last thing he saw was Robin moving forward to break his fall.

CHAPTER THIRTY-FOUR

Angie felt dirty. Even after a scalding hot shower, she felt like she would never get rid of the filth inside.

The look on John's face, the fear, the sense of betrayal, had cut her heart like a jagged piece of metal. Will had carried John to the car, helped him into the backseat like a child getting ready for a trip to the store. Angie had stood there thinking, Here are the two men whose lives I've ruined the most.

She left before Will could stop her.

What was it about John Shelley that made her want to save him? Maybe it was because he was all alone in the world. Maybe it was because he wore his loneliness like a suit of armor that only Angie could see. He was like Will. Exactly like Will.

Despite the fact that she had cleaned her house top to bottom a few days before, Angie put on her gloves and went to work. She used half a gallon of bleach in the bathroom, scrubbing the glistening white grout with a toothbrush. Will had laid the tile for her, putting it on a diagonal because he knew instinctively that this would make the room look larger. He had painted the walls a creamy yellow and used an off-white oil on the trim while Angie had chided him about his decorating skills.

She should call him. Will was just doing his job. He was

a good cop, but he was also a good man and it wasn't right for her to punish him because John Shelley had gotten mixed up in something bad. As soon as she finished cleaning the house, she would call Will's cell, make sure he knew it was the situation she hated, not him.

Angie started on the kitchen next, taking out pots and pans, wiping out all the cabinets. She kept going over what had happened this morning, trying to think if there was a way she could have made it easier.

"Fuck," Angie cursed. She needed shelf liner. It was stupid to wipe out the cabinets when there was probably all kinds of trash underneath the liner. She picked at the corner of the sticky vinyl on the bottom of the sink cabinet, ripping it up in two pieces. The base was clean, but she had already ruined the liner. Angie stood to get more, realizing before she even reached the pantry that she was out.

"Fuck," she cursed again, snapping off her cleaning gloves. She threw them into the sink, offering a few more expletives as she looked for her keys.

Ten minutes later, she was in her car, driving not to the grocery store, but straight up Ponce de Leon toward Stone Mountain. She knew where Michael lived. After they fucked, or, more to the point, after Michael fucked her, Angie had gotten a little obsessed. She had driven by his house a couple of times, seen his wife and kid in the driveway, caught sight of Michael washing his car. This behavior hadn't lasted long—maybe a week—before she realized she was acting like a deranged person. It wasn't Michael she was furious with, but herself, for getting into another bad situation.

The Ormewoods lived in a ranch house that fit the other houses in the neighborhood. Angie parked in the empty driveway. If any of the neighbors noticed her black

Monte Carlo SS was out of place, they didn't come running. Every inch of her skin tingled as she got out of the car.

She was dressed in her usual cleaning attire: a pair of cutoffs, one of Will's old shirts and some pink flip-flops she had slid into as she left the house. The shoes made a popping sound against her soles as she walked up to the garage. The wind was blowing, and Angie wrapped her arms around her waist to fight the chill. She stood on tiptoe as she peered into the garage.

The windows had been blacked out with paint.

A car drove by, and Angie followed it with her eyes, making sure it didn't slow, before heading to the front door. She rang the bell and waited, relishing the thought of Michael's surprise when he opened the front door and saw her standing here. She was going to tell him that John had been arrested, then she was going to ask Michael how he knew John Shelley, why he had told her and the girls to look out for the recently released murderer.

Angie knocked, then rang the bell again.

Nothing.

She tried the door, but it was locked. Forcing herself not to look over her shoulder or do anything else that might make her look like a thief, she walked casually around the house to the backyard, keeping her pace slow, glancing at the windows as if she was a friend who had just dropped by for a visit. She wished she had her cell phone as a prop, but she'd left it at home to charge.

A dog door was cut into the back door. The door looked old and she figured it had come with the house. Michael hated dogs. She remembered this from their first bust together. One of the girls had a mutt that wouldn't stop barking and Michael had pulled his gun when the animal lunged at him. The prostitute had laughed, and so had

Angie. Come to think of it, this same prostitute was the girl who had told Angie that Michael was getting freebies.

Angie got on her knees and twisted her shoulders so she could get through the door. Her breeder's hips caught—thank you, Mother—but she managed to pull herself through. She crawled inside and stood in place, straining her ears, making sure no one was home. For the first time since she had left her own house, she wondered what the hell she was doing. Why would she break into Michael's house? What did she expect to find?

Maybe Will was right. Michael was certainly a jerk, and he beat his wife, and he had probably raped Angie that night she had been too drunk to know better, but that didn't mean he was mixed up in all of this. So why was she here?

"Shit," she hissed, turning around to crawl back out the way she'd come. She stopped mid-crouch as she heard a noise. A whimper? Was that what she had heard? Did Michael have a dog now?

Angie froze, listening. The sound didn't repeat itself, and she wondered for a half second if she was losing her mind. The fact that she had broken into a man's house did bring her sanity into question.

Still, Angie stood up. She might as well finish what she started. She left her shoes by the door. She hated being barefooted, but she didn't want the flip-flop sound to follow her through the house.

She stopped midway through the kitchen, hearing a car drive by. Angie listened, her ears straining. A door opened and slammed shut, but it was across the street. She heard somebody call a hello, a conversation start up, and she unclenched her ass. Christ, all she needed was for Michael to come home and find her snooping around his house.

The living room was what she would expect: an over-

stuffed couch and a big-screen television. She glanced down
the hallway, but Angie didn't want to go into the bedrooms.
She didn't want to see where Michael screwed his wife, know
that this was the place where he probably beat Gina.

Had he beaten Angie? She didn't know. Her arms were
bruised the next day, her privates on fire with pain. She had
passed out in the car and he had done whatever he wanted
to do. The stupid fucker. Couldn't he tell by looking at her
that she could do pretty much anything? It wasn't like he
had to wait for her to pass out.

There was a door at the back of the living room. A hasp
lock bolted it shut. She tried to orient herself, figuring the
garage was on the other side of the door. Why would he
have such a serious lock on the garage door when anybody
could come in through the dog door? And why would the
windows be blacked out?

Angie walked over to the door, put her ear to the cool
metal. The hinge on the lock squeaked as she pried it open.
She put her hand on the knob and opened the door. The
room was pitch-black, and she groped along the wall for the
light switch. The fluorescent bulbs flickered on and off several times, and in the strobe she saw a workbench, a lawn
mower, a pool table.

The lights stayed on. A naked young girl was tied to the
pool table. Her mouth was gagged, her face bloody. Her
eyes opened wide at the sight of Angie, the whites showing
in a complete circle around her irises. Except for the rapid
rise and fall of her chest, she wasn't moving.

Angie's breath caught. She felt a sharp, searing pain at
the back of her skull, then saw a blinding explosion as she
crumpled to the floor. She heard the girl sobbing, a man
laughing, and then nothing at all.

CHAPTER THIRTY-FIVE

Will leaned back in his chair, looking out at the dismal view his office afforded. He picked up his phone and tried Angie's cell again, waiting until it went over into voice mail before disconnecting. He'd been trying to call her for the last hour, first on her home line, then on her cell. She'd told him she was going straight home, and it wasn't like her not to answer when he called. Even if she was mad at Will, Angie would have picked up the phone at least to cuss him out and tell him to stop calling.

She had been right about one thing at least. John Shelley hadn't said a word from the moment Will had put him in the car.

Leo Donnelly knocked on Will's office door, opening it before he was told to. "Lawyer's here."

"Thank you."

"Claims she's a friend of his sister's."

Will stood up, slipped on his jacket. "You don't believe her?"

Leo handed Will a business card, saying, "She's a real estate lawyer." He lowered his voice. "Hot-looking dyke."

Will didn't know what he was expected to say. He stared at the card for an appropriate amount of time before tucking it into his vest pocket.

Leo walked beside Will up the hallway. "I gotta tell you, she's a big loss for our side. Know what I mean?"

Will didn't want to have this conversation, so he asked, "Have you ever heard Michael mention John Shelley?"

"The perp?" Leo pursed his lips, thought about it. "Nope."

"There's a woman who works in Vice—Angie Polaski."

Leo's mouth shot up in a knowing grin. "Yeah, I know her."

Will opened the doorway to the stairs. Leo didn't look pleased that they weren't taking the elevator down the two flights to the interrogation rooms, but the man should be glad Will wasn't punching that grin off his face.

He told Leo, "Detective Polaski said that a couple of months ago, Michael warned her and some of the girls to look out for a con named John Shelley."

Leo's smile faltered as they reached the landing. "Mike knew about this guy before?"

"Seems like it."

Leo continued down the stairs, his fingers trailing the handrail. He stopped on the landing and Will turned around.

"Listen," Leo said. He glanced over the railing, lowered his voice. "This Polaski chick...Mike threw her a bone a while back. He's a married guy, you know, really loves his wife but it's not like he's gonna say no to getting his knob polished, especially by something like that. Know what I mean?"

"What happened?"

"Polaski didn't understand the rules. She was looking for something a little more permanent. Mike tried to let her down easy, but she's had a real hard-on for him ever since."

Will almost laughed at the thought of someone thinking

Angie wanted to be in a serious relationship. He continued down the stairs, asking, "You think she's making it up?"

"I think hell hath no fury, you know?"

"Yeah," Will agreed. "But why would she make up something like that?"

Leo took a few seconds to think of an answer. He finally shrugged. "Women, you know?"

"Didn't you tell me the other day that Gina filed a restraining order against Michael for beating her?"

"Well . . ." Leo stopped again. "Yeah. So?"

Will kept walking. "You didn't seem to think she was making that up."

"No," Leo admitted. He rubbed his thumb along his chin, a tell Will had picked up on within minutes of meeting the detective. He hoped the man never played poker. "It's like this," Leo eventually said, "Mike called me last night and asked me how the case was going."

"He called me, too."

"What'd you tell him?"

Will opened the door to the second floor. "Probably the same as you. We don't have anything to go on."

"Yeah, but then I mentioned that you'd asked me to pull the sex offenders list. He got all hot and bothered about it. Said it was fucking brilliant." Leo gave Will an apologetic half-smile. "I don't think I'm squeezing your toes when I say that going through those files was a Hail Mary if there ever was one."

Will nodded. Shelley had been included in his group of registered offenders, but the parole sheet lacked the details Caroline had pulled for him. If Angie hadn't asked Will to look into the man, then Shelley would probably still be out in the street.

Of course, Michael Ormewood had been the one who told Angie about Shelley in the first place.

Leo's stride was shorter than Will's. He struggled to keep up as they walked down the hallway, saying, "Point is, Mike's been on the job almost as long as me. He knows it's a long shot, too." Will slowed his pace. "And he also knows that some smack-head pross living in the projects ain't gonna be keeping no tidy house."

Will stopped, thinking maybe he'd underestimated Leo Donnelly.

The detective said, "I'd bet my left one that place was scrubbed down before we got there."

"You mentioned this to Michael?"

"He argued with me," Leo admitted. "Mike's usually an easygoing guy, you know? But he got real pissed when I said the place had been cleaned. He wouldn't even put it in his report."

"Maybe he was just being careful?"

"Careful is when you leave out the fact that you found your name in the bitch's little black book, not when you forget to notice somebody's rubbed down the place with a gallon of Clorox."

Will tucked his hands into his pockets. "What are you doing now?"

Leo shrugged. "I got a couple'a three other cases I'm working. Why?"

"You mind going over to Michael's?"

"What for?"

"Pay him a call," Will said. "Make sure he's doing okay."

"I gotta say," Leo began, "the way he's been acting, I'm thinking right now I don't give a shit one way or the other if the guy is okay."

"Just check on him," Will insisted, putting his hand on Leo's shoulder. "I want to know where he is."

Leo stared up at him for a few seconds, then nodded. "Sure," he finally said. "Okay."

Will put his hand on the doorknob to the interrogation room but didn't open it. He closed his eyes, trying to center himself. While he was in that room, he couldn't think about Angie or Michael or Jasmine or anything else that would throw him off his game. John was the target and Will would not settle for anything less than a direct hit.

He knocked once on the door and walked into the room without waiting to be invited. John Shelley sat at the table. His lawyer was leaning across him, holding both his hands in hers.

They moved apart quickly when Will entered the room.

Will said, "I apologize for interrupting."

The woman stood up. Her voice was strong, indignant. She might have specialized in real estate, but she was still a lawyer. "Is my client under arrest?"

"I'm Special Agent Will Trent," he told her. "And you are?"

"Katherine Keenan. Can you tell me why my client is here?"

"I believe you're a real estate lawyer," Will said. "Are you representing Mr. Shelley in an acquisition?"

Her eyes narrowed. "Is he under arrest or not?"

Will started to sit, asking, "Do you mind?"

"Detective, I don't care whether you sit or stand or levitate into the air. Just stop dicking me around and answer my question."

John looked down at the table, but not before Will saw him smile.

"All right." Will sat down across from them, telling the lawyer, "But, if you don't mind, it's actually Special Agent Trent. Detectives work in local PD. I'm with State. The

Georgia Bureau of Investigation. Perhaps you've seen us on the news?"

Keenan was obviously at a loss to the relevance, but John seemed to realize what that difference meant. State turned up the heat. Either the locals couldn't handle the case or the crime involved several jurisdictions.

John said, "I'm not answering any questions."

Will told him, "That's fine, Mr. Shelley. I don't have any questions for you. If I did, I might ask something like, 'Where were you the evening of December third of last year?' Or maybe I'd ask about October thirteenth." If the dates meant anything to John, he wasn't letting on. Will continued, "Then, I might get curious about last Sunday." Now, there was a reaction. Will pushed a little more. "You'd remember that day because of the Super Bowl. And the next day, the sixth. That was a Monday. Maybe I'd ask you where you were last Monday."

Keenan said, "He doesn't have to answer any of your questions."

Will spoke directly to John. "You need to trust me."

John stared at Will the way he might stare at a blank wall.

Will sat back in his chair and listed it off for both of them. "I've got a dead hooker, a dead teenager and two little girls north of here who are trying to figure out how to live the rest of their lives after having their tongues bitten off."

Will was watching the lawyer as he said this. She wasn't as practiced as John, hadn't learned how to hide her emotions as well.

Will continued, "I've also got a missing little girl. Her name is Jasmine. She's fourteen. Lives at the Homes with her little brother, Cedric. Last Sunday, a white man with brown hair paid her twenty dollars to make a phone call."

John clasped his hands together on the table.

"The funny thing is, this man gave her a dime to make the call." Will paused a moment. "I don't think pay phones have cost a dime since at least nineteen eighty-five."

John worked his hands.

Will told the lawyer, "Ms. Keenan, this is the question that keeps coming up: How does John Shelley know Michael Ormewood?"

She literally gasped at the name.

"Kathy," John cautioned.

Will explained the situation. "Last Monday, a fifteen-year-old girl died. Somebody cut her tongue out. I can't help thinking, Mr. Shelley, that twenty years ago, you cut out another little girl's tongue."

Keenan couldn't take it anymore. "It wasn't cut!"

"Kathy," John said. "Wait outside."

"John—"

"Please," he told her. "Just wait outside. Try to find Joyce."

She obviously didn't want to go.

"Please," he repeated.

"All right," she told him. "But I'll be right outside."

"Actually," Will began, standing, "you're not allowed to wait in the hall, Ms. Keenan. Government office, terrorists, you know how it is." He opened the door for her. "There's a room for attorneys one floor down, right by the vending machine. You can make some calls there, maybe get a snack."

She shot daggers at Will as she left the room. If anything, her departure heightened the tension rather than alleviated it.

Will took his time closing the door before sitting back down. He crossed his arms over his chest, waiting for John Shelley to speak. At least five minutes of silence ticked by.

Will waited a little longer, then decided to give in. "How do you know Michael?"

John's fists were still clasped on the table, and the fingers tightened. "What did he say?"

"I'm not asking him. I'm asking you."

John stared all his anger straight into Will.

Will asked, "Is Joyce your sister?"

"Leave her out of this."

"It must've been hard all those years. You being in prison like that, her on the outside."

"She knows I didn't do it."

"That must have made it even harder."

"Stop trying your psychology bullshit on me."

"I was just curious about what it was like."

"What was it like?" John repeated, some of his anger starting to seep out. "What was it like to ruin my family, send my mother to an early grave? What was it like to be treated like some kind of fucking pariah by my own father? What do you think, man? What the fuck do you think?"

John's words hung in the air, his voice echoing in Will's ears. What did Will think? He thought that the pieces were finally fitting into place.

He said, "I want you to do something for me."

John's shoulders went up in a noncommittal gesture.

Will had kept a copy of Aleesha Monroe's letter in his pocket, sort of like a talisman to help him in the case. He unfolded the paper, slid it across the table to John. "Can you read this for me? Out loud, please."

The man gave him a strange look, but curiosity won out. He leaned over the table, not touching the paper as he read it to himself first.

John looked up at Will, confused. "You want me to read this out loud?"

"If you don't mind."

John cleared his throat. Obviously, he didn't know what was going on, but Will took it as a sign of trust when the man actually started reading it.

" 'Dear Mama,' " John began, but Will stopped him.

"Sorry. Third line down," he said. "If you could start with that."

John gave him another look that said he was only going to let Will go so far with this. " 'The Bible tells us that the sins of the parent are visited on the child. I am the outcast, the untouchable who can only live with the other Pariah, because of your sins.' " He stopped, staring at the words like he knew he was missing something that was right under his nose.

John asked, "Who's Alicia?"

"Aleesha Monroe," Will told him, and the expression on John's face showed him everything he needed to know. "I talked to her mother yesterday morning. I had to tell her that her daughter was dead."

John swallowed visibly. "Dead?"

"Aleesha Monroe was raped. Beaten. Her tongue was bitten out."

"It was . . ." John whispered, more to himself. He picked up the letter, stared at Aleesha's words to her mother.

"She wrote pariah twice," Will said, knowing that now was his only chance to get John to trust him. "The first time, she used a lowercase p. The second time, she capitalized it. *Pariah,* not *pariahs.* She meant one person, not a group."

John's eyes scanned the page, and Will knew the line he was reading. *The untouchable who can only live with the other Pariah.*

Will leaned forward over the table, made sure he had John's attention. "Who is the Pariah, John?"

He was still staring at the letter. "I don't know."

"It's somebody Aleesha knew way back when. Somebody she's having to live with now." Will's phone rang in his pocket, but he ignored it. "I need you to tell me who the Pariah is, John. I need to hear it from you."

John knew the answer, had figured it out. Will could see it in his eyes.

All the man said was, "Your phone is ringing."

"Don't worry about it," Will said. "Who's the Pariah?"

He shook his head, but Will could tell he was right on the edge.

"Tell me what she's talking about."

The phone kept ringing. Will didn't move to turn it off. He saw John starting to slip away, the ringing acting like some kind of warning bell reminding the con to keep his mouth shut.

"John," Will prodded.

John stood, wadding up the note and throwing it in Will's face, screaming, "I said I don't know!"

Will sat back in his chair, cursing Angie for picking now to return his call. He flipped open the phone, demanding, "What?"

"Trent," Leo Donnelly said. "I'm at Mike's place."

"Hold on," Will said, then pressed the phone to his chest as he told John, "I'm going to step out and take this call for a minute, okay?"

John shook his head. "Whatever."

Will left the room, putting the phone to his ear as he closed the door. "What is it, Leo?"

"I went to Mike's house like you said."

Will felt a spark of anger. John had been about to crack. If the stupid phone hadn't rung, he'd be laying out the whole story right now.

"I'm knocking on the door, knowing Mike's home because I see his car in the street."

Will leaned against the wall, feeling his sleepless night catch up with him. "And?"

"No answer, but then a DeKalb PD cruiser pulls up with Gina right behind him. Gina's the wife, right? She called them for protection while she gets some of her stuff out of the house."

"Okay."

"She backs into the driveway and it's not like I can duck under a bush, so I go up to her, ask her how she's doing. She looks at me like I'm a turd in her cereal, I guess thinking I'm Mike's buddy."

Will thought about John, sitting in the interrogation room. "Is this going somewhere?"

"You think I'm tugging your root, junior? I got at least ten years on you."

"You're right," Will allowed, leaning back against the wall, wondering how long this was going to take. "Go ahead."

"So," Leo continued. "DeKalb's not happy to see me, right? Apparently, Mike's been giving them the runaround about the dead neighbor. Won't talk to them, won't give a statement, won't let them look in his house."

He had Will's undivided attention now.

"My thinking is they jumped on Gina's call so they could get a peek around."

"And?"

"After she figured out Mike wasn't home, she wouldn't let them into the house." Leo added with some appreciation, "She may hate his fucking guts, but she's still a cop's wife. She knows you don't let nobody poke around unless they've got a paper from the judge."

"What am I missing here?"

"Lemme finish," Leo cautioned. "This cop, Barkley,

he's pretty pissed standing around with his dick in his hand. So, he takes it out on me, tells me to get the fuck off the property." Will heard a lighter flick open as Leo lit a cigarette. "Me, I mosey out into the street. It's a free country, right? Barkley don't own the street."

Will could imagine the scene. You didn't tell a cop to leave unless you wanted him to hang around your neck for the rest of your natural life.

Leo continued, "I'm poking around Mike's car, wondering why it's parked across the street and not in his drive, when the neighbor pulls up with her groceries. Real nosy bitch, but I ask her where Mike is, and she says—" Leo paused to take a drag on his cigarette. "She says that Mike was there about an hour ago. She was getting her mail when he pulled up. He asked her about the car parked in his driveway."

Will stood away from the wall. "What car?"

"Some car in the driveway," Leo answered. "Mike wanted to know how long it had been there. She tells him five, maybe ten minutes, then he just walks away, doesn't even say thank you."

"Then what?"

"The neighbor got inside her house, gets her grocery list and heads back out." Leo took another drag. "Only she notices that now the car in the driveway is facing the other direction. It's backed up to the garage now. She sees Mike standing there, closing the garage door."

"Shit."

"He throws her a wave, closes the trunk, gets in and drives off."

Closes the trunk, Will echoed in his head. Michael had put something in the trunk.

Will asked, "Did she say what kind of car it was?"

"Black. She don't know models."

His heart wasn't beating anymore. "Leo, is the cop still there?"

"Yeah."

"Gina's car is still backed into the driveway?"

"Yeah."

"I need you to go into the driveway and look under the back of her car. Tell me if there's fresh oil on the concrete."

"You want me to get my dick shot off?"

"You've got to do this," Will insisted, his throat hurting from the effort it took to speak. "Tell me if there are any fresh oil stains."

"Jesus," Leo muttered. Will heard him blow out a stream of smoke. "All right, hold on."

Will squeezed his eyes closed, picturing Leo walking across the street into Michael's driveway. There was a man's voice, probably the cop named Barkley, then a few groans as Leo must have struggled to get down on the ground. More yelling from the local cop, Leo yelling back. Finally, he got back on the phone. "Yeah, there's fresh oil. Can't be from Gina's car because she backed into the drive—"

Will snapped the phone closed, tucking it into his pocket as he slammed into the interrogation room.

John saw him and backed up, saying, "What the—"

Will twisted the man's arm around behind his back and smashed his face into the wall. He put his mouth an inch from John's ear to make sure the bastard heard every word.

"Tell me where he is."

John screamed in pain, going up on his toes.

"Tell me where he is," Will repeated, pushing the arm higher, feeling the shoulder start to give.

"I don't—"

"He's got Angie, you asshole." Will twisted the arm harder. "Tell me where he is."

"Tennessee," John whispered. "He's got a place in Tennessee."

Will let go and John dropped to the floor.

"Where in Tennessee?"

John shook his head, tried to stand. "Take me with you."

"Tell me the address."

He pushed himself up, wincing from the pain in his shoulder. "Take me with you."

"I'm only going to ask you one more time." When he didn't answer, Will took a step toward him.

"All right!" John screamed, holding up the only arm he could move. "Twenty-nine Elton Road. Ducktown, Tennessee."

CHAPTER THIRTY-SIX

Angie had vomited at some point, but the gag had kept most of it in her mouth. Judging by the acrid smell in the trunk she had managed to urinate on herself as well. Her head was pounding, and her body ached so badly she couldn't move without moaning in pain. Her hands and feet were hogtied behind her. Even if she had been able to move, she had nowhere to go, no way of helping herself. She was completely powerless.

She tried to concentrate on breathing, keeping herself oriented so that she wasn't sick again. This was hardly her first concussion, nor was it the worst, but the darkness in the trunk made it difficult to keep from panicking, and every time the car stopped for a traffic light or stop sign, she could not calm the fear that burned in her chest like acid.

The car slowed again, and she tensed, listening to the tires crunching against a gravel road. They were off the pavement now. Angie had no idea how long she'd been in the trunk. She hadn't seen who had hit her on the back of the head, but she knew it was Michael. His laughter still rang in her ears. It was the same laugh he'd given the night of Ken's party when he'd shoved her into the backseat of her car.

The girl.

There had been a girl tied to the pool table. Blood and bruises had riddled her small body. Jasmine. It had to be Jasmine.

The car rolled to a slow stop. Angie counted the seconds. At twelve, a door opened. The car shifted as weight lifted from the front seat. The door slammed. Footsteps crunched against gravel. The passenger side door opened, then closed hard as if it had been kicked shut.

Twenty seconds. Fifty. A hundred. Angie had given up counting by the time she heard the key scrape in the lock of the trunk.

She was blinded by sunlight. Angie squeezed her eyes tight against the pain. The fresh air was like heaven, and she opened her mouth wide around the gag, flared her nostrils, desperate to breathe it in.

A shadow blocked the sun. Slowly, she opened her eyes. Michael was smiling down at her, the ragged scratch Jasmine had made down his cheek three days before looking like war paint.

"Have a nice nap?"

She strained against the ropes.

"Settle down," he cautioned.

Angie barked out a "fuck you," around the gag.

He unsheathed a long hunting knife, warning her, "Don't try anything," as he sliced through the ropes behind her back.

She moaned with relief as she stretched her legs as much as she could. Her hands were still tied behind her back, but at least she could move.

"Get out of the car."

Angie struggled to sit up. Michael slid the knife back into the sheath and pulled out his service weapon. He pointed it at her head and she stopped moving.

"Slowly," he ordered. "Don't think for a minute I won't shoot you."

The rope bit into her wrists as she pressed her palms flat against the floor of the trunk. After several attempts, she managed to push herself up. She threw her legs over the side of the open trunk. Groaning, she forced herself out, tottering as her feet hit the ground, but somehow keeping her balance.

She stood up straight, looking around, trying to get her bearings.

"That was pretty impressive," he said. "I'd forgotten how limber you are."

She wanted to rip his eyes out with her bare hands.

"Look around," he told her. She saw rolling hills and snowcapped mountains looming behind a rustic-looking cabin. "You can scream all you want, but no one is going to hear you."

He pulled down the gag and she gulped for air. Her nose felt broken, and when she spit on the ground, a clot of blood mixed with chunks of food from breakfast.

She screamed like a banshee.

Michael just stood there as she doubled over from the exertion, her lungs rattling in her chest. She yelled until there was no air left in her lungs, nothing in her mind except the sound of her own screams.

He asked, "Finished?"

She lunged for him and he brought up his knee smack into her chest. She buckled to the ground, gravel shooting sharp pains through her legs.

He pressed the Glock to the side of her head, put his face a few inches from hers. "Remember this, Angie: you're second-string here."

Jasmine. "Where is she?"

He yanked her up by the hair, dragging her toward the

cabin. Angie struggled against him, pulling the ropes as she bumped against the stairs. "Let me go!" she screamed. "Let me go, you fucker!"

He opened the front door and pushed her inside. "Get in there." He grabbed her arm and threw her into the bathroom.

She fell into the tub, her head popping against the plastic wall. Michael still had his gun in one hand. With the other, he turned on the shower. Angie tried to stand, her legs slipping out from under her as the cold water beat down on her face.

"Take off your shorts," Michael ordered. He squirted a glob of shampoo on her as she struggled to stand. "Get them off."

Even if she'd wanted to, Angie couldn't do anything with her hands tied behind her back. Michael seemed to realize this. He reached in and ripped open the top button of the cutoffs, then pulled down the zipper.

"Underwear, too," he said. "Now."

Her fingers were numb, the circulation cut off. Still, she managed to hook her thumbs in the waistband and pull down the shorts. She kicked them away with her feet.

"What did you do with the little girl?" she demanded, pushing down her panties. "What did you do to Jasmine?"

"Don't worry." Michael smiled, like he was enjoying a private joke. "She won't talk."

Angie lunged again, her head barreling into his gut. Michael fell back into the hall and the gun skipped across the wet floor. In one swift motion, he picked up Angie and threw her across the room. She landed awkwardly, reaching for the empty space behind her to break the fall. Her right hand twisted as her full weight pressed into the wrist and she heard a crack just as a lightning bolt of pain set her arm on fire.

"Get up," Michael ordered.

Her hand was throbbing, needles running up and down her arm. She rolled to the side, sobbing. Oh, God, she had broken her wrist. What was she going to do? How was she going to get out of here?

She heard noises in the next room. Michael was gone. Where was the girl? What was he doing to Jasmine?

Angie pressed her face into the floor, forcing herself to her knees, then her feet. She leaned against the wall as her head started swimming, her vision blurring. She took a breath, braced herself, then moved away from the wall. Her wet underwear was wrapped around her ankle and she kicked it off as she limped into the outer room.

Michael was sitting on the couch, one leg crossed over the other, foot bouncing up and down. The Glock was on the cushion beside him. He knew she couldn't get to it in time.

"Sit down," he said, indicating the rocking chair by the fireplace. Carefully, she sat on the edge of the seat, trying not to fall back.

"What were you doing in my house?"

Angie looked around the room, which was about ten feet by twenty, a living room with a small kitchen at the back. She remembered the mountains outside, the stark isolation of the cabin. He had been right: no one would hear her scream.

She asked, "What are you going to do?"

He had that same smirk on his face, that smile she had seen the night of Ken's party and taken for flirting. "What do you think I'm going to do?"

Angie could not stop her bottom lip from trembling. Her hand was going numb, dull throbs of pain ringing around her wrist. The rope was wet from the shower, somehow made thicker and heavier by the water. The skin felt as if it had been burned away.

She looked at the gun on the couch.

"Don't be stupid."

Angie cleared her throat, feeling like she had swallowed cotton. "John told me everything," she said, wondering how hard she could push before Michael broke her. No one knew where she was. Will was probably still interviewing John Shelley, trying to get to the truth. If John had learned anything in prison, he was keeping his mouth closed. It would be hours, maybe days, before Will even thought to look for her, and when he finally did, there was no way he would know about this tiny cabin in the hills.

Michael asked, "What did John tell you?"

"About Mary Alice," Angie said, praying she'd got the girl's name right. "He told me what really happened."

Michael laughed, but he wasn't smiling. "John doesn't know what really happened."

"He figured it out."

"John's too stupid to figure anything out."

"I told everybody."

"Don't lie to me," he warned. "I'm being nice now, but we both know what I'm capable of."

"Will. I told Will."

He was scared of Will. She could see that in his eyes.

He asked, "Trent?"

"He's my boyfriend."

Michael kept staring at her, obviously trying to decide if she was telling the truth. Finally, he shook his head. "Uh-uh." He didn't believe her.

"It's true," she insisted. "I've known him all my life."

He let his gaze take in her body. She was naked below the waist, her legs braced apart so that she would not fall.

He told her, "You need to remember there are a lot of different ways you can die."

"The scar on Will's face," she tried. "It goes down his jaw to his neck."

Michael shrugged. "Anybody can see that."

"His hand," she said. "He was shot with a nail gun. I took him to the hospital."

Anger flashed in his eyes. He stood slowly from the couch and walked over to where she was sitting. Angie tried to lean back as he put his hands on either side of her, bracing himself against the arms of the rocking chair. His voice was a low growl when he asked, "What did you tell him?"

Fear tightened like a band around her throat. "Everything..." She heard the terror in her voice, knew he would hear it, too, but her mouth would not stop moving, the words would not stop coming. "John told me...and I told...I told Will..."

He was gripping the arms so hard that the whole chair seemed to vibrate. "Told you what?"

"That you knew Aleesha!"

"Fuck!" Michael pushed himself away from the chair so violently that it almost tipped over. Angie's legs flailed as she scrambled not to fall. "God damnit!" He lifted his foot to kick over the coffee table but stopped himself at the last minute. Slowly, his foot went back to the floor, but his fists were still clenched at his sides and he shook with fury.

Angie stared at his back, breathless with fear. Carefully, she stilled the rocking chair, inched her way closer to the edge of the seat. The floor creaked as she shifted her weight.

Michael turned and backhanded her so hard that she slammed onto the floor.

Angie lay there. She couldn't move. Her head was still echoing from the impact.

"Get up."

He didn't have to threaten her. Angie tried to sit up but couldn't. She pressed her face to the floor and closed her eyes, waiting for the punishment.

Nothing came.

"My dad left me when I was ten."

Angie opened her eyes. She must have passed out, missed something. Michael was at the kitchen sink. He took a metal tin out of one of the cabinets.

He said, "You know what that's like?"

Angie didn't answer. She watched him open the tin, check the contents.

"John thought he had it hard. He didn't know what hard was." Michael waved a bag of white powder in the air. He was back to being that guy again, that normal guy he projected out to the world so that they wouldn't figure out what a monster he was.

He said, "This is good stuff. You want some?"

She tried to shake her head.

"You didn't want that last drink, either." He smiled like it was funny. "Remember that, Angie—Ken's big party? I got you a drink."

She couldn't remember, but she nodded anyway.

"Roofies, baby." He sat down on the couch, putting the tin on the coffee table between them. "You gulped down a mouthful of roofies."

Rohypnol. He had drugged her.

Michael laughed at her expression. He took a razor blade and a small mirror out of the tin and tapped some of the powder onto the glass. Angie watched as he chopped the coke with the blade. "You ever have a kid?" he asked, not looking at her. "I bet you've had about sixty abortions by now." He kept cutting the coke, businesslike. "My son has problems. You know that."

Angie willed her body to move. She was gasping with

pain by the time she managed to sit up. At least she had managed it, though. At least she was no longer lying helpless on the floor.

"He's retarded," Michael told her, cutting the powder into four lines. He took a rolled dollar bill out of the tin and inhaled one of the lines. He made an "ahh" sound, then told Angie, "This is some good shit. You sure you don't want some?"

She shook her head again.

"Don't like being out of control? That's what you said at Ken's party when I handed you that drink." He chuckled. "You drank it anyway, didn't you? Could have put it down, but you gulped it like a damn fish." He held out the mirror, offering, "Sure?"

"You broke my nose."

"Your loss." He put the mirror back on the table.

"Just let me go." She was trembling so hard she could barely speak. "I won't tell anybody."

"You can't honestly think you're getting out of here."

"Where's Jasmine?"

"You'll find out soon enough." He leaned his head back on the couch, studying her. "Don't you want to know about John?"

"What about him?"

"Half that prison plowed John's ass. I bet he has AIDS."

Angie took deep breaths, coughed from the effort. Her wrist was throbbing with every heartbeat. The rope was tightening around her skin as it dried in the heat of the cabin.

"So, Tim, right?" He let out a short breath. "We got the diagnosis six years ago."

Angie tested the ropes around her wrists, gently pulling to see if there was any give. "That must have been . . . hard."

"It's always about money, isn't it?" He indicated the

mirror on the table, the lines of coke. "That's how I paid for it. Give the girls a little bump, let them help pay for my boy to learn how to tie his fucking shoes. State insurance won't cover half the shit he needs. What am I going to do, let my child waste away in some home?"

Angie didn't answer. Her mind processed his words, tried to make sense of them. Had Michael been selling dope to the girls, taking it in trade when he felt like it? He had been in Vice for at least ten years. His son couldn't be more than eight. Tim had nothing to do with it.

"Then I had all that cash and nowhere to park it. Can't put it in my account because Uncle Sam might get curious. Can't leave it lying around because Gina might ask questions." He pointed his finger at Angie. "Then, I figured, why not open up some accounts for my good old cousin Johnny? I already had his social security number from all that court shit my mom had lying around."

Cousin. Angie didn't know if Michael meant they were related or he was just using slang.

Michael said, "Wasn't like I had to worry about him getting out."

She felt her eyes wanting to close and fought to stay awake.

"Where are your questions, Angie?" The coke had made him more alert, talkative. "Come on, girlie. Ask your questions."

Angie's mind reeled. She couldn't think of anything but, "You knew Aleesha Monroe."

"Yeah, we go way back."

Angie waited for him to figure out that she had lied before, but he was too wrapped up in his own story to take apart hers.

He said, "First day in uniform, I got a call to the

Homes—got stuck in the freaking elevator. All the old-timers were busting a gut by the time they got me out, and there was Leesha, laughing right along with them. At least, she was laughing until she recognized me." He wagged his finger. "Nobody laughs at Michael Ormewood, Angie. Nobody laughs at him, and sure as shit nobody pushes him away."

Angie felt a trickle of blood sliding down the back of her throat. She gagged at the taste of it.

Michael said, "She was a whore in high school and she was a whore fifteen years later. Bitch would suck off a dog for the swill in a spoon." He was smiling again, that smile that said he was in charge. "What they don't realize is you have to control it. Take it when you want it, not when you need it." He meant the coke. "Don't smoke it, don't shoot it, don't get too greedy."

Michael was stupider than she thought if he believed he could control an addiction. She asked, "Why did you kill Aleesha?"

"She pissed me off. Tried to change the rules."

"You didn't want to pay her." Angie had been around enough prostitutes to know the score. "Did Jasmine piss you off, too?"

"Jasmine…" He smiled. "I wonder what your boyfriend would think if he found out I stashed her up in Aleesha's place while I drove him back to the station?" He watched her closely, seemed to be feeding off her reaction. "Remember when we were going over my reports? You were wearing that tight skirt up to your slit, flashing your tits every time you leaned over? She was in my trunk the whole time, Angie. The whole time you were rubbing up against me, she was in the trunk of my car, pissing herself thinking about what was going to happen."

Angie parted her lips, let some of the blood drip out.

One of her back teeth was throbbing. It was probably broken.

He had stopped speaking, and she wondered if the coke was starting to wear off. She couldn't tell how much time had passed since he'd snorted the line. Maybe he was one of those people who had the opposite reaction to the stimulant. Maybe he was so in control of himself that it didn't matter.

He was silent for so long that Angie felt her eyes closing, felt her body relax into some kind of sleep. Michael started talking again and she jerked awake.

"They all act like they're so fucking good, but all it ever takes is one hit, one snort, and they're hooked. They keep coming back, begging at your feet. All of them. Especially John."

Angie had to clear her throat a few times before she could talk. "Is that why you framed him?"

"That was Mom's idea, but he got what he deserved. They all got what they deserved." He glanced down at her. "Just like you."

Angie felt her eyes wanting to shut again, her muscles start to loosen. She fought it off, biting her split lip until she tasted more blood, using the pain to keep her alive.

"Once you get a taste for it," Michael was saying, his voice low, thoughtful, "you can't do it the other way. You need that fear, the way they push against you, the panic in their eyes."

Angie tested the rope again. The bones in her broken wrist shifted against each other, made a clicking sound that echoed inside her head.

"I got Johnny some credit cards," Michael continued. "Got this place." He meant the cabin. "You think I'm stupid, but I'm not." He tapped the side of his head. "Think, right? What's the first thing you do when you're trying to pin down a perp to the scene? Check their credit card receipts: gas bills, hotel bills, all that shit. Place the perp close to the scene, right day, right time, bingo, you've caught 'em." He shook his head. "They won't find nothin' on Michael Ormewood, that's for sure. Not in Alabama, not in Tennessee, sure as shit not in Atlanta. I'm just a family man, taking care of my poor retarded boy, looking after my wife, home every night in front of the tube."

"You sold them drugs," Angie said, thinking about all those girls she'd met on the streets, all those addicts who did anything to feed their addiction. A cop had supplied them. A cop had exploited their need and filled his own. How many had he raped? How many had he killed?

"I should be mad at you, but I'm not." He rubbed his jaw, kept his eyes on her. "Stupid people let their emotions get the better of them; that's when they make mistakes. I'm in control here, Angie. I'm the one who's going to decide how you die."

He stood up from the couch and she braced herself for more pain, but he went over to the fireplace, rested his hand on the mantel. Angie remembered being with Will three nights ago. He had stood at the fireplace in her house and she'd looked at his back, his strong shoulders, and wanted nothing more than to put her arms around him. She would never have that moment with him again. He would never know how she felt.

Michael said, "You don't know what it's like to have this dream in your head that you're gonna have a perfect life, a perfect family, and then something like Tim happens and you feel like you're just a fucking failure."

She breathed in as much air as she could, tried to keep her thoughts clear. "How did it start?"

"You know about Mary Alice."

"The other ones." There had to be other ones.

"How far do you want to go back? Eighty-five? Ninety-five? Last year?" The smile was on his face again. "Hell, I can't even remember which states they were in. Your boyfriend's into that profiling shit, right? I guess he'd say I escalated when old Johnny got out. Took the gloves off because I knew when the heat was turned up, all I had to do was point the finger back at him."

"They were just kids."

"Believe me, they were a lot more experienced than they let on. Real mature for their ages." He shook his head, as if he could not get over the irony. "Bunch of prick teases is what y'all are."

From out of nowhere, Angie felt shame welling up inside of her. How many of her mother's boyfriends had said the same thing about Angie? How many times had she accepted their stuffed animals or their nice meals out or their pretty clothes and then been told she was going to have to pay for it with her mouth?

Michael told her, "Most of those girls have been drilled so many times they can't even feel it unless you pound it into them." He was looking at her again, appraising her. "You were exactly like Mary Alice. You know that? You tease me, let me kiss you, touch you for a while, and then you push me away like I'm not good enough for you." He snorted his disgust. "You play it all innocent, but then when I'm inside you, I feel like my cock's in a fucking vacuum."

Angie stared at the gun on the couch.

"The whores are good for that. You can do anything to them, right? I mean, that's what you pay for." He had turned his back to her, his hands pressed into the mantel. Angie kept her eyes on the Glock, hoping the weapon wasn't some kind of trick her mind had played on her. "All I wanted was to blow off a little steam with Aleesha before the game. And then she gets all uppity with me, chases me out of the apartment and into the stairway like I'm some kind of punk. I don't pay for that shit. She kept pushing me and pushing me, and then she learned the lesson. Michael Ormewood does not pay."

Angie pressed her face to the floor, willing herself to endure this.

"Yeah, I let her get my temper up." She heard his footsteps, could feel him standing inches from her face. "But, nobody really cares when a whore dies, right? Nobody cares about you."

She squeezed her eyes shut. She had let him get into her head, let him have control, just like he wanted.

Angie said, "All that John had to do was tell them." She took a chance, adding, "You're his cousin."

"Oh, sweetheart," Michael tsked. "You actually think John would've had the chance to open his mouth in a courtroom?" He shook his head, telling her, "I've been playing with him all along, just tugging his strings whenever I wanted to." He chuckled to himself. "Sure, I almost shit in my pants when I opened that toolbox, saw what he put in there, but that's nothing compared to the shock I had planned for him. I was gonna have some wicked fun with that little girl, then lay it all back on Johnny's door—or, more specifically, that shithole room he lives in."

"It wouldn't have worked," she said, knowing that it probably would have.

" 'Hero cop catches serial killer in the act.' My DNA all over the room from holding the poor little dead thing in my arms. Cops busting in, seeing Johnny dead, me wailing in grief. I would've gotten a fucking promotion for killing that bastard. Do you know how much it costs to put a man on death row? I'd be saving the city twenty million bucks, easy."

"They would've found out."

"From who? All his friends? His loving family? His devoted, dead mother?"

"People would remember you."

"*Nobody* remembers me," Michael snapped, and she could tell she'd cut close to the bone. "John's the one who always stood out. I was just in the background—always in the background. Nobody ever noticed me, and you know what? Now, the only thing they're going to remember their precious Johnny for is being a killer."

"But John's not a killer, is he?" When he didn't answer, she looked up.

Michael was standing in front of a closed door that she assumed led to a closet. He reached up, feeling along the sill at the top, and pulled down a key.

She saw the dead bolt. Her heart stopped mid-beat. "What are you doing?"

"Enough talking," he said, slipping the key into the lock.

Angie's leg muscles trembled as she forced herself to stand. She backed away from him, pushing toward the couch.

Michael read her mind. He scooped up the gun. "Move." He used the muzzle to nudge her toward the closet. "Go on."

Angie took small steps, the closet coming into view. It wasn't a closet at all. Stairs led down to what must be a cellar.

"You fucked it all up," Michael told her. "That little girl and me, we were having a real good time."

The stairs got closer. If he put her in that cellar, Angie knew she would be dead.

"Move."

She stopped walking and he bumped into her from behind. "Don't do this."

His breath was hot in her ear. "I'm gonna fuck you, Angie. I'm going to fuck every hole you've got." He kept forcing her toward the cellar. "You sit down there and wait for me. Think about what I'm gonna do to you."

"No!" She dug her bare feet into the floor, pushed back against him. Her soles skidded across the wood. She tried to twist away, but he grabbed her by the waist, lifting her, closing the distance in two steps. She screamed "No!" bracing her feet against the doorjamb, fighting as hard as she could.

"Stop it!" he yelled, jerking her up again. Her legs swung wild as he threw her down the stairs. Angie careened against the walls as she fell. She landed in a heap at the bottom of the stairs, weeping from pain.

The overhead light flicked on, a single bulb illuminating what must have been a root cellar at one point. Jasmine was in a corner, curled up into a lifeless ball. Angie tried to go to the girl, but something held her back. She looked down, saw the shard of glass that impaled her upper arm. More glass stuck up like shark's teeth where broken bottles had been cemented into the bottom stair.

The glass made a sucking noise as she tried to move.

"Think about it," Michael called from the open doorway above. "Think about what's going to happen to you."

The light went out. The door closed. The bolt slid home.

She was going to die.

CHAPTER THIRTY-SEVEN

Will kept his cell phone to his ear as he drove, praying that Amanda would be in her office. He had brought John with him because he needed to hear his story, wanted to know what kind of animal he would be dealing with when he reached Tennessee. For his part, John was more than willing to oblige. All of the man's recalcitrance had disappeared, and Will's head was spinning from his theories.

Caroline finally answered the phone, saying, "Amanda Wagner's office."

"I need Amanda now. It's urgent."

She put him on hold. Will kept his eyes on the road, speeding up Interstate 75 in the HOV lane thirty miles over the posted speed limit.

"Will?" Amanda said. "What's going on?"

"I'm on my way to Tennessee."

"I don't recall signing off on a vacation request."

"I think Michael Ormewood is the killer."

"All right," Amanda drawled. "Break it down for me, Will."

Will told her John's story, how Michael had tried to lean on the parole officer, how John's sister had told him about the cabin in Tennessee. He finished with the oil stains in Michael's driveway and what the neighbor had told Leo Donnelly.

"You checked Polaski's house?"

"I had a cruiser go by. She's not there. Her car's not in the driveway."

Amanda was silent. Will had introduced her to Angie once—not by choice. She had taken him to the hospital when Amanda had shot him with the nail gun. Inconceivably, the two women had gotten along.

Finally, she spoke. "So, what you're saying is, based on some unanswered phone calls and a few spots on a driveway, you're taking a convicted felon over state lines to look for an Atlanta police detective who may or may not have snatched another detective in broad daylight?"

"You need to search his house."

"This is the house in DeKalb County's jurisdiction? How do you propose I get a warrant, Dr. Trent? Not that your mysterious oil stains in the drive aren't compelling, but I doubt there's a judge alive who would sign off on it."

"Amanda," Will said, trying to control his voice. "You are a nasty, horrible person, but you have always had my back every time I worked a case. Don't do this to me now."

"Well, Will," she countered. "You are a high-functioning dyslexic who reads on a second-grade level, but let's not throw stones."

Will felt all the saliva in his mouth dry up. When had she found out?

Amanda said, "I don't have many friends in Tennessee, Will. I can't reach out to them to help you with nothing more to go on than the bad feeling in your gut and we both know Yip Gomez would rather eat his own shit than give you a hand." Yip was Will's old boss in the northwest field office. She added, "This is why I keep telling you not to burn bridges," as if now was the time for one of her lessons.

"I don't know what you want me to say," he admitted. "You're right. This could be nothing. I could get there and it could be just a waste of time, but I can't stand around not doing anything, Amanda."

"You put out an APB on Polaski's car?"

"Yes."

She was silent for a few seconds, then asked, "Tell me, this Detective Donnelly, he was the last person to leave Ormewood's house?"

"Yes."

"Well, look at this," Amanda exclaimed, her voice raised in mock surprise. "Caroline just handed me a message. It's an anonymous tip. A concerned citizen has noticed that Detective Ormewood's back door has been busted open. I think I should check on it myself, don't you?"

Will felt a wave of relief. Amanda was going to help him. He could almost hear her thinking it through over the phone.

"Thank you," he breathed. "Thank you."

"I'll let you know when I get there."

Will ended the call. He kept the phone in his hand as he drove, taking the exit onto 575 with an abrupt jerk of the wheel that made John Shelley grab the side of the door like he was afraid they were going to roll. Will had been in such a hurry that he hadn't even considered how he was going to find the cabin until John had asked for a map. The five-minute detour to the gas station had seemed like a lifetime. If what the neighbor had told Donnelly was right, Michael had about an hour on them. But, then, Michael was probably driving the speed limit, staying under the radar. Will wasn't being so careful.

John asked, "What did she say?"

"You could have prevented this," Will told him. "You could have stopped this four days ago."

"I don't know what you're talking about."

"Michael was with me when Cynthia Barrett died."

John looked down at the map he had spread across his lap. "I heard she was running across the yard and tripped. Hit her head on a rock and died."

"Then cut out her own tongue?"

John didn't offer an answer.

"You should have done something then."

"What?" John demanded. "Gone to you? You don't even believe my story now, man. What am I going to do? Turn in a cop? Who's gonna believe an ex-con who works at a car wash?"

Will kept his hands tight around the wheel. John had brought this down on Angie. She would be safe now but for the man's arrogance and stupidity. "You were baiting him. You knew exactly what you were doing."

John snapped the map along a crease, folding it into a smaller section as he kept trying to defend himself. "You tell me what I should've done and I'll get back in my magic time machine and do it. Tell you what, though, let's don't stop at four days. Let's go back twenty years. Give me my youth back. Give me my mother and my grandparents and my family. Hell, throw in a wife and a couple of kids for me while you're at it."

"She was running away from something in that yard."

John was still working on the map, but Will could hear the anguish in the other man's voice when he said, "Don't you think I know that?"

Will looked back at the road, watched the signs blur by, the mile markers with their bold numbers popping up along the landscape. He hadn't thought this through; hadn't considered that he might be endangering John.

Will said, "It violates your parole to go over state lines."

"I know."

"You could be arrested. I can't help you in Tennessee."

"You can't help me in Atlanta, either."

Will chewed his lip, staring at the black pavement, the other cars on the road. He had driven back and forth between Atlanta and the mountains for the last two years, so he knew exactly where all the speed traps were. He slowed down through Ellijay, not resuming his speed until he crossed Miciak Creek. He coasted by the new Wal-Mart and the old one, then past several outdoor flea markets and a couple of liquor stores. At the town of Blue Ridge, he took a left. He was flying down Coote Mason Highway, just beyond the apple orchard, when the phone rang.

He flipped it open on the side of his leg. "Amanda?"

Her tone was grim. "We found blood in the garage. Two different types and lots of it."

"Angie?"

"She's not here, Will."

His mouth opened, but words failed him.

"Here's how this is going to work," Amanda said. "I've called Bob Burg at the Tee Bees." The Tennessee Bureau of Investigation. "He's putting together a team right now. They're about forty minutes out from the cabin."

"I'm closer."

"I figured you would be," she said. "Let me speak to the pedophile. I've got directions to Elton Road."

CHAPTER THIRTY-EIGHT

Angie had almost passed out when she lifted her arm off the shard of glass cemented to the bottom stair—not so much from the pain, but from the sensation of the glass sliding out of her flesh. There wasn't much blood, and compared to the throbbing in her wrist, the wound was manageable. She had been lucky. Her right wrist was the one that was probably broken and she had by some miracle fallen on her right shoulder at the bottom of the stairs. Like Will, Angie was left-handed.

"Jasmine?" she whispered, her voice echoing in the pitch-black cellar. "Jasmine?" There was no response.

Angie pressed her good shoulder against the wall and stood. She took a moment to catch her breath, then carefully slid her bare feet across the dirt floor, searching for the girl.

"Jasmine?" she repeated, her foot making contact. "Are you okay?"

The girl was either too terrified to answer or was dead.

Angie knelt down, put her head to where she thought Jasmine's mouth and nose might be and tried to listen for signs of life.

Nothing.

Angie turned around, reaching blindly with her fingers. She felt along the girl's naked body, touching sticky blood, finally feeling the shallow up and down of Jasmine's chest laboring to breathe. Angie didn't touch her mother much, but the few times she'd visited Deidre in the home, this is what she had felt like: deadweight, just a shell that looked like a body.

"Jasmine?" Angie whispered.

The girl did not stir as Angie touched her face, her hair. Angie's fingers slipped under the scalp and she recoiled.

"Oh, Jesus!" Angie bent at the waist, trying not to vomit again. She'd touched the girl's skull, felt the splintered bone and the soft, wet, gray matter underneath.

They had to get out of here. They had to get help.

Angie stood again. She paced out the cellar. Ten feet wide, maybe twelve feet deep. Before the bulb had been switched off, she had glimpsed crude wooden shelves built into the walls. With her hands tied behind her back, it was difficult to check the top shelves. Her fingers felt nothing but vacant space as she checked the lower shelves for anything that might be used as a weapon.

The cellar was empty. Even the packed dirt floor was swept clean.

Maybe her wrist was not completely broken. Angie could still move her fingers, though they felt swollen and hot as if an infection was already working its way through her bloodstream. She was becoming used to the pain, almost welcoming it because it took her mind off the pounding in her head, the roiling in her stomach. The dark helped, too. There was nothing for her eyes to focus on, nothing to throw her balance.

Michael was upstairs. She thought he might be making a meal, lunch or dinner. She didn't know what time of day it was or how long she'd been in this fucking hole.

Every noise he made—a chair sliding across the floor, joists squeaking as he walked around—intensified her fury.

Angie seethed with hatred. He had gotten to her. He had worked his way into her mind and made her feel like a useless piece of shit. She'd had more men inside her body than she could count, but not one of them had ever gotten into her head like this.

She would kill him when he came back. She would kill him or make him kill her. Those were the only two options.

Angie braced herself, sliding down the wall until she was on her knees. Two paces to the stair, the broken glass embedded in the tread. She turned and felt for it with her hands, careful not to slice her already shredded fingers as she positioned the thick, knotted rope over the biggest shards. She sucked in air through her teeth, trying not to think about the pain as she sawed the rope against the glass.

Michael's handcuffs were on Jasmine. He had used rope to tie up Angie.

"You fucker," she breathed, a mantra to herself. Michael Ormewood didn't make mistakes. He was always in control, always on top of everything. Everything but the fact that glass could cut rope.

"You stupid fucker."

Blood soaked her hands, wet the rope that bound her wrists together. Angie stopped sawing, trying to catch her breath, take it slow. She'd almost passed out the first time she'd tried to cut the rope, but with each new attempt, she honed her technique, learned more about the knots he'd tied, the way the rope bound her wrists. She could feel that the rope had shifted down a little, was rubbing raw a new section of skin. Her blood was acting as a lubricant.

She would get out of this. She would saw off her own hand if she had to.

"Oh!" She gasped as the rope skipped down the glass, her hands slipping, the razor-sharp edges slicing into her fingers.

Angie held her breath, listening for Michael. God, she had never hurt so bad in her life. She couldn't stand it, couldn't take the feeling of the flesh being sliced off bone. She leaned forward, her forehead touching the ground as she cried.

"Will," she whispered. She couldn't pray to God, not after everything she'd done, so she prayed to Will. "I'm going to get out of this," she promised him. "I'm going to get out of this and..." She didn't say the words, but she knew them in her heart. She would leave Will for good. She would finally let him escape.

Overhead, footsteps walked across the floor. Angie reared up, her hands fumbling for the glass. She furiously worked the rope, fear anesthetizing her against the pain.

"Angie?" Michael called. He was on the other side of the locked door. "Answer me. I know you hear me."

She stretched the rope taut, wrenching her shoulders, desperate to break free. "Fuck you, motherfucker!"

"Get away from the stairs, Angie. I'm gonna open the door, and I've got my gun trained right on you."

She didn't answer, couldn't answer. Faster, faster, she sawed the rope up and down the jagged glass.

The key scraped in the lock.

"No," Angie whispered, forcing herself to hurry. "Not yet, not yet."

"Get away from the stairs," he said. "I mean it."

"No!" she screamed, jumping away from the glass just as the door flew open.

The light blazed on. Angie looked at Jasmine, saw the girl's face was turned toward her, the eyes slit open but unseeing. Her mouth was open. Blood pooled around her head.

"Don't try anything," Michael warned. He stood at the

top of the stairs with the gun in his hand. He was bare-chested, jeans and sneakers the only thing covering his body.

"Fuck off," Angie told him. She'd felt the rope give, but not enough. Blood wet her hands like water. She was still trapped, still helpless.

He tucked the gun into the waist of his jeans, then reached into his back pocket.

"Go away," Angie told him.

He put on a black ski mask, holes cut out for the eyes and mouth.

"Go away!" she screamed, backing into the wall, scrambling to stand.

He took out the gun and started down the stairs. Slowly, one tread at a time.

Angie's shoulders tensed to their breaking point as she pulled at the rope. She had felt it give before. She had felt it give.

He kept up his steady pace down into the cellar. The ski mask was unnerving, more terrifying than anything he could have said. The gun stayed trained on her chest, and she saw the knife sheathed at his side.

Angie's throat tensed. She could barely speak. "No..."

He stepped over the last stair and stopped. His eyes were dark, almost black. She could see dried blood around the mouth of the mask.

The sight of him sent an uncontrollable tremble through her body.

He looked at Jasmine lying in the corner, then took a step closer to Angie. They both stood there facing each other, the room quiet but for the short breaths Angie was taking.

His voice was so soft she could barely hear him. "Michael is going to hurt you."

"I'll kill you," she breathed. "I'll kill you if you touch me."

"Lie down."

She kicked out at him. "You sick fucker."

He still spoke gently. "Lie down on the floor."

"Fuck you!"

He brought up his gun and slammed it down on her head.

Angie slumped to the ground. She couldn't keep her head up, couldn't remember for a moment where she was.

He cupped her chin in his hand, his words still soft; the tone he would use with a child who was misbehaving. "Don't pass out on me," he whispered. "You hear me?"

She saw Jasmine lying behind him, her body limp. What had Michael done to her? What had the child endured before her body simply gave up?

"Look at me," Michael said, gently, as if this was some kind of seduction. "Keep looking at me, Angie. Look at Michael."

Her head rolled to the side. She couldn't make her eyes focus.

"Come on, darlin', don't pass out." He cupped her chin with his hand again, tilted up her face. "You okay?"

She nodded, mostly to prove to herself that there was still some part of her body that she could control.

"That's good," he soothed, placing the gun on one of the shelves above her head, high out of the way. He took the knife out of the sheath and knelt down, holding the blade to her face so that she could see.

"No . . ." she begged.

He used his knife to cut open her shirt—Will's shirt—pushing it back on her shoulders. She tried to watch him, tried to see his hand as he traced his fingers across her breasts, but she could only feel what he was doing.

"No," she pleaded. "Don't."

"Lie down," he coaxed. "Lie down and I'll be sweet to you."

She rolled back her head, trying to look at his face. Who was behind the mask? Was it John? Had she tricked her mind into thinking it was Michael when it was really John?

"Angie?" He was so calm. Like Will. He knew that was the best way to make her angry. She would fly off in a tantrum and he would just stand there, patiently waiting her out, staring at the floor. Oh, God, Will. How would he live with this? How would he live with himself knowing that he'd failed to stop this bastard?

"An-gie," he sang. "Look at me."

She knew that voice, knew that body.

"An-gie..."

She squeezed her eyes shut, seeing Will's arm, the angry scar where the razor had cut into his flesh.

"Okay," she said. "Okay."

She fell to her side, her uninjured shoulder thumping into the packed-dirt floor. He helped her lie flat on her back, tugging at her shirt when it got caught around her arms. All of her weight rested on her hands, her pelvis arching up as if it was on display for him.

"That's good," he whispered, straddling her legs. She saw his tongue dart out of his mouth as he traced the tip of the knife down her abdomen, stopping just shy of her snatch.

Where was the gun? Where had he put the gun?

"Look at me." He leaned over her body, pressing the knife against her neck.

The shelf. He had put it on the shelf.

"Look at me."

She looked at him.

"Kiss me."

Too high. The shelf was too high.

"Kiss me," he said.

Her whole body shook, but she leaned up, pulling at the rope as hard as she could as she brought her mouth to his. He was still trying to be tender, his lips soft against hers. She could taste her own blood, feel his heart pumping against her chest as he pressed against her. When he put his tongue in her mouth, she gagged, instinctively trying to jerk away, but he pressed the knife harder against her throat, and Angie had no choice but to let him kiss her.

He made a smacking noise as he sat back up, satisfied. "If you'd kissed me like that in the back of the car, maybe it would have gone differently."

Angie looked up at him. The bare lightbulb made a halo behind his head. She turned, saw Jasmine, saw the blood in the girl's mouth, the dead look in her eyes.

"Angie," Michael whispered, tracing his fingers along her face, down her body. Will had touched her like this a long time ago. Why had he stopped touching her? When had she started pushing him away?

Michael leaned over her again, his weight pressing her into the ground.

"Please . . . Please don't . . ."

He kissed her again. She pushed her weight into her right hand, pulling as hard as she could with the left to stretch the rope. Her stomach muscles shuddered, her breath caught, as the skin started to peel off her hand like a glove. He jammed his tongue farther down her throat, his teeth clashing against hers. She could feel the shattered bones in her right wrist grind against each other. The pain was so unbearable that she finally gave in to it, let it rush through her body like a red tide.

Michael sat back on his heels, watching her.

"No . . ." she breathed. "Oh, God, no . . ." She was going to pass out. She couldn't stop it. Her eyelids flickered. Her vision blurred.

She felt him press harder into her, excited by her pain.

"Take it off," she panted. "Take off the mask."

He shook his head.

"Let me see you."

"No."

"Will," she whispered. Where was Will?

"What?"

She shook her head, blinking, forcing herself to stay lucid. "Oh, Will . . ."

"It's not Will," he said, using his free hand to peel off the ski mask. He threw it on the ground. "It's Michael. I'm the one who's doing this to you."

"Will."

He twisted her head, forced her to look at him. "Who's doing this to you, Angie?"

"Will . . ."

"Look at me," he repeated, his voice stern. "Look at me, Angie." His weight shifted, pressing her harder into the dirt. Angie moaned as the broken bones shifted.

"Help . . ." she whispered, her voice nearly failing her.

"That's it," Michael said. "Yell for help."

"No . . ." Angie writhed underneath him, whimpering, "Please don't hurt me . . . please."

He dropped the knife and fumbled with the button on his jeans. He was reaching into his pants when she reared straight up and slammed her head into his.

The blow stunned him, and she scooped up the knife in her left hand before he could regain his senses. She was the one straddling him this time. She was the one holding the knife at his throat.

"You stupid cunt," she slurred, blood and saliva spraying his face. "The glass on the stairs. I cut the rope on the glass."

He didn't speak, but she saw it in his eyes. *No.*

Her body shook with rage as she pressed the blade harder against his flesh. Michael didn't flinch, didn't struggle; the brutal rapist, the violent murderer, and he'd given up just like that.

How many men, Angie thought. How many men's faces were seared into her brain, their twisted mouths grinning as they pounded it into her, their big hands pressing into her wrists so hard that the next day she almost hurt more there than she did between her legs?

Even if Jasmine made it out of here alive, she would always have this bastard's face in her head, always feel his hands on her body every time another man touched her. Even if she loved that man. Even if she wanted that man more than anybody else in the whole world, it would always be Michael's face she would see when she closed her eyes.

Being raped wasn't the hard part. Surviving was what killed you.

"Angie!"

There was a loud crash upstairs, splintering. The front door had busted open.

"Angie!" Will yelled. "Where are you!"

She put her face close to Michael's, making him look into her eyes as she whispered, "Kiss this, you stupid motherfucker," and jammed the blade up under his ribs.

Michael's mouth opened just as Angie's did. She let out a bloodcurdling scream, pulling out the knife and plunging it back in to the hilt, yelling, "Help! I'm down here!" She drew back the blade and slammed it home again and again, screaming until her throat was raw. "Will! We're down here!"

"Angie!" The cellar door buckled as Will tried to break it down.

"Will!" she pleaded, twisting the blade into Michael's gut. "Help me!"

Three gunshots splintered the lock off the door. She used the knife like a handle to shift Michael's weight onto her just as footsteps pounded down the stairs.

Will grabbed Michael from behind and threw him against the wall like a bag of trash.

"Angie!" Will was breathing so hard he almost couldn't speak. "Did he hurt you? Are you okay?" He tried to take the knife from her, but her hand would not let go. "Did he hurt you? Baby, please talk to me."

"Will," she whispered, wanting to touch his face, wipe away the tears streaming out of his eyes.

"It's okay," he told her, gently prying open her fingers so she would let go of the knife. "It's okay now. I'm here."

"Will..."

"Your hands," he said, horrified. "What did he do to your hands?"

Someone else entered the room. She saw a man running down the stairs. John Shelley stopped just before the bottom tread. He looked at Michael, then Jasmine, as if he couldn't make up his mind what to do.

"Angie." Will held her in his arms, cradling her. She didn't stop him even though it hurt all over. "Oh, Angie."

John went to the girl. He checked her pulse, looked at the wound on her head.

Angie could only watch Michael. She wanted him to see her, wanted the image of her face to haunt him.

His eyes were open. He blinked once, twice. Blood pooled on the floor in front of him like a river flowing out of his body. Pink translucent bubbles sputtered on his lips as his lungs filled. His breath whistled through the holes Angie had made in his chest.

He knew what was happening to him.

He was terrified.

Will pressed his lips to her forehead. "You're all right," he whispered. "You're okay."

Michael's eyelids fluttered. A gurgling noise filled the room as he began to choke on his own blood. His mouth gaped open, a thin line of blood tracing a path down his cheek.

Angie pursed her lips and blew him a kiss good-bye.

CHAPTER THIRTY-NINE

You" was all Lydia Ormewood said when she'd opened her front door to find John and Joyce standing there.

Michael's mother had aged well, or more likely she'd spent enough money to make sure she looked like it. Though John knew the woman was in her late sixties, the skin on her face was smooth and healthy-looking. Even her neck and hands, the usual giveaway, were as smooth and young as Joyce's.

Life had obviously been very good to her. She lived in Vinings, one of Atlanta's more expensive suburbs, in a brand-new, three-story house. White walls loomed over everything, white carpets scattered around the bleached oak floors. A gleaming white grand piano was in the living room, and two black leather couches faced each other by a marbled fireplace. Cream silk curtains hung in the windows. Abstract art with bold primary colors hung on the walls, all of it probably original work. Lydia herself was monochromatic. She wore black. John did not know if this was her regular attire or if she was in mourning for her son.

Joyce had been at the DeKalb County courthouse when John was arrested, going page by page through old records, looking for Lydia. Since then, she had taken days off work, digging through all the public records she could find. Lydia had married and divorced twice since her husband Barry had died. Her surname had changed each time, but Joyce had finally managed to trace Michael's mother through a contact who worked at the social security office. Uncle Barry had been fully vested in the system when he died. Lydia had started to collect his social security checks four years ago.

Joyce had the woman's address in her hand three days later.

They sat in front of the fireplace, Joyce and John on one uncomfortable couch, Lydia on the other. Their aunt sat with her spine straight, knees together, legs tilted to the side, like a photograph out of Miss Manners. She looked at John with open distaste.

He knew he looked like hell. Ms. Lam had knocked on his door at five o'clock that morning. She'd handed him the specimen cup, then started searching his room for contraband. He'd come back from the toilet to find her holding the picture of his mother in her hands. John had stood there holding his own piss, feeling a slow shame burning inside him. This was just one more degradation he had forced on Emily. When would it end? When would his mother be able to rest in peace?

Joyce said, "We're here about Michael."

"He was my son," Lydia told them, as if it was that simple.

Joyce stiffened beside him, but John shook his head, willed her to be patient. He loved his sister, but she lived in a world of black and white. She didn't know how to deal with the grays.

John told Lydia, "The little girl he kidnapped is going to be okay."

"Well," she said, dismissing this with a shrug of her narrow shoulders. John waited, but she didn't ask about Angie Polaski, didn't seem interested in the health of her son's last victim. As a matter of fact, she didn't seem interested in anything.

John cleared his throat. "If you could just—"

"He hated you, you know."

John had already figured that out, but he needed to know. "Why?"

"I don't know," she answered, smoothing her skirt with her hand. She had a large diamond ring on her finger, the gold band at least half an inch wide. "He seemed quite obsessed with you. He kept a scrapbook." She stood suddenly. "I'll get it."

She left the room, her slippers gliding across the white carpet.

Joyce hissed out air between her teeth.

"Calm down," John told her. "She doesn't have to do this."

"She's holding your life in her hands."

"I know," John said, but he was used to having other people control his life, whether it was his father or Michael or the guards at the prison or Martha Lam. John had never known a moment in his adult life when he wasn't trying to keep somebody happy just so he could live through another day.

Joyce started to tear up again. He had forgotten what a crier she was. "I hate her, John. I hate her so much. How can you stand to be in the same room with her?"

He used the back of his finger to wipe away her tears. "We need something from her. She doesn't need anything from us."

Lydia returned, holding a large photo album to her chest. She put it on the low leather ottoman between the couches as she sat down.

John saw a photograph of himself pasted to the outside

of the book. At least, he thought it was his photograph. The face had been scratched out with an ink pen.

"My God," Joyce murmured, sliding the album over. She opened the cover to the first page, then the second, as John looked over her shoulder. They were both speechless as they saw pictures of John from junior high—class pictures, team photos, John running in his track uniform. Michael had catalogued each moment of John's teenage life.

"It was Barry who made it worse," Lydia said. Uncle Barry, her husband, their mother's brother. "Barry talked about you all the time, used you as an example."

"An example of what?" Joyce demanded, obviously horrified by the scrapbook.

"Michael went down the wrong path after his father left. He had problems at school. The drugs...well, I don't know. There was an older boy at school who got him interested in the wrong things. Michael would have never done anything like that on his own."

Joyce's mouth opened but John squeezed her hand, warning her not to speak. You didn't get what you wanted from someone like Lydia Ormewood by telling her what to do. You came with your hat in your hand and you waited. John had done this all of his life. He knew that one false word could ruin everything.

Lydia continued, "Barry thought you would be a good role model for Michael. You always did so well in school." She sighed. "Michael was a good boy. He merely gravitated toward the wrong crowd."

John nodded, like he understood. Maybe, on some level, he did. John himself had gotten sucked into Michael's crowd. So had Aleesha Monroe. She had hung around Michael's house all the time, had even been there the night of the party. She'd had good parents, siblings who were always at the top of their classes. Would John have ended up like Aleesha if Mary Alice hadn't died? Would his life have been wasted like hers no matter what had happened?

Lydia's chest rose and fell as she sighed again. "I made him join the military," she told them. "I didn't let him sit around after you went away. He fought in the war. He tried to help keep those Arab people safe and got shot in the leg for his trouble."

Joyce was so tense John could almost hear her humming like a piano wire.

Lydia picked at a speck of fuzz on her skirt. "And then he came back to Atlanta, settled down, had a family." She looked up at Joyce. "That girl he married, she obviously had something wrong with her. Tim was *not* Michael's fault." She spoke vehemently, and John looked around the room again, trying to find photographs of Michael or his son. The mantel over the fireplace was bare but for a glass vase of silk flowers. The stark metal table on the back wall held nothing but a neat stack of magazines and one of those princess phones like Joyce had in her room when they were growing up. Even the thick cord dangling from the telephone hung in a straight line, as if it, too, was afraid to displease Lydia.

The whole place was like a tomb.

"He got a commendation for saving a woman's life," Lydia continued proudly. "Did you know that?"

John's reply almost caught in his throat. "No. I didn't."

"She was in a car accident. He pulled her from the car before it exploded."

John didn't know what to say. Michael may have saved one woman, but he had ruined countless others, selling drugs to the working girls, raping and murdering for his own sick pleasure.

"Michael *was* good," Lydia insisted. "That other part of him"—she waved her hand, dismissing the evil her son had wrought—"that wasn't my Michael. My Michael was a good boy. He had so many friends."

So many friends he got hooked on hard drugs, John thought. Like Aleesha.

"And such promise," she continued.

"You can't do this." Joyce's voice shook with anger. "You cannot sit there and tell us what an angel Michael was. He was an animal."

"Joyce," John tried. She didn't know the rules, didn't know how to give up her control. She had never had someone throw feces in her face just for looking the wrong way. She had never tried to go to sleep while the sixty-year-old man in the next cell whispered about what a beautiful body you had, told you in minute detail what he wanted to do to it.

Lydia raised a thin eyebrow. "You should mind your brother, young lady."

"Don't you dare talk about my brother."

Amusement flashed in Lydia's eyes. John knew they had lost. In that one moment, they had lost everything.

Lydia asked, "Are you threatening me?"

Joyce exploded off the couch, yelling, "You knew John didn't kill Mary Alice!"

"I knew no such thing."

"How can you defend him?" John tried to pull her back to the couch, but Joyce slapped his hand away. "How can you just sit there—"

"You don't have children so you don't know," Lydia snapped. "You and your . . . lady friend."

Joyce clenched her fists. "No," she answered. "I don't have children. You're right. I didn't raise a child. I didn't raise a rapist and murderer, either."

Lydia looked as if she had been slapped. "You've no right to speak to me in that tone."

"Did you tell Mama?" Joyce demanded. "When you went to the hospital, is that when you told her what happened, that your child murdered Mary Alice, not hers?"

Lydia advised, "Let the dead rest in peace."

John didn't know if she meant Emily or Michael. For his part, John wasn't sure if Michael's death brought him any peace. Standing there in that cellar, he had wanted with every ounce of his being to fall to his knees, beat the life back into Michael's chest, do whatever it took to bring him back to life so he could kill him again with his own hands.

But, he hadn't. John had saved Jasmine instead. She had stopped breathing, and John had breathed for her, giving her CPR for over forty minutes until the ambulance had arrived at the little cabin Michael had bought in John's name. The same hands that had mutilated Cynthia Barrett had given life to another little girl. There had to be some kind of justice in that. There had to be some kind of peace.

John watched his sister as she walked to the other side of the room, putting some space between herself and the woman who had destroyed her family. Joyce was just trying to defend him. He knew that. He also knew that she had ruined any possibility they had of clearing his name.

Still, he had to try. John had learned patience in a way his sister never had to. He had also learned how to talk to the people in charge.

"She's upset," he told Lydia, a half-apology he knew she was waiting for. "It's been hard for her."

"You've got your freedom," Lydia pointed out. "I don't know what you want from me. I'm an old woman. I just want to be left alone."

"It's not that easy."

"You're out, aren't you?" She said it as if it was a simple thing, as if John wasn't always looking over his shoulder, always waiting for those cuffs to be put back on, for those guards to throw him into a cell with Zebra. He had nearly shit his pants when Will Trent slammed him into the wall. There were some prisons you never got out of.

John took a deep breath, made himself explain to the former criminal lawyer how the justice system worked. "I'm a registered sex offender. A pedophile. I can't get a decent job, buy a home. I'll never have a life."

"What about Michael?" she demanded. "He doesn't have a life, either."

Joyce made a noise of disgust. She was standing by the piano, arms crossed over her chest. She looked just like their father.

John turned back to Lydia, speaking gently, trying to lead her through it. "Michael killed a woman named Aleesha Monroe."

"She was a prostitute."

So, she had been watching the news.

"He kidnapped a police officer," John continued. "The bones in her wrist are so badly broken that she may be permanently disabled."

Lydia didn't have an answer for that one.

"He kidnapped a little girl and raped her, nearly beat her to death."

"From what I've gathered," she said tartly, "the girl was hardly inexperienced."

"He bit off her tongue."

Lydia smoothed her skirt again, keeping silent.

"Michael bit off her tongue, just like he bit off Mary Alice's."

If John hadn't been looking at Lydia, he would've missed her reaction. For just an instant, he was certain she had been surprised.

John said, "I know about the report the state's dental expert wrote."

Her chin went up in challenge. "I have no idea what you're talking about."

"I think you do."

"I have no recollection of a report." She added, "And even if I did, there's nothing I can do about it now."

"You can give me my life back." John tried, "All you'd have to do is make a sworn statement—"

"Don't be ridiculous."

"That's all I want, Lydia. Swear under oath that it was Michael who killed Mary Alice and not me. Convince them to clear my record and I'll just—"

"Young man," she interrupted again, her tone clipped. He could tell from her posture that it was over. She pointed to the door. "I want you and your sister out of my house right now."

John stood automatically, always one to follow orders. Joyce was still at the piano. Tears of defeat welled into her eyes. She had fought so hard for him and now she had finally realized that there was nothing more that she could do.

She mouthed, "I'm sorry."

He looked around the house, the mausoleum Lydia had built with the money she'd earned from suing corporations and doctors and anyone else who had made a mistake she could profit on. She'd spent hours with John at the county jail trying to fabricate his defense. Twenty years ago, she had told him not to testify on his own behalf. She had handled the lab tests, the experts, the character witnesses. Lydia was the one who came to Coastal that day to tell him that it was over, that there were no other legal avenues left to explore. She'd started crying, and he had tried to comfort her.

John also remembered another day at Coastal, that first visit his mother had made after Zebra had ripped him in two.

"You will not give up," Emily had ordered, gripping John's hands so hard across the table that his fingers started to go numb. "Do you understand me, Jonathan? You will not give up."

You didn't go through twenty years of hard time without learning something. Prison was nothing but a big clock that never stopped ticking. All any of them had was time, and they spent that time talking. There was trash-talk—plans of escape, plans to shiv the bastard who disrespected you in the lunch line—but you could only bullshit for so long. Invariably, everyone ended up talking about how they'd wound up in the joint. All of them were innocent; framed by some crooked cop, fucked over by the system. All of them were working some angle, some way to snatch that get-out-of-jail-free card.

In 1977, the United States Supreme Court handed down a decision that led to the establishment of adequate law libraries in all state and federal prisons. No one knew exactly what adequate meant, but the library at Coastal rivaled any law school's, and every man in the joint eventually ended up with his head tucked into some case book, searching for an obscure passage, an arcane edict, any loophole they could exploit. Most cons knew more about the law than the lawyers the state had appointed to represent them—a good thing, since you usually got what you paid for.

John picked up the vase of flowers on the mantel.

Lydia stood, spine stiff as a board. "Put that down."

He hefted the vase in his hand. Leaded crystal, heavy as a brick. Probably worth its weight in gold. That was the only thing Lydia cared about now—money: how much she could make, how much she could hold on to. Four marriages, a son, a grandson, and all she had to show for it were these cold little objects scattered around her pristine mansion.

He said, "You've got a nice place, Aunt Lydia."

"Both of you. Get out of my house this instant."

"Your house," John repeated, sliding out the flowers, dropping them one by one on the expensive white rug. "That's an interesting way to put it."

"I'm going to call the police."

"Better duck first."

"Wha—" She was old but she moved fast when she saw John raise the vase. He threw it well over her head, but the shards of glass that shattered off the wall rained onto the couch where she had been sitting.

Lydia shrieked, "How *dare* you!"

The vase was probably worth more than he'd made since leaving the joint, but John didn't give a shit about money. There were rich people all over the world who were living in their own prisons, trapped by greed, shut off from the world around them. All he wanted right now was his freedom, and he was going to do whatever it took to get it back.

He asked his sister, "How much do you think this house is worth?"

Joyce stood frozen in place, her mouth gaping open. Any conflict in her life usually consisted of heated negotiations and thinly veiled threats made across a polished conference table or martinis at the club. A veiled threat didn't count for much at Coastal State Prison.

John guessed, "Quarter of a million dollars? Half a million?"

Joyce shook her head, too shocked to respond.

"You!" Lydia said, her voice shrill with anger. "You have exactly one minute to get out of this house before I call the police and have you arrested."

"A million bucks?" John prodded. "Come on, Joycey.

You handle real estate closings all day. You know how much a house is worth."

Joyce shook her head like she couldn't understand. But then she did something that surprised him. She glanced nervously around the room, took in the two-story cathedral ceiling, the large windows looking onto the graciously manicured back lawn. When she looked back at John, he could tell that she was still confused. But she trusted him. She trusted him enough to say, "Three."

"Three million," John echoed, incredulous. He'd thought he was rich when he cleaned out the thirty-eight hundred dollars Michael had left in the fake John's banking account.

He said, "Divide that by twenty years, you get— what—about a hundred fifty thousand bucks a year?"

Joyce was slowly getting it. "Yeah, Johnny. That's about right."

"Doesn't seem like nearly enough, does it?"

His sister's eyes sparkled. She smiled. "No."

"What do you think she has in the bank?" He turned back to Lydia. "Maybe I should be directing these questions to you?"

"You should be walking out of that door if you know what's good for you."

"What kind of car do you drive? Mercedes? BMW?" He felt like a lawyer on a television program. Maybe he could have been a lawyer. If Michael Ormewood had never entered his life, maybe John Shelley could have been a doctor or a lawyer or a teacher or a . . . what? What could he have been? He would never know. No one would ever know.

"John?" Joyce sounded concerned. He had gone too quiet.

His voice was not as strong when he asked Lydia, "How about that ring on your finger? What's that worth?"

"Get out of my house."

"You're a lawyer," John told her. "You've obviously made a very good living by suing people for everything they've got." He indicated the house, her useless things.

"I want you out of here," Lydia commanded. "I want you out of here right now."

"I want this house," he told her, walking around the room, wondering what would make her break. He pulled a monochromatic canvas off the wall. "I want this," he said, dropping it to the floor as he continued his stroll. "I want that piano."

He walked over to Joyce's side, thinking that no matter what happened, nothing would be more valuable to him than knowing she believed in him. Michael had tried to destroy him, but he was gone now. Nothing could change the past. All they could focus on now was their future.

He asked his sister, "How many times did Mom yell at us about practicing our scales?"

"All the time."

John trailed his hand along the keys. "She'd like this," he said, playing a couple of notes he remembered from a million years ago. "She'd like the idea of me taking up the piano again."

"Yeah," Joyce agreed, a sad smile on her face. "I think she would."

"You can stop right there," Lydia barked.

John warned, "I think you should be careful how you talk to me."

Lydia tucked a hand onto her hip. "You don't have nearly the grounds you need for a criminal conviction. Even with this recent...innuendo...you have leveled against my son, you don't have proof of anything."

"The burden of proof is lower in a civil suit. You know that."

"Have you any idea how many years I can hold up

depositions and hearings?" She gave a crocodile grin that showed pearly white teeth. She made her voice softer, frail. "I'm an old woman. This has been a terrible shock. I have my good days and my bad..."

"I can freeze your assets," John told her. "I'm sure you'll have plenty of bad days living in a one-room condo on Buford Highway."

"You can't threaten me."

"What about the press?" he asked. "Joyce found you. I'm sure the reporters can, too. Especially if she gives them a little help."

"I am calling the police," Lydia warned him, walking stiffly to the phone.

"All I'm asking for is a sworn statement. Just tell them Michael framed me, that he killed Mary Alice, and you'll never see me again."

"I'm calling the police right now to remove you from my house."

"How would you like a bunch of reporters camped out on your doorstep? How would you like to explain to them how you knew your son was a killer and you didn't do anything to stop him?"

She took off one of her chunky gold earrings and put the receiver to her ear. "I knew nothing of the sort."

"Michael told me a funny thing in that cellar, Aunt Lydia." Her fingers hovered over the keypad but she did not dial. "He knew he was going to die. He was absolutely certain that he was going to die and he wanted to tell me something."

The cord slapped against the metal table as Lydia let the receiver slide to her shoulder.

"Michael told me that he killed Mary Alice and that you knew all about it. He said it was your idea to frame me. He said that you planned the whole thing from the very beginning." He gave her a wink. "Deathbed confessions aren't considered hearsay, right? Not if the person knows for sure he's going to die."

She clutched the receiver in her bony hand. "No one will believe you."

"You know that cop he took—the one he kidnapped, nearly beat to death and was about to rape and kill?" He lowered his voice as if he was telling her in confidence. "I think she heard him say it, too."

The table banged against the wall as she sagged against it. Her eyes blazed with outrage.

John asked, "Who do you think the prosecutor is going to listen to when he's trying to make the decision about whether or not to file charges against you for obstruction of justice, false imprisonment and conspiracy after the fact?"

A noise came from the receiver, a recorded voice advising her that if she would like to make a call, to please hang up and dial again.

"The prosecutor will come to us," John continued. "He'll ask me and he'll ask Joyce whether we want to pursue criminal charges against you or just drop it." The phone started to make a loud busy signal that echoed in the cavernous room. "Let me tell you one thing I've figured out, Lydia: Michael was a predator, but you were his gatekeeper. You were the one who knew what he was and still let him out in the world."

"No..."

"Go ahead," he dared her. "Dial the number. Make the call."

Lydia stared at him, nostrils flared, eyes wet with angry tears. He could almost see her thinking it out, that fine legal mind of hers working all the angles, considering all of the options. Somewhere in this pristine white prison of a house, a clock was ticking. John silently counted the ticks in his head, biding his time.

"All right," she finally agreed. "All right."

John knew what she meant, but he wanted to hear her say it, wanted to be the one who *made* her say it. "All right what?"

Her hand trembled so badly that she could barely replace the phone in the cradle. She could not look at him. Her voice was choked with humiliation. "Tell me what I have to do."

CHAPTER FORTY

Will was listening to Bruce Springsteen's *Devils & Dust* as he brushed the dog. He wasn't certain why his neighbor had insisted on the brushing. Betty's fur was short. She didn't shed much. Will had to assume the origin of the task was somehow connected to the little dog's pure pleasure in the sensation; however, the neighbor had never struck him as particularly interested in the animal's comfort.

Not that he was assigning a personality to the thing, but there was no denying she liked a good brush.

The doorbell rang and Will stopped mid-stroke. It rang again, and then there was a staccato of knocking.

Will sighed. He put down the brush and rolled down the sleeves of his shirt. He scooped up Betty in his hand and walked to the door.

"What the fuck took you so long?"

"I assumed it was you."

Angie grimaced, which was hard considering her face was still healing. She had butterfly bandages on her forehead and her cheek had turned from black to yellow. Band-Aids on each of her fingers covered more sutures. A neon pink plastic cast was wrapped around her right arm, metal bolts sticking out around her wrist where the bones had been screwed back together.

He looked over her shoulder and saw her car parked in the street. "Did you drive here?"

"Arrest me."

"Why?" he asked. "Do I need to lock you up so you won't skip town?"

"Not this time."

"You're not leaving me for John?"

She laughed. "He's already had half of his life fucked up by some asshole. I figured I'd let him live the other half in peace."

"You didn't sleep with him?"

"Of course I slept with him."

Will's chest fell, but he couldn't say he was surprised. "Do you want to come in?"

"Let's stay out here," she suggested, awkwardly bending down to sit on the porch.

Reluctantly, Will joined her. He kept the dog close to his chest, and Betty tucked her head down, her snout dipping inside his vest.

"It's Saturday," Angie told him. "Why are you wearing that suit?"

"It's a good look for me."

She bumped her shoulder into his, teasing, "You think?"

He tried to make a joke of it. "You know, I'm not wearing any underwear."

She gave a deep, bawdy laugh.

He smiled, relishing the ease between them. "How come it's sexy when you say it, but not when I do?"

"Because the type of man who doesn't wear underwear usually hangs around playgrounds with lots of candy in his pockets."

"I've got candy in my pockets," he told her. "You want to put your hand in and see?"

She laughed again. "You are all talk, Mr. Trent. All talk."

"Yeah," he admitted. "You're probably right."

They both stared out at the street. Traffic noise from Ponce de Leon followed the breeze; car horns blaring, people shouting. Will heard wind chimes clanging in the distance, and a bicyclist rode by the house.

"I love you," Angie said, very quietly.

Betty stirred. He felt a flutter in his chest. "I know."

"You're my life. You've always been there."

"I'm still here."

She gave a heavy sigh. "I talked to you when I was in the cellar. Before you came." She paused, and he knew she was thinking back to that awful place. "I promised you that I would leave you if I got out of there alive."

"I've never expected you to keep your promises."

She was quiet again. Another cyclist rode by, the metallic whiz of the turning wheels sounding like a field of grasshoppers. Will thought about putting his arm around her shoulders, then remembered the gash from the glass. He was about to put his arm around her waist instead when she turned to him.

"I'm really bad for you."

"Lots of things are bad for me." He listed some examples. "Chocolate. Artificial sweetener. Secondhand smoke."

"Passion," she said, holding her fist to her heart. "I want you to have passion, Will. I want you to know what it's like to fall in love with somebody, to stay awake at night thinking you're going to die if you don't have them."

All he could say was, "I've stayed awake plenty of nights thinking about you."

"*Worrying* about me," she corrected. "I'm not an old pair of shoes you can wear for the rest of your life just because they're comfortable."

Will didn't know that there was anything wrong about being comfortable, but he held his tongue on the subject, asking instead, "Where am I going to find another woman with your low standards?"

"Isn't Amanda Wagner available?"

"Oh," he groaned. "That's just hurtful."

"You deserve it, you illiterate shit."

He laughed, and Betty stirred.

"God, that thing is ugly." She patted Will's leg. "Help me up."

Will hooked his hand under her good arm to help her stand. "Where are you going?"

"To look through the want ads." She indicated her broken wrist, her torn hands. "I'm not going to sit behind a desk for the next twenty years and even the city of Atlanta isn't desperate enough to give me a gun." She shrugged. "Besides, it'd be nice to find a job where I don't have to dress like a whore unless I want to."

"You don't really need a job," he offered.

She barked a surprised laugh. "You jackass. Do you really think I'm going to stay at home cooking and cleaning while you go to work?"

"Worse things could happen."

"I doubt it."

"Betty could use a mother."

"She could use a plastic bag over her head."

"I—"

Quickly, Angie stood on her toes and pressed her mouth to his neck. Her lips were soft against his skin. He could feel her warm breath, the soft tips of her fingers pressing into his shoulders.

She said, "I love you."

He watched her walk down his driveway, the pink cast

held out at her side. She turned around once to wave at him, then got into the car and pulled away.

She was almost proud of the cuts that riddled her face and hands. It was as if she had finally found a way to show on the outside what she'd been feeling on the inside all along. He had not asked her about what happened in that cellar, had not wanted to look too closely at the angle of Michael's wounds or count the number of times the man had been stabbed. Will had just wanted to hold her, to lift her up in his arms and carry her up the stairs and keep her safe for as long as he could.

And for at least a couple of hours, she had let him.

Will wasn't sure how long he stood there looking into the empty street. The Boss was singing "Leah" and Betty was snoring against his chest when a tan Chevy Nova pulled into his neighbor's driveway.

Betty woke up when the car door slammed.

Will walked across his yard toward the woman, who was hammering a wooden stake into the ground with the heel of her shoe.

He asked, "Can I help you?"

She startled, putting her hand to her throat. "God, you scared me to death."

"I'm Will Trent." He indicated his house. "I live next door."

She was looking at the dog, her lip curled in distaste. "I thought Mother said that thing was dead."

"Betty?"

"Yes, Betty. We moved her to a home."

Will felt his brow furrow. "I'm sorry?"

"Betty, my mother." The woman was impatient; she clearly didn't want to be here and she sure as hell didn't want to explain herself to Will. "She's living in a home now. We're selling the house."

"But," Will tried, "I heard her..." He looked down at the dog. "At night sometimes," he began. "She—your mother—would yell at someone she called Betty."

"She was yelling at herself, Mr. Trent. Did you never notice that my mother is nutty as a fruitcake?"

He thought about the midnight yelling, the way she would sometimes spontaneously burst into show tunes while watering the plastic plants on her front porch. These things had not struck Will as particularly odd, especially considering the eccentricities of the neighborhood. It was hard to stick out on a street that had six hippies living in a one-bedroom, rainbow-colored house; an abandoned Weiner Mobile up on blocks in front of a Mennonite church; and a six-foot-four functional illiterate who walked a toy dog on a hot pink leash.

The woman had a staple gun, which she used to attach what looked like a homemade For Sale By Owner sign to the wooden stake. "There," she said. "That should do it." She turned back to Will. "Somebody will come by in a day or so to clear out the house."

"Oh."

She slid her shoe back on, then threw the stapler into her car.

"Wait," Will said.

She got in her car anyway, rolling down the window as she cranked the engine. "What is it?"

"The dog," he said, holding up Betty—if, indeed, that was her real name. "What should I do with her?"

"I don't care," she answered, her lip curling up again as she looked at the dog. "Mother couldn't stand the little rat."

"She told me to brush it," he said, as if this would alter her memory.

"She probably said to flush it."

"But—"

The woman turned shrill. "Oh, for the love of God, just take her to the *pound*!"

She glanced over her shoulder then backed straight out of the driveway, nearly running over a passing jogger. Both men watched as the car careened into the street, sideswiping Will's trashcan.

The jogger smiled at Will, asking, "Bad day?"

"Yeah." Will wasn't as polite as he should have been, but he had bigger issues to deal with at the moment.

He looked down at Betty. She leaned her head against his chest, her bug eyes half-closed in ecstasy, tongue lolled to the side, as she stared back up at him. If she had been a cat, she would have purred.

"Crap," he muttered, heading back toward his house.

He remembered what the woman had said, could still hear her screeching voice ringing in his ears. Inside, he put Betty down and she skittered across the floor, jumped on the couch and settled in on her usual cushion.

Will closed the front door with a heavy sigh. A man who has grown up in an orphanage cannot take a dog to the pound.

Even if it is a Chihuahua.

AUTHOR'S NOTE

Being an author has given me the great pleasure of traveling to some of the most beautiful places in the world, but there is no city I love more than Atlanta, my hometown. I've always felt that writers are basically professional liars, and I think good liars know how to blend fact and fiction so that their story rings true. With this novel, I have tried to capture the flavor of my city—the areas I love, the ones I wouldn't walk through after dark, and everything in between. I have also taken great liberties with streets, buildings and neighborhoods, so if you are looking to visit our fair city, I would highly recommend you buy a map.

City Hall East was at one point a Sears department store and while there are several city agencies in that building, it's by no means the operation I have described. At the time I wrote this, Grady Homes was slated to be torn down. As with most major metropolitan cities, we are slowly but surely eradicating all low-income and subsidized housing. "Loans Until Payday" schemes tend to charge anywhere from 300 to 500 percent. The monthly rent I cited for Chez Pedo is the going rate, as was the state fine. Bus passes, clothing, and various other luxuries of the low-wage worker were all verified.

Fortunately, I have never had occasion to visit Coastal State Prison, and much of the information I have related about this facility comes from the Internet (www.dcor.state.ga.us). The death row inmates mentioned were real people and their ages are correct to the best of my knowledge. Atlanta has consistently ranked in the top ten most violent cities in America. Over a thousand rapes were reported last year within the Atlanta metro statistical area (www.ganet.org/gbi). Nationally, approximately 44 percent of rape victims are under the age of eighteen and 15 percent are under the age of twelve (www.ncvc.org). In the United States of America, it is estimated that every minute, 1.3 women are raped.

There is a car wash on Piedmont Road with a waving gorilla outside, but that is as far as any similarity goes. The Falcons were not in this year's Super Bowl. Ducktown is a real city in Tennessee. Former DeKalb County Sheriff Sidney Dorsey was indeed convicted of arranging the murder of his elected successor, Derwin Brown. The mayor of Blue Ridge actually had a ringside recliner at the cockfights. He has been quoted as saying that he's getting old and might soon "retire from politics and chickens."

Oh—and, trust me, dogs really should not eat cheese.

ACKNOWLEDGMENTS

Two years ago, I decided that I wanted to write a book outside my Grant County series. This was a risky proposition, and I knew that people would either think I was really smart or really crazy. So, first thanks goes to Kate Elton, Kate Miciak and Victoria Sanders for not having me committed—yet—and for letting me get this story out of my head.

As usual, Dr. David Harper kindly checked over the medical details for me. Trish Hawkins answered myriad questions about learning disabilities and Debbie Teague shared her firsthand knowledge about living with dyslexia. JS explained to me the uphill battle of the convicted felon and verified some drug facts. Jeanene English talked to me about that enigmatic little beast known as the Chihuahua.

At Delacorte, I would like to thank: Irwyn Applebaum, Nita Taublib, Barb Burg, Susan Corcoran, Betsy Hulsebosch, Cynthia Lasky, Steve Maddock, Paolo Pepe, Sharon Propson, Sharon Swados, Don Weisberg, Caitlin Alexander, Kelly Chian, Loyale Coles and the Random House sales team. Lisa George, thank you for forcing me onto unsuspecting friends.

At Random House UK: Mike Abbott, Ron Beard, Faye Brewster, Mike Broderick, Richard Cable, Georgina Hawtrey-Woore, Clare Lawler, Simon Littlewood, Dave Parrish, Gail Rebuck, Emma Rose, Claire Round, Susan Sandon, Trish Slattery and Rob Waddington.

Billie Bennett-Ward, Rebecca Keiper, the real Martha Lam, Fidelis Morgan and Colleen Winters have been supportive friends. My daddy took care of me in the mountains and DA was always there when I came home.

If you enjoyed Karin Slaughter's TRIPTYCH,
you won't want to miss any of her
internationally bestselling crime novels.
Look for them at your favorite bookseller.

And read on for an electrifying early look
at her next novel

BEYOND
REACH

Available now in hardcover from Delacorte Press

KARIN SLAUGHTER

a novel

BEYOND REACH

BEYOND REACH

ON SALE NOW

SARA LINTON LOOKED AT HER WATCH. The Seiko had been a gift from her grandmother on the day Sara graduated from high school. On Granny Em's own graduation day, she had been four months from marriage, a year and a half from bearing the first of her six children and thirty-eight years from losing her husband to cancer. Higher education was something Emma's father had seen as a waste of time and money, especially for a woman. Emma had not argued—she was raised during a time when children did not think to disagree with their parents—though she made sure that all four of her surviving children attended college.

"Wear this and think of me," Granny Em had said that day on the school campus as she closed the watch's silver bracelet around Sara's wrist. "You're going to do everything you ever dreamed of, and I want you to know that I will always be right there beside you."

As a student at Emory University, Sara had constantly looked at the watch, especially through advanced biochemistry, applied genetics, and human anatomy classes that seemed by law to be taught by the most boring, monosyllabic professors that could be found. In medical school, she had impatiently glanced at the watch on Saturday mornings as she stood outside the lab, waiting for the professor to come and unlock the door so she could finish her experiments. During her internship at Grady Hospital, she had stared blurry-eyed at its white face, trying to make out the hands, as she calculated how much longer she had left in thirty-six-hour shifts. At the Heartsdale Children's Clinic, she had closely followed the second hand as she pressed her fingers to a child's thin wrist, counting the beats of his heart as they ticked beneath his skin, seeking to discern if an "achy all-over" was a serious ailment or if it just meant the kid did not want to go to school that day.

For almost twenty years, Sara had worn the watch. The crystal had been replaced twice, the battery numerous times, and the bracelet once because Sara could not stomach the thought of cleaning out the dried blood of a woman who had died in her arms. Even at Granny Em's funeral, Sara had found herself touching the smooth bezel around the face, tears streaming down her own face at the realization that she could never again see her grandmother's quick, open smile or the sparkle in her eyes as she learned of her oldest grand-daughter's latest accomplishment.

Now, looking at the watch, for the first time in her life Sara was glad her grandmother was not there with her, could not read the anger in Sara's eyes, know the humiliation that burned in her chest like an uncontrollable fire as she sat in a conference room being deposed in a malpractice suit filed by the parents of a dead patient. Everything Sara had ever worked for, every step she had taken that her grandmother could not, every accomplishment, every degree, was being rendered meaningless by a woman who was all but calling Sara a baby killer.

The lawyer leaned over the table, eyebrow raised, lip curled, as Sara glanced at the watch. "Dr. Linton, do you have a more pressing appointment?"

"No." Sara tried to keep her voice calm, to quell the fury that the lawyer had obviously been stoking for the last four hours. Sara knew that she was being manipulated, knew that the woman was trying to bait her, to get Sara to say some-thing horrible that would forever be recorded by the little man leaning over the transcript machine in the corner. Knowing this did not stop Sara from reacting. As a matter of fact, the knowledge made her even angrier.

"I've been calling you Dr. Linton all this time." The lawyer glanced down at an open folder in front of her. "Is it Tolliver? I see that you remarried your ex-husband, Jeffrey Tolliver, six months ago."

"Linton is fine." Under the table, Sara was shaking her foot so hard that her shoe was about to fall off. She crossed her arms over her chest. There was a sharp pain in her jaw from clenching her teeth. She shouldn't be here. She should be at home right now, reading a book or talking on the phone to her sister. She should be going over patient files or sorting through old medical journals she never seemed to have time to catch up on.

She should be trusted.

"So," the lawyer continued. The woman had given her name at the start of the deposition, but Sara couldn't remember it. All she had been able to concentrate on at the time was the look on Beckey Powell's face. Jimmy's mother. The woman whose hand Sara had held so many times, the friend she had comforted, the person with whom she had spent countless hours on the phone, trying to put into simple English the medical jargon the oncologists in Atlanta were feeding the mother to explain why her twelve-year-old son was going to die.

From the moment they'd entered the room, Beckey had glared at Sara as if she were a murderer. The boy's father, a man Sara had gone to school with, had not even been able to look her in the eye.

"Dr. Tolliver?" the lawyer pressed.

"Linton," Sara corrected, and the woman smiled, just as she did every time she scored a point against Sara. This happened so often that Sara was tempted to ask the lawyer if she suffered from some unusually petty form of Tourette's.

"On the morning of the seventeenth—this was the day

after Easter—you got lab results from the cell blast you'd ordered performed on James Powell. Is that correct?"

James. She made him sound so adult. To Sara, he would always be the six-year-old she had met all those years ago, the little boy who liked playing with his plastic dinosaurs and eating the occasional crayon. He'd been so proud when he told her that he was called Jimmy, just like his dad.

"Dr. Tolliver?"

Buddy Conford, one of Sara's lawyers, finally spoke up. "Let's cut the crap, honey."

"Honey?" the lawyer echoed. She had one of those husky, low voices most men found irresistible. Sara could tell Buddy fell into this category, just as she could tell that the fact the man found his opponent desirable heightened his sense of competitiveness.

Buddy smiled, his own point made. "You know her name."

"Please instruct your client to answer the question, Mr. Conford."

"Yes," Sara said, before they could exchange any more barbs. She had found that lawyers could be quite verbose at three-hundred-fifty dollars an hour. They would parse the meaning of the word "parse" if the clock was ticking. And Sara had two lawyers: Melinda Stiles was counsel for Global Medical Indemnity, an insurance company to whom Sara had paid almost three and a half million dollars over the course of her medical career. Buddy Conford was Sara's personal lawyer, whom she'd hired to protect her from the insurance company. The fine print in all of Global's malpractice policies stipulated limited liability on the part of the company when a patient's injury was a direct result of a doctor's willful negligence. Buddy was here to make sure that did not happen.

"Dr. Linton? The morning of the seventeenth?"

"Yes," Sara answered. "According to my notes, that's when I got the lab results."

Sharon, Sara remembered. The lawyer was Sharon Connor. Such an innocuous name for such a horrible person.

"And what did the lab results reveal to you?"

"That more than likely, Jimmy had acute myeloblastic leukemia."

"And the prognosis?"

"That's out of my realm. I'm not an oncologist."

"No. You referred the Powells to an oncologist, a friend of yours from college, a Dr. William Harris in Atlanta?"

"Yes." Poor Bill. He was named in the lawsuit, too, had been forced to hire his own attorney, was battling with his own insurance company.

"But you are a doctor?"

Sara took a deep breath. She had been instructed by Buddy to only answer questions, not pointed comments. God knew she was paying him enough for his advice. She might as well start taking it.

"And surely as a doctor you know what acute myeloblastic leukemia is?"

"It's a group of malignant disorders characterized by the replacement of normal bone marrow with abnormal cells."

Connor smiled, rattling off, "And it begins as a single somatic hematopoietic progenitor that transforms to a cell incapable of normal differentiation?"

"The cell loses apoptosis."

Another smile, another point scored. "And this disease has a fifty percent survival rate."

Sara held her tongue, waiting for the ax to fall.

"And timing is critical for treatment, is that correct? In such a disease—a disease that literally turns the body's cells against themselves, turns off apoptosis, according to you, which is the normal genetic process of cell death—timing is critical."

Forty-eight hours would not have saved the boy's life, but Sara was not going to utter those words, have them transcribed into a legal document and later thrown in her face with all the callousness Sharon Connor could muster.

The lawyer shuffled through some papers as if she needed to find her notes. "And you attended Emory Medical School. As you so graciously corrected me earlier, you didn't just graduate in the top ten percent, you graduated sixth in your class."

Buddy sounded bored with the woman's antics. "We've already established Dr. Linton's credentials."

"I'm just trying to put it all together," the woman countered. She held up one of the pages, her eyes scanning the words. Finally, she put it down. "And, Dr. Linton, you got this information—this lab result that was almost certainly a death sentence—the morning of the seventeenth, and yet you chose not to share the information with the Powells until two days later. And that was because . . . ?"

Sara had never heard so many sentences starting with the word "and." She imagined grammar wasn't high up on the curriculum at whatever school had churned out the vicious lawyer.

Still, she answered, "They were at Disney World for Jimmy's birthday. I wanted them to enjoy their vacation, what I thought might be their last vacation as a family for some time. I made the decision to not tell them until they came back."

"They came back the evening of the seventeenth, yet you did not tell them until the morning of the nineteenth, two days later."

Sara opened her mouth to respond, but the woman talked over her.

"And it didn't occur to you that they could return for immediate treatment and perhaps save their child's life?" It was clear she didn't expect an answer. "I would imagine that, given the choice, the Powells would rather have their son alive today instead of empty photographs of him standing around the Magic Kingdom." She slid the picture in question across the table. It glided neatly past Beckey and Jim Powell, past Sara's two lawyers, and stopped a few inches from where Sara was sitting.

She shouldn't have looked, but she did.

Young Jimmy stood leaning against his father, both of them wearing Mickey Mouse ears and holding sparklers as a parade of Snow White's dwarfs marched behind them. Even in the photo, you could tell the boy was sick. Dark circles rimmed his eyes and he was so thin that his frail little arm looked like a piece of string.

They had come back from vacation a day early because Jimmy had wanted to be home. Sara did not know why the Powells had not called her at the clinic, brought in Jimmy that day so she could check on him. Maybe his parents had known even without the test, even without the final diagnosis, that their days of having a normal, healthy child were over. Maybe they had just wanted to keep him to themselves one more day. He had been such a wonderful boy—kind, smart, cheerful—everything a parent could hope for. And now he was gone.

Sara felt tears well in her eyes, and bit her lip so hard that the tears fell from pain instead of grief.

Buddy snatched away the picture, irritated. He slid it back to Sharon Connor. "You can practice your opening statement in front of your mirror at home, sweetheart."

Connor's mouth twisted into a smirk as she took back the photograph. She was living proof that the theory that women were nurturing caretakers was utter bullshit. Sara half-expected to see rotting flesh between her teeth.

The woman said, "Dr. Linton, on this particular date, the date you got James's lab results, did anything else happen that stood out for you?"

A prickling went up Sara's spine, a spark of warning that she could not suppress. "Yes."

"And could you tell us what that was?"

"I found a woman who had been murdered in the bathroom of our local diner."

"Raped and murdered. Is that correct?"

"Yes."

"That brings us to your part-time job as coroner for the county. I believe your husband—then ex-husband, when this rape and murder occurred—is chief of police for the county. Both of you work closely together when cases arise."

Sara waited for more, but the woman had obviously just wanted to get that on the record.

"Counselor?" Buddy asked.

"One moment, please," the lawyer murmured, picking up a thick folder and leafing through the pages.

Sara looked down at her hands to give herself something to do. Pisiform, triquetrum, hamate, capitate, trapezoid, trapezium, lunate, scaphoid . . . She listed all the bones in her hand, then started on the ligaments, trying to distract herself, willing herself not to walk into the trap the lawyer was so skillfully setting.

While Sara was in her residency at Grady, headhunters had pursued her so relentlessly that she had stopped answering her phone. Partnerships. Six-figure salaries with year-end bonuses. Surgical privileges at any hospital she chose. Personal assistants, lab support, full secretarial staff, even her own parking space. They had offered her everything, and yet in the end, she had decided to return home to Grant, to practice medicine for considerably less money and even less respect, because she thought it was important for doctors to serve rural communities.

Was part of it vanity, too? Sara had seen herself as a role model for the girls in town. Most of them had only ever seen a male doctor. The only women in authority were nurses, teachers, and mothers. Her first five years at the Heartsdale Children's Clinic, Sara had spent at least half of her time convincing young patients—and frequently their mothers—that she had, in fact, graduated medical school. No one believed a woman could be smart enough, good enough, to reach such a position. Even when Sara bought the clinic from her retiring partner, people had still been skeptical. It had taken years to carve herself a place of respect in the community.

All for this.

Sharon Connor finally looked up from her papers. She frowned. "Dr. Linton, you yourself were raped. Isn't that correct?"

Sara felt all of the saliva in her mouth dry up. Her throat tightened and her flesh turned hot as she struggled with an unwelcome shame that she had not felt since the last time a lawyer had deposed her about being raped. Just like then, Sara's vision tunneled and blurred in such a way that she saw nothing, just heard the words ringing in her ears.

Buddy shot to his feet, arguing something, stabbing his finger at the lawyer, at the Powells. Beside him, Melinda Stiles from Global Medical Indemnity said nothing. Buddy had told Sara this would happen, that Stiles would sit silently by, letting opposing counsel tear into Sara, speaking only when she thought Global might be exposed. Another woman, another failed role model.

"And I want that on the goddamn record!" Buddy finished, pushing his chair away from the table as he sat down.

"Noted," Connor said. "Dr. Linton?"

Sara's vision cleared. She heard a whoosh in her ears, as if she had been swimming underwater and suddenly pushed herself to the surface.

"Dr. Linton?" Connor repeated. She kept using the title, making it sound like something vile instead of a position Sara had worked for all of her life.

Sara looked at Buddy, and he shrugged as he shook his head, indicating there was nothing he could do. He had predicted that the deposition would be nothing more than a fishing expedition with Sara's life as bait.

Connor said, "Doctor, would you like a few minutes to

collect your emotions? I know that your rape is a hard thing for you to talk about." She indicated the thick file on the table in front of her. It had to be the trial transcript from Sara's case. The woman had read everything, knew every disgusting detail. "From what I gathered, your assault was very, very brutal."

Sara cleared her throat, willed her voice to not just work but to be strong, fearless. "Yes, it was."

Connor's tone turned almost conciliatory. "I used to work at the district attorney's office in Baton Rouge. I can honestly say in my twelve years as a prosecutor, I never saw anything as brutal, as sadistic, as what you experienced."

Buddy snapped, "Sweetheart, you wanna quit with the crocodile tears and get to the question?"

The lawyer hesitated for just a second, then continued, "For the record, Dr. Linton was raped in the bathroom of Grady Hospital, where she was working as an emergency room intern. Apparently, the perpetrator accessed the women's room through the drop ceiling. Dr. Linton was in one of the stalls when he literally dropped down on her."

"Noted," Buddy said. "You got a question in there, or do you just like giving speeches?"

"Dr. Linton, the fact that you were brutally raped figured greatly into your decision to return to Grant County, did it not?"

"There were other reasons."

"But would you say that the rape was your primary reason?"

"I would say that it was one of many reasons that figured into my decision to return."

"Is this going somewhere?" Buddy asked. The lawyers exchanged words again, and Sara reached for the pitcher of water on the table, poured herself a glass with hands she willed to be steady.

She felt rather than saw Beckey Powell stir, and wondered if the woman was feeling guilty, seeing Sara as a human being again instead of a monster. Sara hoped so. She hoped Beckey tossed and turned in her bed tonight, realized that no matter how much she and her lawyer vilified Sara, nothing would bring back her son. Nothing would change the fact that Sara had done everything she could for Jimmy.

"Dr. Linton?" Connor continued. "I imagine in light of the brutal rape you experienced, it was quite an emotional ordeal to walk into that bathroom and discover a woman who herself had been sexually assaulted. Especially as it was almost ten years to the date that you were raped."

Buddy snapped, "Is that a question?"

"Dr. Linton, you and your ex-husband—I'm sorry, husband—you both are trying to adopt a child now, aren't you? Because as a consequence to this brutal rape you experienced, you cannot have children of your own?"

Beckey's reaction was unmistakable. For the first time since this had started, Sara really looked at the woman. She saw a softening in Beckey's eyes, a stirring of joy for a friend, but the emotion vanished as swiftly as it had come, and Sara could almost read the rebuke that cancelled it: You have no right to mother a child when you killed my son.

Connor held up a familiar-looking document, stating, "Doctor, you and your husband, Jeffrey Tolliver, filed papers for adoption with the state of Georgia three months ago. Isn't that correct?"

Sara tried to remember what they had put on the adoption application, what they had said during the state-mandated parenting classes that had taken up every free minute of their time over the last few months. What incriminating evidence would the lawyer wring out of the endless, seemingly innocuous process? Jeffrey's high blood pressure? Sara's need for reading glasses? "Yes."

Connor shuffled through some more papers, saying, "Just a moment, please."

The room was tiny, airless. There were no windows, no paintings on the wall to stare at. A dying palm tree stood in the corner, the leaves drooping and sad. Nothing good would come of any of this. No pound of flesh would bring back a child. No verdict of innocence would restore a reputation.

Sara looked down at her hand. Dorsal metacarpal ligaments, dorsal carpometacarpal ligaments, dorsal intercarpal ligaments...

Sara had visited Jimmy the week before he died, held his frail little hand for hours as he haltingly talked about football and skateboarding and all the things he missed. Sara had been able to see it then, that look of death in his eyes. The look was the mirror opposite of the hope she had seen in Beckey Powell's, even though the woman had heard the prognosis, had agreed to stop treatment so as not to prolong Jimmy's suffering. It was that hope that kept Jimmy from letting go, that fear that every child has of disappointing his mother.

Sara had taken Beckey to the cafeteria, sitting in a quiet corner with the bewildered woman and holding her hand just as she had held Jimmy's moments before. She'd described to Beckey how it would happen, how death would claim her son. His feet would get cold, then his hands, as circulation slowed. His lips would turn blue. His breathing would become irregular, but that shouldn't be taken as a sign of distress. He would have difficulty swallowing. He might lose control of his bladder. His thoughts would wander, but Beckey had to keep talking to him, engaging him, because he would still be there. He would still be her Jimmy until the very last second. It was her job to be there at every step, then—the hardest part—to let him go on without her.

She had to be strong enough to let Jimmy go.

Connor cleared her throat and waited for Sara's attention. "You never charged the Powells for the lab tests and subsequent office visits after you made James's diagnosis," she said. "Why is that, Dr. Linton?"

"I didn't, in fact, make a firm diagnosis," Sara corrected,

trying to get her focus back. "I could only tell them what I suspected and refer them to an oncologist."

"Your college friend, Dr. William Harris," the lawyer supplied. "And you didn't bill the Powells for any of the lab work or any subsequent visits following the referral."

"I don't handle billing."

"But you do direct your office staff, do you not?" Connor paused. "Do I need to remind you that you're under oath?"

Sara bit back the sharp answer that wanted to come.

"According to the deposition of your office manager, Nelly Morgan, you directed her to write off as a loss the almost two thousand dollars the Powells owed you. True?"

"Yes."

"Why is that, Dr. Linton?"

"Because I knew that they were facing what could be crippling medical costs for Jimmy's treatment. I didn't want to add to the pile of creditors I knew that they would have." Sara stared at Beckey, though the woman would not meet her gaze. "That's what this is about, isn't it? Lab bills. Hospital bills. Radiologists. Pharmacies. You must owe a fortune."

Connor reminded, "Dr. Linton, you're here to answer my questions, not ask your own."

Sara leaned toward the Powells, tried to connect with them, make them see reason. "Don't you know it won't get him back? None of this will get Jimmy back."

"Mr. Conford, please instruct your client—"

"Do you know what I gave up to practice here? Do you know how many years I spent—"

"Dr. Linton, do not address my clients."

"This is the reason why you had to go to Atlanta to find a specialist," Sara told them. "These lawsuits are why the hospital closed down, why there are only five doctors within a hundred miles of here who can afford to practice medicine."

They would not look up at her, would not respond.

Sara sat back in her chair, spent. This couldn't just be

about money. Beckey and Jimmy wanted something more, an explanation for why their son died. The sad fact was that there was no explanation. People died—children died—and sometimes, there was no one to blame, nothing that could stop it. All this lawsuit meant was that a year from now, maybe five years, another child would be sick, another family would be stricken, and no one would be able to afford to help them.

No one would be there to hold their hand, to explain what was happening.

"Dr. Linton," Connor continued. "As to your failure to bill the Powells for the lab work and office visits: isn't it a fact that you felt guilty for Jimmy's death?"

She knew the answer Buddy wanted her to give the question, knew that even Melinda Stiles, the silent advocate for Global Medical Indemnity, wanted her to deny this.

"Dr. Linton?" Connor insisted. "Didn't you feel guilty?"

Sara closed her eyes, could see Jimmy lying in that hospital bed, talking to her about skateboarding. She could still feel the cold touch of his fingers in hers as he patiently explained to her the difference between a heelflip and an ollie.

Interphalangeal joints. Metacarpophalangeal joint. Capsule, distal, radioulnar joints...

"Dr. Linton?"

"Yes," she finally admitted, tears flowing freely now. "Yes. I felt guilty."